END IT IN A LIE

BY

PETER M. ATKINS

END IT IN A LIE

Name changed from "End It With a Lie" August Copyright © 2016

Author: Peter M. Atkins 2016 Bourkeite
Cover art by Leanne Kuulkers Copyright © 2015

"End it In a Lie" and "Short Stories in Rhyme" eBooks available at Smashwords.com

Produced with the assistance of
www.loveofbooks.com.au

CHAPTER 1

The summer in eastern outback Australia had been the driest in Simon's experience. Wide cracks in the topsoil gave it a shattered appearance and offered stark proof of how much water the ground was prepared to accept. An old hard black ground, made up of layers of sediment brought by swirling and seldom occurring floods over centuries of time and hundreds of kilometres. To where they finally settled in the slower and sometimes still waters that soaked the flood plains.

The river lay like an avenue. Low leveled, slow and bound between banks studded with River Red Gums that stood with heavy knotted trunks; as if they sought to form a barrier. To protect the lifeblood of the outback from the drought that held the surrounding flood plains firmly in its moisture-sucking grip.

The country around the river portrayed a scene of death.

Tumbleweeds of burnt brown and desiccated yellow grasses crackled underfoot. At times their shattered debris lifted when whirling-winds came to life. The pieces carried and then dumped to the earth again as the varying winds lost momentum.

Simon looked out toward the horizon where heat haze shimmered, and through it saw an old fox moving slowly over the rough ground. It travelled almost lamely towards the cool waters of the river, head bowed down as if in silent submission as it carried its bony body in a weary trot. The animal had seen better days and Simon wondered if the wretched survivor would see good seasons again. Knowing, as probably the old fox did that the rains would have to come eventually, if not this day, then maybe the next.

Hope was the knot tied in the end of the tether in this drought ravaged outback.

Simon also knew the old boar was not far away, having seen him briefly less than an hour earlier. The pig had warily drunk from the still waters of the river, before moving back into one of the many dry tributaries away from the oppressing hot sun. The boar, like the fox, also carried itself wearily.

Simon felt coolness on his face as the breeze picked up a little more. It caressed his moist skin as it carried from the direction of the river away to his right. He made a mental note of the advantage it gave him, as it blew his scent away from where he expected the boar to be. Simon lowered his nose towards his armpit and sniffed as he smiled to himself at the thought that scent was probably not the best word.

He had nothing personal against the wild boar; it was just a victim of circumstance. The circumstance being that the grazier who owned the land allowed Simon to live in the old homestead for token rent, and a promise to carry out 'a bit of pest control' now and then.

The grazier had two pet hates in his life. One being the wild pigs which ate his lambs while they were being born, and although no less fierce than the first, his second hate was for the crows who pecked the eyes from the ewe, as she lay tired from the exertions of birth.

Simon heard a sound.

A slight scratching sound drifted feebly to him across the wind. Then a muted snuffling grunt that suggested to him he was undoubtedly much closer to the boar than he had realized.

The sweat rolled down Simon's chin and dripped away to impact on to the thirsty ground below.

He tensed; like he always did when close to these powerful animals and the dagger like sharp tusks they carried in their lower jaws.

His hands were slippery with sweat as the heat of the day sucked at the pores of his skin. He wiped it away onto the material of his trousers before slowly working the rifle bolt, quietly pushing a bullet into its breech.

Simon was crouched at the base, amongst the roots of an old Coolabah tree when the sound came again. He strained his ears to listen, and gained knowledge of the pig's general direction before he rose in a half crouch.

Stealthily he moved a foot forward, careful that small twigs and dry leaves on the ground made no sound as they crushed to particles under his heavy boots. After some twenty short slow paces he could see the far bank of the tributary. A sloping bank probably three metres lower than the side he approached from.

The advantage of height over the boar suited him.

Simon crouched lower and then easily dropped to his knees as he heard another snuffling sound. He placed his free hand to the ground and lowered himself until he lay stretched out face down on the hot black soil.

With his rifle held in two hands he deliberately and slowly crept forward on his elbows, knees and toes. His belly protected from the sticks and insects that lay in his path by a heavy drill shirt.

A red bull ant walked across his intended path. It was within reach so he sent a curled finger out to meet it, flicking it out of his way as a louder snuffling sound touched his ears, and then his curiosity.

He eased his head up slowly to peer over the edge of the bank, and although his field of view was greatly expanded, it did not include the animal. He decided it must be directly below him. At the base of the high bank on whose edge he lay, and shared with at least one bull ant.

A fly buzzed and then settled.

Simon licked his lips, and his dry tongue rejoiced in the moisture made available by the salty sweat, which had until then clung to his upper lip. He lay in the hot sun, while the heat that had baked the earth prior his arrival radiated up to him and offered only more discomfort.

He was about to move forward a little more when suddenly a movement caught his eye, causing him to still himself in all but his shallow breathing.

Something small moved again. He stared at the object before realizing that it was the fold at the base of the pig's ear, just visible over the rim of the creek bank. The animal was indeed directly below him, and too close to the lower wall of the steep bank to bring the rifle to bear.

Simon slowly lowered his head until his chin touched the ground, before cautiously moving back from the edge of the bank. He then brought the rifle to an approximate firing position and quietly released the safety catch.

Once more he began to inch forward, stopping only when the rifle's barrel began to extend over the edge of the bank. With stilled body he slowly raised his head until finally he could see the whole of the pig's ear.

It was a big animal. Its large ears flapped as it tossed its head to deter the moisture-seeking flies, who sought the living spring which soaked its lightly coloured eyes. Simon could see the bush ticks that clung to the boar's tough hairy hide, and once again he curtailed his breathing as the old animal lifted its head to concentrate its sense of hearing.

Still as a post it stood, almost as if it were feeling its surroundings.

After a minute Simon saw the animal relax again. It glanced briefly at the bush on the far side of the creek before it flicked its tail and walked a few more steps. Once again it dropped its snout to the soft sandy creek bed. Where with each breath, there shot up a spurt of dust that hung in the air briefly before disappearing on the lifting breeze.

Now that he could see the animal clearly he noticed a severe swelling at its shoulder. A large blackened lump had swollen to the size of a cricket ball, restricting the animal's movement and causing a slight limp. Simon could make out the yellow pus and body fluid that dribbled down the animal's swollen foreleg. It attracted a horde of flies that settled, swarmed and then settled again to do what came naturally to them. Possibly an old bullet wound Simon thought, before he wondered if he'd ever euthanized a pig before.

The boar was moving again. Slowly and heavily towards the far bank, shoveling a trough in the creek bed as it went in search of the juice laden roots.

Simon lay prone and relaxed in a shooting position. He gauged where he expected the boar to go, and believed he just had to wait until it moved in front of the rifle sights.

Some leaves fell from a Coolabah tree as the boar lifted its head and flapped the big ears again, disturbing the cluster of greedy moisture seeking black flies. The falling leaves caught Simon's attention, and he became aware of the breeze steadily building in force. It delivered to his sun drenched back a noticeably cooler temperature.

He wanted to turn his head and check the weather, but decided to stay perfectly still. At the pig's present rate of movement, he would soon be in the rifle sight.

Simon's sense of fair play whispered to him, and he wondered if he should make a sound to alert the boar. Give it the opportunity to escape. The whisper had barely voiced its comment before he argued that the fair play avenue might lead to the risk of only wounding it again, and ultimately a slower and painful death.

No. It was better this way. A quick shot, dead before it hit the ground and forever free of pain.

He chose a spot to sight on and then waited some seconds as the flies swarmed as if they suspected that an ill wind was about to fall.

Simon inhaled gently, and then let the air slide slowly from his nostrils. As he did the rifle barrel touched the banks crumbling edge and dislodged a small piece of sun-hardened dirt, which rolled down the steep sided earthen wall, taking other smaller pieces with it as it went.

The pig lifted its head and stilled its chewing as it looked over its shoulder. The instant it realized danger was the instant a rifle explosion filled the air. A split second later a puff of dust and a small cloud of flies erupted from its hairy hide.

By the time Simon had ejected the spent shell and pushed another bullet into the rifles breech the boar had fallen on its side. Its wound offering a small red fountain of fresh moisture to the already descending flies.

It gave another high-pitched squeal as its four legs stiffened to full length, before it quivered and then lay still.

The sudden silence, thick after the loud explosion was broken only by the buzzing of the bush flies as they jostled for position in an excited unsettled swarm.

Simon lay still for a moment and gazed thoughtfully at the big animal. He always had the same feeling after he had killed something, and the same thought. One minute you're standing minding your own business, the next you've gone to oblivion.

Simon thought he understood the speed of death, for there had been times when he'd come close to it. Each time there had been no time for prayer, and from that he believed it was practical to live life a minute at a time.

He was still holding that thought when his attention was caught by the falling of more leaves and the now very cool, light wind on his back.

He turned and looked over his shoulder.

Damn he thought. Dust storm.

The sky had turned to a thick ochre red; its blue blotted out by dust from the central Australian deserts from where it had been swept up by cold relentless winds. It had crept up and taken him by surprise, just as he had taken the grunter by surprise.

Typical he thought, lying here minding my own business...

Dust storms like these were less common than twenty years ago, but now and then one would come, and it would be followed by thunder, lightning and hopefully, rain.

Simon looked down to the creek bed and decided the base of the bank from where he shot the boar would have to do for shelter.

He ejected the bullet from the rifle, caught it, and removed the magazine before reinserting the unused bullet back into the magazine. The bolt pushed home easily along its well-oiled slide, while at the same time he pulled the trigger to release the firing pin and avoid cocking the rifle. He pulled the trigger again to double check before slotting the magazine back into its place. His father had shown him to do it that way, and his father had been right in many other things.

This was no time to be choosey about one's company he thought, as he jumped down into the tributary not far from where the boar lay. The steepest part of the bank stood protectively between him and the approaching dust storm, and he crouched down against its lower wall. Basic physics told him that most of the wind would blow directly over him. About the wind currents within the creek he knew not what to expect, but he'd soon find out he reckoned, as it would be upon him within minutes.

He was stuck here for now, so he rolled a cigarette and leant back against the wall of black dirt to wait.

It began with a wave of leaf litter. Many small sticks and particles of sand, which blew forcefully over the edge of the embankment immediately dropped into the vacuum below.

Simon spat out dust and dirt, feeling with annoyance the grit between his teeth as he squatted on his haunches, his hat pulled down low on his head. Its large brim offering some protection to the back of his neck as it covered his upturned collar.

He squinted into the maelstrom as dust and pieces of bush debris swarmed about him, before he nestled his nose into the crook of his elbow and clenched his eyes tightly shut.

Seconds later he felt the wind try to pull his old hat from his head, and with humour he wondered about those who wore toupees.

The howl in his ears was the fierce song of extreme power, and he heard what he thought was the sound of a tree or its branches being thrown to the ground with a weird crashing noise.

He heard a similar noise again which seemed a lot closer.

The thrashing wind seemed to go on for more than just the ten minutes as his wristwatch suggested, and he wondered how long it would last. He had in the past sat through many of these storms, but then he had waited them out in good shelter where he'd felt no need to measure their time span.

All at once the wind dropped to a constant rushing flow, and he knew that soon the thunder and lightning would let loose.

This was the really scary part.

Simon lifted his head slightly and looked out at the trees just ten metres away. Their ghostly shadow outlines stood feint in the thick fog of sand.

He would wait a few more minutes and then start the dash back to the house, and although he wasn't looking forward to the march, he had to make a move.

The day would soon darken as nearly all the sun's rays were lost and distorted by the millions of particles of grit, which whistled as they were tossed at random through space.

The first rumble of thunder in the distance told him in its grumbling ungrateful tone that his scamper for cover could not be put off any longer. He had to move now although the dust was still bad. Shouldering the rifle, he climbed out of the tributary to where, upon the banks top he was forced to involuntarily squint as he went against the gritty tide.

He walked as fast as he could while taking care to avoid the large River Red Gums as much as possible. They were well known to drop their heavy termite ridden branches at any time.

With firm step he leant into the wind, allowing his bodyweight to help push through the sandy soup. Suddenly there came a flash, which automatically drew the attention of his eyes as lightning struck down to the horizon. It startled him, and he jumped as every nerve ending triggered.

He loved thunderstorms but they scared him.

Too much chaotic power, especially when he was as exposed as he was now. Amongst trees which could shatter from a lightning bolt at any moment.

More lightning hit and it looked much closer this time. A massive crash of thunder sounded out its cry of fury, almost before the momentary glare of the giant spark had completely disappeared. The ground itself seemed to vibrate and Simon once again realized his insignificance in the whole universal scheme of things.

The flashes of lightning came with more regularity now, and as the low light of evening fell they helped guide his feet through the mess of exposed tree roots. They lay like tentacles over the rough and uneven ground between trees that looked eerie in the stark blue light.

He reached the road which ran from the house to the river and turned onto it just as the first cold raindrops fell. Large drops drove into his back and quickly drenched him.

His stride strengthened at the thought of a cold beer and a taste of the wild duck he'd left cooking in the camp oven.

There were no lights on at the house, so he guessed Ray had not stayed around. He would have seen or smelt the approaching storm and returned to town post haste. Ray wasn't caught out like that; he was too much of a good bushman and in tune with his outback surroundings.

Ray the foxhunter also used the grazier's old homestead, as a base for his enterprises. He came from town each day to feed his horses, and at times make up batches of cyanide baits. Baits he used on his regular trips into the bush to kill foxes and feral cats.

Simon had once asked him about the money in fox skins, to which Ray replied, *"There isn't any Simon. Not now. There used to be, twenty odd years ago, when some disease went through the animal population in Europe. They were screaming out for skins then, and the money was good. These days I might tan the odd winter skin, but mainly I just kill them because they're not native. Although, I suppose that during this drought I'm probably doing some of them a favour."*

Simon understood, and he had on one occasion gone out into the bush with Ray. They had dragged road kill to leave a trail some kilometres long, and along it they'd buried condensed milk coated cyanide baits in shallow holes. Ray had marked each site, so unused baits could be retrieved early the next day.

He liked Ray. An easy bloke to be in the company of, and one who without knowing it always seemed to be teaching. Whether it was bush craft, mechanics or the stars which displayed themselves against the ebony outback sky. A listener to Ray's quiet voice always came away from a meeting having learnt something.

He was a wiry man, not tall, who wore a uniform of the traditional Australian stockman. Western style shirt, jeans, riding boots and a belt which when coupled the correct way, doubled as a pair of horse hobbles. There was nothing flash about Ray. He was just a down to earth Aussie bushman who knew and loved the bush. His only desire in his late life was to be as close to the bush as often as possible.

Ray loved the bush with a passion similar to the passion Simon had for the sea, but Simon loved the bush too, while Ray thought little of the sea.

It worked out.

As Simon stepped up the stairs to the old house his thoughts moved to food, drink and a hot shower. His sodden shirt had warmed due to the rise in his body temperature brought about by his brisk walk. Now as he stood wet under the iron roof of the veranda he welcomed the feeling of rainwater on his skin.

It had been so long in coming that he looked up into the darkness, toward the clouds that undoubtedly hung beyond the falling veil of water and whispered quietly, "Thank you."

The sound of his footfall, while mostly lost to the rattle of rain on the iron roof, was also muffled by the thick coat of mud, which acted like a second sole on his boots. His muddy track ended at a welded steel frame. It held his boot's heels while he eased his feet free from the hollows within the sticky mess, before he made his way to the kitchen and retrieved a bottle of beer from the refrigerator.

Simon noticed that Ray had left some mail on the kitchen table. He didn't bother with the three envelopes. Instead he went bare footed down the kitchen stairs to a corrugated iron lean-to, which offered weather protection to a forty-four gallon drum hot water heater.

Using his hat to protect his hand from the hot fencing wire handle, he lifted the camp oven from the dying embers and carried it inside the house. Placing it by the lounge room fireplace, before he threw paper and wood onto the iron grate, then with a small pour of kerosene he brought a fire to life.

Simon lifted the lid off the camp oven, and his saliva glands responded to the steamy cloud of aroma which arose from the cast iron pot. Pleased with the sight of the roasted wild duck he pinched a small sample of glistening brown skin, along with a portion of the juice-filled meat. Content for the moment with its taste on his tongue, and the thought of what was waiting for him on his return; he replaced the lid and sat the oven by the fire to keep it warm.

He had to walk past the kitchen table to retrieve his beer bottle by the sink and was tempted to check the mail, but decided he would prefer to shower under hot water first.

The three letters, one of which would redirect his current course in life, would have to wait his return.

CHAPTER 2

Simon rested Gidgee on the open fire, where pine kindling crackled as its leaping yellow flame was highlighted against a backdrop of the soot covered black stone. The hearth was wide enough to allow long logs, and its mantelpiece high enough to avoid head contact for even tall people who tended the fire.

It wasn't really cold enough to warrant a fire, but Simon grasped at the age-old pleasure of flickering flames and glowing coals whenever the opportunity allowed. It had been some time since he'd had a fire at his feet as he sat contentedly in an armchair.

There had been plenty of campfires after his days of work on the bulldozer, but those had been a necessity for cooking and hot water, and therefore more of a chore than a pleasure.

As well, the chairs he'd sat in at that time were not comfortable, and as with all open fires their smoke always followed beauty, to the extent that they often became a pain in the bum.

Whereas, this open fire tonight with flickering flames and shadows, complimented by the constant sound of the rain on the corrugated iron roof could only be seen as pure smokeless luxury.

The duck had gone down well, and the two glasses of wine which followed it left a contented feel in his belly.

He would sleep well tonight.

Simon filled a glass with some reasonable port and sat back into the old decrepit armchair. His feet in fresh socks presented sole first to the yawning open mouth of the stone fireplace. The chair he likened to the barber's cat, in that it was better than it looked. Even more so on this wet and windy night.

The blue flashes, which entered through the window created their own forms of surrealism in the room. They came at longer intervals now, and with less thunder.

He picked up the three letters, and as usual he didn't look at the front of any of them. Just held the three as a pack and opened them all with three quick movements of his pocketknife. The one on the top was junk mail, where someone tried to point out to him the benefits of their country style furniture. Simon smiled to himself as he looked about the room at the existing furniture. It had stood the test of time and proved its old world quality.

He crumpled the brochure and threw it at the fire.

The second letter was from the boat company on the east coast. Where his thirty-two-foot ocean going sail boat had just completed a three month fit out. From new sails and rigging, new diesel engine, new sonar, depth sounder and radio, new solar panels and deep cell batteries, auto pilot, right through to the thorough lacquer job on her well-built wooden hull. She was his pride and joy. Beautiful in the water, and she now had a whole lot of new toys for him to play with.

It had originally been rebuilt and equipped in Canada by a German named Hans. He'd explained to Simon, that his wife had left him because he, in his words had, "*Spent all der time mit der boat.*"

Hans had eventually finished the work, and left his wife behind as he sailed to Australia. From Cairns he had sailed around the top to Broome, from where with a newly acquired crew of two women he'd set out on a voyage to Bali.

Simon had met the crew, and he had to admit he was not impressed with the attitude they had of Hans when he was out of earshot. It had appeared to Simon they would go to any lengths to achieve their aim of a free yacht ride to Bali. He'd wondered, when he'd heard the story later about Hans being washed overboard somewhere between Broome and Bali. Simon had met Hans in Broome a few months before he went missing, and even though he liked him he didn't go much on the crew who managed to return.

Simon had paid top dollar for 'der boat', which was small compensation for Hans' wife who'd played second fiddle to it for all of those years.

He supposed der boat was why he was still in the ranks of the single. For boats he reckoned were like women. It was difficult to juggle two at the same time, either two women or a boat and a woman. It was okay if you found a woman who could handle the isolation of the sea, but they were few and far between. They both needed time and energy, nurturing and maintenance and of course, a woman needed those added extras, security and a nest.

Simon loved women, some like lovers, while for many he felt something akin to brotherly love. He didn't love boats; a boat was just a possession one used to celebrate life. It was a tool with which one expressed one's gratitude for the privilege to be alive.

When the time came for explanation, it came at the same time as the realization that the thin edge of the wedge had found a crack in the relationship, and soon after that came the inevitable 'me or the boat' ultimatum. Simon had heard many of them, and was fairly sure the boat was just a means used by some who needed to exercise their importance. Turn the freewheeling adventurer into the perfect example of domesticity.

What type of love has to be proved by the sale of a possession? Will the time come when the same expectation will arise over a set of golf clubs or a surfboard?

He didn't blame women though. He understood, he thought. They were subject to the will of a dictatorial maternal instinct that used any means necessary to repress revolt. Simon admitted to himself that he was far from being an authority on the subject, but it appeared to him that it was somehow along these lines.

Suddenly, the thought flashed into his mind of one woman. As it did, he took his eye from the letters to gaze at a small blue feather of flame that fluttered like a flag over an orange glowing Gidgee coal.

Sarah. She was unique, and one who had it seemed, won the fight against the tyrant. She had shown her scorn by going off and exploring the world.

He wondered where on the planet she might be.

She was like him in a way. As she had once put it, "As soon as I could walk as a toddler, I was out the door to see what was outside the house. Mum says she spent half of her time bringing me back in again. That's the way I've always been Simon, always looking to see what's around the next bend. I don't know if I'm searching for anything in particular, I think that I'm just making the most of my time in life." Simon understood, for it could have been him she was talking about, and for that reason when the time came for her to go, he'd not asked her to stay, where she was going, nor if she'd be back.

They were two travellers who may one day meet again, and Simon never questioned coincidence. He'd travelled enough to know that old acquaintances could turn up in the least expected places.

He reminisced for a few moments before he returned to the letter. It pointed out to him that the fourth and final payment for the refit of the 'Patricia Anne' was due.

'Patricia Anne' was the name that Hans had given her, and Simon had seen no reason for it to change, although he always referred to it as 'der boat'.

He looked forward to being with the ocean again. Although, when the time came he knew also, that he would miss the bush, but he would return again. Part of being free was the ability to go where you wished when you wished.

His decision to come to the outback was because of the sea. He came to work in this part of arid Australia so that he could make the money to enable him to go back to the sea. A situation which had now changed course, due to his unearthing of a treasure trove of startling coloured Australian opal.

Simon's two skills in life were sailing and earthworks machinery. The difference between the two was that he would sail for free, whereas for driving machinery he expected, and received a high rate of pay.

Part of the reason he commanded a higher rate of pay was because of the difficulty facing employers in finding operators prepared to spend long periods in isolated areas.

Simon, being a sailor was used to isolation, and had over long years become used to solitude. It mattered little to him whether that solitude was to be had on the rolling high seas or on the hard packed Western Plains.

Now after four months of dusty working days in the outback, his bank balance was very healthy. He had enough to cover the refits final payment and he'd not have to work many years to come. This fact was not only because he had worked hard and for many hours. Mostly it had to do with his good fortune when his employer had contracted him and the dozer to a grazier at Lightning Ridge to build an earthen dam.

He'd been in an area well known for opal mines for about a week, and had dug the dam down almost to its required depth when he'd struck a patch of white chalky clay. Over the next few days he'd searched that patch as he had cut it away. He knew nothing about opal mining, but he did learn on this occasion that knowledge was unimportant when one accidentally turned up a small fortune. Particularly when with each cut, the white earth yielded another layer of precious stone. He'd bagged a lot, and just a cursory glance as he grabbed at it showed a lot of the high valued red colour.

He did wonder at the time whether he was in fact stealing it.

The fact he'd hidden the white patch by raking a thin layer of red dirt over it suggested so.

After a few more days he'd finished the Ridge job, and had moved to the small village of Byrock and to a new contract. Spending another week clearing woody weed infested bush for a new fence line before returning to Bourke, where he'd put in his notice to finish up. Without his opal discovery he would have had to stay dozer driving for at least another three months, and he felt elated at having been saved from at least that amount of work.

He could leave the outback right now if he'd wanted to, but the precious stone discovery had somehow taken away the need to rush. He'd become a wealthy man, and had learnt already that although wealth couldn't buy more time it did allow him the freedom to take his time. His time was his, to be used at his own pace and shared with whomever he chose, rather than at some other persons pace when it was traded for a weekly pay packet.

At some stage of the game he would have to march to another tune, but now with the newfound wealth, that hovering knowledge seemed to have faded into insignificance.

Of more significance at this moment in time was a basic need to have a week or three doing absolutely nothing. That is, nothing other than make the most of his days in the outback, because when 'der boat' was back in the ocean it may be years before he had the chance to return to this harsh, dry and broad landscape.

A short holiday after four months of dust, dirt and flies seemed fair.

He'd had time off over that period of course, due to the odd dozer breakdown when he'd had to wait for spare parts, but not all of it had been quality time. Except for some days he'd spent with a single, professional woman whom he'd met at a local bush poet's night.

She was a newcomer to the outback, and was taking the opportunity offered by this small country town to begin her own private practice. She hoped, when it was built up and sold on, it might bring enough profit to enable her to buy into a Sydney practice.

He sat considering her for a moment, and suggested to himself that he should call her.

Soon, he thought.

For now, he just wanted to relax and adjust to holiday pace, sleep in, do a bit of fishing.

A smile came to his face at the memory of her when he'd offered to be her chaperone on her first excursion into the bush. They'd travelled out to the Warrego River to catch yabbies, and he'd watched with fascination as absolute feminist dealt with waving yabby claws, mud, leeches and a smoky campfire.

He'd wondered as their day had progressed whether in fact she was enjoying the outing. He was reassured at sun down as he delivered her safely home, when she had reached across the car to touch his arm and thank him for an excellent day.

He'd not known Beth for very long, but it was long enough to know that she had a heart of gold.

Simon put 'der boat' letter down and reached over to pick up the third and last envelope. It immediately caught his interest as it carried a postage stamp of an animal he'd only seen in picture books.

He grasped the single page and withdrew it from the envelope. Unfolding it he found it was addressed to someone by the name of Garry.

Simon looked to the envelope again.

"Uh, Oh," he croaked. It was addressed to a man by the name of Garry Sudovich.

The post office box number was the same as Simons, but the place of its supposed destination was a suburb of Sydney, though the postcode was Simon's postcode.

He studied the handwriting, whose large and very loopy scrawl would be easy to misread. The Post Office staff could be forgiven for the letters incorrect destination. The fact the envelope held the post code of Simons town rather than that of its intended destination wouldn't have helped much either he thought.

Simon learnt at that moment that these things obviously did happen at times. He was sure misdirected mail was a thing of the past with the introduction of new technology, but nothing could overcome an incorrect postcode.

He looked at the good quality paper of the letter itself. The letterhead told him it had begun its travels in a city he had heard of, and he decided he would have to check the atlas later.

He read the loopy hand with difficulty.

My good friend Garry,

How are you my good friend? It has been a long time since I have called on you in this way. A necessity for the time of trouble has yet again come to my country.

An uprising which started in our north some months ago is becoming more serious by the day, and of the future for me or for any of my colleagues in this government I know not.

The possibility of an over throw hangs over all our heads now, and because of the fear and suspicion that many may be sympathizers of the rebellion, I must be guarded in my contact with you my friend.

I use this method of communication because of the uncertainty of the security surrounding my private and official communication systems. There are many ears alert for the sound of treachery.

If the government falls I must escape, for my life would be considered worthless by the leaders of the uprising. My timing must be perfect, for if I make my move too early then my President will most certainly view my intentions as disloyal.

As you know my good friend, my position in government allows for certain fund transfers and I have at this moment another viable plan. The necessary government ministers are aligned to sign the papers to achieve a smooth result.

I need from you now a facsimile number to be able to further my communication with you. The facsimile number posted at the top of this page is direct to my office, and even though I use it with apprehension it is necessary to do so this once, and one time only. I will brief you as to a more secure line the next time I contact you.

I remind you that your interest in this venture has risen due to the time factor; to 25% of the sum of $32.6m (U.S.) I think this will be to your satisfaction.

I bid you farewell my friend, and I stress once more that time is short and that this plan must be put into effect immediately.

Best Regard

Abu Mohammed

Simon sat back in the old chair and for a moment gazed at a large huntsman spider, which hung on the far wall. He considered the letter for a while, and then decided on a nightcap before moving down the corridor to his bedroom.

He lay on his bed and stared at the ceiling for a short time, until with the welcome sound of lightly falling rain in his ears he drifted off to sleep.

His last thought in an awakened state was of Abu, and he spoke quietly to him in the darkness, "Got your fingers in the till have you mate?"

He smiled.

CHAPTER 3

The morning sun woke Simon early.

At dawn, it stared across from the far horizon and into his sleeping face. His eyes registered the bright light through closed eyelids and opened, before quickly closing again to the glare of the huge golden eye, which rested upon the windowsill.

He awoke slowly.

Starting a day was something he believed should be done slowly and cautiously. There would be plenty of time to speed up as the day progressed. This idea was reinforced by the stories he'd heard of people waking up on their boats, sleepily walking out on deck and stepping straight over the side. If not a good reason to Simon, then at least it was a good excuse to lie in for those extra few moments.

There was an extraordinary feeling he'd dreamt of an African country and its intrigue. As he swung his legs from bed, he glanced at the letter on the bedside table and allowed its existence to introduce that feeling to reality.

Simon showered under water still warm from the previous night's fire, and considered the day ahead over a cup of hot sweet tea.

After the last nights rain the roads would be soaked and impassable. It would be necessary to use the small outboard motor boat to get to town, and once there access a facsimile machine. An electrician friend had one, and Simon believed he knew the man well enough to ask for the use of it.

If it came down to it, there was always the fax service at the local post office, or just go and buy one of the things. They'd become a lot cheaper over the years as far as he knew.

To do this he would need international direct dialling.

His didn't have this function. He considered the different facets of telecommunications, and he couldn't help but wonder why this Abu fellow didn't just use E-mail. Surely the internet would be the most efficient method for direct and secretive affairs.

Simon couldn't figure that one, and decided he would have to follow the African's lead. The first card had been played and Simon was obliged to follow suit. He picked up his phone hand piece and dialed enquiries, and after wasting some minutes of his time following various prompts he was finally answered.

"Good morning, telephone and information services, Kerry speaking. How may I help you?"

Simon liked the voice. An easy one to listen to this early in the day, and he wondered whether the same could be said of his voice.

"Hello. I wondered if you might tell me about International Direct Dialling please, and if this phone I'm using is capable of using it?"

Simon wasn't sure if his question would be understood. He sometimes felt uneasy when trying to find the words to describe something he knew nothing about.

"If you give me your number I can find out for you, Sir."

He told her his number, and then waited for some moments before she replied.

"My screen reads that your line is not linked to the I.D.D system, Sir."

Simon thought a moment.

"I see. Could you tell me the waiting time between application and connection? That is, if it's possible to apply through you now?"

"Yes it is, and the waiting time is four days."

Too long, Simon thought.

He thanked her for her help and she wished him a nice day before he put down the phone.

Simon rolled another cigarette and decided the electrician's fax was his best bet, although more to the point, his only option.

He'd ruled the Post Office out because of the lack of confidentiality. It was a small town and who knows who might read his message. Besides, he had to expect a return facsimile. If he was going to carry this thing through, then he had to act quickly.

Up until now he'd not made the commitment, but once he had sent a fax to the African he was on the roller coaster, which may be hard to stop. It may be that the whole idea might prove to be incredibly easy. There was always the possibility of danger of course.

And as far as the law was concerned? He questioned quietly.

He didn't know, and as he had no way of finding out it was a waste of time thinking about it.

The African was obviously thieving from his government. Was there a law against thieving from a thief? Whose law? African? Australian? In his case the African was hardly going to go to the police to report a theft.

He picked up the phone and dialled the electrician's mobile phone number.

"Gidday mate."

"How're you going Simon? Good rain, eh?"

Simon agreed and they spoke of happenings around town for a few moments until he felt the bush had been well beaten,

"I wondered if I might be able to use your fax machine."

"Can't see any reason why not Simon, it's right to go whenever you want to use it."

"Does it have International Direct Dialling, do you know?"

"I'm not sure, it may have. The wife ordered the machine, so she probably bought every attachment and connection known to mankind." The electrician suddenly threw a surprise question that for a moment caught Simon off guard. "Why do you need International dialling?"

"I've decided to write a book and I need to do a bit of research, so some of the information for it will have to be gained from overseas sources," Simon added weakly.

"Half your luck, I wish I had the time just to sit down somewhere quiet to read one."

"Yeah I know what you mean; life can get to be a bit hectic at times."

"You know Simon, you'd have to be the only bloke I know who can get away with working part of the time, living an easy lifestyle while still paying your own way. Don't ever get married mate."

"I don't think I'd be able to live that way, married I mean, although I am kind of married anyway. My boat can be a bit demanding now and then."

"Speaking of demanding, I'd better be getting back to work."

"Would it be alright to use the fax today sometime?"

The electrician told Simon he would find the key to his office under a house brick at the corner of the building nearest to the door. They spoke a little longer and decided that a beer at the Oxford Hotel would be in order at about five o'clock that afternoon.

Simon put his phone down and looked out the window. There were a lot of birds out this morning. Some performed aerial ballet to catch flying insects while others pecked and scratched the soft moist ground. The parrots walked pigeon toed through dead but damp grasses in search of seed.

Their bright green feathers stood out on a background of burnt brown and golden yellow. Birdcalls and high-pitched whistles came to him from rough barked branches, where leaves shone bright now that the dust of years of yesterdays had been washed away.

Simon loved this country. It was a land of great extremes which balanced like a see saw. On one end the torrid tyrant who burned and scorched the earth from horizon to horizon. While on the seesaws other end, the tyrant torrent that drowned and flooded all that stood before it from billabong to open plain.

Simon remembered the lines he'd heard delivered by a local bush poet, and as he looked out to the far horizon he spoke the words loudly. They echoed through the rooms of the old homestead.

From rain and plains of green

to floods, no banks between

Then dry with heat extreme

or fire, blazing queen

Simon's mood was good, as would be everyone's in the district he expected, rain usually brought out the best in all people. Except for those who are bogged, he chuckled. Particularly as it was only fifteen hours ago that rain had seemed to be so far away.

Like Africa.

The thought was a jolt back to reality, and he trod through the house for the few items he needed to take with him to the small outback town.

The sky was blue and the air smelt fresh in his nostrils, complimented by a light cool breeze, which carried a butterfly across the unkempt garden.

He walked the four hundred metres to the river in short time, even though the black soil clung to his boots. It forced him to pull up at times to scrape his heels across a log or tree root to remove the claggy mess.

The riverbank was slippery as he made his way down to a small aluminum boat whose motor started easily. He pushed its nose towards the main channel, away from the potential propeller damaging submerged logs in close to the riverbank.

The surface of the river itself was a mess of small twigs, leaf litter and old gum nuts that had been washed off the riverbanks by the storm. It formed floating islands that water striders zipped around.

He was rewarded with pleasant thoughts of his sailboat as the gentle waves pummeled the bow of the small aluminum boat. Those thoughts began to pale as they were overtaken, and replaced by the sight of the natural colour and beauty of the river.

It amazed him sometimes.

The ride lasted twenty minutes, and ten minutes after that he had the key inserted into the office doors lock. He let himself in, and in a short while had the fax machine uncovered. Its single green eye stared out at him, suggesting it was available to his every command.

He eyed the typewriter on the desk and wondered if the African was familiar with Garry Sudovich's handwriting. The letter he'd opened the night before and now held in his hand didn't suggest so.

A piece of paper rolled into the typewriter easily and he typed slowly with one finger, Abu. Below that he typed in the International access code for Australia, the Australian country code, the area code and then the electricians fax number. He signed it with a simple capital G, thinking that if the African was jumpy about security, then maybe he would expect some kind of code.

It was the best he could do under the circumstances he decided, as he placed the typed paper into the facsimile machine.

He pressed the touchpad numbers with the index finger of his right hand. The fingers of his left hand followed across the top of the Africans letter, as he double-checked the number and then pressed 'start.'

Simon looked at the machine and wondered at its age. He didn't see himself as an authority on facsimiles, but this one appeared to him just by its design to be an early model.

"I suppose that in the world of electronics you are probably comparatively about my age," he told it almost apologetically. The machine made some electronic noises, then a few more strange sounds before a short delay.

Simon watched as nothing happened, and waited as his heart pounded. It seemed to work overtime in his chest, until finally it felt as if it skipped a beat as the paper began to move through the machine.

He knew then, that whatever it was he was starting had begun, when he looked out of the office window, uneasy with the thought that he now had reason to look over his shoulder.

CHAPTER 4

Abu Mohammed stood looking out of his large office window and down over the well-tended garden area of the courtyard. He was a big man, so looking down on his immediate surroundings was to him quite normal. He noticed the guard had been doubled, and he watched as uniformed troops positioned sandbags around a heavy machine gun.

Every Government official and employee understood that a day is a long time in politics. The same could be said about revolutions, where situations changed at very short notice, and the term 'early retirement' took on a whole new meaning.

It was still dark, and powerful floodlights lit the whole area, leaving little shadow.

It was not unusual for Abu to be in his office at this time of night. Many of his activities had to be carried out under the cover of darkness. Not only for his sake, but the people with whom he had dealings felt more at ease under a cloak of night.

His expensive gold watch showed the local time to be near two o'clock in the morning before he gazed again out over the high compound wall. To where the bobbing lights of a fishing vessel reflected off the wide dark waters of Freetown's natural harbour.

He lifted his eyes and allowed them to follow the street lit, but night filled black spine of the Sierra Leone Peninsula. Its seaward tip touched the Atlantic Ocean and rose through to the wooded hills known as the Lion Mountains.

Abu had spent much of his childhood on the Sierra Leone River, whose fast flowing current scoured silt away from the bottom of Freetown's harbour. It had also strained the motor of his father's small boat, as he'd returned upstream from the bustling markets after delivery of vegetables and tobacco. His Father and his Grandfather had tried to instill in him some of their wisdom and experience, but Abu had learnt at a young age that there was more to be expected from life than what could be gained from delivering vegetables.

Their endeavours met with little success, partly because of the markets of Freetown, where Abu befriended those who extended their incomes in the diamond smuggling trade.

It was these smugglers who used the overland river route to carry out their private business affairs that caught the attention of the teenage Abu. He chose to follow a similar path to them in an attempt to gain wealth and local prestige.

Freetown also taught him about political turmoil. How its impact, in the form of wholesale slaughter and widespread hunger could lead to the making of an entrepreneur.

He had his first taste of upheaval and despair at the age of seven. In 1967, Siaka Stevens All Peoples' Congress was deposed by Juxon-Smith, who, one year later became the victim of mutiny, and Stevens was reinstated to office.

The rest of the decade was stormy.

In 1971, Sierra Leone became a republic, and the countries rapid decline became more apparent with each passing day, as Steven's supporters enriched themselves at the public's expense.

Stevens retired in 1985 and his successor governed under 'the business as usual' principle. Corruption flourished while the economy deteriorated further, until a coup toppled the successor in 1992.

Worse was still to come.

In 1997, Major Johnny Koroma released six hundred captives from the capital's top security prison and overthrew the government of President Ahmad Tejan Kabbah. Lawlessness spread throughout Sierra Leone, bringing with it the international community's immediate condemnation, until Nigeria finally led a regional force to restore Kabbah. In early June their naval vessels bombarded Freetown, and Abu learnt firsthand the power of an artillery shell over a human body.

Nigeria's occupation of Freetown failed to restore Kabbah, and a stalemate ensured. Clashes between Koroma and Kabbah supporters continued into 1998, when Nigeria tripled the number of its forces in the country.

It was at this time, when his smuggling operations in the diamond rich eastern part of the country became threatened by Pro-Kabbah forces that Abu was forced to choose sides. He threw in his lot with Kabbah, and through insight and carefully chosen accomplices, he'd achieved a place in Kabbah's new government after Koroma was forced to flee.

Abu's position in government was not high, but it afforded him access to senior ministers and freedom to carry on business as usual.

He'd also expanded his interests into other areas such as drugs, and the acquisition of the weapons that became available by the disarming of Koroma's rebel militias.

There was also money to be made out of international community who offered humanitarian assistance.

Abu had been brought up in an environment where coup d'état prevailed, and its consequences of corruption, disappearances and torture were seen by him to be everyday occurrences. One thing had changed however. Now it was Abu himself who made torture and disappearances everyday occurrences. Nothing personal against the lost souls, but business was business and through necessity he had learnt to be good at it.

To a certain extent he forgave himself for his wayward ways, because he had been forced to accept that the traditions of his forbears had gone. Now the world had changed to one where the creed was to grab what you can, while you can and be vigilant. His choice of this particular office was based on vigilance. It was to the front of the Government building where it gave him a good vantage point to see the comings and goings through the compounds stone arched gateway.

He noted the movement of troops below him in the courtyard, and then looked toward the east where the brooding mountains were touched by the brilliant glow of a full moon.

Out there, in the dark bush of the mountains whose silhouette Abu could see from this very window, was a new rebel whose name was Imbo.

Imbo was following the same path that Juxon-Smith and Johnny Koroma had. His plots and plans were made under the same moon and with the same destination in mind.

Now Abu knew the feeling of uncertainty that was probably felt by the previous occupiers of this Government building. They may have also looked out of this window and into the quiet before the storm.

He'd sunk into the false sense of security allowed by the fact that it had been nearly ten years since Johnny Koroma had issued his challenge. Now that comfort, like ice in warm water, was slowly taking on a whole new form.

Abu had also kept up his contacts in the drugs trade and it had become obvious to him two months earlier that something was in the air. Someone with access to good quality drugs had suddenly begun to compete heavily in his market. A sign that someone had the need to build a strong cash base, and Abu's concern had grown until suddenly his black market weapon sales began to spiral. New rumours reached his ears about the man named Imbo.

Abu considered the irony that the weapons he was selling to Imbo now, were supplied by the dealer whom he'd been meeting in Cape Town in 2001 when he'd met the man whose facsimile he waited for now.

He had been staying at the hotel where, coincidently, Garry Sudovich was enjoying his second honeymoon. After several chance meetings in the hotel bar they'd struck up conversation, and learned the similarities between their business interests.

In 2002 Abu had contacted Sudovich and outlined a plan, which they'd then carried out successfully, to the tune of three hundred thousand dollars.

Another year had passed before Abu felt it safe enough to try again, this time for higher stakes. They were successful again and netted a little over eight hundred thousand dollars. Hopefully this year would be good for them too. Abu tried to visualize the look on Sudovich's face when he realized the value of his share.

Abu smiled at his own reflection in the darkened office window as he contemplated his retirement plan. Suddenly his face became blank as he glanced again at the machine gun.

He was approaching his fifties, and although he didn't feel old, there was something somewhere within him that felt tired, a feeling that was exacerbated by his fear of uncertainty.

Imbo.

It didn't matter to him that the arms he traded were the weapons used by the rebels who were slowly sweeping across the country. Maybe Imbo himself was holding a weapon that had Abu's fingerprints stamped firmly upon it.

After all, if he didn't supply them, then someone else would.

He just had to make sure he got out of the country before he became the victim of one of those weapons. With Sudovich's help he would reap his reward and then find somewhere on this earth where he could retire and enjoy stability.

He still had that thought in mind when suddenly the facsimile machine began to spit out a sheet of paper.

It was only a short message.

His ticket to freedom.

CHAPTER 5

Having a clear picture in mind of what he would do with this fortune was one thing, being in the position to do what he pictured was another, and the two hinged on the most important factor. He had to acquire it first. To do that, Simon would need some legal advice.

He looked at his watch and decided it would be around eleven o'clock the previous night African time. The African had suggested in his letter that time was short. If that was the case, then Simon just had to rely on the man's need for speed.

Five o'clock this afternoon would be around four in the morning African time. Hopefully, if the African was an early riser and on the ball Simon might have the information tonight.

He left the electrician's office, replaced the key below the house brick, and then with time to kill he walked towards the town's main business area.

Beth was sixteen years younger than Simon and they'd met in the crowded bar of the North Bourke hotel a few months earlier. A bush poet's night had been held, and due to the lack of seating Simon had been forced to ask if he could sit at her table.

She'd been unsure at first, but after a hesitant first step they'd talked for nearly an hour during which time he didn't say a word out of place. He'd been clothed as an outdoor worker, and although she could see that his calloused hands were ingrained with soil of some sort, his fingernails were clean, and that to her was good sign.

They'd had good rapport, while Simon endeavoured from the outset not to send any signals that might suggest he expected anything more than friendship. He'd been down many roads before, and believed he understood relationships well enough at a glance to know that the distance between the two of them was too great.

Simon was not one to view prospects with a critical eye, but he did face facts. The facts as he saw them in this case were that his boat, his old blue Ford and his close to nature life style were way too far removed from her gleaming B.M.W, her stationary well to do career and the established neighbourhood that she sought in Sydney of all places. To him there would be too much compromise, and compromise in Simon's eyes led to pressure. The last thing a relationship needed, he thought

They had enjoyed each other's company at the bush poet's night, and after that a day out catching yabbies. Since then they had met on the few occasions that Simon had been in the town. He'd discovered that he loved her as a friend, but that was as far as he would like it to go, as he was planning to be sailing the Whitsunday passage soon. A point he'd gone out of his way to make plain on several occasions, and one he hoped she would understand without need for an in depth explanation.

The right man for her was out there somewhere, and Simon secretly wished for her sake, that whoever he was he'd get his act together and turn up.

He crossed the main street and pushed open the door to Beth's reception area where he spoke across the room to Lynette who was working at her computer.

"Hello young one. How's your day?"

Lynnette was a dark haired beauty whose smile was as broad as the day is long, and it shone. Not only from her white even teeth, but also from her shining large pupil brown eyes. She was about twenty-two he guessed and a lover of life. Her father owned a large sheep station about a hundred and fifty kilometres west of Bourke.

"Hello Simon," she said with some surprise. "Must be a bit of cocky in you eh? Straight into town as soon as it's rained. Or did you miss me?"

"No and yes," he answered.

She moved across the room and looked up at him. He saw with the help of the overhead lights her eyes change until they glowed like polished copper. "Who's the lucky girl then?"

Simon grinned.

"It's business, so I don't have the luxury of choice."

She laughed.

"I'll accept that. You got out of that one pretty well didn't you?" She called over her shoulder as she walked back to her desk. She spoke to Beth on an intercom before she returned again to stand behind the counter before him where she said, "She enjoys her time with you Simon."

He held her gaze for a brief moment before he looked toward Beth's office door.

"Is she free at the moment, or will I be interrupting?"

"She has a bit on today, but she'll make time for you. Go on in." Simon walked across the room and was about to knock when the door opened. Beth met him and drew him into her office. She didn't return to the chair behind her large desk, leaving them to sit facing each other in the two client's chairs.

"How're things Simon?"

"I've been taking it very easy," he smiled, "Just a spot of fishing and some quiet time in the bush." He paused for a moment before he added, "I have to make the most of it while I can. I received a letter in the mail yesterday telling me that der boat is ready for sea. How about you?"

She considered his question as she wondered at his reaction if he ever had to choose between the ocean and the bush. "Pretty quiet. You know how it is, life in a small town where not much happens. I like the country lifestyle, but it would be nice sometimes to be able to nip into the city for the theatre and the restaurants." Simon pictured himself at the theatre, trying to work out an opera.

She laughed and Simon saw beauty as her face beamed in the shaded office light.

"I'd love to know the thought that just went through your mind?" She said, still smiling.

"Can't give too much away," Simon grinned.

She amazed him again and as usual caught him off balance. He still didn't know if she could read his mind, the look on his face or if she just knew the right time to throw semi questions like that into conversations.

They chatted.

"Are you busy for lunch?" He asked.

"I'm free now until 2 o'clock. There's plenty that I should be doing, but to tell you the truth I am hungry."

The restaurant was within walking distance and they had time.

The building itself was an old, well-manicured structure with a bull nosed awning. Its interior was decorated with old style furniture. Each piece covered with lace doilies and ornaments of fired pottery.

It was quiet as the lunch hour rush hadn't started and they chose a table whose window gave them a view of the street outside. When they were both seated and had given their orders for lunch, Beth looked at Simon.

"Well?"

"Well what?" Simon said.

"You've something on your mind. What is it?" Simon smiled into his wine glass, not quite sure of his feelings when he was read so easily. He would like to have had the opportunity to ease the topic into the conversation.

A shy grin amplified his tanned dimples.

"Ah, I need a favour actually. I've decided to write a book and I need help with some of the legal angles of the story."

"Love to help you. What do you need?" She probed.

He told her as much as he felt she needed to know. Most of what was true; after all it was only a story line. Like one that might be seen on film at the movies.

Only in this case he was the author, and the actor.

More deception as the day wore on and aimed at this beautiful trusting woman. He felt his appetite for lunch leave him.

"What I need to know is the procedure to move the money into Australia legally, that is, after the books character has acquired it." He looked at his food, then back into the large pools of pupil, which stole away the blue in her eyes.

"You're in luck Simon; I've spent the last year studying corporate law." She lowered her voice into a business tone of quiet discussion and Simon hoped to remember all the information in her answers.

He'd better. He could not afford to make mistakes. Prison and loss of his freedom was a thought that sickened him.

"The central character must be confident the fortune can be imported into his country and into legitimate business. He must be able to lose all the money in a corporate structure," he said when she'd finished.

"In other words, launder it," Beth suggested as she looked at him questioningly. Simon was taken aback as he was struck by the implication of the words. He played for time by reaching out for the wine bottle before he answered,

"Yes. I suppose that is the correct term, isn't it?"

"Sounds like your character might need a good solicitor either way," she smiled again.

"Either way?" Simon asked.

She raised an eyebrow.

"Well if he's successful in his bid he will need a corporate lawyer, and if he's not, then he may need a more than an average defence lawyer." She sipped her wine before she added, "If you meet him in real life let me know. I'd love to get involved practically in corporate law."

Simon noted her statement, and then laughed as she joked.

"Either way."

He walked her back to her office, where a light breeze touched her hair and with the sunshine a new blue in her eyes.

"You know Simon, when you first mentioned this book, I wondered if it might be an autobiography?"

Their eyes locked and he smiled at her.

"No. It's just a novel about a bloke whose quest is for a worthy cause." Simon reached out his hand and Beth took it in hers as Simon said in his quiet appreciative manner, "I enjoyed lunch and your company. Thanks for your help."

He turned away and for a moment she watched him go until he rounded the next corner. She sighed, and as the breath escaped her lips it carried with it the unheard words.

"Take care Simon."

CHAPTER 6

Simon had a beer with the electrician at 5.15, and at 6 o'clock was walking back towards the office and the fax machine. He found the key under the brick and opened the door. Some sheets of paper hung from the machine and Simon tore them off, found which end was the top of the page and began to read.

He felt strangely nervous as his eyes focused on the opening lines of the facsimile

My good friend Garry,

This letter is to be on a letterhead, signed by company officials and stamped with a company seal.

The Director General,

Project Implementation Division,

Ministry of Aviation,

120 Narrow Road.

Freetown.

Dear Sir,

RE: CONTRACT No MVA/P.I.R./94/0622

(A) TARMAC PRECONSTRUCTION AND COMPUTERISATION OF TOWERS AT HASTINGS AIRFIELD

(B) SUPPLY, ERECTION AND SYSTEM OPTIMISATION OF HANGARS

With reference to your letter of 19th July 2008, we take the liberty of submitting for your consideration, this letter for the sum of thirty-two point six million U.S. dollars ($32.6M), being the final payment due to us following completion of the above mentioned contract.

We wish to state that in arriving at this claim, we have taken cognizance of the mobilization fee already received from you and have also affected all necessary discounts in relation to variation orders issued and approved by consultants during the execution of the contract.

In accordance with terms of the contract and all relevant amendments thereto, and to enable to discharge our obligation to our numerous sub-contractors, we kindly remit the above stated amount in full to our under mentioned bank:

Account number:.........................

Bankers name:..........................

Bankers address:........................

Bank facsimile No:......................

Beneficiary:............................

Thanking you in advance for your co-operation:

Yours Faithfully,
Managing Director

Simon was stunned and he sat back on the desk to stare at the document. There was more to read on the other pages, but he had seen enough to know the gist of it.

All he had to do was prepare some false letterheads, type in the letter the African had faxed him and send it back to the

African. He would put it through his government offices and Simon would be $32.6m dollars richer.

He folded the paper and put it into an old envelope he retrieved from the waste paper bin, turned the fax off and left the building. He would have tonight and tomorrow to read the rest he thought.

The sun was low as he started the boats motor and set off up stream. As he motored along he didn't take note of the river, its tree lined banks or the birdlife jostling noisily for the best night perching places.

He was different somehow, and he drove the boat fast, not hearing the blaring outboard motor he usually found annoying.

CHAPTER 7

Simon awoke early after a late night. The coffee he'd siphoned during the course of those awakened hours was, he suspected, only part of the reason for his restless sleep. During the night his mind had worked over time on the plan he'd concocted. Each time he woke with a new thought until finally he got out of bed and started on a list of things to do.

It was going to be a very long week.

He stepped to the window and looked out. He took delight in the thought that it was sure to be a fine day. A few puffy marshmallow type clouds floated overhead, while nearer the horizon a heavier cloud formation was highlighted by the sunrises reddish pink glow.

As he gazed toward the river, a man's figure stood out against the bush background and the unexpected sight startled him.

Getting jumpy already, Simon? He thought as he looked closer and realized it was Ray. Simon watched as the man walked an indirect course from the river, and understood as he stopped now and then to kick mud off his boots. He'd obviously failed to successfully negotiate some of the still wet patches.

As Ray approached the house Simon called,

"Suppose you'd be in the market for a cup of tea?"

"Gidday Simon. A cuppa would go down well."

"You're early today?"

Ray put down the box he'd been carrying.

"Yeah, I'd set a few cod overnight lines yesterday, and seeing the track is still a bit wet I brought the boat out and checked them on the way. I didn't expect much because the waters not cold enough, but I thought that maybe the rain might have stirred something up." He paused for a moment before a hint of agitation touched his voice. "I heard on the news that common sense hasn't stirred up though. Someone else got lost again, and didn't have a disposable cigarette lighter for their two nights stay in the bush. It's amazing how a fire at night can make misadventure a bit more like a camping trip with a bit of warmth and light. Keeps the mind focused too, with the fire tending and wood collection, not to mention that bugs and lizards taste better cooked. Easy to signal search aircraft too, with a bit of smoke, especially during bushfire season, and all for a three dollar lighter."

While Simon knew Ray liked his fish, and of course common sense, he also understood the difficulties in catching the elusive Murray cod. Fishermen in the area usually baited lines with freshwater yabbies and set them in the deeper waters of the Darling River. These lines were nearly always tied to rubber bands made of tyre tube rubber which were attached to a tree or a log. Their design being to absorb some of the fishing lines stress when subjected to violent attacks by these large freshwater fish.

Simon smiled to himself as he remembered a tall story of a particular fish, which when photographed, the negative of film weighed thirty pounds.

They talked and smoked cigarettes until Simon heard the kettle whistle.

"I reckoned I'd make up a few fox baits for tonight. Would you mind bringing the tea out back while I get me gear ready?"

"Yeah I can do that mate. Want some toast or cake or something?"

"No. Nothing for me thanks," Ray replied.

Simon fixed the tea and stepped down from the veranda to where Ray had his gas cooker set up on the concrete swimming pool surround. The pool had seen better days, and now was only used as a reservoir for the garden sprinkler systems muddy Darling River water.

Simon handed him a large pannikin of black sweet tea and then watched as Ray pawed through the cardboard box. He lifted a block of white wax and broke it into smaller pieces, then dropped the pieces into an old pot on the single gas burner. When the wax had melted Ray turned down the flame, picked up a knife sharpening steel and dipped about four centimetres of its tip into the melt. When he pulled the steel from the wax he thrust it into a bucket of cold water, where with cooling, the wax solidified and Ray was able to pull off the steel a wafer thin wax capsule.

After he had made about thirty of these capsules, he lifted the lid from an old tin. It was filled with cyanide, and with it and the aid of a small scoop he filled each capsule, before sealing their open ends with more melted wax.

Tonight he would drag an animal's carcass behind his car, and lay baits as he went along its dead scented trail. Simon liked to watch him work. Every movement of Ray's hands was precise. He knew Ray had been trained in explosives during the Vietnam War. The fact he had a full complement of fingers suggested he'd been precise in that type of work too.

As Ray finished filling his wax capsules, the conversation picked up with Simon stating he had to fly down to Sydney. He'd leave on the plane at 10 o'clock in the morning and would Ray mind feeding the animals while he was away.

"No worries Simon. How long will you be gone?"

"Not really sure, couple of days, maybe a week. If it looks like being longer, I'll give you a ring and let you know."

After Ray had gone down to the paddock to check his horses, Simon walked over to the kennels with food for the sheep dogs. The dogs wagged their tails and strained at their leashes in their eagerness to be near the hand that fed them.

The grazier's ever faithful working dogs. They would follow and shepherd sheep all day for their master.

Run all day, until their paws grew painfully sore from the burrs of the outback and then when called on to do so, they would run some more.

Simon read the ingredients on the side of the dog food box, and thought the dogs probably had better tucker than many of the people on earth.

His mind shifted to Africa and he wondered if this 32.6 mill had been skimmed off the foreign aid which flooded in to feed the masses.

The children whose distended bellies and haunted eyes could be seen on the seven o'clock news on T.V.

He finished feeding the dogs and walked back to the house, to his comforts of home and lunch. His mind was still on the seven o'clock news and he had to remind himself not to let conscience get in the way.

There was a lot of work to be done over the next week and no time for distractions.

Ray saw to his horses. Measuring an amount of oats for each one and throwing a wad of lucerne into each stall. As he leaned against the rails of the horse's stalls watching the animals eat their green he considered Simon.

He knew Simon wasn't himself. His mind was elsewhere, and he was not anywhere near as talkative as usual.

Ray wondered if it had anything to do with the African postmarked letter he'd delivered on the afternoon of the rain.

The fact that Simon had not even mentioned the letter suggested to Ray that this man Garry Sudovich might not ever see its contents, and Ray could not help but to wonder why.

He turned his head towards the house as Simon was walking across its yard. As Ray watched him go, he thought he would wait and see. His life in the bush had taught him well the art of patience, and as the old saying 'time reveals all' crossed his mind he spoke quietly to his horses.

CHAPTER 8

He was known as the N.C.O. A nickname he'd earned, and one used so often his real name, Henry Horton was rarely heard.

At five feet and nine inches tall, but with many years behind him in gyms throughout the world he had become proud of his physique.

As a boy at school he'd been skinny and was looked down upon as the odd boy out. It led to him being picked on by an entire team of schoolyard bullies.

He learnt well at primary school. Being shunned by the other students on a daily basis was to his advantage, as he found refuge in books, after discovering the library was the safest place to be.

The schoolyard bullies had taught him how to fight and he became a practiced hand. Unfortunately, it wasn't enough against a pack, but he found it gratifying at times to see bruises and black eyes on some of the individual players the day after a chance meeting.

It was especially gratifying when a pack member would be absent from school altogether. A reminder to those present that stragglers beware.

Horton survived primary school, but by the first years of secondary school he had become withdrawn and insecure. To the extent he believed that everyone who spoke was speaking about him, and that every sound of laughter was aimed at him.

He'd taken it as a compliment when the girls at school became quiet as he passed. Mistaking their silence as respect rather than the steps they saw necessary to take, so as to not mistakenly provoke, 'Weird Henry.' The nickname was whispered, and it had been a long time before he had found out what it was he was called behind his back. The day he found out was in his third year of high school and the place was the science laboratory.

The students were working with acids in small uninspiring experiments when Weird Henry made a comment to the one girl in the class who was pleasing to his misguided eye. The girl was annoyed enough to tell him of his nickname in front of the whole class. Amid the snickering, Weird Henry wanted to shrink from view, but instead he lashed out at the girl. She had been holding a beaker which was partly filled with acid, and as he attacked her she instinctively flung the contents into his face.

He been badly burnt, and after a short time in hospital he'd returned to his home, where he told his Mother not to worry about him before he walked out to see the world.

After several low paid jobs in various fields, Henry joined the British army with the goal being the high prestige of the S.A.S. However, the army discovered almost immediately that Henry was a loner, and not nearly enough a team man. It was here he acquired a new nickname; one that Henry decided could only be a compliment. He had no idea where the name originated. When the men around him began to call him the N.C.O he just smiled in his ignorance and took it as a sign of respect. Not knowing, and never finding out that the real meaning of the letters was, 'Never Count On' Horton.

He would never follow the team plan to the letter, which is fair enough after the shooting starts. It is then that any plan can go haywire. He was seldom where he was supposed to be and rarely in place on time, in effect he couldn't be depended on and this impacted on the morale of his team members.

They knew Horton had balls and the ability to back anyone up in trouble, but would he be in the right place to do so if the situation ever arose?

He was a loner and even the army couldn't change that, although it did teach him two fundamentals toward the end of his army career. One being that he would never be S.A.S and two, that the freelance life of the mercenary was the next best thing.

He'd quickly gained contacts and now twenty-six years later, he was a survivor trying to survive another fight in someone else's war. It didn't matter whose war. He was employed for his expertise not his conscientious support. As long as Imbo kept feeding his bank account, then Horton would continue to supply his tools of trade.

That was part of the reason anyway; the root of it all was that Horton was addicted to his work. He needed the action, the sound of battle, the noises associated with it, the sound of men dying and the adrenalin rush.

He'd had seen a lot of wars and he'd decided to stay alive to see a lot more. He justified his actions with the obvious fact that each and every one of his wars was intent on the death of a tyrant or the overthrow of a dictator.

Of course he knew nothing of the characters who replaced the deposed. He expected the countries that'd been under the previous leaders control had at least the chance offered by a new beginning.

The death and carnage which littered the road to these new beginnings did not concern Horton. His motto was simple. 'No pain, no gain.'

He'd taken up temporary residence in this jungle three weeks earlier and had spent most of it bored out his mind. The rebels who made up Imbo's revolutionary force had no discipline at all. Horton had discovered very quickly he needed to be up front to lead them, whilst at the same time in the rear to rally them forward. As the weeks had passed, his followers had been thinned out in the often short skirmishes with the Government troops. Until at last the 'best' were left standing and Horton had at least something pliable to mould.

Against the government troops anyway, for their only cause was self-preservation and for this reason they had a tendency to break off engagements early, when with a little more push they may have won the day.

He scraped out the last of the baked beans cold from the can and hoisted the tin into the bush. Then after checking his weapon for dirt, he brushed the soil and leaf litter from his clothes, swung his back pack into place and called to his 'team.'

"Righto you mob, on your feet. It's time to go back to work." The fact that most of them spoke little or no English didn't matter. The command sounded alright to him.

Most of them had seen Horton check his personal gear and had risen, ready to go when he called. A lazier few tagged onto the end of the band as it moved off in the direction of Freetown, thirty miles away.

These were noted by Horton who sized them up as he ran his fingers over the heavy bristle which would never grow into a decent beard. He would remember the 'tail taggers' when some shit or dangerous jobs came up.

They were expendable.

*****

At the same time thousands of miles away. Garry Sudovich was caught up in heavy traffic snaking its way through Sydney's heat. The fact that someone had broken into his car the previous night and stolen all his C. D's didn't help to improve his day. He was about to turn his car's radio off, when the national news burst out and he decided with some resentment to give it one last chance to offer satisfaction. The last item of news caused him to concentrate.

"West African sources report the Sierra Leone Government is once again under threat of hostile takeover. Members of the African Union have called on the United Nations to send representatives to the country to evaluate the deteriorating situation. The calls come amid speculation that the actions of the rebel forces could lead to a situation, similar to that of the late 1990's when civil war broke out. It is estimated that over half a million people were killed, and neighbouring countries were forced to accept a similar amount of refugees." The newsreader went on with some more, but Garry was not listening as he had to brake heavily to narrowly avoid running into the car ahead.

He wished the day was over.

It was going badly.

His mind went back to the news bulletin and he wondered without care how Abu was going. Sudovich didn't like the African, and the fact he was thousands of miles away suited him. Sudovich had liked his percentage of the African's misappropriations though. Easy money which had fallen into his hands at a time when he was riding a wave of successful ventures and his confidence was at its peak.

A period in his life when everything he'd touched turned to gold. It had appeared that life was his oyster until the day it had been gutted by misadventure on the stock market. The monetary cost had been great, and its loss had forced him to enlist the services of a 'silent partner'. One whom he'd soon learnt was more like a vampire, determined to suck the very lifeblood from him.

Sudovich hated the man, but his back was to the wall and he had nowhere to run. He needed the 'silent partners' capital to survive. The banks would not look at him because the company's books, in their words, "Didn't appear sound." He was in no position to show them the second set of ledgers. He had to accept the situation as it was or face ruin.

If he was able to drive a wooden stake into the heart of the vampire, he would and not miss him at all. If the African met a similar fate in whatever was going on in Sierra Leone, then to hell with him too.

It had been over twelve months since their last contact, and the man had nearly slipped his mind. Now with the radios reminder of his possible existence he wondered if maybe he should give the African a call. If he was lucky there may be something to be gained out of the whole affair, especially if the African was under pressure.

Sudovich suddenly decided to ring the African right now; it would at least give him something to do until the traffic speeded up. As he reached for his mobile phone there came the realization that the C.D bandits had taken it too and were probably running his phone bill up to the sky.

He cursed loudly and wondered if the day could get worse.

CHAPTER 9

Simon checked his stuffed overnight bag. He was travelling light and would buy items, such as clothes as they became necessary. The plane was due to depart from the small outback airport in an hour, and after another glance at his wrist watch he decided he had little time to spare.

He reckoned the track from the house to the main road should be passable. The sun and the breezes would have dried it although there would be patches he'd have to negotiate with care.

His old Ford would be left locked at the airport. The airport caretaker, to whom he'd telephoned, had assured him it would still be there when he returned.

The homestead door was half closed behind him when the phone rang. Or it would have been called ringing on the old phones; the noise these new ones made was not 'ringing.'

He dropped the overnight bag onto the weathered wooden veranda floor before stepping back through the doorway. To where the telephone was perched on a rickety table of so light a construction, that Simon wondered if the ringing might one day cause it to collapse.

Out of habit he held the corner of the table to steady it while he picked up the hand piece.

"Hello, Simon here."

"Simon. How are you going, you old pirate?" Simon's life stopped for a second as he recognized the voice.

"Sarah? Sarah is that you? How are you? Where are you?"

"Come on Simon, no need to sound so surprised." Simon didn't have to try to sound surprised, he was overcome. Typical of Sarah though, out of the blue with no warning. He climbed back on track, and sat on the chair beside the phone.

"Sorry. I... you caught me off balance. Where are you?" Her gentle, but straight forward voice always had a place in his ear.

It did again.

"I'm in Brisbane, just flew in from New Guinea. I went scuba diving for a month. I'm ringing from the airport." Simon was still lost for words.

"I'm guessing by the area code of this phone number that you're back on the Darling. Will you be there long?"

Simon explained his estimations.

"What are your plans?" He asked.

"Well I promised Mum I would spend some time with her, after that I don't know." She paused a moment and then said, "Simon, I would like to spend some time with you. Can I come down there?"

Simon almost laughed with delight. "Sarah, do I have to say please?"

Her laughter floated down the phone line to him.

"I'll stay with Mum about a week and then catch a plane to Sydney. After that, I guess I'll find a bus or train or something up to good old Bourke."

Simon looked at his watch. He had to get moving.

"Listen, I need to go. You've just caught me walking out the door to fly to Sydney. I'm not sure how long I'll be down there, but I will ring you when I'm about to return."

He had her mother's phone number. Sarah had obviously been in contact with her as she had this phone number. He'd left it with her some months earlier when he'd been in Brisbane to organize 'der boats' refit

Sarah had been in Canada at the time taking part in the World hang gliding championships. They would have a lot to talk about.

"It's been a long time. I've looked forward to seeing you again."

"I've missed you too Simon. More than you know. I'll see you in a week or so, take care."

He put the phone down and looked again at his watch as he rushed out to where his overnight bag lay. After closing the door firmly behind him he strode to the wide wooden staircase. Its worn and cracked timbers reminded him to tread carefully as he stepped down.

As he drove away from the old farm house he found the concentration necessary for the negotiation of muddy spots was a little impaired. He had to at times, force thoughts of Sarah from his mind in order to focus on the tricky and in parts slippery bush track.

It was during the drive it suddenly dawned on him that for the first time in days he'd forgotten all about Africa.

Simon had bought a one-way ticket to Sydney. He hated the thought of going there, but he assured himself the days would pass quickly as there was much to do.

Organizing the African's paperwork would most certainly occupy his mind and his time.

The fact he liked flying made it easier, although as the aircraft lifted him into space his thoughts were still with Sarah.

He remembered the time they'd canoed down the Darling River from Bourke to Louth during a flood. The river had been flowing at a flood level of eleven metres and it carried them swiftly.

Two hundred and fifty kilometres of sun filled days in cool winter months, with nights spent by big open fires under clear star studded skies. She had proved to be as good in a crisis as any man, not slack when the work was to be done and practical in her method.

Simon loved her, although he didn't ever tell her so. She was a freedom child and like the wind; she would stay for a while, then blow off in another direction and onto a new adventure. He understood this, because she was as he was.

He looked out the window and down at the airport. Its windsock appeared to have male menopause as it drooped toward the galvanized burr that covered the red sandy ground.

Some moments later he looked down at the town where corrugated iron roofed buildings reflected varying shades. From grey through to silver amongst an oasis green of gardens and tree lined streets. He wondered momentarily about the people there and everywhere in this great country.

The Australian lifestyle would be like an elusive precious gem to millions of people in strife torn countries around the world. A lifestyle that Simon felt was taken for granted by many the people who lived here.

The thought stayed with him until the township disappeared from his windows field of view. Then feeling relaxed in the warmth, he thought again of Sarah until finally, as if lulled by the steady drone of the aircrafts engines, he slept.

He awoke as the plane was about to touch down at Mascot airport, and after collecting his bag he took a taxi into the city. He didn't feel like talking, but he had to tell the taxi driver the hotels address a few times.

Simon hoped the man's driving was better than his English, and found out as they went along that it was a debatable point.

The hotel room was like a hotel room, a small fridge, heaps of towels and a carpet that showed signs of wear in the doorway.

Room service brought food and copies of the cities phone books. He showered and then sat down to scan each copy, making a list of the addresses he would visit the following day. It took shape in the hour before his nodding head signaled it was time to sleep, and he took to his bed knowing the next day was shaping up to be long, and probably interesting.

CHAPTER 10

Simon left the hotel early and took breakfast later at a cafe with clean windows, before he again entered the outside world of city streets.

He caught a taxi and gave the driver an address he read from the list written the previous night. Then sat back in the rear seat and watched the traffic.

The taxi pulled up outside the suit hire place and Simon went inside the glass fronted shop. After enquiring as to his obligations, a large girthed man who smelled of baby powder measured him up. The tailor then showed him a sample of colours and materials available. It didn't matter much to Simon as he reminded himself that he was hiring only and might only wear the suit once. The tall thin man who stood at the counter told Simon he could pick the suit up at three o'clock the following afternoon, and asked Simon for a deposit.

Simon paid from his wallet in cash, having seen enough movies in his time to know not to leave a paper trail by using his credit card.

He left the tailors shop and walked to the nearest Post Office, which he reckoned would house the quietest public phones. At least the building itself offered shelter from the noise of the city street.

The list of telephone answering services he'd gleaned from the phone book provided him with four names. He'd chosen the ones which carried the smallest advertisements, as he felt they might be easier to deal with.

He tried the first one on the list.

It was answered and Simon explained what it was he wanted.

"Yes sir, we can provide that service. Now, if we can just get some of your details."

"What do you need?" Simon asked.

"We just need to know your name and address for accounting purposes."

Simon thought a moment. This is no good. He nearly hung up on the voice, but instead he thought on his feet.

"Sorry mate, can I get back to you? Something's just come up here that needs my attention."

"Of course sir, please feel free to call us at any time," said the voice unconcernedly.

Simon put the telephone hand piece down, wondering at the same time if the person on the other end of the phone had found him to be somewhat suspicious. His hands were trembling as he rolled a cigarette, and he again looked over his shoulder before closing his eyes and inhaling the cigarette smoke deeply. As he opened them again he told himself quietly he would have to try to keep calm.

Stay on top of things. Take it slower; remember that unexpected questions will come out of the blue over the next week or so. Until this thing is over.

He finished his cigarette and punched in the numbers of the second service. The voice that answered was one of an older woman. It sounded as if it had spent a lifetime soaked in cigarette smoke and he explained what he wanted.

"Yes I can do that," the older voice said.

Simon wished he'd called this one first.

"How do I make payment to you?"

She replied that a postal note in the mail would do.

"Does that mean I can use this phone number in my communications as of now?" He asked, not believing it could be so easy

"I will take calls for you as of now, but I will expect payment from you before I will make any messages available to you," she replied.

Simon doubted she would get any calls for him. He only wanted a phone number to put on the business letterheads. Although it would come in handy, as it was one way of knowing if anyone was following up on his activities. He asked of the cost of the service and then listened as she explained.

"I will put a postal note in the mail to you today and pay you for a month in advance. Will the address in the phone advertisement get you O.K?" He asked.

"Yes, that address will get me. What is your name?"

Simon paused a moment.

"Munroe. James Munroe."

Jimmy Munroe owed him $100 so he wouldn't forget the name.

He walked into the Post Office and purchased a postal note, printed her address on the envelope and dropped it into the post box. She'd have it tomorrow he thought as he walked towards the street in search of another taxi.

The car took him to the first of the printers on his list of addresses. An impressive building of sandblasted concrete whose heavy tinted glass doors, shielded him from the warmth of the day outside.

He approached the front desk and derailed the receptionist's train of thought. She stopped writing and looked up at him with a smile of white even teeth. Simon immediately thought of the dentist he should have visited some time ago.

"Can I help you?" She asked.

"I'd like some business cards printed please."

She asked him if he'd mind waiting a moment, while she, at the same time pointed to chairs which lined the wall on the far side of the room. Simon stood for a few minutes while she spoke to someone on her phone and as she hung up, she said.

"Mr. Curtis will be with you in a moment."

At that moment, Mr. Curtis stepped out of an office which led off from the reception area. Almost as if he'd been listening at his door and heard his cue.

He was a retiring man who showed the effects Simon thought, of a life spent in an office where he lived out his days without sunshine.

The pale man ushered Simon into the small office where he seated himself behind a desk and produced a large catalogue of business cards. He slid it across the desk to Simon as he flicked over some pages, revealing a card which Simon thought would do the job. Simon pointed to the particular card.

"This one will do." He produced a piece of paper from his pocket and handed it to the pale man. "This is what I'd like printed on it." The pale man looked at the paper and read that Simon was an engineering consultant. It also held the name of an engineering firm which Simon had found in the telephone directory the night before, along with a Sydney phone number.

Simon handed the pale man a second piece of paper which stated that Simon was also a company director for the same firm.

"I'd like a second lot of cards, to be printed with the information on this paper please," Simon said.

The pale man wrote something on his order form, then changed his mind and wrote a fresh form, so as to, 'Not have any confusion downstairs.'

Simon then passed the pale man a third piece of paper and asked him if he could have letter heads printed also. Simon pointed out that the letterheads were to be as he had drawn them.

"Would you use the best quality paper?" He said to the pale man.

The pale man ran his eye over the third sheet and agreed he would have it printed as Simon asked and that the whole would be ready the following day. Simon smiled, glad that he had all the printing under control and at one place.

He thanked him for his help, left the building and searched for another taxi.

After a short ride across a suburb, Simon was again side stepping people as he moved through a shopping centre. He found the address of the business equipment hire shop and instead bought a second hand typewriter.

"Reconditioned," the bloke behind the counter pointed out. It seemed to be in good order and Simon suggested that the seller fit a new ribbon. The bloke behind the counter agreed with that.

Simon asked the typewriter salesman if he could direct him to a place where he might have a rubber stamp made, and the typewriter salesman pointed to a shop across the road. The typewriter was a light weight electric, and Simon hoped it would prove to be user friendly. It nestled under his arm as he crossed the street to the rubber stamp shop, where he ordered a company seal.

The rubber stamp man told Simon the seal could be picked up the next day, and mentioned in the course of conversation that he could also provide a stamp pad for a small additional cost. Simon had not even thought about a stamp pad and was glad the rubber stamp man had mentioned it.

He told the man so.

"All part of our service, sir," the man replied,

Simon bought an office manual/dictionary, liquid paper and a few other items of stationery. Then after a short walk he found an arcade coffee shop where he ordered a late lunch.

He rested his feet and took aspirin for the slight headache which had been nagging him all morning. Almost certainly due to the amount of exhaust gases trapped in the city streets. The hurry, noise and vibration, along with the blank defensive faces in crowds and the flashing of traffic lights were all alien to him.

Somewhere further away a siren demanded attention.

Here in this place the bushman and the sailor were out of tune with their environment.

He watched it for a while.

Each sound made in the city, both the quiet and the loud seemed to him to blend, to become a steady hum.

Like that of a giant machine of transport, communications and services. All generated by power and money and seemingly governed by law.

He felt tired and his legs ached a little. It had only been a few days since his first knowledge of the African, but somehow it seemed longer. Time was in 'swift' mode and he felt a little disorientated by it all.

He paid for his lunch and easily found another taxi.

Twenty minutes later he was asleep in his hotel room.

CHAPTER 11

By 4.30 the next afternoon, Simon had collected his suit, cards, letterheads, and then stayed up until nearly midnight typing the Africans papers. He'd written a letter which was an exact copy of the letter the African had faxed. This letter was addressed to the Ministry of Aviation.

The bill for services rendered Simon called it. It was signed by four company directors.

He'd signed on behalf of the other three. His own personal signature had been easy but the other three had taken a little practice on a scrap of paper. He'd used a different type of pen for each signature, so each bore something resembling individuality. He typed four copies, signing each of them before stamping them with the company seal.

The second letter was similar to the first. A letter signed by the four company directors authorizing the bearer, Simon, to open an account for the deposit of the proceeds of the bill for services rendered. He stamped it with the company seal.

He wrote another, authorizing the bearer whose signature appeared below to transfer the funds to where the bearer wished, on presentation of the letter. This third letter he signed only three times, leaving the fourth directors space blank. He left his own space blank to belay the possibility of him forgetting the style used by one of the others.

He made four copies of this letter, put two copies into each of two envelopes and addressed them to himself in the outback.

He wrote a fourth letter, authorizing Abu Mohammed access to 75% of the funds held in the account. The four directors signed this letter of account and Simon thumped it with the company seal.

No bank would see this letter. It was for the Africans eyes only and Simon knew he would have to find a way to make the

African feel that he was in control. A bank letterhead would do the trick, if he could acquire one from the bank he ended up using in Europe. Then he would only need to find access to a typewriter in Liechtenstein and mail it to the African from there. Whether the African would inquire about this with the bank official when the final transaction for the transfer of funds took place Simon could not know.

Surely he wouldn't oversee that directly.

That job would come under the responsibility of a senior government official and not the minister himself. Wouldn't it?

He felt certain that the African and Sudovich must have some trust with each other, at least on a business level?

Simon leaned back in his chair, rubbed his eyes and tried to think of anything he may have forgotten.

He decided he hadn't overlooked anything and started to clear up all the bits and pieces. He placed the letters in a folder, chose to keep only about twenty of each of the business cards and retained the pen he had used for signing his own signature.

He dropped the other three pens, the unused letterheads, business cards and every scrap of paper he'd used, along with the ribbon from the typewriter into a plastic bag. He tied the bag closed and placed it near the door ready for disposal in the morning.

CHAPTER 12

Abu was feeling the tension. His appetite for food had slowed and he found he had a tendency to pick at portions, rather than his normal whole hearted attacks on large plates.

It was midnight and he sat in his large overstuffed chair staring at the plate of food untouched on his desk. He wondered if maybe he should have gone home, but immediately understood why he hadn't.

He felt more secure here in the ministry with the troops and guards watching his back for him. His nervousness was almost at a point where he might pack a suitcase and escape the country with what cash he had. The fact he had only about $100,000 American in his safe was the anchor that held him fast.

He had much more in his country's currency, but it was almost valueless off shore.

There were of course, the diamonds and a small amount of gold which might bring another $500,000 U.S. That amount would not bring to him the lifestyle he desired, even when added to his quarter share of previous misappropriations which was tucked away in a Swiss bank account.

Access to that account needed four signatures. His and the ministers aligned, thus giving him a quarter share, and that depended on all of them surviving long enough to sign.

Abu had pleaded with them to make changes to this arrangement. "It was stupid." He'd argued. "Even if one of the ministers aligned did not survive. Those who did may have to wait years for proof of his demise before their access to the account was allowed. Particularly in a country like this where it was easy to prove a disappearance. People vanished every day. The fact they weren't there anymore was proof enough they had disappeared. Proving that a vanished person was dead was a different thing altogether."

Abu understood his partners in crimes reasoning. It was a very basic form of insurance against unforeseen accidents.

Access to the money was important, but not as important as surviving long enough to actually spend it.

That's the problem with the world these days. No one trusts anymore. He thought quietly.

The six hundred-thousand-dollar quarter share seemed to be a trivial amount compared to the $32.6m, minus of course, Sudovich's share of 25%. He calculated and came up with a figure of around $24m.

That sounded better.

It would have to be enough.

He was despondent at the loss he would incur when he escaped. His house in Freetown, his Mercedes Benz and particularly the mansion he'd had built in the countries interior. It had become a very personal place where he'd felt at home and far from the world and its trouble. He was stuck as the English say, 'between a rock and a hard place.'

He wondered at his lack of recall as he rubbed his fingertips into his brow. Was the stress of the situation beginning to affect his concentration? If so, was it also the reason behind his recent mood swings and lethargy? He was unsure, but with thought he diagnosed the symptoms. They would have to be viewed as small hurdles, rather than road blocks lying on the path to his overall success wouldn't they?

Success should only be about two weeks away, and he wondered how far away would the rebel army be by then?

He hoped they'd be far enough away to allow the ministers aligned enough time to unknowingly sign over their shares to him.

'The ministers aligned' was his pet name for his accomplices who would sign the necessary papers and allow the $32.6m to go through the proper channels.

For their cooperation they expected their full and fair share. Abu tried to picture their shock and anger when they learned the truth.

Abu and the ministers aligned went back to the very beginning. Back to the time when all four of them joined Axele the outlaw, who had become Axele the revolutionary. Each one of them had played their part for Axele. So well that in the end they had won a bloody coup and been rewarded a place in the countries government.

Each one of them owed to each other his life many times over during those dangerous days. The bond between them had been strong, but to Abu not so strong that it could not be severed by the vast fortune which was almost in hand.

CHAPTER 13

The city sounds came crashing through Simon's sleep, and he woke through a dream of car loads of fraud squad agents, braking noisily to a halt outside his door. He sat up sharply and then rubbed the sleep out of his eyes as he remembered where he was. The bedside clock brought the realization that it was the latest he'd slept in for some time. A vacuum cleaner whined as it sucked at the floor somewhere in the hallway outside his door as he made tea.

After a refreshing hot shower and dressed in casual clothes he opened the door leading to the hallway. The whining vacuum cleaner was by now at the far end of the corridor.

He left his door open and walked towards its sound. The girl pushing the vacuum cleaner ignored his presence, and it was not until he spoke that she looked up from what she was doing.

She glanced at the typewriter he carried and a questioning expression came to her face.

"Hello. Do you know how to type?" He asked,

"I can type," she said, in a 'who wants to know' tone.

Simon smiled and asked her if she had a typewriter.

"I do have an old one, but it has seen better days." She replied as she turned the vacuum cleaner off.

"I bought this one yesterday and today I have no more use for it, so I wondered if you'd like to have it."

She looked at him warily and stepped around behind the vacuum machine, defensively.

"At what cost?"

Simon could see where the conversation was leading.

"It will cost you a dollar." He added, "I can also write you a receipt, to show you its above board."

"Is it hot?" She asked.

"No, it's not hot. I bought it yesterday and now today I have no more use for it."

She thought for a moment as if trying to view it from another angle.

"Where's the receipt?"

Simon pulled his notebook from his pocket, asked her name and wrote the receipt. He passed it to her and she handed him the dollar.

He held his hand up in the manner of a Star Trek salute.

"Spock's honour," he mimicked.

She smiled at last, and a sparkle came to her eye.

"It needs a new ribbon, but other than that it works alright. Hope it serves you well," he told her.

"Thanks. It'll have a good home."

As Simon walked back to his room, he wondered where the world had gone to when a person has to ask the cost of accepting something for nothing.

Leaving the hotel he walked to the nearest Post Office to send the two self-addressed letters to the outback, posting two sets in case one got lost in transit, before he found a waste paper bin in an alley to deposit the bag of stationery.

He made his way back to the street and asked a shop owner for directions to the nearest travel agents.

Two hours later he was sat back in a comfortable chair and listened while a stewardess showed him how to operate an oxygen mask.

Fifteen minutes after that, while looking out the window on Sydney, he heard the pilot over the intercom. The plane would touch down in Melbourne, before flying on to Changi airport in Singapore, then travel nonstop to London.

CHAPTER 14

Simon was new to international travel, so he had taken the advice given by the girl in the travel agency and bought a connecting flight to Rome. She'd advised him that a connecting flight would allow him to just change planes in London and save the hassle of custom checks at Heathrow.

He left the Qantas plane at Heathrow, where he boarded a British Airways flight to Rome, then flew Swissair to overnight in Zurich.

He was weary from the flight when he caught an early morning train from Zurich Central to Sargans, then rode a bus to Vaduz. It was through tired eyes that he first saw the fairy tale landscape of Liechtenstein.

Simon booked into the first hotel he came to and would have slept, but for the church bells which rang out at half hour and hourly intervals.

He'd never had jet lag before, so he presumed it was why he felt like he did now as he stepped from the hotel. He'd buried his head under the hotel beds pillows as long as he could. A vain attempt to dampen the sound of church bells and after a light breakfast he'd set out in search of a bank.

There were plenty of them about. Though many of the doors he tried were bolted, and at first he thought that maybe they had unusual business hours. He found out as time passed, that these banks with bolted doors operated on an appointment only basis.

He had expected old style facade buildings, but found as he went that they all in the end just looked like banks.

Not knowing where to start, and after walking past several, he decided to just enter the bank which was the closest to hand.

The heavy door opened easily and he immediately caught the attention of the woman behind the counter. She spoke

English quite well, but she was either having a bad day or she just couldn't give a rat's rear end if the whole place just disappeared. She suggested that Simon should wait, rather than ask him to wait and Simon did. A few minutes later a big man in a suit which looked very expensive stepped gracefully down the stairs and escorted Simon into a large and very ornate office.

The big man didn't talk unless there was something to say and Simon didn't really know where to start. So he removed the letters he'd typed in Sydney and laid them out in front of him. He put them in order and then turned them about so the big man could run his eyes over them. Simon remembered his business cards and pulled one from his wallet. It described him as a company director of the firm detailed on the letterhead.

He was nervous and for a moment he wished he was far away on the Darling River until he put the thought aside and instead, said, "I'm here as a representative of my firm. My colleagues in that firm wish to open a business account for the deposit of the funds owed to us by this government." Simon pointed to the bill for services rendered. He felt his own voice in his ears and thought it sounded strained, so decided he should try to soften it. He took a deep breath and then exhaled slowly, but still felt a lump in his throat.

The big man finally spoke and Simon found the mild voice easy to listen to, his English was good so Simon understood him without effort.

"I understand that this particular government is at the moment fighting to survive a rebellion. Do you feel the government will pay this account before it realizes its own success?"

Simon thought a moment as his mind searched for an answer.

"My company has made arrangements with their Government officials." He tried to made it sound like he'd made the below the counter payments necessary for smooth transition without actually saying so. "All the paper work is in order as you can see."

The big man looked back at the papers.

"It seems to me that you are not in a position to spend much time in search of a bank which will carry out this transfer of funds?" Simon looked back at the big man with the thought he was about to be squeezed and then his heart began to sink as the big man spoke further, "My bank would not be prepared to expose itself, but as my bank cannot help you, I do know of a person, a lawyer, who may be available to give you satisfaction."

Simon nodded and the big man picked up his phone and dialed a number. He spoke for a short time, listened to the reply for a moment and finished the conversation with a Danke.

He placed the phone back on its cradle before looking at Simon.

"My friend is in a meeting at the moment, but he is certain he can be here within the next hour. If you would care to wait, then you will be welcome to do so here. My secretary will bring you coffee."

"Yes, that would be alright. Thank you."

The big man smiled.

"Please make yourself comfortable. If you would like to freshen up, then behind that door are facilities." He pointed to a door in the far wall before turning to leave the room, closing the main door quietly behind him.

Simon could feel the silence.

He walked to the window which overlooked the Aulestrasse and gauged the drop if he needed to get out. Leaning out the window he checked the way he would go if it came to that. He pulled a chair to the window where he sat down and gazed out towards the distant Alps. They were certainly impressive, and brought to mind a trip he'd done to New Zealand twenty odd years earlier.

Forty minutes later he was getting anxious, and started to have visions of Interpol turning up to take him away. With every second that ticked on the big clock which hung on the far wall, Simon's apprehension grew, until he was on the verge of jumping out of the window and running away. There was no thought of where he might run to if he did jump out of the window. Just get away.

Who was the man who was coming to meet him? He thought.

What kind of man?

One who might do a bit of questionable work obviously, but then again so was he, "Simon the criminal." He said it out loud to hear what it sounded like, "Simon the crim."

Suddenly the door opened and his mouth went dry.

A shorter, thick set man came into the room, saw him by the window and crossed the room in greeting. He tugged Simon's hand and introduced himself as Karl, before he suggested they leave the place and go to his own office. Simon returned the chair he'd used, and then followed as they left the bank. He didn't see the big man again and the woman behind the counters day appeared to have not got any better.

He was shown to a Mercedes, and after closing his door the driver pulled away from the parking place noiselessly. While Karl drove he talked to Simon, and as Simon listened he tried to remember the route they were taking, just in case.

Karl's office showed less expense but more taste than the one at the bank and its warmth more welcoming. The short man offered Simon a chair, poured two drinks and then walked behind his desk, loosening his tie a little as he went.

Simon noticed that the short man was always moving. Everything about him was quick, even his smile flashed on and off.

Karl asked for the paperwork and Simon passed it all to him before he studied the man closely as he read carefully until he finally looked to Simon.

"My colleague tells me there is a revolution brewing in this country. He suggested also, you have made certain arrangements with officials there?"

"Yes that's true; the only thing that can stand in the way is the banking system. Once an account is made available then the transaction will move ahead quickly."

The short man looked at Simon with one eyebrow lifting, this being the only expression on his face.

"You sound sure of these people. Many would say that you are very trusting. No?"

"Shall we say the transaction is also in their best interests?"

The short man understood. He rubbed his hands together and smiled lightly, then sat back in his chair.

"I can organize an account for you. The bank I will use is reputable, and it will supply a bank nominee to transfer the funds at the African end. I can have the paper work prepared for you by 10 o'clock tomorrow morning."

Simon listened.

"And the cost?" He asked.

The short man looked Simon in the eye.

"My normal rate is two and a half percent. For this particular venture I would ask for 5%." Simon did some high school arithmetic; it worked out in his mind to around $1.63m.

"I take it that nothing can go wrong, in a way that the funds might fall into the wrong hands?"

"If you mean the possibility of the paperwork being written in such a way, that it may all fall into my hands? Do not worry, because the reputation of the whole banking system in Liechtenstein depends on fair dealing, and one spot of tarnish could destroy all our livelihoods."

"From where I sit, your credentials seem to be in order. If a situation should arise, then I have been merely employed by your firm to transfer funds. The extra 2.5% commission will be there to cover expenses, if any questions should arise."

"You can rest assured my friend that you are in good hands, and 5% is a very good wage for me. Now if we might have a drink on the deal, I will then give you a ride back to your hotel. I assume you have booked in somewhere?"

Simon told him the name of the hotel, while thinking at the same time that he was beginning to like the man.

The short man poured two more drinks and he and Simon raised their glasses in salute.

The deal was made.

"I will work on the paperwork tonight and pick you up at your hotel at 10 o'clock tomorrow morning. After we have the necessary papers signed, it will be up to you to see that the money is readied at the African end. Here is my card; this phone number will be answered day or night. I will also need to know where to contact you in Australia?"

Simon wrote his name and address on the back of one of his bogus business cards, then added the electricians fax number before the short man checked it to make sure he understood.

Simon slept easier that night, secure in the knowledge that the hard part was over and progress was being made. He'd presumed the bank account part of his venture would be a major stumbling block. The fact it hadn't been, proved once again that worry was based on worst case scenario.

His dreams, like disjointed motion pictures still persisted, but now they were more like dreams and less like nightmares.

He smiled once during his sleep when a vision of Sarah passed through his mind. He called her name, then was silent again as was Vaduz, except for the church bells that rung out at regular intervals.

Simon didn't hear them.

CHAPTER 15

Simon pulled his coat closer. There had been a light fall of snow during the night, and although there was no visual evidence of it this morning, it had left its chill behind.

He was glad when the grey Mercedes pulled up in front of the hotel. More glad when once in the car he found the cars heater had warmed its interior.

Karl greeted him cheerfully, and Simon proved the feeling mutual. They chatted about the weather as they drove on moistened roads to his office.

It too was warm, for a large open fire burned and crackled in a stone fireplace. Simon was at home for a time.

Karl had certainly done some homework. The evidence of this was loaded into a fat file which lay on his desk. Simon glanced at its cover and saw his name, along with some reference numbers that he didn't understand. Karl opened it and pulled from it three papers.

Simon understood about the banks with bolted doors. A letterhead of one of them was amongst the papers in the file. He realized then, that Karl must have opened an account during the night.

They certainly did have unusual trading hours.

Simon imagined the response he would get if he knocked on his bank managers' door at even two minutes after closing time.

Karl explained to Simon the significance of these three documents until he was content that Simon understood the facts. He asked Simon to sign all three. There were three more exact copies for Simon to keep. He shuddered with excitement at the one that held the account numbers, and address details of the bank which Simon needed for the bill for services rendered.

It wasn't this information that excited Simon, but the banks letterhead which was what he needed to forge a letter to send to Abu. A letter Simon felt absolutely necessary in order to allow the African to feel at ease.

It took all his self-control to not stand up, like a spectator when his team scored and shout, "Yes."

*****

He was still on a high when he boarded the bus which would take him to Feldkirch. The views from the bus were spectacular, and they continued to be so after he left the bus and boarded a train. It took him to Innsbruck where he changed trains and headed for Verona.

An overnight train took him to Florence, and he arrived in Rome the next morning. It was from there he caught a midday flight to Sydney via Bangkok.

Simon had always been unexcited about overseas travel, but now after seeing some of the scenery he knew that at some stage in the future he would have to return and see more.

Now, as he lay in his bed in another Sydney hotel he wished he'd had more time to spend there, but he had to move. Keep on moving, for it had been over ten days since his first electronic introduction to the African and he wondered if time was running out.

Today he would have to find a small time printer, maybe a one-man operation. He flicked through the phone book and made a list of the names which looked the most promising.

With this done he showered and shaved before venturing out onto the busy city streets to hail a taxi. He gave the driver an address and sat back as he swallowed a pill for the headache which seemed to have dogged him for the last week.

The first thing to do was find a colour photocopier.

He met with success at a news agency and laid the documents in their machine. A carefully placed blank sheet of paper concealed everything except the letterheads, and he printed copies of both the banks and the short lawyer's documents. Then with the copies tucked under his arm in a large envelope, Simon left the newsagents and sought the first address on the printers list.

Simon supposed it was ink he could smell when he entered the small printers shop. There was no one at the counter and while he waited he looked about the room.

It looked a bit of a mess really. A rough counter held evidence of past ink spills, each of these spills had left designs which might appear to be the work of children.

He glanced at the cobwebs in the corner of the ceiling, before he allowed his gaze to drift down and across the wall to the doorway which connected to the buildings rear. He was about to ring again when a figure appeared in the doorway Simon greeted the older man with a smile and suggested that it was a nice day.

The older man agreed that it might be a nice day for some, so Simon came to the point.

He removed the two letterheads from the envelope and brought them to the older man's attention.

"I wondered, if it might be possible to have exact copies of these made?"

The older man looked at and read each and every word, then peered at the emblems at the top of each page.

"Same colour?" He asked as he blinked his eyes.

"Close as possible please."

The older man rubbed the side of his nose.

"I can handle them alright. It may turn out a bit fluffy on the edges of the emblem though," he said.

Simon considered a moment, and expressed his opinion that it would be alright.

"How many do you want?" The older man asked as he put the pages down on the counter.

"Four copies of each one."

The older man eyed Simon through dusty spectacles.

"They'll cost $50 a copy. Half of that in deposit, just in case you get caught up in something and don't get back."

"When can I have them?" Simon asked.

"When do you want them?"

"This afternoon?"

"For an extra hundred you can pick them up at 4 o'clock this afternoon." Simon pulled at his wallet, extracted $300 and handed the money over. The older man wiped his hands on his ink stained apron and accepted the cash.

"I will see you at 4 o'clock then."

The old man said nothing and walked out to his workshop.

CHAPTER 16

At 4 o'clock Simon collected the papers from the printer and returned to the business equipment shop. The owner was glad to see him, and enquired jokingly as to why he needed two typewriters in such a short period of time. Simon had to lie again, and said that the first one had been stolen.

This time he decided to hire a machine for the night. The owner didn't ask for any identification on the rental as he already knew Jimmy Munroe from the previous receipts. It wasn't until Simon had left the shop that he realized he'd nearly painted himself into a corner, and was relieved the rental shop owner hadn't asked for such.

By 5 o'clock Simon was sitting in his hotel room typing a letter to Abu on the Banks letterhead. The letter stated that a bank account was open in the name of the engineering firm which Simon had taken the name of. It explained that the bank held a letter of authorization for Abu Mohammed, who was to have access to 75% of the funds in that account. It also stated that the above mentioned Abu Mohammed should have in his possession an identical letter signed by Mr. Garry Sudovich. Simon listed the bank account number which was on the bill for services rendered. He thought of a German sounding name, typed it in and then signed it in that name.

The second letter was the letter of authorization signed by a Mr. Garry Sudovich. It was written on the letterhead of the engineering company which Simon had printed prior his trip to Europe.

He wondered about the signature of Sudovich, and practiced it a few times before he decided to enter a scrawl, hoping it would slip by the African's attention. Even then, it might not come out clearly after a trip through a fax machine.

Simon sat and looked at the two letters for nearly an hour. Checking his mental notes, trying to see if he'd made any slip ups along the way. He couldn't see anything wrong.

He typed a third letter directly to Abu and also on the engineering letterhead. Saying that the accounts were open, and all the necessary documents would be posted express mail in the next few hours.

They couldn't be sent until tomorrow morning, but he reckoned the African would appreciate the belief that the documents were virtually on their way. He signed it with the letter 'G.'

Simon put the copy of the bill for services rendered into a large envelope, along with the original copies of the letters of authorization. Then double checked the postal address which was the one on the original fax he'd received from the African.

He wrote clearly, because he didn't want it ending up at the wrong place. It would be posted tomorrow from the Post Office the first letter he'd received from Abu had been addressed to.

A return address might be in order he thought, but he refrained from its inclusion in the hope it would draw the Africans attention to Sudovich's post mark and therefore allow his mind to assume all is well.

After he had removed all the papers from the hotel room table he rang the front desk and asked if there was a fax machine available for customer use.

The lady on the phone said there was, and if he wanted to use it, all he had to do was turn up at the front desk.

He did.

Simon asked about payment for the use of the fax and the hotel lady told him it would be billed to his room. He fronted the machine. It looked user friendly, but he allowed the hotel lady to tutor him in the art of faxing anyway. His nerves were strung taut as he keyed in the African's number.

He hoped that nothing would go wrong. Not now, after all of his effort.

The number he used was the more secure line the African had promised him, and Simon prayed it was still secure. He held his breath as the machine made its electronic comments, then let the breath slide slowly from his lips as the connection was made and the paper began to move through. He lined up the second sheet and it moved through in the same way, followed by the third sheet.

Simon gathered his papers, thanked the hotel lady and returned to his room.

Lying on his bed he looked at the ceiling and thought. I'll be glad when this is all over.

He felt sick in his stomach as he was not used to being in a nervous state, and wished there were something he could take for it. He knew in his heart that the only antidote was to walk the straight and narrow.

Then you never had to look over your shoulder.

CHAPTER 17

Abu had decided that now was the time to visit his mansion in the jungle, and a platoon of government troops went with him. He didn't want to be there. Not right now. Especially now, with rebels having a tendency to pop up out of the bush at any tick of the clock.

His mountain retreat was important to him, but not that much to risk his neck for.

He had to be here, as this was where he hoped to hear from Sudovich on a secure communication line. The papers and the valuables he held in stock here were not of a value to risk a life for, but the reason to be here would afford him the excuse to retrieve them, and thus add to his, as yet, very small fortune.

It was ten o'clock in the morning, and he sat in a large room which was well lit by brilliant sunshine.

His mansion as he liked to call it was a sprawling affair. Made of heavy timbers, most of which had been cleared from the very land the house was built upon. Where there wasn't timber there was glass. Huge panes from ceiling to floor that allowed a full view of the gardens and the dense jungle which formed his perimeter.

He would miss this place, all there was in it and the life he would leave behind.

His thoughts finally drifted to Sudovich. Why was it taking so long? It had been ten days and no word on activities, no reports at all. Was there something wrong? He couldn't believe the possibility Sudovich may have overcome his greed, and not be interested at all.

Abu had met Sudovich once, and that had been six years ago. They'd spoken but a few times, the necessity was not there anymore. After the first and the second money transfers, the operation had been fine tuned to run at its own pace, with just a fax letter to set the wheels in motion. In a way, that allowed both men to keep the contact between them very discreet.

Both Abu and Sudovich had a fear of the insecurity of telephones. They worried a lot about who might be listening with Abu's fear stemming from Axele and the power he had over him. He and the ministers aligned.

One foot out of line in the loyalty game, and there were no second chances.

Sudovich worried about the Australian Federal Police and the information they might have on him. He worried about the possibility that the very next piece of intelligence about him might just tip the balance, and begin a full blown investigation. Abu shuddered as he thought of Sudovich's minor worry compared to his. At least the Australian Federal Police didn't cut you to pieces, and let you watch in agony as those pieces were fed to the crocodiles.

Abu looked at the phone and wondered if he should make contact. It was dangerous, and the cruel face of Axele crossed his mind as he made a resolution. First he would go to the toilet, and then ring Sudovich straight after. No more delays.

As he peed into his personalized urinal, his gaze focused through the window to the jungle beyond the clearing. The dense greenery brought to mind pillaging rebels who may well be roaming the mountains.

His other fear.

As he stood gazing out the window with the thoughts of his two main fears foremost in his mind, the fax phone suddenly sounded. Seemingly loud in the quietness, and somehow out of place in this steamy jungle environment.

His heart for a moment startled, and Abu nearly ducked to the floor with fright. He finished his business, and with wet stains on his trouser front ran back into the room.

Was this it?

He scanned the pages, and then, almost in tears with relief he began to laugh.

Abu fell to his knees before the fax machine, clutched the fax paper to his chest and laughed.

*****

The next day Simon secure posted a large padded bag to the African. At the last moment he decided to write on the back of the envelope a senders' name and wrote the name of the company he had used. He put the imaginary address from its letterhead on with that name.

If it went missing then Simon didn't want it coming back to him, and he had backup copies for a second postage if it became necessary.

After this was done he decided there was one thing left to do. He found a good quality restaurant and ordered lunch. He was still without appetite so he began to force himself to eat, and after some mouthfuls gathered momentum to finish the meal. It took longer than it would have done a fortnight ago, but he felt better for it and became a little more alive.

He bought some Lebanese food to take away, two bottles of wine from a pub, a batch of newspapers and returned to the hotel room. With the door closed behind him he did nothing but watch television, read the newspapers and sleep.

One of the newspapers gave a little information about a probable coup attempt on a dictator called Axele, but as far as news sources were concerned there was no immediate danger.

Simon saw that the newspaper was twenty-four hours old before he checked the phone directory. It offered a 1900 number news headline service whose recorded voice made no mention of new trouble.

Relaxed with help from the wine, he slept easily and awoke early the next morning to a full breakfast. When he'd looked closely at the face in his mirror the previous night, he'd noticed that it was showing signs of strain. Maybe it was strain, it could also be the tiredness he still felt, or the fact that he'd been without appetite for ten or more days.

He rang Sarah's mother who told him Sarah had flown down to Sydney the day before, and could be in the outback by now.

Simon wished he'd phoned her yesterday, and wondered if Sarah was still in Sydney. He wouldn't know where to begin to look if she was, so he put the thought aside while he rang the airline people and booked a ticket on the next plane out.

Sarah was still on his mind when he boarded the small two engine plane and while he made himself comfortable he looked up at the next boarding passenger. Straight into the eyes of a friend whose face broke into a broad grin.

"Simon."

Simon tried to stand to meet her, finding out as he partly lifted from his seat that his seat belt was secured. He unbuckled and rose quickly to bump his head squarely on the low aircraft ceiling. She laughed, and then as she fell into his arms she felt she had finally arrived to where she had waited a long time to be. A quiver rushed through her body.

Simon held her, not only because she asked, but because he wanted to, and also because he felt the loneliness of the last ten days' flood away as he did. He smelt her perfume and kissed her hair, before remembering where he was and he looked toward the cockpit. The pilot grinned at him and gave a faint nod.

"I think the pilot wants to fly."

She looked Simon in the eye and grinned.

"You know; it was worth flying halfway around the world just to see you wrestle your way out of that seat."

Simon laughed.

The other passengers on the plane didn't mind the wait and they'd heard Sarah's comment, while taking note of her clothes. Khaki shorts, blouse and lightweight bushwalking boots, they knew they were looking at a woman who could probably be capable of walking half way around the world. An older lady passenger smiled as if seeing a memory. A younger woman envied the way Sarah filled the clothes she wore and the pilot envied Simon.

Simon let Sarah have the window seat, and ten minutes later they were above the city and flying away from the morning sun. They talked quietly for about an hour, bringing each other up to date.

Simon didn't add too much to that part of the conversation, but he added to the conversation in other ways. He asked with interest about her travels, and answered her questions about this part of outback Australia.

As they flew further inland, they sat nearer to each other, each relishing the closeness. This was a time when words were not needed.

Simon's car was still at the airport; he had wondered about it over the last few days, and was glad to see it parked as he had left it. Still intact, but in need of a jump start. In sitting idle it had brought to Simon's attention the fact that he would need to buy a new battery. They threw their gear in the car, and drove to a nearby store where they bought supplies. Then after driving some miles they pulled off the bitumen road and drove to the gate which opened onto the grazier's pasture.

Simon noted that even after the rain prior to his departure, the country was again drying off and he searched the sky for cloud.

There were none.

The day was warm. Probably in the early thirties he reckoned and the house was dusty. After a light lunch they cleaned up a little and then decided on a swim.

The river was running a good current because of heavy rain in Queensland a couple of months earlier, so they drove in the dusty old Ford through a forest of Coolabah trees to a nearby billabong.

After cooling in the fresh water, they sat on a blanket and talked until finally they kissed and then came together; losing themselves from a world whose openness surrounded them.

The birds that frequented the waterhole whistled as if they condoned the movement of love which was now in their domain.

*****

The next day, Simon and Sarah stayed in the old house, lazed, prepared food, loved and slept in each other's arms.

The day after that, Sarah picked up her hang glider from a local transport company who'd delivered it from Brisbane, and they travelled to a nearby mountain where she flew with the eagles.

Simon loved to watch her as she drifted through the sky. Gliding high over the sun burnt wide land while he secretly worried, like a parent for a child who might fall. He knew she would scold him gently if he spoke of this worry, and knew also, she was an expert at gliding, so really his fears were unfounded.

She had once told him.

"My time will come one day my love, and if I die flying, then I've gone out doing what I enjoy." Simon remembered she had touched his face and continued the sentence with a gleam in her eye, "There is one thing that I enjoy as much, my friend Simon, but I doubt you'd appreciate me doing that to you."

Simon saw her point and also the funny side of her statement.

He knew also that there were dangerous days sometimes at sea, and if he were sailing when his time came, he too would prefer it that way.

*****

Abu had gathered together all the possessions from the mansion he was able to carry, without leaving his platoon of troops behind. He cursed the fact the men took up so much room as he rode in the transport truck on the return trip to the capital.

Now, four days later he stood in his office and planned his next step. He'd opened the express envelope from Australia, checking carefully beforehand that the envelope had not been tampered with.

He pressed the intercom button and summoned his secretary who almost immediately appeared at his door. He asked her to bring her typewriter into his office; she smiled questioningly and did as he ordered. As usual Abu thought, a good secretary who carried out his instructions without question.

There was a colour photocopier in his office and he photocopied the letter of authorization which gave him access to the Liechtenstein bank account.

It came out a little light coloured, so he enhanced the tone and was happy with his second attempt. With the next copy, he laid a piece of his blank office stationery under the letter of authorization and was reasonably happy with the outcome.

After three more attempts he had the page of the letter blank except for the letterhead.

He positioned himself behind the typewriter, placed the blank page in the machine and typed, looking as he went at the letter authorizing his access to the Liechtenstein bank account.

Abu typed word for word until he got to his name. At this point, he typed in the names of the ministers aligned before his own. He thought this might give the other parties a secure feeling, in seeing their names to the top of the list.

When he had finished, he used different pens and signed the document with the names that appeared on the original letter. He fudged the first copy and had to start over again, but an hour later he had it done, and he smiled as he looked over his handiwork.

As he was putting the original copies into his safe, he called to the secretary to take the typewriter away. After she had gone from the room he sat by his fax phone and called each of the ministers aligned, asking each of them to secure their fax machines and to stand by to receive.

Each one of them did, and twenty minutes later they all wore smiles of joy as they walked with a little more lightness in their step.

For each of them understood the possibility of the government forces failing to defeat the rebels, and each had an escape route planned.

Once the money was in the bank account they could all leave at a moment's notice.

Not too early, and not too late.

Abu sat back in his chair and wondered at the feelings in these fool's hearts. All believing they were rich. They couldn't even access the $2.4m account, because they would need his signature and he would be gone.

Abu put the bill for services rendered into the system that day, and as each of the ministers aligned knew it was moving through the departments, they gave it priority, signing the necessary papers that sent it quickly on its way. The last minister making sure it made the Nation's bank by having it delivered by the hand of his personal secretary. By lunch time the next day the whole amount, minus banking fees, was in a bank in Liechtenstein.

The short lawyer was happy, the knowledge that he was $1.63m or thereabouts richer gave him an intense thrill. A feeling he'd nearly forgotten as the economic climate of late had been weak. He'd had thrills in the past when he'd closed on deals.

But $1.63m in one go?

His colleagues would go green with envy. He smiled as he thought of the looks that would be on their faces as he placed a call via the fax to Simon in Australia.

As he punched 'send' on his machine and watched the good news go on its way, he hoped that if Simon ever came up with another idea such as this, he would not forget his good friend in Liechtenstein.

CHAPTER 18

It seemed like such a long time since she and Simon had canoed the 250 kilometres of the muddy swirling water downstream to the small outback village of Louth. The Darling had been in flood, so she and Simon had drifted with the current for four days.

Four days of sunshine when they had floated on the river by day, and camped by open fires under clear starry skies at night.

Of all the places she had been in her life. From the rivers in Borneo, the mountains of Scotland, the Rockies in Canada or the Kimberley in Western Australia her fondest memory was the trip down the Darling River with Simon. Now she was here once again with the lazy moving river where she'd left part of her heart. She had not returned to retrieve it, but to be with it, to make it whole again.

She'd spent her life in the good times of travel, and had known and held fond memories, but now she felt weary.

Her soul was tired from the exertions she'd asked of it over the long years, and she needed to have somewhere to call home. She knew that if she were to go to a doctor then the doctor would prescribe Simon.

She knew that he was the remedy. These first days back with him had been excellent, although Simon seemed to be withdrawn and sometimes quiet, almost moody. She wondered if it was because of her.

Was it because he'd come to expect that she would be here today and maybe gone tomorrow? If that was the case, then the only way to solve the problem was with time. How would she find out if he was prepared to give her that time?

What happened if she left herself open and accepted that here with him she would stay, only to find that he was used to her arriving and then going again. Until the next time around and they would start over?

Would he want her around full time?

He was a free spirit like her in many ways.

She looked up and saw a large bird gliding over the river, a hawk of some kind. It lifted and turned, and its shadow passed over her as it spiralled to a River Red Gum where it settled lightly on a high branch. There was a nest in the same tree, though whether it belonged to the bird or not she couldn't tell. Maybe the nest was an old one, whose sticks still balanced on the branch which swayed lightly in the wind.

Whichever way it was, Sarah saw a connection between the hawk and its home, whereas she was a traveller without a home. She looked back at the water, and watched a log moving along with the current as she told herself that time would tell. As the sun went down in red and gold she stood up and went to the house to find Simon, quietly assuring herself that everything would work out, and that she was just being silly.

She was suddenly surprised at herself and her doubt.

Doubt was a new sensation in this usually confident woman's mind.

She was near the house when she heard the phone sound and Simon was replacing its hand piece as she walked through the doorway.

"I didn't know if it might have been Mum?" She asked.

"No, it was a mate of mine in town. He just rang to tell me there is a fax for me."

Sarah noticed that Simon was a little jumpier this evening and she wondered again if it were because of her. He was also in a hurry to get out of the house and into town.

"I need to see what this fax has to say. The electrician says he hasn't been in his office for two days, so I don't know when it arrived and if it may be important. Do you want to come for the drive?" It was the longest sentence she'd ever heard him say and she noticed he was perspiring.

"No. You go and I'll see if I can rustle up something for us to eat when you get back." Simon hurried out the door, and was gone before she realized he'd not kissed her good bye.

She turned to the kitchen and found the two fish she and Simon had caught at dawn that morning.

It was a bit over an hour later when she heard the Ford return. Simon was driving fast; changing gears at times, then speeding up to almost hurtle through the bush. Sarah watched as the headlights of the car seemed to pass by the tree trunks very quickly.

He pulled up outside the house and she heard him walk across the veranda floor boards before he stepped through the doorway and into the kitchen. The grin on his face spread from ear to ear, and although he appeared a little more relaxed she sensed that he was inwardly excited.

"It went O.K then?" She asked.

He watched her play half-heartedly with the fish and went to her as she faced the kitchen bench. He knew he'd been strained during the last couple of days and knew also, that it must have been noticeable to her.

He took her waist in his big hands and turned her to face him. She had flour on her hands and a little more on the end of her nose and he smiled.

"I know that in the past we've been together for a little while, and then we part again to go our separate ways. It's the way we are and we both understand that. In a few weeks I'll be ready to put to sea and I want to know if you'll stay this time and come to the Whitsunday's with me? Sarah, will you stay this time?" Sarah looked at his kind face, then buried her face into his chest and started to cry. Simon held her close as her body quivered and heaved as if she had broken free of some demon and loosed it from her.

After a while she straightened and looked at him.

"Simon, I've been a wanderer all my life, and now, tonight, I think I'm finally home."

"There's one thing you probably should know."

"What's that?" She asked.

He looked deep into her eyes.

"You've got flour on your nose."

With tears still drying in her eyes she laughed.

CHAPTER 19

Horton stood among a thick belt of bush that held fast to the steep banks of a small creek. It flowed down the lower gradual slopes of the forested mountains, and in the pale moonlight he could see glistening water rippling over black rocks. Looking down into the valley it was easy to make out the fortified area, it was active with movement of troop transport trucks and smaller jeep type vehicles.

Away to his left, further up along the valley he could just make out the lights of another of the encampments, which he knew, would also be alive with troops and armaments.

In the distance to his right he noted a glow on the skyline which gave away the position of the capital. He reckoned it would be less than ten miles to its outskirts. From there it was about another three miles to the government administration offices, where he was to eliminate certain ministers when the rebels took control of the capital.

Most of the Government officials would escape, while others would fall into the hands of the rebels. In some cases, his job would be done for him, although he hoped he would find two in particular. Dead or alive, it made no difference to him.

The attack on the two encampments would begin at dawn, and he looked to the east where the sky had begun to lighten. A glance at his watch told him he would have less than half hour to wait.

He walked back up the trail and called his band together, speaking out some instructions to his single interpreter. This was the first time he'd informed them of what was about to go down and they listened intently, nodding that they understood.

Horton led them to where they quietly positioned themselves in the thick belt of bush. It screened them from the clearing they would have to cross as soon as the sky lightened.

He felt good, as he always did before battle. Some part of him came alive.

He licked his lips and was ready.

The mortars started first, and he listened as they whooshed overhead, before plumes of dust and dirt heralded their arrival.

A young voice screamed and a truck exploded.

He counted the bombs, 6, 7, 8...

They'd only had 12 for each of the camps, and he knew that what had started here, would surely have started at the other camp by now.

...9, 10... He stood and began to run across the open area, hoping the last two bombs didn't fall short.

The African who he'd instructed to cut the wire was at it already, and had snipped through the last wire, enough to give them quick access.

Horton's target was the sand bagged machine gun just the other side of the wire.

...11, 12. The last of the bombs exploded and he knew they would be enough to keep the gunners' heads down.

His timing was spot on, and as the gunners lifted their heads to ready their fire Horton shot the three of them down.

The Africans who followed him jumped the sandbags and finished unnecessarily what he'd already accomplished, and although Horton questioned their methods he understood their madness and their hatred.

Five minutes later it was all but over as the camp fell to the rebels, with only the odd shot ringing out as they killed off the wounded. There weren't many of these sounds, as Horton knew these people would do most of their killing with the big machetes they carried.

The same big blades he'd seen them use on the villagers.

Men, women and children alike had fallen to the long blades before their belongings, and the supplies delivered by the Red Cross were carried from their burning villages.

Horton had heard the blades as they whispered out their bludgeoning sounds of death and disfigurement many times. He heard it again now as a scream filled the air, and then a hoot of laughter. Smoke and flame roared from a truck as its fuel tank erupted. A dying man moaned and Horton walked to him and shot him in the head, cursing as blood and brains splattered on his boots.

A couple of the trucks had been smashed beyond repair. Two more had received minor damage, while some had come away unscathed. These were loaded with weapons and ammunition the government troops would need no more, along with their food supplies and jerry cans of spare fuel.

Horton noticed there were many more rebels today, and figured the fence sitters were joining up with the rebels. Now that it seemed almost certain the government troops would be defeated.

When the trucks were loaded, the ragged army left the burning camp and headed up the highway singing their song of victory. They travelled slowly, for they knew that although a battle was won, the war was still in progress. Only a few miles had passed before the singing died down and tension began to mount, as they began to encounter small pockets of resistance.

Horton looked back at the smoke which rose above the burning camps and knew it would be visible from the capital. If not, then word would soon spread that the rebels were almost upon the city.

*****

Garry Sudovich sat in his office whose windows overlooked industrial buildings, upon which hovered Sydney's summer heat haze.

He gazed into the shimmering rooftop heat as he took stock of his day.

It was three-thirty in the afternoon and he'd just finished his last meeting for the day. In which he'd learned the ship carrying cargo from Britain on behalf of one of his new business partners was having engine trouble. It was somewhere on the seas between Tokyo and Sydney, with a possible two-week delay in its expected arrival. He thought of the money involved in this import deal. The amount of money he was being paid suggested the cargo was, if not unclean, then maybe a little tainted.

The people who owned the cargo also rented premises from him in Sydney, so regardless of whether the cargo was clean or not, he was connected to them.

If the shit hit the fan, then he'd just tell the truth. Deny knowledge of everything, other than importing in good faith. If things went smoothly, then his new yacht was as good as paid for. There had also been talk of industrial strife brewing at the wharves. He wondered if the ship would arrive just in time to become one more of the unloaded in a harbour closed down by the unions.

Hence even more delay, and an even later payment.

He'd hoped the deal would have been concluded earlier, because of the risk that his silent partner might find out.

Tom Lee was not a man to be crossed, and the less he knew the better.

Sudovich existed because of Lee. Their dealings had come about initially because Sudovich had hit a rough spot on the share market, and without Lee's capital input he would have been hard pressed to survive.

Now Lee owned fifty-one percent of his soul.

Sudovich risked his life by skimming the profits and private deals. He knew the cost of being discovered, but his need to live the high life and be seen by others to be successful was too great. It was almost like an addiction. He wanted to stop, but he just couldn't take his hand from the till.

His copy of the days Financial Times informed him that his share prices were holding.

The shares he'd bought in an oil company should have gone through the roof by now, he thought. He'd read in the same newspaper a week ago that the company had reported good results while drilling on the Canadian-Alaskan border. Information backed up by an Australian Stock Exchange report.

He decided to give it a few more days, and began to read an article about another Australian Company. One who had interests abroad, in Africa, who was now slowing operations because of unrest in the country under the control of President Axele.

The thought of Abu's ugly fat face sprang into mind. He wondered how the big African was handling the situation, and then remembered his intention to call him on the day he'd been stuck in the traffic. This thought brought to mind the C.D bandits and the loss of his mobile phone. He cursed them again.

He opened his desk drawer and extracted a small book. It held the phone numbers of people he would rather not have in his normal business directory. He normally kept it in his secret safe, and made a mental note that he should put it back in there and not leave it lying around.

He flicked it open to find the initials A.M, beside which was the Africans phone number. He lit another cigarette and waited impatiently for a connection.

The answer came with the sound of a heavily accented woman's voice.

"Office of the Minister of Overseas Affairs, can I help you?"

"Yes, I wonder if I could speak to Abu Mohammed." "Is he expecting your call, sir?"

"No he's not, but if he is there, could you get a message to him. Tell him that Garry is on the phone and needs to speak to him urgently. He will talk to me." The line went silent and Sudovich wondered how many ears were maybe listening to this call. He hoped none, and that could possibly be right because this phone he used was a new line. One he had changed every month or so, trying to keep a step ahead of the people who 'listened'.

Sudovich heard a grunt on the line and then the Africans deep voice.

"Who is this that I speak to, please?"

Sudovich refrained from using his whole name.

"It's me Garry, in Australia."

Abu voice lightened.

"Garry. How are you my good friend?"

The way that Abu said, 'How are you,' sounded more like he felt the need to call out the greeting because of the distance, rather than the basic close to the second party. 'How are you?'

"I am well Abu, and how are you?" Sudovich had a way, that to him sounded like he needed to speak like the foreigner he spoke to, and sometimes he wondered if he over enunciated.

"It is dangerous times my good friend. I thought that would have been obvious in the letter I wrote to you?"

Sudovich stopped short and tried to remember a letter from the African. "What letter?"

Abu noted the confusion in the Australians voice and replied, "The letter I faxed to you after you replied to my original fax telling you to set the wheels in motion for another transfer of funds."

"I know of no letter."

The Africans voice went cold, "Do not play games with me my friend. I have long arms and I can reach out to you." Abu said in a cold voice.

Sudovich didn't know what to say, and by now he had forgotten any fears of the 'listeners'.

Something was terribly wrong.

"Abu, I have no idea of what in the world you are talking about. You talk in mystery riddles."

A cold hand touched Abu's heart as his fist tightened on the phone hand piece.

"Do not play games with me. You know of what I speak. You set the wheels in motion." Abu said again. This time his voice became more venomous as he almost hissed over the phone, and reached a higher note as Sudovich moved the phone away from his ear, "You are trying to steal from me."

Sudovich was by now confused.

"Abu, I am at a loss. I have had no communication with you since the last transfer. When was that? Twelve months ago?"

Abu's curse came down the phone.

Sudovich held the phone away again. He waited until the verbal storm had passed.

"Abu, calm down a minute, this is getting nowhere. Tell me what has happened?" It was quiet at the Africans end of the phone, except for the fast and heavy breathing.

Sudovich listened as the African calmed. There was a quaver in his voice as he told of everything that had happened, from the time of the first fax to the money transfer to Liechtenstein.

Sudovich couldn't believe what he was hearing. The story sounded so incredible. Someone had ripped off the African, easily, and the African had helped them. At the end of the tale of woe, silence hung in the air.

"We have to find the money. Have you any idea as to whoever has taken it?"

The African was close to tears, and Sudovich could hear the quiet sobs which evolved from deep in the Africans chest.

"Abu, get it together, we must search. Do you still have all the paperwork used in this transfer?" Sudovich almost said, 'Monumental fiasco', but at the last moment caught himself.

"Yes. It is all in my office safe." Abu sobbed as Sudovich leaned back in his chair. He told the African to get the papers, and then listened to the sounds of the African as he left his chair and moved about his office.

A few moments later the African picked up the hand piece.

"What now? What can you do from there?" Sudovich thought a moment, not really knowing the answer to that question himself. He paused again as he formed a plan.

"Do you have the original fax from the thief?" He asked.

He heard a shuffle of paper and then the Africans voice.

"Yes, it is in my hand now."

Sudovich directed the African to look at the very top of the page.

"Is there a name or a number, which is normally encoded into fax machines evident there, at the top of the page?"

There was a moment's pause as the African squinted at the very fine print.

"Yes, there is no name, but there is what appears to be a telephone number."

Sudovich asked of the area code and listened as the African spoke while he lifted a telephone book from the bottom drawer of his desk. He opened the book, found the listings of area codes and ran his finger down the column until he finally came to a matching set of digits.

"I've found the number. It covers a large area of outback New South Wales. Abu, do you have any other documents at hand which may point to the name of the thief?" Abu replied that he had, and Sudovich asked him for all of the names on all of the letters. Knowing it was unlikely the thief would use his real name, but maybe the paper which gave authorization to the bank account would give a clue.

Sudovich wrote the names associated to the signatures on the authorization document, and then tried to soothe the African. He lied that he would find the thief, retrieve the money and give Abu half. Abu didn't like the idea of losing 50% of the money, but he was in no position to argue.

Sudovich finished the conversation.

"Don't worry Abu, I will look into this and get back to you."

As Sudovich put his phone down, he leaned back into his chair and decided that he would find the thief and take it all.

He made his plans, then picked up the phone and punched in some new numbers. He waited some moments before his call was answered, and a calm voice sounded in his ear.

"Hello, directory assistance. Which town please?"

*****

The African sat on the edge of his chair and stared at the floor, before he wiped tears from his eyes with a large handkerchief. The tears had stopped flowing now, but the anger still built in his chest.

He called his young secretary and motioned her into his office, requesting she close the door behind her before she approached his desk.

Abu rose from his chair and walked around to stand behind her. She felt his large paw like hands clutch her waist, and they stilled her startle as she tried to turn. He held her firm and pushed her head down hard, until it thumped onto the desktop.

Bent over the desk she was vulnerable to him, and she felt the weight of his hand as it pushed her forehead into the desk top.

Abu held her there as he fumbled with his trouser belt, then lifted her dress until it lay over her back. As her under garment was torn away from her, it caught the corner of her eye as it landed like discarded waste upon the floor. She whimpered under the pressure of him forcing himself against her, and felt pain as he gained access to her inner sanctum. Her attempts to squirm away from the torture of his violent thrusts were in vain. Her pleas were like drumbeats to the oarsman as he drove into her brutally, until he felt his anger and frustration drain away.

Finally, he stepped away from her, and she whimpered as she limped to the door and closed it behind her. While Abu sat on the edge of his desk and gazed wearily at the light under garment on the floor at his feet.

Rape was not new to him, and he knew there was no complaint his secretary could make against him. Her life would be worth nothing on the street if he chose to put her there, and he had the power to do that.

He poured whisky, and as he drank he thought of the pain and suffering he would put the thief through if he could get his hands on him. Suddenly, a feeling of desolation enshrouded him as he remembered he'd have to rely on Sudovich for retribution.

For this only, because he knew he could not rely on him, or trust him to even consider returning his share of the money.

Abu dropped into his chair, and as he buried his face into his hands he wondered, 'surely things cannot get any worse than this?'

Lost in his thoughts, he didn't even hear a distant sound of thunder.

CHAPTER 20

The small private plane vibrated on the wet tarmac. Its powerful heart strained against the brakes which held it in check, as the pilot completed the final stages of his pre-flight procedure, until it was let loose to fly.

A light shower of fine droplets of rain had fallen, causing the lights of the airport through the planes windows to become like twinkling starlight. He watched as some of the droplets slid across the windscreen. Their wet trails glistening behind them as the planes thrust eased him back into his seat and lifted the aircraft into the air.

It stayed up there for a little over three hours before descending to an airfield of a mid-western city.

As the pilot taxied the aircraft to a halt, a car slid silently from the shadows beside a hangar. The quiet spoken passenger alighted sure footedly from the plane, and folded himself easily into the car's rear seat. The pilot felt a civilized dislike for their type of person as he watched the car leave the airfield. Of all the passengers he carried in this well paid job, those bastards were the worst. They always interrupted his concentration; he could feel them there behind him.

He had carried many of them over the past year, yet he still could not get used to them, and he'd noticed there had been more of them travelling lately. He watched as the cars tail lights turned through a gate and off down a darkened highway. Be it this town or one in the close proximity, someone was in really deep shit.

He tried to put the thought and the passenger from his mind as he taxied to the fuel bowsers to ready for the return trip south.

The passenger was driven for some kilometres along a near deserted highway to the outskirts of the city, where the driver pulled to the side of the road, leaving the car idling and the air conditioner on low.

It wasn't really hot this night, though the draught the air conditioner produced in the car was comfortable, and the man in the grey suit appreciated its cool touch on the exposed parts of his skin.

The driver turned to him.

"There's a small caliber semi-automatic in the glove box. You shouldn't need it but you never know." The man in the grey suit answered with a tone that touched on amusement. He knew his power and chose this moment to make it known, "This country bumpkin shouldn't be too much of a hand full." There was no hint of question in the statement.

The driver disregarded the passenger's small talk and handed over an envelope.

"There's some money for expenses, a plane ticket to the Gold Coast and a map from Sudovich. Just follow this highway and it'll take you to where you need to go." The driver then opened his door and walked off into the night. He didn't think anymore of the man in the grey suit. His job was done.

Scott was the name of the man in the grey suit, and his job began by climbing over the console to make himself comfortable in the driver's seat. When he had done so, a heavy bladed knife appeared from beneath his windcheater and he used it to slit the top of the envelope.

The heavy bladed knife disappeared again and he extracted a map from the envelope.

The name of a small outback town etched into his brain, as he turned off the car's interior light and looked into the headlights of an approaching car. They cut the darkness and highlighted the road which stretched out in black before him.

It was just after sunrise when he sighted the outback town, after a long four-hour drive on a particularly straight stretch of road.

The monotony had been broken though, by the many times he had to brake heavily to avoid bounding kangaroos. They appeared out of nowhere, and then just as quickly disappeared again into the darkness. He didn't look forward to the drive back, though his kind of person didn't look forward to too much at all in life, just one minute to the next.

A hearty breakfast at a roadhouse gave him second wind as reread his instructions and awaited his second cup of coffee.

It came with a young waitress.

Scott noted her. His guess was that she'd be about thirteen and he immediately desired her. His initial grooming began the moment he'd read the address of his target, by asking the girl its direction, as he noted again her young ripeness.

After paying for his meal, he bought fuel for his car and drove around town to familiarize himself, before returning to the roadhouse and from there followed the girls directions.

She was accurate.

"Good girl", he whispered.

He looked to the buildings at the address. It was an electrical tradesman's small business premises, and he noted the yard which was very open and easy to observe. There was an office and sheds which were of old design. Nice house though, he thought, as his eyes travelled to the rear of the yard. To his professional side he noted the surroundings and possible points of access. The house was two stories high, with a pitched roof and plenty of windows. All the better to see you with he thought, as a vision of little red riding hood visited his mind.

A well-built man came out of what might be an office and pulled the door closed behind him. He placed the office doors key under a house brick at the corner of the building, before driving away in a truck.

The man in the grey suit yawned and decided to find a motel.

He booked into a place close to the electrician's office, choosing a room whose window over looked the motels entrance road. A three-day booking should do he thought as he took in his rooms surroundings. Deciding on the best available escape routes was second nature to him. He slept for three hours and then showered before driving back to the roadhouse for lunch.

He was disappointed when he found that the young girl was not there.

Afterwards, and not wanting to rely on the motel switch board for his calls security, he walked to a public phone box and rang Sudovich's new number.

"Are you ready to go ahead?" Sudovich inquired.

"Yes. I've already located the place. It's a business premises and thanks to the owner, an electrician, I have access to his office," said Scott.

Sudovich was impressed, but didn't say so.

"The bait can be laid tomorrow. Call this number when you can see this electrician on his premises and I'll do the rest from here."

"If there's no luck tomorrow, what do I do then?" Scott asked

"Then you sit there until there is," came back Sudovich's harsh voice. "And don't go getting into trouble either. You're there for one reason and one reason only. That's to identify and deal with the thief. Understand?" Scott said that he understood, unperturbed by the lie.

He left the phone box and decided to walk to the roadhouse, it would be dark soon and he was hungry. He liked the roadhouse, not only for the food, but the thought of sweet, young meat.

*****

Abu sat in his large chair and contemplated time. Wondering how much he still had available; he was spending most of what he had in the office now, close to his communications. He needed to be close to them, for he had problems on two fronts.

His loss of a fortune, and the fact the rebel army was getting closer by the minute acted as a crystal ball might in foreseeing his future.

He held another whisky in his hand as he waited for his phone to ring. Either from his spies around the capital, who kept him informed as the events unfolded in the rebel war, or from Sudovich.

Sudovich would give the signal to send the fax which would hopefully locate the thief.

Abu looked at the message he'd printed. It was a simple and to the point. *'Call me one more time, Abu.'*

He startled as the sound of the ringing phone rang out through the room and then grabbed at the hand piece.

"Who is this?"

An answer came from across the world.

"It's me, Garry."

Abu did not greet Sudovich in his usual manner.

"Is it time?"

"Yes, it's time Abu, send the fax now."

"I will send it immediately," and then added, "I have lost the game my friend, now all I ask of you is to kill the thief for me." Abu listened as Sudovich promised, and then dropped the phone down. He rose from his chair and walked with a slight sloping of the shoulders to the fax machine where he dialled the electrician's Australian number. It made its necessary electronic tones before the message clattered through it and on its way.

He returned to his chair to wait and silently welcomed the knock on his door.

"Come," he called

His new secretary's head poked around the door to inform him that that rebel forces were within ten miles of the capital. He thought about this information, and remembered his revolution of eight years ago. He and Axele had covered that last distance into the capital in less than two days.

Time was getting short, and soon he would have to leave.

CHAPTER 21

Scott sat in his parked car under a shady peppercorn tree within sight of the electrician's office. He looked at his watch, then back to the open yard and watched with steely eyes the electrician as he walked to his office and disappeared inside.

A few minutes later he emerged again holding a piece of paper in his hand.

The piece of paper was rolled, which suggested it to be a fax and most probably the bait that Sudovich had organized, he thought.

He readied himself to drive while he watched the electrician walk to the truck. A cloud of black diesel smoke escaped the rear of the vehicle, announcing that the electrician was about to roll.

His own car started as the truck pulled out of the yard and onto the street. It was easily followed to a road which headed in a northerly direction away from town, and kept to this course for about four miles. Finally, it turned off to raise dust on a bush track, before it disappeared into a forest of stunted eucalypts.

Another track led him under a small bridge which straddled a dry billabong. He parked in its shade where he had a clear view of the main road and its junction with the farms dusty bush track. He waited an hour, until the sun glinted off the windscreen of the truck, heralding its return.

Some minutes later, after the truck had left on its way back to the town, a second vehicle swung onto the main road. It was an older model blue coloured Ford whose swirl of dust lingered over the track behind it.

Scott followed it discreetly back into town, and then again until it stopped at a supermarket.

He noted the driver of the blue ford, reckoning he'd be a bit over six feet tall and athletic in build. His face was shrouded in shadow thrown by a wide brimmed hat so he couldn't make out his features clearly.

Having waited outside a moment, he crossed the street and entered the supermarket himself. Walking to the rear of the shop where he found fresh fruit juice, and with this in hand he moved across the aisles, looking up each one as he went until he saw the driver of the blue Ford.

Scott trod lightly along the aisle, until he stood next to Simon, where he noted everything about the man. From the scar on his lower leg to the single red rose tattoo on his fore arm.

The aisle was narrow, and he purposefully bumped into Simon to get a good look at the face under the broad brimmed hat.

As planned, Simon looked around at the person who'd bumped him and looked right into cold and unsmiling eyes as the person apologized gruffly.

"That's alright mate," Simon said as he went on his way down the aisle.

Scott stopped at the checkout to pay for his items.

"I have a feeling I've met the man in the wide brimmed hat. You wouldn't by any chance know his name would you?"

The girl looked up from the groceries she was packing to see Simon's wide brimmed hat.

"That's Simon. Everyone knows Simon."

Scott thanked her, and returned to his vehicle to wait until Simon left the building, then followed the old blue Ford until it turned off again onto the dusty dirt track.

Upon returning to the phone box he noted the graffiti on its wall, and as he waited for a connection he wondered what kind of good time he could have with someone named Cathy.

He heard Sudovich's voice.

"I've identified two targets and their locations," he said

"Good work," offered Sudovich, "Will you take one tonight?"

"No, I think I'll do both jobs together tomorrow night. The out of town one first, as I will probably have to spend more time on him. I've found out that his first name is Simon. Does that fit in with the names you said you have?"

Sudovich looked through his papers.

"One of the English names on the documents is James Munroe. It could be him. No doubt you'll find out when you question him." Sudovich reminded Scott, "Make up a map showing both men's locations and include their descriptions. Post it to me on today's mail."

Scott understood that Sudovich was readying, just in case.

"I don't like you suggesting that I might fail. I don't..." Scott began defiantly.

Sudovich's voice cut him short and turned steely.

"Just do as I say. Make the map and post it to me, then do what I pay you to do. Make this Simon, or whatever the arsehole's name is, talk. Try to get hold of any paperwork as well as information. I need access to the man's bank account." Sudovich paused a moment before adding, "And remember, none of your baby pussy chasing on the side either. Just do what I tell you to do, then get the hell out of there. Is that clear?"

Scott looked at Cathy's name and lied again.

"Yes, boss."

At the roadhouse a short time later he forgot all about Cathy as he turned his attention to the young girl. With careful questions he found out her name, where she lived and what time she usually left the roadhouse at night.

He made her laugh a trusting young girl's laugh.

Later, as he lay on his bed at the motel he devised his plan for the next day. Not noticing the late night news or its mention of a President Axele, whose government, according to reliable sources was likely to fall.

He formed his plan.

A drive down the dusty road to find a place to hide the car, then walk the final kilometre or so to the farm which must be down there somewhere. Lie up under cover for the day to watch the goings on before moving in. Just on sundown would be a good time. He could spend some time on the Ford driver, and then go to the electrician and deal with him. After that he'd go by the roadhouse, snatch the girl and take her back to the place down the dusty road.

If he had trouble extracting the information from the blue Ford driver, then he could leave him tethered and finish him when he came back with the girl.

His fingers touched lightly on the heavy bladed knifes honed edge before he lay it on the bed beside him. When the young girls form began to fill his mind's eye, he reached for the zipper of his trousers and took his hardness in hand.

He awoke early the next morning refreshed, and after an early morning jog past the electrician's house he ate breakfast at the roadhouse. Then returned to the motel to shower and prepare his work gear.

Donning a dark coloured tracksuit he threw his tool bag in the boot of the car and drove to the dusty track.

At the turn off, he checked his rear view mirror, and seeing no one in sight drove down the dirt track, awkwardly handling the rough road. He drove until he saw buildings in the distance through the trees, at which point he left the track and directed the car towards some thick scrub nearby. Once there, he opened the cars boot and extracted an olive green army surplus parachute car cover.

It covered the car completely and he changed from his tracksuit to a pair of olive green overalls. Unzipping the tool bag in the boot of the car he reached into it and retrieved the pistol. Checking its load, and then weighing it in his hand as he decided he would take it with him. There may be dogs he thought, as he fitted its silencer.

His eyes roved over the contents of the bag as he made a last minute check of the tools of his trade, field glasses, long cable ties, a half dozen short pieces of cotton rope and a roll of wide duct tape.

He jammed a lead shot filled waddy into his back pocket and put the sandwiches he'd bought at the roadhouse, along with his canteen into the bag. A final check saw that the car cover was secure before he walked toward the buildings beyond the bush in the distance.

An old tree with even shade, whose heavy roots protruded from the hard ground provided some cover, and he settled upon a thin layer of its leaf debris where he had a good view of the house.

The dusty blue car was in sight.

As he played the field glasses over the area around the house and sheds, he heard a motor start. A moment later an old truck drove into sight from behind the horse stables.

Even with the field glasses it was difficult to make out the driver; the fact he could not see a wide brimmed hat suggested it was probably not the man he sought.

The old truck drove on the road leading towards town and disappeared amongst the trees. It returned around mid-afternoon and he watched as a wiry man lifted a cardboard box and a gas bottle from the vehicle. He was lost to sight for some moments as he carried them to the rear of the house, before reappearing again to make his way to the horse stables.

It was quiet all afternoon with no movement except for the wiry man who spent his time feeding and exercising horses.

Scott ate some food, and then spent the rest of the afternoon squashing ants as they crawled on him, or swishing flies. His gaze at times followed kangaroos as they passed nearby on their way to the river for their late afternoon drink.

In the evening the dusty blue Ford left and took the road towards town.

Simon and his wide brimmed hat stood out, and Scott hoped he wouldn't stay away too long.

By now the wiry man had left the horse stables and had moved to where he'd left the gas bottle. Scott watched as the wiry man poked a rod into the container on the gas bottles stove top, removed it, and then poked it into a plastic bucket.

The wiry man had obviously been out in the sun too long he thought, and as he grew weary with watching him, he put the field glasses down and rubbed his eyes.

Sometime after sundown, he left the place amongst the tree roots and made his way over the last few hundred metres to the house. On his final approach he heard an engine start and suddenly lights came on. He realized the motor must be a lighting plant. Good. That will cover the sounds of the dogs if they start to bark, he thought.

The wiry man walked from the shed where the noise of the motor seemed to come from, and returned to his place by the gas bottle. Where it was easy for the stalker to approach from the wiry man's rear, and let the waddy fall firmly to his head.

The wiry man fell forward with a flailing right hand. It upset the gas bottle, causing the tin pot which had been heating on its top to hit the pool surround. Spewing its contents of liquid wax in a wide fan on to the cooling concrete where it quickly solidified.

The intruder applied cable ties to Ray's wrists and ankles, before slapping a short piece of duct tape over his mouth.

As he dragged him into what appeared to be a feed shed, a sound caused him to stop short and listen.

Suddenly a light came on in the house, and he quietly cursed his lack of professionalism as he realized there was someone he hadn't accounted for.

He bundled Ray into the feed shed and made his way around the side of the house, to where he found a window. He looked through it, and saw a tall woman with long reddish curls of hair that reached for the base of her back. He ran his eyes over her with interest.

She had good shoulders and a trim waist.

He liked what he saw.

CHAPTER 22

Sarah had had a good day. Simon had been cheery and a little more relaxed, even after the electrician had delivered yet another fax.

Now, after Simon had related the story to her about the money, the faxes and his trip to Europe, she understood his restlessness over the past days. The initial disheartenment she'd felt when she learned of his theft had passed as he'd explained his plan. Now she smiled to herself at the memory of his explanation for not kissing her good bye the night he rushed to town to read the fax from the African. She reviewed the conversation of that afternoon as she and Simon had lain in the cool of the house.

She listened to his explanation again as it reeled in silent words through her mind.

"Sarah, if I could put into money terms an excuse for not kissing you goodbye that night. How much would you accept as a reasonable excuse?"

"I don't know. I would prefer a reason rather than an excuse." She laughed and asked, "What's all this about Simon?"

"How much?" He persisted as he kissed her gently and asked again,

"I don't know."

Simon stroked her hair and said,

"The excuse... Sorry. The reason I have for forgetting to kiss you goodbye was 32.6 million dollars American."

"Are you serious?" She asked incredulously.

It was then that Simon related his story to her.

She was smiling to herself when she heard a sound behind her. She'd begun to turn when she saw a movement from the corner of her eye. Something touched the side of her head, and then blackness.

Scott caught her as she fell, and lowered her to the floor where he used cable ties on her wrists and ankles. A third cable tie held her wrists to her ankles behind her back before he gagged her with duct tape.

While dragging her still form to the pantry, his eyes were drawn to her bared chest. It had become exposed when the buttons of her blouse had torn away as he'd caught and broke her fall.

His lips were dry, and he was about to touch when he saw a reflection of light on the far wall of the darkened dining room. It drew his attention to the window where he saw headlights of an approaching car.

He looked down at the woman who as if in sleep lay on her side at his feet.

"I'll be back for you later. Don't go away now, will you," he whispered.

Her upper most breast hung from her chest like firm fruit, and before he left the pantry he gave it a rough squeeze.

Quickly leaving the house, he made his way to the swimming pool area, where he took in the situation before backing away into the shadows. Leaving the blue flamed gas bottle on its side, as he reckoned the returning man would be drawn to it, like a moth to a light.

From where he stood in the thick shrubbery he could see clearly the blue flame of bait.

*****

It was 9.15 when Simon finally drove back to the farm. It had been a good day and he felt better now as he had told Sarah what he had done.

His worry had been she might object to his actions, and it appeared at first that she would do so, but she had come around to his way of thinking when he'd explained to her his intentions.

The road he drove was really a track of twists and turns and gullies. Each small hazard had to be negotiated rather than driven, and he always looked forward to doing just that.

The lights of the house glowed vividly through the night, and he wondered if Ray might be still there, as the lights were also on in the swimming pool enclosure. He parked the car and made his way towards the kitchen end of the house.

While passing the pool gateway he saw the gas bottles blue flame fluttering alone into the night. Odd he thought, as he walked past the feed shed and towards the overturned gas bottle.

He stepped up to it and righted the near empty bottle before turning the gas off. Noticing as he did so, the wax, where it had spilt from the pot and spread in a smooth shiny glaze over the dirty concrete. At the same time, he saw the lidless cyanide bucket standing dangerously close to the edge of the pool.

Fearing fumes, he carefully lifted it by its handle, and at arm's length made to move it from the water's edge. As he did he wondered where Ray might be.

Suddenly it dawned on him that something was wrong. He was about to put the cyanide bucket down near the gas bottle, when he caught sight of movement out of the corner of his eye.

He was still holding the cyanide bucket in his left hand as he straightened, and as he turned, the movement became that of a black shadow of a man. It slipped out of the darkness and moved swiftly toward him.

Simon froze. Then his right arm whipped up to protect his head from the small club in the attacker's hand. It rose, and reached out for him as the shadowed figure moved smoothly perilously close. Simon felt like prey in the sights of a skilled predator.

No thoughts of death entered Simons head. He was transfixed, mesmerized.

His minds vision was resolutely clear, reality in a time slowed. The predator's face sneered at him. Its triumphant grin distorted by the shadows thrown as leaves of a single tree were entertained by a light breeze under the pool enclosures single yellow light.

At last Simon moved. Stepping to his right as the shadow came on. Sure of itself.

Suddenly the grin of victory vanished, immediately replaced by one of confusion as the attacker's foot began to slip on the spilt wax. It tried to right itself, but only slid further into failure. Desperately it tried to grip Simon's arm.

Simon stood fast while the shadowed figure lost grace. Its half grip became no grip, and as Simon pulled away from the violent clutching fingers he too spun out of control, in turn losing the cyanide bucket.

It hung in the air while the shadow landed on its back in the water. A second later it fell, as if it intended to follow the struggling shape, hitting the water and spewing its deadly contents over and through the murky broken surface.

The shadow sunk down with momentum and then found its footing. Its powerful legs propelled it upright, and Simon watched the dark head break the surface. Its mouth wide open as it gasped for air.

It filled with water instead, and cyanide.

The shadow seemed to ready itself for another attack. Suddenly it just stopped in mid-stream. Its eyes popped open as it gurgled, and sank back into the water.

Simon felt as if every emotion he'd ever known had visited him, all in the space of a few short seconds. He felt hot and cold, laughing and crying, weak at the knees, tight in the belly and he had a thick taste of something on his tongue. He gained a grip on one of Ray's chairs for support and stared at the pool and its ripples. Almost expecting the shadow to break free of its dark, wet shroud and attack again.

The sound of knocking brought him back to reality and hairs stirred on the back of his neck as he realized he was not alone. He turned toward the noise and ran quickly to the feed shed to swing open the loose fitting door. In the darkness he could make out a body lain out on the earthen floor. It kicked, and dust rained down as riding boots came in contact with the timber wall.

"Ray! Are you alright?" No answer came from the man, other than a moan and a grunt as Simon realized he'd been gagged.

Ray was lying on his side with his face away from Simon and flinched when Simon touched his shoulder.

"Ray, it's me, Simon," he said, as he bent over and spoke clearly into the bonded man's ear

With this Ray settled, and remained still while Simon removed the duct tape which clung stubbornly to his stubble face. Simon pulled free his pocket knife and cut the cable ties, allowing Ray to struggle to a sitting position, where he rubbed circulation into his wrists.

"Simon. Bloody hell! What happened?" Ray stopped short at this point, looked at Simon, and said a word that made Simon's warm blood run cold.

"Sarah."

Simon backed out of the feed shed and ran to the house. Mounting the steps to the veranda with long strides and discounting in his haste, the loose and risky boards. He called her name as he entered the house, and the cold hand of fear touched his heart when silence was the only reply.

He came to the kitchen and was greeted by the signs that she had been here. Her sandwich ingredients were sitting on the breakfast bench. Simon noticed the pantry door was slightly ajar, though the light was not on. He pushed the door gently and it opened on squeaky hinges. The first he saw of her through the darkness of the room was her bare hands and feet.

He pulled his pocket knife and cut the cable ties.

Simon put the knife away and touched her shoulder to turn her. Suddenly she leapt like an animal and lashed out, catching him square in the eye with her balled fist. He fell back and she was on him in a flash, her fingernails going for his eyes until he managed to grab her by her wrists.

"Sarah, Sarah, it's me."

She relaxed her attack and looked at his face, finally recognizing him. At that moment Ray stepped into the doorway and saw Simon flat on his back with Sarah sitting on his stomach. She with red hair aglow in the kitchen light, her chest exposed and fire in her eyes. Simon lay with a scratch on his face and an eye which was quickly swelling.

Ray turned away out of respect for the woman's exposure, then leant on the kitchen table where he allowed a relief of laughter to explode from deep within him.

Sarah looked down at Simon, and taking in his wounds she lowered her head and he felt her hair caress his face as she snuggled into him. She lay there a moment before rising again as if to say something, then stopped as her hands felt the reason for her silence.

Simon didn't know what to say so he remained quiet and began to nurse his eye.

Ten minutes later the three of them stood by the pool looking at the body of the man in the water.

They opened cans of beer and for a time each was lost in their own thoughts.

Ray broke the spell.

"Has this got anything to do with the letter I delivered to you the night of the rain Simon?"

Simon looked at Ray, and before he knew it he was pouring the story out to him. He'd known Ray for a long time and felt he could trust the man. Although under different circumstances he may have considered that the amount of money involved could buy some men's souls.

Simon closed the story with the plan he had for the disposal of the millions, which were safe in the bank in Liechtenstein.

Ray looked at him disbelievingly and then smiled as he saw the look of truth in Simon's eyes.

They all remained quiet for a while until Ray spoke.

"Well it looks like you've got someone on your tail. So I suppose the best thing to do now is to get this clown out of the pool and see if he's got any I.D on him." He paused for a moment before asking, "Who'd like another beer?"

It wasn't long before they were rifling through the dead man's pockets, and came up with a wallet and credit cards that explained his details. They also found a plane ticket, the address of the girl who worked at the roadhouse and a list of instructions authorized by the initials G.S.

The night was still reasonably young so they sat and discussed the body. Sarah thought that to just bury it somewhere was a bit callous. She stood by this idea until Ray pointed out to her that the girl from the roadhouse was his niece. It appeared to him that the dead man was not only a killer, but he possibly had sinister intentions in mind regarding my niece. Thankfully we've stopped that from happening." He nudged the dead man with his boot, "Now to me, there's no such thing as callousness where scumbags like this are concerned."

Sarah hadn't thought of what was obvious to her now that Ray had pointed it out. It brought to the surface a memory of a secret scar which had marked her heart since she was a young girl.

"Don't get me wrong Sarah. I'm not an evil man, but people like this don't deserve a Christian grave. Anyway, what about the questions it'll raise with the authorities? We'll have coppers everywhere poking about in things, court cases, lawyer's costs and our time." Ray paused for breath, and then continued, "The time that I have left on earth is limited and I don't really want to waste it on a scumbag like this. He died while attacking people with intent. He died because people fought back in self-defense. You know that, and I know that. Why is it necessary to prove it to some judge or jury when we know in our hearts that it was his own fault he died?"

"He must have had a car. It may be hidden around here somewhere. Shouldn't we find it first?" Sarah suggested.

Ray thought for a moment and gave another of his ideas.

"What about if you and Simon take a drive and hunt around for his car, while I get rid of the body?"

"Do you want a hand to dig the hole?" Simon asked.

"No I'll be alright. I can have this bloke under eight foot of dirt in less than half an hour, with the help of the grazier's back hoe. You two will have to find the car and see if you can dispose of it."

Ten minutes later Simon and Sarah drove slowly along the dusty track until they arrived at the boundary gate, then Simon turned the car around to cover the road from that direction.

He hadn't picked up any tracks on the way out, and hadn't expected to. A greater chance of discovering them lay in traversing the track from the direction the dead man had taken.

His bush experience was rewarded, and as he rounded a slight bend he could see clearly where car tracks left the road. He followed them until they led him directly to the car.

Simon left his car and walked around the deserted vehicle. Peeling the car cover back and peering into its windows without touching any part of the car itself.

He returned to his own car, and from its boot he took a pair of leather oil riggers gloves before he leaned into Sarah's window.

"I'll drive it into town and leave it there somewhere. You follow me. When I've found a place to park it I'll turn off the lights and walk to where you've stopped. Don't drive too close to me, and if you see me pulled up by the coppers or something, then drive around the block and check again. I can't see that anything can go wrong Sarah, but if it does, then get out of the place and tell Ray O.K?"

Simon got out of his car and Sarah slid over to the driver's side. Simon closed the door and then leaned in through the window and kissed her softly. "Sarah, I'm sorry I got you involved in this. I was scared when I couldn't find you this evening and I...." He didn't finish and instead of trying to find the words he kissed her again and whispered, "I always had hope you would return to me Sarah, but tonight I had a terrible fear you might be lost to me forever."

Sarah could see that he was shaken. She and Ray had not seen their attacker, so they had not experienced the fear of direct frontal contact with his intent. Their headaches were still felt from the dead man's club, but Simon felt something more, and it showed in the expression on his face. She loved him more at that moment, and knew then, that she would soothe him in her own way when they'd returned to the farm.

Simon found the keys to the dead man's car in the ignition. Started it, and drove it through the gateway, then closed it again after Sarah had driven through. He locked it. Thinking it might save Ray being interrupted by unexpected visitors.

As he got behind the wheel of the car, he suddenly realized where he had seen the dead man before. The face came back to him as the one who had bumped into him in the supermarket.

The steep learning curve he was on suddenly taught him that he would have to look over his shoulder more often. Take careful note of any strangers he saw. Sudovich had sent one man to find him, and he might send another when he found this latest one missing.

Simon drove directly to the end of town pedestrians didn't use at night, and left the car in the shadows. Expecting the street kids would have it in pieces by morning.

He walked around the corner to his own car, and noticed that Sarah drove more quickly than her usual on their return to the farm. Fatigue seemed to overtake him as he tried to relax his head on the headrest until he welcomed Sarah's voice as it came to him over the noise of the car.

"Simon."

"Mm?" Simon, still with his eyes closed, murmured,

"The fax that came from the African this afternoon, what does he want?"

"I don't know Sarah. The message just asked me to contact him one last time."

"Will you?" Sarah asked.

"Yes I think I will. Mainly out of curiosity, but also because I shouldn't let the bloke entertain the thought that we Australians have bad manners."

She looked at him, and in the low cabin light she could make out a tired grin on his face, and they both chuckled.

CHAPTER 23

Her name was Che'anton. She had come to know the dangers of the militia first hand, and her initiation to their methods was when she was just 12 years old. She had watched helplessly her father's murder, whilst he tried to protect his family during Abu's revolution 8 years ago.

Being the oldest girl in a family of six, she had carried the burden of helping her mother raise the young of the family. Working hard over the years since that tender age of twelve, she had learnt by experience to survive the terrible days that followed the revolution.

On the way she had gained some education, and it had stood her in good stead in gaining easier and better paid work. Life had become better for her and the family she provided for. She had felt better in her own heart until three months ago, when her younger brother had disappeared.

He'd been taken off the streets by the gangs of thugs who went under the guise of Government militia. More than likely he'd been tortured, and was by now most certainly buried in an unmarked grave somewhere in the jungle. The stories were that all those who disappeared died horribly, and eventually ended up in unmarked graves.

She'd tried not to listen to the rumours and stories she'd heard. As the memory of her brother was still fresh in her mind, she preferred to remember him as he was before he disappeared. She'd struggled on, and prayed to God that her life and the lives of her people would get better.

Prayed the revolutionaries would put her country and its people before themselves and their greed.

She knew she asked a lot of God, but her faith had been strong. A faith she'd carried for many years, and through it believed that God had smiled upon her when she'd achieved the position as secretary in the government. She'd carried the faith right up until the time that Abu the corrupt had pushed her down and splashed her legs with her own virgin blood.

The blood she had cherished, and had been saving to give in sacrifice to the one she was to marry in two months' time. Now even that had been destroyed, by the same regime that had taken her father and her brother.

She would extract payment from the one responsible, and knew that when the time came for the rat to leave the sinking ship, where the rat would run to.

Her time normally spent in prayer was now spent in grievance, and for the first time in her life she felt the dark shadow of hate and revenge creep into her gentle heart.

✳✳✳✳✳

Abu stalked his huge ornament of an office. He moved about the floor with anger in his heart, as he emptied his safe and quickly counted his American dollars. His earlier estimation had been close to correct.

His new life would be difficult.

There was always the money in the ministers aligned account he thought, but they would undoubtedly suspect him of theft when he tried to explain that the money had actually been stolen from him. He wondered how he would react if the foot was in the other shoe, and knew then that his chances were slim.

One thing he did know. They needed him as much as he needed them. The four signatures were in the end necessary to empty the account, so he could still come out of this with something.

There was a sound of gunfire in the distance. It was still a fair way away, but he knew that time was quickly slipping by.

A call to his new secretary produced nothing, so he walked to the door of his office and looked to her desk. It had been cleared. He decided that she too had heard the gunfire and had left the building, as she'd have realized that she would be treated as any government official if caught by the rebel army.

Abu treaded back into his office and pulled the curtains apart slightly. Smoke was clearly visible as it curled in huge clouds across the far side of the city.

He stared at the smoke for a moment, hoping he had not left it too late to make his escape. With this fear in mind he was about to turn away from the window when an explosion rent the air. It was closer, and he realized that the government armory had just been turned to ashes.

Abu picked up the bag which held his possessions and made his way to the door.

As he passed the secretaries desk the phone rang. He had no time to waste and was on the verge of ignoring it, but finally picked up the hand piece.

"Who is this?"

A voice came back in a foreign accent.

"I'd like to talk to Abu Mohammed."

"I am Abu Mohammed. Who is this that I speak to?"

"My name is Simon. You sent me a fax asking me to call you one last time."

Abu stiffened, as he growled down the line.

"You stole from me. You took what was mine."

"Yeah, you're right that I stole from you, but I didn't take what was yours you prick."

Abu wasn't quite sure what to say to the man on the phone.

"I have this morning mailed to the Federal Police in Australia documents which show your activities in the theft of my countries money, and I know that even in your country that fraud is looked upon as a more serious crime than murder, so I have won in the end my friend," he threatened with a lie,

Simon listened to the voice of the African as it shook with anger and laughed.

"Look mate, I've been keeping up with the news, and I know there are rebels in your capital right now. In fact, I'm surprised your phone lines are still open. Let alone the chances of your countries Post Office employees turning up for work half way through a revolution. So save me the bullshit, eh?"

Abu exploded and cursed Simon loudly, furiously, until commotion from across the city brought pause to his speech.

"Sudovich will get you then. You have crossed a very dangerous man and when he has you in his hands you will beg for death, he hissed. You, you..."

Simon chuckled into Abu's ear and stirred the African a little more.

"He has already tried and failed Abu. So if you think he will carry out your revenge for you then, you'd best think again."

Abu stamped his foot heavily on the carpeted office floor as he raged with more curses. Suddenly the sound of another explosion came to him from across the city and the phone went dead.

Undeterred, he ranted and cursed into the hand piece, words and profanity which were lost and heard by no one but him. Finally, he threw the phone down and watched as it shattered against the office wall.

He drew himself to his full height, and drawing on all his being, he spat a heavy glob of sputum and saliva towards the place where the phone had landed.

Abu had to lean against the desk for support as he rubbed a hand over his sweat wet face. Massaging his closed eyes, he groaned an animal like noise as he retrieved his bag of valuables and retreated from the room.

CHAPTER 24

To the few people who knew him well enough, he was just known as Quinn. A bungalow by a beach which was caressed by a gentle blue ocean in the Central South Pacific was his home.

After spectacular sunsets he would feel sea breezes, and listen to the waves break on pristine sand not ten metres from where he now sat. He sipped something magic from his glass, and reflected on the thought of how much he hated to leave this place. As in the past, he was called upon again to carry out small favours for powerful people.

The funds made available to him in return for these favours allowed him to live here in this beautiful South Seas paradise.

He missed the freelance mercenary work he used to do, but the retainer he was on made life comfortable. It was not a desirable situation to be retained by these people, but resigning his position was near impossible.

Quinn had tried with no success.

His reason for failure in this was that one of the powerful people had sent him a list of his Sydney based family members. Along with an 'I know where they live' threat if Quinn happened to step out of line.

So Quinn stayed in line, and bided his time. He knew that at some stage of the game the tide would turn, and the rules of the game would change to his advantage.

He would do the work. He was good at it and after all, it did pay the bills.

Quinn's first taste of war had been in Vietnam.

One day he'd been working as an assistant chef at an up market hotel. The next day his National Service Papers had arrived, and his life had changed.

He'd easily passed his medical, and very soon afterwards he was in a training camp. Then suddenly he was in some Asian country he'd never heard of, where people he didn't know were trying to kill him.

He fought back in order to survive.

In the end he came away unscathed physically, but bruised mentally. Wondering at his good fortune at being alive when so many of his friends had their lives or their limbs blown to hell.

Even if he had gone back to his old job after it was all over, he doubted if he would ever be able to work with red liquids or sauces.

So he had followed his new found career and had discovered the meaning of the term, 'this is the last one'.

His knowledge of war, its strengths and weaknesses had taken him into many battles in many countries. Where either a government had rebel problems or rebels had government problems. Either way it made no difference to him. It was his job and he would carry out his duties for whoever was his employer. He had, on numerous occasions declined work with drug people, as he had seen too many of his friend's lives destroyed by drugs.

The only reason that would bring him into working contact with drug people would be if he was employed against them. He doubted it would ever happen, because the Drug Enforcement people weren't allowed to use the tactics which would give them an even chance of winning.

He sipped his drink and looked at the fax which had arrived an hour ago.

You're booked on the 10 am flight tomorrow, your time. A car will pick you up at Mascot airport. Garry.

He knew that Sudovich and his mates were druggies, but he was stuck with them for now.

One day, he thought.

He didn't need to pack anything other than clothes, as all the tools of his trade were in storage in Sydney, so he bedded down early in preparation for the long day ahead.

He told his only true friend, his caring and beautiful Polynesian lover that he would have to be away for a while.

"Is this the last time? Is it nearly over, so you can come home and stay with me?"

Quinn touched her with gentleness that he reserved only for her.

"That day is getting closer all the time. It may be closer than we both know, but for now you must be patient while I fly to Sydney to find out. Will you wait a little longer for me?" He consoled her quietly,

She came to him, and with the smile he always carried with him while he was away.

"I will wait for you and I will hope that the day has come."

He held her close that night, as he always did before going to work because he needed her.

She was his only true friend.

She held him close that night because she loved him, and she was fearful for him when he went to work.

*****

Quinn's flight was on time. So was the car that picked him up at Mascot airport. It took him to the address he'd given to the driver at the airport and while he was transported, he read the instructions the driver had given to him from Sudovich.

The information was about a man who lived on a small farm in the New South Wales outback. A complete physical description, the type and colour of car he drove, and a map of where he could be found.

There was also a description of a secondary target at a different address.

The car pulled into Quinn's first destination as he was viewing a map of the state of New South Wales. They parked near a set of garages where normal people with normal lives usually stored motorcars and personal household goods.

Quinn opened number four with a key which hung on a chain he wore only while he was at work. It stood as a constant reminder of his work and his need for vigilance.

He went into the garage, stayed some minutes before he reappeared carrying a back pack and a team sports bag.

After relocking the garage door and loading his gear into the car's trunk, he was driven back to the airport. Where he boarded a small private plane which shortly after takeoff headed towards the state's North West.

As the plane gained height he glanced again over Sudovich's instructions. He couldn't know of course, that the photocopy he was reading was once the property of a predecessor, who was last seen refuelling a car at an outback roadhouse.

CHAPTER 25

The pilot watched as the passenger boarded the plane and thought, *shit, another night person.*

He'd expected the brood-like silence or the blatant arrogance, but was surprised when within ten minutes into the flight the passenger asked if he could sit up front. Even more surprised when the tanned and very fit looking man asked questions and chatted amiably.

The pilot thought it interesting that he had delivered two of the same kind of people to the same mid-western city in a matter of days. Up until this morning his instructions had been to fly to this city, pick up the man in the grey suit, and transport him to Sydney in time to catch a plane to the Gold coast.

Sudden changes in plan usually meant that something had gone wrong.

He wouldn't miss the first man, but this second one was different.

*****

Quinn stayed overnight in the city, and rested while he waited for transport. It was delivered to him just before sunrise the next day, and he arrived in the small outback town in time for lunch. He ate at a roadhouse and then got down to work.

At three o'clock he was about 300 metres from the old house described on the map. A Coolabah tree gave him sparing shade, but its root base offered excellent cover for the one who needs to hide.

Quinn watched the two people on the veranda of the old house, scrutinizing the man carefully as he took off his wide brimmed hat, before he considered the woman; she looked like a good sort from where he lay, but not a patch on his Polynesian girl, he thought.

He allowed the powerful binoculars to roam over the house and the yard, taking in the horse stables and the pool enclosure. He saw nothing out of the ordinary and it appeared the two people were the only occupants.

Quinn decided he would wait, watch the house for the rest of the afternoon, and then if things looked O.K move in tonight.

He swung the binoculars back to the couple on the veranda, saw the woman laugh and decided to give his eyes a rest for a while.

Simon and Sarah stayed in the shade of the veranda where they had afternoon smoko. They talked about their upcoming trip to the Whitsunday Passage, and both agreed they should be there now. Sarah brought this point up. "It would be nice to be up there now, wouldn't it? I mean, the weather is not really all that bad at this time of year is it."

"We've both lived through wet seasons, haven't we? In another month the dry season will start and that'll be better. I'm finding it hard to wait too." He was quietly thoughtful for a moment and then continued, "As Ray suggested, it'd be a good idea to wait and see who turns up looking for me next. If I leave here now, then he'll be on his own which would be unfair on him I think, especially when I'm the one responsible for his involvement." They were both quiet for a while before Simon asked her, "Would you rather be out of here, I mean, away somewhere safer until it's over?"

She rubbed her hands together slowly and displayed a light smile.

"No. I'm alright. It's probably just the waiting, not knowing when it'll start up again. Being wary all the time, when I just want to relax with you and enjoy our time together."

Simon leaned over the small table and touched her hand.

"I know. It's a pressure that won't go away until the ..." He blinked and looked out over the country to the south to where he was sure he'd seen a light. As if the sun had flashed off a piece of glass or something shiny. "I think it may have started my love. Don't look around, but I just saw the sunlight glint off something in the trees, way over. I think it would be a good idea if we act naturally, clear off this table and go inside." She followed Simons lead when he stood up and again, when he pulled her to him to give her a hug.

An eyebrow rose as she grinned.

"Is this a real hug or just a pretend one for the benefit of whoever might be watching us?"

He held her to him and smiled into her face.

"Does that feel real enough?"

She could feel his hardness as he pressed against her.

"You perk up at the most interesting times don't you?" Sarah laughed and then more seriously. "You'll have to keep yourself under control big boy, at least until we find out about the flashing lights."

They separated and carried the afternoon tea cups and plates inside to the kitchen.

Simon went to his room and found his binoculars, then walked to the centre of the room and focused them through the glass of the closed window. He couldn't see anything at first, but then he noticed some birds there were upset about something or other. Maybe a goanna, he thought, as he made a mental note of the place. He collected his rifle and checked its load.

He turned to Sarah and told her that she should find Ray.

"Let him know what's going on. Tell him to keep out of sight and be ready."

Sarah listened and kissed him. She didn't have to tell him to take care.

CHAPTER 26

Quinn had been comfortable enough until he'd felt a stinging pain in his right arm. He'd searched his shirt sleeve and had found a large red bull ant. The sting was enough to interfere with his concentration, allowing the scrim netting to fall away from his binoculars and expose its lens to the sunlight. He cursed the ant, and tried to rub the pain away, but it stayed with him as he squashed the offender with the handle of his folded pocket knife.

By the time he'd focused his binoculars back on the veranda, the man in the wide brimmed hat and the woman were gone.

He wondered if he'd been spotted, but no good worrying about that now, he thought, as the pain of the ant sting persisted.

Simon loaded the rifle and donned the heavy drill shirt he usually wore when he knew he'd be crawling around in the dirt. He stood at the closed window again, and focused the binoculars on the place amongst the roots of the Coolabah tree. There may be something he thought, as he played the binoculars over the area.

A billabong ran along behind the trees. It would give him the cover he'd need to creep up near the gnarled old trees exposed and shadowed roots.

Simon left the house and kept it between him and his destination, while he made his way to the river. He made quick time and worked his way downstream for some minutes, before he followed a tributary which connected to the billabong that ran behind the target tree.

The billabong was as dry as a bone and Simon followed its left bank. He reckoned he would come up directly behind the target tree, and hoped that whoever may be lying under the tree would still be looking in the old house's direction.

Moving from tree to tree he stopped at times to check his bearings, making sure the coast was clear through the scope of his rifle before he progressed.

He reached a gully which had to be crossed and dropped into it. Followed its far bank for a short distance, until he turned into a shallow tributary whose sloped bank gave little cover.

His shirt front scraped heavily against the hard earth, as he tried to keep his body profile as low as possible. The tree he sought was not more than fifty metres from his present position, and he brought the rifle to his shoulder to view it through its scope.

Simon concentrated on the thick roots. He could make out an indefinite shape in the shadows and stared at the place until his eye began to ache, then rubbed the ache away and looked again.

At last he was sure.

There was definitely something there. He slowly moved towards another tree about five metres away; it too had heavy exposed roots. Simon slithered across the ground with the rifle in the crook of his arms. The drag of his shirt on the rough earth seemed noisy in his ears, and with his heart pounding he finally sought cover behind the tree. He wiped stinging sweat from his eyes, and then with breath held he began to edge around the trunk of the tree.

He wanted to just turn around, go home, sit down in the old chair and read, or eat, or drink wine, because life had become complicated lately.

As he left the comfort of the tree he couldn't believe his ears.

"Stop right there or drop right there, it's your choice." A voice whispered and the metallic sound of a pistol slide emphasized the words.

Simon froze.

It was as if his heart would explode, and his feet seemed to cling to the ground as if they tried to sink into the dirt. Taking Simon down, so he could find some security in the folds of the womb of Mother Earth.

The voice spoke again as if in general conversation.

"Not a bad effort. I didn't pick you up until you dropped into that gully; it was right in the open so don't feel bad about it. Now, put the peashooter on the ground. Slowly, just lean forward and put it on the ground." Simon aimed to please.

"What's in the pockets of your shirt?"

"Not much," Simon said.

"Empty them." Simon did so.

"Now lift your shirt up so I can see your waistband." Simon did that too.

"Now pull up your trouser legs so I can see your sock tops." Simon wondered how far this would go and began to turn his head toward the voice.

"I didn't tell you to move your head, so stay still. Who else is at that house other than your girlfriend?"

"There's only Sarah."

"Are you absolutely sure? I don't like liars." The voice went quiet for some seconds as if it was giving Simon time to reconsider his answer. When Simon was not forthcoming it began again with another order, "Now I want you to march slowly and carefully towards the house. Remember, if you've lied to me then you're the first to go. Understand?"

The silence was broken only by the scuffle of boots on the hard black earth, and the buzzing of flies.

Worry for Sarah weighed heavily upon him.

Simon on command slowly opened the gate to the old house's front yard, and moved through the gateway. The long untrimmed branches of the overgrown and unkempt hedge fell in behind him as his raised hands waved them away. He stepped into the house's front yard.

The armed man followed.

Simon kept walking slowly while the armed man stopped in the gateway and ran his eyes over the garden area. He then came on, while his gaze roved the hedge line in both directions away from the gateway.

All of Quinn's instincts heightened. He looked ahead at the fruit trees and could see nothing that might explain his feeling that something was about to happen. His years of experience screamed at him.

Adrenalin rushed as he looked to the ground and saw that some sand had been smoothed down.

He tried to step back, but he knew it was too late.

The ground exploded in front of him.

His eyes filled with dirt as his face was assaulted by its sand storm. He felt himself being torn from the ground, as would a tree before a violent wind. The pistol flew from his hand as his back hit the ground and he lay there stunned.

Simon felt the blast at his back and was pushed forward violently, but with less intensity than the man three metres behind him. He fell to his knees and then his face hit the ground.

Strange sounds rang in his ears and dust besieged his nostrils as he lifted his head. His hand involuntarily went to the back of his neck which felt as if it had been sun burnt.

He rolled over onto his side and looked back to where the force had come from.

Ray was on his knees, leaning over the body of Quinn who was spread-eagled on his back. Simon gained his footing, lurched to Ray's side and looked at the face of the fallen man.

"Is he alive?"

Ray's look was one of derision.

"Of course he's alive. I put enough putty down to knock him out, not kill him." The tone in Ray's voice stressed indignation that Simon might suggest that he, a professional, would use too much explosive.

"Shit, what did you do?"

Ray cut the question short.

"Talk later. First thing we have to do is get this fellow trussed up before he comes around. Get his pistol, and keep him covered in case he does before we get it done."

Simon picked up the gun and then watched as Ray and Sarah loaded Quinn into the wheelbarrow. They wheeled him to the steps which led up to the veranda, and from there they man handled him to the spare bedroom.

Simon left Sarah and Ray to tend to Quinn while he retrieved the backpack and raked smooth the loose sand that had been dislodged by the detonation.

By the time he'd returned to the spare room, Ray had Quinn secured to the bed, so Simon brought beer. While they drank, they stood over the man and studied him.

He was tall and filled the bed with his body bulk. His face had a look of calm, but the lines which contoured and spread about his face suggested a life of hard going, touched also with the grimace of determination.

After some time he stirred, then sighed as his eyes flickered open. He clenched them shut again, and then blinked many times before squinting up at the trio.

Quinn began a movement with his right arm, as if to bring it down to rub the grit from his eyes. Then realizing he was tethered he tugged at the bonds before he relaxed and offered a wry smile.

"Where did you learn that one?" He directed at Ray.

"Are you hurt anywhere in particular?" Ray asked.

Quinn stopped, as if to think about this a moment, then moved his limbs as far as the lashings would allow.

"No. Except that my eyes and my face feel like shit." His eyes went to Sarah and he said, "Sorry, but I don't know how else to describe it."

He looked at the beer bottles.

"Throats a bit on the dry side though."

Simon went to the refrigerator, brought another bottle and tipped it to Quinn's lips.

Quinn gratefully licked the excess from his lips.

"What are you going to do with me now?"

Ray thought about this for a moment.

"We are going to ask you a few questions. If you can't answer them, then fair enough. If you won't answer them, then I can easily start the back hoe and dig another hole down in the back paddock."

Quinn went quiet as he noted the way the wiry man mentioned, 'Another hole,' and was reminded once again that it was not always preferable to know exactly where you stand.

He knew the wiry man was serious.

CHAPTER 27

Simon brought more beer, and after giving one each to Sarah and Ray he twisted the tops from two and tipped one at intervals, to the lips of Quinn.

"Who do you work for?" Ray started in a low voice,

"I work for a company based in Sydney."

"Whose company, what's its name?" Ray asked.

"It's called Sudovich Holdings." Quinn replied.

"Who runs it?"

"His name is Garry Sudovich."

"We met one of his associates I think, a fellow by the name of Scott. He's the one who's in the first back hoe hole."

Quinn coughed on his half swallowed beer.

"Now, it seems to me that your problem is. You know something about us now, and that raises the question as to whether you can be allowed to leave here or not?" Ray questioned. Quinn swore quietly. The last thing that a prisoner needed to hear was that those who held him captive had nothing to lose. They had one back hoe hole occupied, why not two, or a dozen for that matter. If they were ever caught, then what charges would they face? Covering up the outcome of an act of self-defense against home invaders? He felt a rush of sadness at the thought of his existence ending this way.

"Did you know this Scott bloke?" Ray asked.

Quinn didn't give an immediate answer, instead looked into the eyes of each of the three people who looked down at him. He decided then, that they held all the cards.

"If you've done the deed on Scott, then you've done the parents of many children a favour. It's a pity the fact cannot be made known so they can rejoice. You've killed an animal." He quietened momentarily before he asked a question, "Scott was good at his work though. You must have had some luck?"

"Maybe Sudovich expected country bumpkins?" Simon said. Quinn had no reply.

His mind up until now had been on escape. Finish the job he was paid for and be out of here, but now the game had changed. Maybe the day he spoke of to his Polynesian girl was closer than he'd expected.

Spill the beans he thought. Maybe he would get lucky and still find a way to escape, leave these people and get out of this place. If he was really lucky, maybe they'd get rid of Sudovich for him.

He could only hope.

Quinn opened up and told all that he knew. Some things about Sudovich were unknown to him, but just his own basic knowledge of the man was a lot.

Eventually he looked at Ray.

"The driver who picked me up at the airport told me he guessed that someone had intercepted one of Sudovich's money transfers. My job was to find out from that man, where the money is and how to get it back to Sudovich."

Simon, Ray and Sarah left the room and moved to the hallway. Quinn strained his ears to understand their muffled voices, but a frog outside the window shattered the silence and stole away any chance.

"What do you reckon Simon?" Ray asked.

"I believe what he says Ray. It fits in with what I already know. Where do we go from here?"

Sarah had been quiet for a while.

"I will tell you both exactly where we go from here." Ray raised his eyebrows and Simon grinned as she finished her statement. "We go directly to the kitchen, where you and Ray cook those yellow belly fish that are in the fridge and I will open a bottle of wine."

Ray laughed as he grew fonder of her and her ways.

"That sounds like the best idea I've heard all day. Let's do it."

He had no doubt that Simon was a lucky man. She reminded him of a woman that he used to know, and for the first time in a long time he rang his wife.

She'd appreciate the call he thought, as they'd not seen a great deal of each other lately. He knew he was mostly to blame and he was thankful that Sarah and Simon had lit a new fire in him. Their closeness had brushed off and onto him, and their adventure was giving new life to him.

His life, like Simon's, was changing.

*****

Abu left the huge Government building, ran to his car and drove out of the back gate. He'd made it his business to acquire a key to the tradesmen's entrance. As well, he'd made earlier arrangements with an officer who was a flight instructor with his countries new and inefficient air force.

That officer was the key to his escape.

He drove to an airfield which was within a mile of the government buildings, but instead of driving through the main gates, he took a back road which skirted behind the air field to a disused air craft hangar.

It had been built by the French during a 'conflict' they'd been involved in many years earlier with another country further inland. The permission needed for the French to build the structure was given by the government in power before Abu's revolution eight years earlier.

It was old, and had no real maintenance in its time. A fact obvious, as it stood like a rusting hulk. Its skeletal frame had been robbed at times by the locals who made use of its corrugated iron for their housing.

Abu's car rolled onto the skirt of concrete which spilled out of its large double doorway, where standing in his path was a helicopter. It was big to Abu, who had only known the smaller machines used by the oil companies.

The helicopter had no doors on its opened sides, and it looked to Abu to be some kind of troop or cargo carrier. He looked around for the aviator, and was startled when the man walked around the corner of the hangar.

Abu greeted the pilot, and then watched as the aircrafts long blades slowly gained momentum, before he bent his head to run towards the aircraft. Suddenly he felt a stabbing pain in his back, and he cried out as he turned and saw Che'anton. Her face was a picture of tear stained fury and the knife she held glinted in the sunlight.

Abu tried to hit her as he backed away, but his flailing only caused her aim to fail as she continued to slash with the blade. He felt the knife dig into his hand and he roared in pain.

He turned to run, but slipped and fell.

His huge body stood out to her as an easy target and she swooped in to deliver another slash. Suddenly there was a single loud shot, and Che'anton fell heavily onto the hard concrete with blood staining her shirt.

She'd spun in her fall, and now lay where she could see the face of her aggressor. She was frightened, and wished her mother were here to comfort her.

The knife had fallen from her hand and she raised her bloody fingers as she tried to cry out to the man who had stolen her chance of revenge.

No sound came as her mouth formed the words.

"Non-justice."

Then her facial features relaxed to a little girl's softness, as her soul slipped away and she went to meet her God.

Abu sat in his tears and self-pity on the concrete. It seemed to be as cold and hard as his life had become of late.

His hand was badly cut and it bled profusely. Its drops of blood drained into his groin and quickly soaked a small area of his trousers. He was in shock, and through his pain he knew he must escape. He'd heard the gunshot, and his fear of being a victim was as great as his fear of losing the contents of the bag he carried.

Too many things had happened too quickly, and in his confusion Abu decided that he must stall for time. Allow his mind to catch up and get a grasp on the situation. Firstly, he must thank the person who had saved him. Try to talk his way around whoever it was, and get on board the aircraft.

He fought his way to his feet, and as he turned toward the aircraft he came face to face with Horton.

"Who are you, my friend? You have saved me from that witch."

Horton gave a sneering grin.

"Out of the frying pan, eh?" He said as he prodded his rifle into Abu's soft belly and asked shortly, "What's in the bag?" Abu winced at the thought of being robbed and wondered if he had the strength to run to the aircraft that idled nearby.

He knew he couldn't make it, and the realization offered an instant vision of inevitability.

"Please, it is all I have," he pleaded through quaking lips.

Horton prodded him again with the rifle and ordered him into the helicopter. Abu's knees were weak as he led the way to the aircraft. He clutched his bag to his chest as tears of torment rolled down his cheeks.

They both climbed on board and Horton motioned the pilot to lift off. When the craft rose to about fifty feet he motioned to the pilot again.

"Hold it at this height," he called as he unsheathed a large hunting knife to emphasize the order.

The pilot complied.

Horton moved again to Abu, turning him so he was facing the open doorway.

"I will not steal your bag, but it seems that a situation has arisen where you will be kind enough to give it to me, or you might fall from the aircraft." Horton called loudly over the noise.

Abu could feel the breath and spittle of the scarred face man as he yelled at him. He couldn't make out a word he was saying over the noise of the aircrafts motor, but he knew what the man wanted. Through his tears he saw the ground a lifetime away below him.

He loosened his grip on the bag, passing it back to the scarred man as he begged for his life.

Horton ears were closed as he reached for the winch switch, pressing it to let out wire rope into loose coil at his feet. He looped the end the thin cable around Abu's neck, hooked it on to itself and gave Abu a push.

Abu's knees were on the verge of giving in on him altogether, and the pressure on his back was enough to buckle them and send him out the door.

Nothing happened for an instant. Then suddenly the craft lurched awkwardly, and for a moment it appeared the pilot might not hold it in the air.

A shudder tore through the machine and Abu's head shot up into view outside the doorway. It hung in the air for a moment, and then was gone again.

"Into the fire," Horton called as it dropped out of sight, then with a laugh he motioned the pilot to put the aircraft down again.

The pilot felt fear, and it showed in his control as the aircraft landed heavily.

Horton appeared not to notice the landing as he sat on the floor in the back of the craft and pawed through the African's bag. Its content's value was greater than his expected pay, and he decided then to take this aircraft and escape to wherever the machines fuel would allow.

The fighting here was all but over, and it was nearly time to leave anyway. He looked to the pilot as the blades slowed overhead,

"What is the range of this heap of shit?"

The pilot answered and Horton thought for a moment before he told the pilot where he wanted to go. As the machine lifted off again, he made himself as comfortable as he could and counted his new found wealth. He found some of the African's documents very interesting, and new schemes came to mind as he stuffed them back into the bag.

CHAPTER 28

Sarah, Ray and Simon ate their fish and then fed Quinn, who was by now into his third beer.

"What was that toy in the path?" Quinn asked.

"Just a little trick I picked up in Vietnam."

"What year?" Quinn asked as he stopped chewing his fish.

"1969."

"Bad year, where were you?"

"I was there in January, if that's what you mean. Khe Sanh." It was Ray's turn to question and he asked, "You were there too?" Quinn told Ray where he had been and who he was with. Ray questioned Quinn about things that people would have to have been there to know. In the end Ray was satisfied that Quinn was telling the truth.

Simon and Sarah left them at this point and they talked well into the night. They were like two long lost brothers. Brothers in arms, and Ray found he liked the relaxed Quinn, who opened up as the hours passed to tell Ray more of his situation with Sudovich.

They called it a night after Ray had loosened Quinn's right hand, and had given him a container to relieve himself in.

"Have you decided what to do with me?" Quinn asked.

"Simon has come up with an idea which should see you up and about around lunch time tomorrow. So you can sleep easy. Me, I'll sleep light like I always do, and remember, I know how to use this." He weighed the pistol in his hand.

"Don't worry about me. I'm not going anywhere, so you can sleep easy too."

Simon's walls were the borders between Ray's room and the one that Quinn found himself in. He heard Ray walk to his room, then checked the lock on his own door before he put his head to the pillow and listened to the silence.

Simon rose early the next morning, and he and Ray talked about what they would do with Quinn.

By the time they'd finished breakfast they had a plan.

They took coffee to Quinn and Ray again untied his right hand. He allowed Quinn to use the container, and then left his hand loose so he could eat his breakfast.

While Quinn ate, Simon wrote on two sheets of paper. Quinn's name which he discovered from his passport to be Peter Quinn, his description, the address he carried in his wallet of his island home and his passport number.

Simon left the room and returned with an old Polaroid camera. He took two photos of Quinn, and put one and a piece of the paper into each of the two envelopes.

"These two envelopes will go to friends of mine in town. Their instructions will be that they be opened in the event of anyone of us not making contact with them at a time I'll not disclose to you," Simon said when he had sealed them. Quinn nodded that he understood, and Simon left the farm to deliver the two letters to town.

When he returned he approached Ray and Quinn at the stables where they were talking.

"I think Quinn has found a solution to ours and his problem." Simon looked to Quinn's matter of fact face.

"I thought about it last night and decided I will have to deal with Sudovich personally. I should have done him in a long time ago. I didn't, but now I think the day has arrived to escape him once and for all." Simon thought about what he was hearing and found himself shocked. He wanted to close off the sound of the man's voice.

Sudovich was by all accounts a son of a bitch, but by the same token he was a human being, and here was Simon listening to Quinn's plan on murder.

Simon wished he could escape his part in it, but what could he do. The dice had been cast and he, Simon, had cast them when he'd answered the first letter from Abu.

For a moment Simon forgot his reason and wished he could go back and regain his freedom of conscience. Change the past and escape the sickness he again felt in his belly.

"I'll need my car. It's parked away over in the bush and my tool bag is in it." Simon gave away his thoughts of innocence and said he would take the man to his car.

An hour later Simon showed Quinn to the work shop where Quinn pulled from his tool bag a crossbow.

"I need a fishing rod reel and a golf ball. Would you have any of these things lying around the place?" Quinn asked. Simon, although confused by the request found an old reel, and after some searching came up with a golf ball.

The golf ball was old and had a small crack in it.

"Doesn't matter, it'll do the job." Quinn said.

Simon wanted to ask, *how it would do the job*, just out of curiosity, but thought better of it and decided he didn't want to know.

"I wonder if you might do something for me," he asked instead. Quinn listened intently as Simon put forward his request.

Simon looked at his feet as if he didn't know how to phrase the request. "It's probably best if Sarah doesn't know about this part." Quinn understood Simon's feelings, and knew full well from experiences passed the necessity of mistruth.

Simon turned to leave Quinn to his work. As he left the workshop he heard the sound of the cordless drill, whining quietly as Quinn drilled small holes in the stock of the crossbow.

CHAPTER 29

Sudovich was worried.

Quinn should have called by now, *"Was it possible that these country bumpkins had disposed of two of his people?"* His mental question was hard to believe, but stranger things had happened.

The thought of the money goaded him onto the next phase of his plan. Somehow the thought of it worried him.

He pondered his situation.

Should he have contracted the services of better quality people at higher rates of pay? If so, did it mean he was moving up to another level of success, or did It mean he was losing control of the immediate situation?

A lot of things seemed to have gone wrong lately.

He rubbed his hand over his forehead as he wondered. Was he still in control and just maybe going through a rough period? Was he losing his grip? Was he on the edge of a slippery slope and about to begin sliding down?

He'd slid down a slope once before, and it had cost him a lot of money. It had hammered his confidence, and worst of all it had cost him his independence. With the loss of his independence, came a lull in his self-esteem, and with that loss of self-esteem, there came a hatred of Tom Lee.

Sudovich's podgy fist came down heavily and crashed onto his desk top at the thought of the man's name.

Tom Lee was one of Sydney's biggest and most successful drug lords who Sudovich believed to be at the pinnacle of success. Sudovich had envied him, had believed that his own goal in life was to be the possessor of a position like Lee's.

Something had gone wrong, and even now Sudovich was unsure what had started his slide down the slippery slope.

It seemed to have started with the Asian gangs moving in on his turf. They were much too clever, and they leaned to the extreme in ruthlessness.

Now in hind sight, Sudovich realized that he'd been too slow in getting in on the ecstasy market. Then to top it off, the taxation department went through his legitimate business like a dose of salts.

Even the money he'd acquired through Abu had been gathered in by lawyers who he'd needed to keep him out of gaol. He'd hated the idea of paying them, but in effect they had kept him alive. There were a lot of enemies in gaol, and he probably would not have lasted long.

He knew with some certainty what had stopped him at the bottom of the slippery slide though. He'd crashed into a need for capital, and the only capital available was through Tom Lee. At the time he'd believed he was capable of level pegging Tom Lee.

By the time he'd measured his capabilities it was too late. Tom Lee was like a virus which multiplied and eventually took over a system. Even now Sudovich still felt the pain.

Tom Lee owned his soul, and for Sudovich the only glimmer of hope was Abu's lost fortune. To retrieve that fortune, he would have to pay for better quality professionals. He had the cash that he'd gotten from Kane, and if he had to invest it on one last effort, then that's what he would do.

Sudovich felt like a punter who'd lost heavily, but hoped the next roll of the dice would win him the day. He must win, because Travers, Lee's accountant, would soon start to ask questions about the company's plane trips to the outback.

He was still worried when he finally lifted the hand piece and punched in the telephone number of an answering service. The voice of an older woman answered his call and he asked the whereabouts of one of her clients.

"He has not called in for messages in three weeks, but you might have some success if you call his other answering service in Auckland," she said.

Sudovich asked her to get the client to call him the moment she heard from him and gave to her his new contact number. He touched the disconnect button on his phone, and then rang the New Zealand answering service.

Another woman answered, and Sudovich immediately disliked the short burst of New Zealand accent which came through his earpiece.

"I'm trying to contact a client of yours. Mr. Weston?"

"Yes Sir. He called just this morning and I can reach him for you, if you would like to leave a message." Sudovich left his name and new number, thanked the woman for her time and put the phone down.

He had never in the past called on any professional people in this man's league. Sudovich realized Weston's existence only because he'd had his ears open, and his memory in gear when he'd heard Lee and Travers organizing the man's services just some months earlier.

Sudovich was used to small time operators who were amateurish and small time crooks. Although he was somewhat taken aback that Quinn had apparently failed.

As far as Scott was concerned, Sudovich was not totally surprised. Scott was far too sure of himself, and it was only a matter of time before he under estimated an opponent and got knocked back a peg or two.

This thought resounded in Sudovich's head. Thinking that maybe he had been too sure of himself also, believing the thief in the outback would be an easy mark.

There was an old saying that suddenly came to mind. 'Never under estimate an opponent and never over estimate an ally.' He, Sudovich, had certainly under estimated Tom Lee, and had the mental and financial scars to prove it.

Sudovich sat back in his soft chair, and gazed out of his window at the grey clouds that hung low over the city of Sydney.

His mind drifted back to his hatred of Tom Lee, and he wished yet again as he ground his teeth for something he could use to destroy him.

*****

Late that same afternoon Quinn readied to leave the farm for the long drive to Sydney. Ray and Simon stood by as he placed his gear into his vehicle.

Sarah didn't witness the departure. She knew she would have done under different circumstances, but she couldn't find it in herself to respect, or even like what Quinn stood for.

Ray told Quinn that if he was ever in the neighborhood to call in, unless of course he was on business.

Quinn saw the funny side.

"I'll remember, but I have to tell you that when this is all over I'm off to my island and my lady for good. So I doubt I'll see you again. Thanks anyway."

Quinn turned to Simon.

"I don't know what you can expect from Sudovich now. He might have enough time to organize another 'enquirer' between now and the time I get to him. No one can take anything for granted in this business. If I do get him in time, then you might be lucky enough to find that your problems are over. Depending of course that Sudovich was freelancing. If he wasn't, and he has the backing of his partner Tom Lee, then you are never going to be sure that it's over. My advice to you is that you get out of here now and find somewhere quiet to keep your head down for a while. Use cash only and no credit cards. Change the name on your car registration. Leave no trace. Tom Lee has people in information places. You hear what I'm saying?" Simon's nerves were at fraying point, and the advice was the last thing he wanted to hear. He took it anyway, and thanked Quinn.

Quinn settled into the driver's seat and buckled up.

"If you don't mind me asking Simon, what in the world is a bloke like you going to do with all the money the driver told me about?" Simon smiled lightly and told Quinn of his intentions.

Quinn looked at Simon's face and noticed the strain around his eyes.

"I'm glad then, that this has worked out in your favour. My life will be better having known you."

Quinn looked again at the tiredness in Simon's face, recognizing signs he'd seen many times before, on many men, though not usually in peace time.

Simon straightened at the compliment and was silent as Quinn's car was hidden behind a billowing cloud of dust.

CHAPTER 30

Quinn was in Sydney by 4am. He drove directly to a suburb on Sydney's north shore, and parked within sight of a large house where he slept at the wheel of the car, until he was awoken by the sound of traffic.

He wiped the sleep from his eyes as he watched the house. A short time later its front door opened and Sudovich walked from it to his Mercedes motor car. Quinn noted the man's manner of dress and was glad to see that the businessman had not changed his routine. With this knowledge in mind he followed the Mercedes through the tree lined streets to Sudovich's destination. Where Sudovich parked his car, and took a golf bag from it to a large building.

Quinn checked his watch and noted the colouring of the sky in the East, guessing that the sun would be up in probably fifteen minutes.

He reckoned he'd seen enough, and left the car park to drive his car around the golf club's landscaped perimeter of lush trees and thick bush.

After a short reconnaissance he decided it was time to sleep, and a motel close to the golf club suited his needs. He pulled into its car park and booked a ground floor room which gave him a view of the bush land. He slept until midday and then returned to the clubhouse. Hired clubs and played each of the fairways until he found a good place to lie up.

Quinn rested at this spot and allowed some other players to play through, watching where their balls landed at this juncture.

The fairway was narrow and bunkers on the far side could be avoided by playing to this side of the fairway. It was bordered by bush thick enough to give good cover and he memorized the spot for he would have to find his way to it in the dark.

There were not many players on this part of the course now, so he ducked into the bushes, chose a secure area and checked its field of view.

He was happy with what he saw.

Quinn moved further into the bush until he came upon a fence line. He climbed it and fought more bush until he came to a track.

His motel was in sight, and he got bearings from the surrounding landscape which would help guide him to this place during darkness.

He remembered that the moon was waning, and should be high when he made his trek across the bush land to this point on the fence line. Satisfied with his plan, he returned to the fairway and finished his round of golf.

*****

Sudovich looked at the carriage clock at the far side of his office and decided he had waited long enough.

It had been a long day and he was tired.

Having not heard from Weston, he would have to be patient until tomorrow and then wait again.

He wished that people were easier to contact, but understood that the man's work probably involved a certain amount of travel. To God only knows where, and to adventures that Sudovich felt he was most definitely too old for.

Sudovich was in the situation where he needed Weston badly. He needed the man to be placed in the small outback town now.

Right now.

Time was slipping away, and he knew that when Simon left where he was now known to be, he may be hard to locate again.

His office window overlooked the highway traffic. It was thinning out as the rush hour had passed, and would offer little difficulty on his way home.

He looked again at the clock, and made a move to collect the few papers he needed to take home to revise for tomorrow's business.

Sudovich was like all other humans in taking the future for granted. He put the papers into a small attaché case, along with a mobile phone and a new set of C.Ds. He kept them with him now, and he smiled as he noted his cleverness in thwarting future thefts by the C.D bandits.

"Bastards!" He spoke aloud.

The phone sounded as a call came straight to his office. His secretary redirected calls onto overnight extension as the last of her office duties each working day. He picked up the hand piece, wondering whether this phone was still secure. It had been only connected up for a short time, but he wondered anyway.

He dropped into his soft chair.

"Sudovich," he answered.

The English accented voice that whispered into his ear sounded tight lipped.

"Ah! Mr. Sudovich. My name is Henry Horton."

"I don't recall your name Mr. Horton. What is it that you want?"

"Mr. Sudovich I've just flown in from Sierra Leone by way of South Africa. I think you may familiar with that part of the world. Sierra Leone, I mean."

Sudovich was stunned.

Unable to, at short notice, come to terms with the way that the conversation was heading. He felt an overwhelming need to field his way carefully, like a barefooted man who found himself in a patch of burrs.

He couldn't control the slight tremble in his voice, so he tried to steer the conversation on a different course.

"What is happening over there? I heard on the news there was a revolution or something. Is the government still in power?"

Horton stated easily as if Sudovich had asked for the time of day or simple street directions.

"It doesn't exist anymore."

"Are you sure?" The question seemed to speed from Sudovich's slack lipped mouth.

Horton replied casually in a way that to Sudovich sounded weary.

"I'm absolutely sure. I organized redundancy packages for some of its members personally."

Sudovich's heart quickened. The sound of the man's voice seemed to crawl into his open ear, and he wondered if at any moment he might shiver. He didn't, and was left with the feeling that one has after a succession of sneezes. Sure that there will be one more sneeze, hoping in a way that there will be and kind of disappointed when it doesn't come.

Sudovich's confusion willed him to just tell Horton to stop pissing around and get to the point, but his nervousness restrained him. Horton's mention of Sierra Leone could mean only one thing, and that thing was most certainly Abu's lost fortune. The fact that he was even having this conversation suggested to Sudovich that Horton was also searching for it.

Now he needed Horton to confirm it for him, but he delayed in asking the man outright. Almost as if he believed that if he didn't raise the question, then maybe the question wouldn't be raised at all and the man might just go away.

Sudovich had buried his head in the sand at times in the past. It hadn't worked then either.

Horton furthered the conversation.

"Mr. Sudovich, a couple of days ago I met with an associate of yours. He gave me a bag of valuables. Along with these valuables were some documents which show of your dealings with him. These documents suggest to me that you and maybe another associate of yours relieved Mr. Mohammed of a certain sum of money. I would have liked to further my discussions with him, but unfortunately he fell out of a helicopter. Of little consequence normally, but on this occasion the helicopter was some distance from the ground." The shiver finally came upon Sudovich. Not because of Horton's voice, but because of the fact that he'd suddenly been placed at the top of another slippery slope. Sudovich at that moment felt very much afraid, and he silently cursed the man named Simon West.

Horton listened to Sudovich's silence for a moment, knowing that he had driven his point home.

"Mr. Sudovich, Mr. Mohammed insisted that I take all that was his. Now taking into consideration that your partnership with him was probably based on a fifty-fifty split, it would appear that you owe me a little over sixteen million American dollars."

Sudovich squirmed in his seat as a panic swept through his brain.

"But I don't have the money. I didn't get it."

"Come now, Mr. Sudovich. Mr. Mohammed dealt with you, and the money left on its way to you. Are you trying to tell me that it got lost in transmission?"

"Yes," he stumbled. "No. No. It was stolen, and I have people searching for it now." Sudovich was thankful for the silence which presented itself from Horton's end of the line. Fleeting moments, and each one of them graciously accepted as a short interval that allowed him to try to sort the thoughts which raced through his brain.

The fleeting moments were soon over.

"Mr. Sudovich. Are you a family man?"

Sudovich was unsure what to expect next, but he had a feeling deep in his gut that the time for threats had arrived. He remained silent as he waited.

"Mr. Sudovich. Your silence suggests to me that you are. I find that to be very interesting, because I see in the telephone directory there are only three listings for the name Sudovich in the city of Sydney. I can only presume that your family lives at one of them? I can also presume that this moment in your life is probably the only time in your life that you wish that your name was Smith, or something similarly common."

Sudovich listened intently to the pause.

"Do you have any children Mr. Sudovich?"

Sudovich felt a chill. It seemed to frost him to the bone as a vision of his three teenagers flashed through his head.

His kids gave him a headache at times. As teenagers will, with their fluctuations of manner, temper and general revolt, but they were his kids. He could lose the money and still live, but if he lost his family, then no amount of money would allow him the same quality of life.

For the first time in his existence he realized the enormity of affection that he felt for them, and his basic need to be part of a family.

He felt his back to the wall, and then a certain resolve seemed to descend upon him as his priorities suddenly became clearer. His family came first, and all other things were just general factors in life.

He sat up in his chair and spoke clearly into the telephone.

"Listen, whoever the hell you are Horton, I will tell you this, and I will say it once only. I don't know where the money went; I mean I don't know where it is. I do know it was stolen from Abu Mohammed. Someone intercepted a communication from Abu, which was supposed to come to me. The person who intercepted the communication stole the money. I knew nothing of the theft until the African told me about it, and then he asked for my help in finding it."

Horton was silent for some seconds.

"What proof can you give me to back up what you say?"

"The man who has stolen the money is called Simon West, and I can give you precise directions that will lead you directly to him."

Horton's voice changed and Sudovich couldn't quite guess if it had gone quieter or just colder.

"Mr. Sudovich, I did ask for proof, not directions. How do I know that you are not just sending me off on some wild goose chase?"

Sudovich felt he was finally gaining some control of the situation. He could feel it in his bones that he was about to be in his element. They'd been through the introductions, now it was time to talk business and talking business was what he knew best.

The threat had passed.

He sat back in his chair and spoke quietly into the telephone.

"I very much doubt that your name is Horton, but until the time comes that you have to tell me your real name I will call you that. Now as far as..."

"What makes you think that I will have to divulge my real name to you?" Horton interrupted.

Sudovich smiled to himself as he had played his only ace.

"Mr. Horton. Do you understand the basic rules of international banking? I mean I will give you Simon West, but when you find him, don't expect that he'll be carrying thirty million dollars around with him in a suit case." Sudovich paused for some seconds to allow this information to sink in before he continued, "I've no doubt that West has it stashed in a bank somewhere."

Sudovich's voice lowered into a matter of fact tone, almost like a teacher who explained a small problem to a pupil.

"Mr. Horton. When you deal with a foreign government and use the method that the African usually used, the monies owed by that foreign Government are paid from bank to bank. West would not have seen any cash; he would have only made his presence known in order to sign the documents necessary for the transaction to be completed. As they say, the proof is in the pudding. In this case, Simon West is the pudding and the proof is in his head. When you catch him you will have to remove this proof from his head in whichever way you find practical. Then, when you have that information you will need to make your identity known to me because I think you will need my experience and expertise to acquire the money."

Sudovich felt that he could almost hear the man thinking, until once again he heard Horton's voice. It too seemed thoughtful.

"What makes you think that I will need you to help me to carry it through?"

Sudovich knew that this was going to be the tricky part.

"Before you go off to where I'm sure that West is, I will make available to you a document that you will have to get him to sign. It will give us the authority to access his account. I already have a Swiss bank account, an empty one unfortunately, but it will suit our needs. I will also make available to you another document which will allow you access to that account. Basically, it will be worded in a way, to say that you are the beneficiary of half, and only half, of the amount that is deposited. For example, if we deposit thirty million U.S dollars then fifteen is yours. The document will also state that I will only be able to withdraw fifteen million dollars; we will have both of our arses covered. I will write the document that way, because you did say at the beginning of our conversation that your main interest was in the African's share."

Horton was interested; Sudovich could hear it in his tone.

"If I agree to this arrangement, where do we go from here?"

"I will give you directions to where our company's plane is located at Mascot airport. The pilot will be waiting for you, and he will have the banking documents for you to look over. After you have done this, he will call me and I will make known to you West's location. When we are both agreed, then the pilot will take you to the outback town's airport. You will be given an untraceable car which you will drive to the thief's location."

Horton was impressed.

"You are a very clever man, Mr. Sudovich."

Sudovich thought to himself. *Perhaps that is your arrogant way of admitting that I am as clever as you, arsehole.*

"There are one or two other things Mr. Horton."

"And they are?" Horton answered cautiously.

"I may appear to you to be very clever Mr. Horton, but unfortunately I'm not infallible. You will be the third person who has gone to find Simon West. The first two appear to have disappeared for I've not heard from either of them. This may suggest that Simon West is a dangerous man, or maybe he's just very persuasive."

Horton was slow to reply, and Sudovich was glad of the man's silence, because it showed a lack of bravado. Bravado to Sudovich was a weakness, a weakness which more often than not led to carelessness.

"Mr. Horton, there is one thing more to understand. Simon West's precise location was known to me yesterday; he may, or may not be still there today. I say this because, I want you to be assured you will be furnished with the correct information which should lead you to him. After all, my share in the bank account depends on you finding him, and relieving him of the information that we need. Proof I hope, to you that I have no desire to send you on a wild goose chase. If West has relocated, then I have no idea where he may go, or for that matter how we might relocate him. That will be in your hands mainly as you will be on site. If I can give you any assistance, then you have only to call this number. I will also give our pilot my mobile telephone number. Would you say that up to this point we are agreed to go ahead?"

Horton was surprised at the way that Sudovich had taken a direct threat to his family, completely turned it around and twisted it into a simple business arrangement. Usually he had to at least carry out part of a threat to gain compliance. In this case Sudovich had countered his basic thrust, and used it to form a plan which should be in both their interests.

"Mr. Sudovich. I am impressed, and most certainly agree."

"Very well Mr. Horton. When the pilot gives you a sealed envelope you should open it and view its contents. You will notice a space left for you to print your real name. A space will also be left for you to sign the document. Beside your signature, the pilot will sign as witness to your signature. Make sure you date the document."

Sudovich spent the next few minutes giving Horton directions to where he would find the plane, and finished his side of the conversation.

"Good luck Mr. Horton."

"And good luck to you too Mr. Sudovich." Sudovich put the phone down and sat back in his chair. He felt good. Almost elated, and he smiled to himself as he took a fat cigar from a drawer in his desk and lit it.

He had two safes in his office. He opened the second one and withdrew a C.D which he inserted into his computer. On it was a copy of the directions he had made available to Peter Quinn, and a copy of the document that Quinn was to have had signed by West. There was also a copy of an older bank document that he'd used in the past to cover the African's arse. Minor alterations only were needed, and they would cover his arse also.

He made a call which interrupted the pilot's plans. His instructions were that he would receive two envelopes. The first he was to give to Horton and after it had been signed, he was to call Sudovich. When this call had been made he was to then give Horton the second envelope.

Sudovich then telephoned a messenger to deliver the two envelopes to the pilot within the hour.

He was still on his high when suddenly he hoped, that Lee or Travers didn't need the airplane tonight.

He'd been lucky so far. As far as Lee and Travers were concerned anyway, but it was nearing the end of the month and bills would have to be paid. One being the planes fuel bill and the second was the pilot's wages which were associated with a time sheet. Barrett being the accountant that he was wouldn't fail to note inconsistencies.

He took from the second safe a diary, into which he entered the names of Horton and Weston. He made no other entry as he felt the names only would be enough to remind him of this afternoon's eventful conversation.

After all, he could complete the entries tomorrow. By then he would hopefully have results to record as well.

Touch wood, he thought. He put his cigar down and punched numbers into the telephone, listened to the voice at the other end as it was answered.

"My name is Sudovich. I called earlier, have you heard from Mr. Weston yet?"

It didn't hurt to hedge your bets he thought.

CHAPTER 31

Quinn left the golf course and found a hardware shop where he bought Araldite, the adhesive. There was a travel agent in the same shopping centre, so he took the opportunity to purchase a plane ticket to New Zealand for eleven o'clock the next morning.

The effects of the long trip from the outback dulled his senses, forcing him to return to the motel and to sleep for the rest of the afternoon.

He awoke at 7 pm and dined at the motel's restaurant. The food was good, and he asked if the motel would provide him with some sandwiches. A midnight snack was usual for him he explained, before he returned to his room to prepare for his bushwalk.

Quinn entered his room, locked the door behind him and pulled the curtains, then dragged his tool bag from under his bed. He opened it and took out the crossbow and fishing rod reel, picked up a screw driver and took care to fit the reel to the stock of the bow.

When the reel was secured to the underside of the bow, he checked the mechanism, satisfied that neither the reel nor its line would interfere with the moving parts of the crossbow.

He'd redesigned its bolt. It now had a small loop of wire attached to its tail end where he tied the fishing line. He checked the firing mechanism again, and was satisfied that the bolt could fly free; leaving behind it a trail of fishing line that would keep it attached to the crossbow.

The smell of the adhesive was one he both liked and hated, but he forgot about the smell as he concentrated on gluing the old golf ball onto the flattened head end of the crossbow bolt.

He held it in place for fifteen minutes before testing it by tapping the ball end onto the concrete floor of the bathroom.

A knock on the door stilled his working hands, and he thrust the bow under the bed before he called through the closed door.

"Who is it?" Quinn felt edgy, a normality for a man in his line of work, for he never knew who would turn up on his doorstep.

He was satisfied that the woman's voice belonged to the one who had said she would prepare his sandwiches.

She held out a package as he opened the door.

"Your sandwiches sir."

Quinn thanked her.

"I wondered what time is the earliest I could get breakfast?"

"We are usually around the place and cooking at 6 o'clock, but breakfast is normally not available until 7 o'clock."

Quinn reckoned from this that he could confidently operate unseen from 4 o'clock.

"About my car, do you ever have any problems with thieves at all?"

"We have a security system in place which allows us to know if anyone is around. It will sound an alarm in the office if anyone as much as walks through the gates or climbs the fences. So you and your car are quite safe."

"I'm glad of that and I will sleep peacefully. Thank you, and thanks for fixing the sandwiches for me. I do appreciate it. Goodnight."

"Goodnight Mr. Scott."

Quinn had used the name Scott in his motel registration. It might put any police investigations off on a wild goose chase, searching for a man, who was, as far as he knew, buried out by the Darling River. The motel owner had taken the cars registration number, and although it might not be traced back to Sudovich, Scott's association with Sudovich might be known to the authorities and confuse the issue some more.

Quinn closed the door and wondered how the hell he was going to break out of the place.

He opened it again and walked to the end of the building near the exit from the motel grounds, where he took a moment to seat on the front fence and watch the traffic.

As he sat, he looked carefully around the entrance and saw the small lens like dot where an infrared light might project. Before searching the place where he expected the light beam to hit on the opposite wall, where he immediately saw the reflector.

"O.K," he whispered.

His only way out was under the infrared light. It meant he would have to leave his room and walk the lighted area of the other room entrances, then crawl under the beam, all while holding the tool bag.

The beam that obviously ran along the top of the rear fence would be more difficult to get around, or in this case, over.

Once back in his room he opened the curtains and tried to see in the poor light where the fence was. It was a well-built fence which stood over the normal six feet, and he reckoned the beam would probably run along the top of it. He discounted it. Without the beam it would have been easy for him to climb over, but the security devices changed the rules.

As he considered his options, he went back to work on the crossbow and fitted the bolt to the bow.

Satisfied that it would be effective he removed the bolt and released the mechanism, before putting the bow back into the tool bag.

One of his towels made good a cover for the crossbow, before he went through his clothes and chose a pair of dark coloured coveralls along with a floppy hat. Quinn took the tool bag to his car and placed it onto its rear seat, taking care not to upset the workings of the crossbow or the fishing rod reel.

The traffic was still brisk, filled with people returning home with their late night shopping he thought, as he eased his car into an outer most lane. The next available side street took him toward the golf club, until he turned off onto the dirt track that skirted the back of the golf course.

When he'd pulled to the side of the track and turned his motor off, he sat in the darkness listening to the quiet. Satisfied he was alone he took the bag from the car and hid it in the under growth, then returned to his car to listen for another ten minutes.

At ease with the thought he hadn't been observed, he returned to the motel and set the alarm on his watch for 3 am.

*****

The pilot was preparing to meet his girlfriend when the doorbell rang. He cursed quietly, and hoped it was not who he thought it to be, and immediately began to work on the excuse he would have to give his girlfriend. She'd be annoyed, but she was probably getting used to it by now, he thought as he answered the door.

It was the same man who usually knocked on his door at odd hours, and as usual the man said nothing. He just handed over three envelopes and then quietly walked away. Not to be seen again until next time.

The pilot looked at the envelopes, opening the one addressed to him and read his instructions. He was to deliver a passenger directly to an outback town, in reasonable close proximity to the mid-western city he'd visited already.

Twice.

He wondered if this meant that the second man had failed, and felt sorry in a way, as he hoped that the one tonight would be of the same value.

With this thought in mind he readied to leave, and was almost through the doorway when he remembered his girlfriend.

*****

Quinn was already awake and had turned the alarm off before it sounded. He'd slept lightly, turning in his sleep many times, until he had finally woken to lie quietly staring at the darkened ceiling.

He rose, dressed and removed the hand piece from the telephone. Not that he expected any calls, but reckoned if the proprietors of the motel tried to contact him, then the engaged tone would suggest his desire not to be disturbed. Hopefully they'd leave it at that, he thought.

Outside the room he gauged the position of the infrared beam, then dropped to his knees and rolled under it.

Once he reached the highway, he broke into a jog and relished the cold night air as it blew into his face.

Some minutes later he was beside the dirt track looking for the team bag. He found it easily, and quickly removed the tracksuit he'd worn for his early morning run to make way for his work clothes.

The feel of the scrim scarf was soft at his neck as he moved into the bush. His team bag, now stuffed with the track suit stayed under bushes near the low fence, and he listened again to the night sounds. Satisfied with his privacy, Quinn moved into the under growth next to the fairway.

The sandwiches were tasty, and he drank from the soft drink bottle, draining it, before he stuffed the sandwich wrapper into the bottle.

He welcomed the firm fit of the soft leather gloves he'd carried with him in his top pocket. Comfortable in their wear, he removed the towel from the team bag and wiped everything he'd touched with his bare hands. Even the tool bags leather handle and the spare golf ball.

After he'd cocked the cross bow he lay in the leaves and watched the night sky, which he thought was clear for a smoggy city. His Polynesian girl crept into his mind, and he dreamt of the freedom that from tomorrow would be his.

CHAPTER 32

The pilot saw the scarred face before he saw the man. When he'd looked into the cold eyes he saw that the man had seen him note the scars, and he shrivelled under his gaze.

It may have just been the light, but the scarred man looked scary. There seemed to be something akin to wickedness in this man's eyes, and the mental vision of it stayed with him throughout the flight.

Once during mid-flight he'd stolen a glance at the man to see if he was asleep or awake, but the man just sat quietly with a look that wasn't a smirk or a smile. It reminded the pilot of a cat. A hungry cat before it snatched the bird.

Horton was tired; it had been a long month and he knew that he looked like shit. His frame was gaunt from weeks of bush living, and his eyes were red rimmed and sore from lack of sleep.

Age was also a factor he thought. He knew he was getting too old for the work he did. He could feel it in his bones, but for now he would have to finish what he'd started and then be free to rest. Fifteen million dollars could buy a lot of rest, he thought.

The look in the eyes of fresh faced younger pilot didn't surprise him. He'd had over forty years to grow used to his scarred features, and had never expected other people to grow used to them in the initial seconds of a first meeting.

Horton could sense the pilot's seemingly nervous state. His presence sometimes did that to people, and he wondered if he should speak to the young man. Maybe put him at ease, after all, it was important to Horton's livelihood that the pilot devoted his full attention to the task at hand. He wondered as to what he might say. Nothing sprang to mind, so he put the whole idea out of his head, deciding instead that the young man would have to get over it.

It was highly likely that the pilot had more reason to stay alive than he did, Horton thought. The pilot would have agreed, and it was during the latter stage of the flight that he decided to take his girlfriend's advice and look elsewhere for employment.

He met people from a world that he didn't want to know on this plane, and some of them, like this one, were just plain scary.

They touched down on the outback airfield, and the pilot was relieved to see the man walking away from his plane. Sorry for whomever the man with the scars was after, and disorientated by the strange sense of foreboding that seemed to permeate his mind.

As if to free his mind, he glanced at his watch.

It was 6 am.

✳✳✳✳✳

The sun was making its way to the horizon, and its glow was easy to see as its light refracted through the cities early morning pollution.

Quinn waited, and heard the golf ball thud as it came in contact with the earth not twenty feet away, directly in front of him.

A few minutes later he heard a grunt as Sudovich dragged his golf buggy to the ball.

Quinn looked at Sudovich's face. Of all the faces that came to mind either during sleep or awake, of people he'd killed, this one he would remember on purpose. Maybe it would help to lose, or replace the faces of those he tried to forget.

Sudovich chose a club and practiced his swing twice, then stood very still as he lined up his ball.

He stood a little side on to Quinn, who wanted his golf ball to hit square on. His finger was tightening on the trigger as

Sudovich took one last look up the fairway, before settling down again to take his shot.

It was at this moment that Quinn applied more pressure, and the golf ball laden bolt left the bow with a soft twang. Sudovich's temple allowed transfer of the impacts energy, and it reverberated through the soft tissue of his brain.

Sudovich was dead before he hit the ground, and in a much better manner than many who had gone before him on his orders.

Quinn reeled in the bolt with its golf ball, and then produced the second ball from his pocket. He wiped this second ball into the small amount of blood that was on Simon's old ball, and threw it out onto the fairway.

He listened for a few minutes for possible witnesses. When none sounded alarm, he rose to his feet, roughed the ground where he had lain and quietly moved away into the bush.

It was impossible for him to know that with the death of Sudovich, there was no one left to control Horton.

CHAPTER 33

The man who delivered untraceable cars didn't enjoy the drive from the mid-western city, but his firm belief in money made it more of a trip and less of a chore.

The delivery was made and his job was done as the man with the scarred face accepted the keys to the vehicle.

Now that it was in the client's possession and being driven away towards the small outback town, he was retired.

His feelings on the subject became immediately obvious as he fell into the plane seat recently vacated by Horton and drifted straight off to sleep.

Horton pulled in at the first roadhouse the town's outskirts offered, and like Scott, he too noticed the young girl who worked the breakfast tables before she left for school. He looked at Sudovich's rough drawn map, and then listened to the girl's directions as she pointed at the road that ran past the roadhouse.

"The place you're looking for is out along the highway towards the airport. When you approach the first bridge about two miles out, you turn off to the right. You'll see a dirt track, follow it and it will bring you to a gate, go through it and just follow the track."

"What's down there, do you know?"

"I don't know what's there. I've only heard Uncle Ray talk about it. I do know that it is straight across the river from the caravan park."

Horton's ears pricked and he asked her for directions to the park. She told him and then walked back into the shop.

He gazed off into the distance, and she wondered as she pushed through the glass doors of the shop front if he'd noticed her departure.

After adding fuel to the car, he purchased three jerry cans, filling each with petrol before he drove to a super market where he bought dehydrated and tinned food.

It was easy to find the caravan park, and he pulled in and booked a cabin for one night. The proprietor of the park asked the normal questions reserved for travellers, but Horton gave little away.

Horton's only question was of access to the river as he felt he might go for a swim later in the day.

The park cabins cool shade revitalized him, and he went to work on his overnight bag. Removing all of his spare clothes he felt the bags base for his pistol and a U.S army issue combat knife.

He cleaned the pistol and filled its two spare magazines. The weapon was in new condition, as it had only fired two rounds in its life, and that was three years ago. Since that time it had lain buried in water proof wrapping by the head stone of someone named Samuels, in an historic metropolitan cemetery.

The bullets were in very good condition too.

Horton had similar weapons buried in cemeteries in many different cities around the world. He'd chosen a 9mm weapon on this occasion partly because the projectiles were metal coated and less prone to corrosion.

He showered under cold water without soap, knowing that if there were dogs at the place he was going, they would surely be alerted earlier to the fragrance of the soap's perfume.

Horton, whose mind was clear, but in a state of near exhaustion, dared not lie down on the bed. If he did he would most likely sleep until the next morning. Not wanting to risk this, he sat in a chair which had a clear view of the doorway and cat napped.

CHAPTER 34

Simon and Sarah had begun their day late, and after breakfast they continued to pack enough of their belongings to travel light. Much of Simon's gear they'd transported the day before to be stored at Ray's place in town.

Now today, there were only the final bits and pieces to be tidied up before they gave the house a clean. The owner would undoubtedly appreciate the work of good tenants. Both Sarah and Simon agreed they may wish to return to the outback again one day.

Ray had the same intention, and had spent most of the day packing his gear to move it to town. Until with time he thought it safe to return.

By three o'clock he had most of the work done, and all that remained for him to do was load his horses.

It had been a long day.

He'd towed his horse float to the stables and lowered its back door before he twisted the top off a beer bottle. As he sat in the cool shade of the stables resting, he told his horses,

"There's plenty of time before sundown."

They seemed content with his decision as they crunched on dry feed.

Simon and Sarah's belongings were in a loose pile on the back veranda, when Simon decided it time to retrieve the two letters concerning Quinn. Before he left he asked Ray if he needed a hand with anything and then drove into town expecting to be away for a half hour.

Sarah watched Simon drive away, missing him as soon as he was lost to sight in a swirl of dust, before she turned back inside to find more things to do.

As she entered the house and walked through the lounge room, she noticed Simon's yellow address book on the rickety table by the telephone.

The telephone beckoned her, as did a thought of her Mother. She didn't feel at all like chatting; just needed to hear her Mother's voice, which would, as always, no questions asked, offer reassurance.

A call just before they left this place would suffice. That way she thought, she would be sure to remind Simon to collect his address book.

As she turned away and walked towards the kitchen, it occurred to her that it had taken a long time for her to decide to make her personal phone call. She had stood looking at the phone for several long minutes, unable to decide, and now in another room of the old house she found herself unable to decide where to start.

Finally she flopped into the nearest chair, and gazed fixedly through the dusty kitchen window pane at a distant point on the tree lined horizon.

*****

Simon drove through the small town and directly to Beth's office. He was greeted by the sound of a computer keyboard and he asked Lynette if Beth was available.

"She's with a client, but they've been in there for a while. I expect she shouldn't be long Simon. If you'd care to wait, I can make you a coffee?"

Simon looked at his watch deciding he didn't want to wait, but under the circumstances he had no choice. He declined the offer and thanked the girl for her suggestion.

There were vacant chairs along the waiting room wall, but his restlessness kept him on his feet, and he paced for some minutes.

"Lynnette, I might wait outside. Would you let Beth know that my need is urgent please?" Lynette saw Simon's agitation and nodded as he turned to leave the room. He lit a cigarette as he went and drew smoke deep into his lungs. His hands trembled and his mind was in turmoil.

He shouldn't be here he told himself. It was stupid not to have just called Beth on the telephone. Ask her to destroy the two envelopes rather than leave Sarah on her own. The few minutes he waited seemed much longer, until finally a call from Lynette brought him back into the office.

Beth met him at her door and ushered him in.

Simon didn't notice the look in her eyes as she took in the sight of him.

She hadn't seen him when he'd delivered the two envelopes, as he had left them in Lynette's charge to be handed on to her.

She thought he looked ragged.

His clothes hung from his body, and he seemed much thinner than she'd ever seen. His skin had a certain pallor that matched the gauntness which showed around his eyes.

She beckoned him to sit.

"Simon. What's wrong?"

"Everything's O.K Beth. I just need the two envelopes I left with you please."

Beth looked at him incredulously and questioned.

"Come off it Simon. You've lost weight and you look like something the cat just dragged in. Something's wrong, and I, as your friend would like to know what it is?"

"Beth, please, there's no time right now. Believe me. You will know the story in a little while. Trust me now, will you? I'd tell you the story, but there's no time right now. I need the two envelopes. Please?"

His hat was wrung in his hands as he continued, "I'll be leaving town tomorrow morning, maybe earlier and I need the two envelopes. Please." She listened to him and knew he was on the verge of breaking down, before she opened the safe and handed him the envelopes.

His hands trembled visibly as he took them from her.

The pressures of the last month were taking over and he was near the end of his tether.

The slow build up from Abu's first letter, until the plan of murder by the second hit man was clearly obvious in Simon's features. His frame showed a weariness which dulled his every movement. Beth felt sadness in her heart at the sight of him. She feared for him as she watched his restless fidget.

He turned to leave, but turned toward her in the doorway.

"Beth I'm sorry. I must hurry, my friends might be in danger and I have to go to be with them. I'm sorry."

With that he was gone and the door closed behind him.

Beth felt helpless as she slowly lowered herself into her office chair. Despondent that Simon believed himself to be beyond her help, and despairing that without his request she was in no position to help.

Until she knew the truth she couldn't even begin to help.

She rubbed her eyes and wished for that knowledge. The knowledge which would help her to bring him back from the nightmare he was obviously in.

*****

Sarah heard at the same time as Ray the black cockatoos which congregated in the River Red Gums down by the river.

They suddenly began to screech, and like Ray she wondered what it could be that disturbed them.

Ray looked in the direction of the river and felt a little edgy, remembering the surprise visitors they'd had here in the recent past.

He stroked his favourite mare. Whistling softly into its ear as it became agitated, and he wondered if there might be a brown snake around.

Turning away from the horse, he walked from the stables at the rear of the building.

Stepped through the low doorway, and turned left towards the lean-to, to replace a bridle. Suddenly he stopped in mid stride as he found himself face to face with Horton. Ray was absorbed by the size of the knife which was waving about in front of his face.

The words, *"Are you Simon West?"* seemed to echo in his ears, and as he had difficulty forming any words himself, Ray slowly shook his head.

"What is your name?"

Ray heard his own speech, and it sounded feeble.

"Ray."

"Where is Simon West?"

"He's not here."

Ray was getting over the shock of the unexpected meeting. His heart pumped hard in his chest, as he thought that this was probably not a good time to have a heart attack, but then again on the other hand. A slight smile crept to the corners of his mouth at the thought.

Horton mistook the smile as some sign of rebellion and he hit Ray in the mouth with the fist that held the knife handle.

Horton wrenched Ray by the shirt front so their two faces were only some inches apart. The tone of his voice raised and some spittle left his lips as he hissed.

"If you want to stay alive you will tell me where is Simon West is."

Ray had a fleeting thought that he was a dead man whatever he said.

"I do want to stay alive, but not on your terms."

Even Ray was surprised at his few words of defiance, but there was no time for regrets. His mind suddenly registered the sound of his name, as Sarah's voice called to him from the direction of the house. The red eyed man cocked his ear to listen as Ray took his chance. He swung the horse bridle and relished momentarily at the sound of the steel bit striking the red eyed man in the ear. Even as it did Ray knew that it was only a glancing blow, and he was going to need a miracle.

None came.

Horton grabbed at the bridle with his left hand and held it fast as he pulled Ray towards him.

Ray wanted to let go of the bridle, but it was looped around his wrist and as he was drawn towards the red eyed man he heard his coarse whisper. "Nothing personal mate, it's just business."

He looked into the red rimmed eyes of the mercenary and realized in that instant, with no time for sadness that his life was finally over. Ray saw the man's right arm swing out to the man's left. Then felt the heavy bladed knife cut a deep wound which started at the corner of his right eye and travelled across his face to the left eye.

It cut through gristle and bone, and left his face wide open as the liquid from his eye balls and mucus and blood from his nose spewed down his face.

In the same movement the knife came around in a graceful arc. It thrust up under his ribs, slicing through his soft belly and pushing up into his chest cavity until at last his heart was divided in two.

Ray was dying where he stood.

He would have fallen, but he was hooked on the knife. Horton held him up and twisted the blade savagely in his chest, until tiring of his over kill he let Ray drop in a heap to the ground.

Horton licked his lips, and unknowingly some blood that had splashed onto them as he stepped over Ray's body and walked towards the house.

He stared as with seemingly sightless eyes.

Windows to a soul filled with intent.

*****

Simon started his car, turned onto the highway and drove towards the outskirts of town. He was near the town's edge when he heard a siren and saw a blue flashing light in his rear vision mirror.

Its intensity was lost for a moment by a plume of dust which arose from the shoulder of the road as he pulled over. Then another plume enveloped the old Ford when the police car came to a halt behind him.

Simon watched as the blue uniform approached his car door.

"I see you have a brake light not working, and you didn't use your indicator on the last turn you made," the officer observed.

Simon felt tethered.

"I'm sorry officer. The brake light I didn't know about until you mentioned it, and you are right about the indicator." Simon admitted to everything in the hope the policeman would just write him a ticket and let him get on his way.

"You appeared to be in a bit of a hurry too." Typical police humour to a captive audience Simon thought, and he felt nervous that the man might hold him up forever with his boring talk.

"I have to get back to my friends."

"Well, they will have to wait a little longer then won't they?" The officer said with a show of teeth.

The policeman walked around the car checking the tyres before he came back to Simon's window.

"I'd like to see your driver's license and registration papers please?" As Simon pulled his wallet and handed the papers to the man, his heart pumped anxiously for Sarah and Ray. He didn't think it possible that Sudovich could have another killer here already, but the possibility existed, and because of that possibility there was potential for panic in Simon's mind.

*****

Sarah had heard the horses shy away with fear and their hoofs as they struck loudly against the walls of the stables. From her vantage point at the window the repulsive sight before her eyes made her shiver to the bone. She witnessed, numb with pity, Ray as he dropped to the ground, and then from pure terror as the bloodied being began to walk in her direction.

Its face swivelled from side to side, as if searching with eyes that were immobile in a head that glistened wet red in the light of the setting sun.

Sarah snapped out of her trance and ran to the rifle rack, where she grappled with the first gun she could lay her hands upon. She knew nothing of weapons, and didn't realize she had taken the smallest caliber, a .22.

She ran back to the window. Where every conviction she'd ever known, every belief she'd ever held about the preciousness of human life came into question. She loaded the gun and aimed to halt the approaching menace.

The bullet brought a splash of blood from Horton's shoulder. He broke his pace, but in effect the sound of gunfire spurred him on.

Sarah was trying frantically to reload, and through her mind's eye she saw that her knowledge of weapons was greater than her hope of survival. As the gun jammed again, she heard the sound of footfall on the veranda floor boards.

The sound entered the house and padded across the wooden floorboards toward her. It beckoned, and she looked up from the useless rifle to stare into the gaping hole in the end of the pistol aimed at her. Cursing the man she lifted the rifle, and with all her effort she cast the useless weapon at his demented face.

As she turned to run to grasp at the second rifle, a gunshot sounded loud in the confines of the room. A split second later she felt pain as her leg buckled under her and she crashed to the floor.

She fell heavily onto her side, and saw momentarily the sharpened end of her thigh bone protruding through her skin. It advertized a severed artery which offered small spurts of red blood a heartbeat at a time.

Sarah's eyes were blind as her tears came in a torrent. The contortions of hopelessness and pain on her face screwed her eyes closed, as her heart felt the coldness of reality.

Her mind was closed to sorrow, and she clenched her eyes shut against a new pain as a fist bound her hair and dragged her across the room. It was there she struggled, as time was stolen from her by weird Henry, who cursed his luck in damaging her artery.

*****

Simon gripped the steering wheel with both hands. He tried to stay calm, but the nerves in his brain cried out to him to drive away and protect Sarah.

His fingers showed white as they held the steering wheel, and an ache began to spread across his shoulders.

Panic suddenly took over as he lost his self-control and as if with a mind of its own, his hand left the steering wheel and turned the ignition key.

He had the car in gear as the engine sprang into life.

It revved loudly until he lifted his foot from the clutch and the rear tyres spewed pebbles and dust from the road side.

The pebbles struck the officers legs as he stood inspecting the rear number plate, while the dust collected quickly in his nostrils and mouth as he cursed loudly.

The blue Ford fishtailed onto the bitumen road until Simon gained control and sped out of town. The car's engine howled as he raced through each of its gears, until he was at last in the open and hurtling down the road to his destiny.

The blue flashing light announced its existence in the distance behind him. It gathered momentum and was closer as Simon spun off onto the dirt track which led to the farm.

With dust spiralling and signalling his direction, Simon made it to the gate. As he left it broken behind him he saw that the highway patrol car was less than fifty metres away.

It was quickly swallowed up in the swirling dust raised by his churning tyres as he sped ahead.

Simon rushed through the bush recklessly, until finally amidst a cloud of dust he braked heavily outside the farm house.

The patrol car slewed to a stop immediately behind him.

Simon left the car and was about to run to the house when a gunshot rang out. He looked up to see a half-naked man run across the front veranda and leap out onto the lawn.

The man's right hand raised a pistol in his direction, and as it fired, Simon saw also, something carried in his left hand.

A brief glimpse of a small, blood smeared yellow object was given to him before a second shot forced him to retreat.

The blue Ford's windshield shattered as he ducked behind its open door. Another bullet left its mark by gashing the bonnet.

Simon screamed.

"Sarah."

More gunfire bellowed from behind him as the policeman opened up on the man who ran away. The fleeing man flashed red in the late afternoon sun. His blood covered body moving quickly toward the stables, from where he could make a frantic dash to the river.

Simon stared bewildered as the figure ran on. Firing its pistol as it went, but showing no sign of faltering under the blaze of fire that followed from the policeman's gun.

A second policeman had come from the patrol car. He too opened fire, but to no avail, until finally the two of them gave chase, loading their weapons as they ran.

The noise of the gunfire exploded in Simon's ears, and each new explosion, as they echoed in his brain heightened his fears.

He turned toward the house hoping Sarah would run to his arms. Show him she was alright, but she did not appear, and as tears of despair watered his eyes he ran to the house.

Quickly crossing the veranda, he entered the old building. Where slowly his eyes grew accustomed to the subdued light of its interior, and through his tears he saw her as she lay. Like some wet red puppet which had been discarded to lie crumpled on the floor.

His first glance assured him that she was lost, there was too much blood.

Her head lolled to one side, and she stared through Simon with sightless eyes. Every memory he had of her suddenly blemished by this single second in time.

He turned away to retch.

While the vision disappeared from his eyes, it stayed stained firmly on his mind. He gurgled, and a moaning sound came from deep within his chest as he dropped to his knees and bowed as if in prayer.

With the coolness of the wooden floorboards on his forehead, he rocked softly as his sobbing slowly steadied to a whimper and he finally broke down.

END OF PART ONE

PART TWO

CHAPTER 1

MARCH 29

Beth suddenly had a mental picture of the last time she had seen Simon. It had been just three days after what had become known as the 'outback murders' and the memory of him was now once again clear in her mind.

The picture of his gaunt frame and fatigued features as he'd entered her office was testimony to the pressure that he'd been under. His secret dealings had culminated in his discovery of the mutilated bodies of his close friend Ray Davis, and his intimate friend Sarah Richardson.

Beth, like her secretary Lynette, had been unable to find the right words to say to Simon, and she'd been secretly glad when he'd quickly got down to business. She'd made welcome his request to form a foundation named the Sarah Ray Foundation on his behalf, and had asked for more information on that occasion. Simon had asked her to trust him this one last time before he explained that everything would become clearer to her in the near future.

The near future has arrived she wondered, as she hoped the contents of this post pack would reveal to her the understanding he'd promised.

Beth thought about the conversation they'd had that day many times, although of late she'd been successful to some extent at putting the whole affair to the back of her mind. Now suddenly it all descended on her again as she held the envelope she'd received from Simon in the mail. She noticed the Brisbane post mark and the date March 25 as she removed three letters from the envelope along with a small cardboard box.

Her curiosity caused her to give the small box a shake, and she'd stopped immediately when a rattle proved loosely packed contents. She placed the small box carefully onto her desk top, and picked up the letter which stated in print, READ FIRST.

She opened it.

My Dear Beth,

I'm writing to you from the deck of the Patricia Anne. It is good to be with her again, and hopefully I will be able to put to sea before the month is out.

There are a few things I must finalize before that can come about though, and most of them have to do with you.

I will be named as a senior director of the Sarah Ray Foundation, and I would like to see you take on the position of secretary. This position will give you most of the work I'm sorry, but I think the position will suit you. I believe that you have the qualities the Foundation can depend upon.

The reason I name myself senior director is, if at any time in the future something should happen to tarnish the name of the Foundation, then I as senior director must take all responsibility. Which will leave you, and any that you see fit to employ free of any cause for concern.

The money which is to be used to form the Foundations economy amounts to around thirty million dollars American. It is at this moment in a bank in Liechtenstein.

If you accept the position of Secretary, I will make available to you the name of the bank and the numbers necessary to gain access to the account. My lawyer in that country will assist you to move the funds into Australia in which ever legal way that you find necessary.

The money is to be invested in Australia. Profits from these investments are to be donated through charitable institutions which carry out work in Sierra Leone, where the money originally came from.

If, for some reason, you feel you'd prefer not to be involved with the Foundation I will understand, and will find another way to trickle it back to the people who own it. Those who now, as you would agree need the funds most.

I have enclosed two other letters. One of these is marked Simon. It is a letter that you must keep in a safe place, as it is the documentation of my role in the acquisition of the money. It should clear the way for you, and accept for myself all responsibility if unforeseen circumstances arise.

The second letter is for you. It is the notification of the success of your employment application for your position in the foundation. I advertised it in the newspaper last week, and have enclosed with the letter a copy of the advertisement for your files.

This I think will also protect you if a problem arises.

I have also enclosed a package of opal, and a business card of an opal dealer you can depend on for a fair price. I have spoken to him and he expects your call. I might suggest to you that it may be a good idea to let him know when to expect you, so he can be sure to have enough cash on hand.

I'm providing this money to you to cover any initial expenses in the setting up of the Foundation. If you find it necessary to relocate, then I have no doubt it will come in handy.

Thank you for your love and your tender care. I shall hold you in a special place in my heart until my time is over. If not for you then I might still be lost.

You helped me to find my way and I thank you.

I will contact you by phone for your decision.

After that I must set the sails and head for the open sea. I hear its call, and it is there that I must try to come to terms with the reason I sail alone.

My best to you,

Simon.

Beth had sat back in her chair, completely overwhelmed by the faith Simon had in her, and the amount of money he'd put at her disposal.

Unsure of her feelings about Simon and the decision he'd left her with, she stood, and then had walked to the door of her office.

"Lynette. Who is my next appointment?" Lynette looked at the diary and said the name of the person.

"Will you try to get him on the phone and ask him if he would mind postponing his appointment until later this afternoon? Then reorganize my schedule so that I have the next couple of hours free please."

Lynette looked at Beth.

"Are you alright, you look a little pale?"

"Yes, I'm alright. I've just been offered a chance of a lifetime and I'm not quite sure where to start. I may move to Sydney. I wonder if you'd be interested in coming with me as my personal secretary."

"Have I got time to pack a bag?"

Beth smiled at her. Understanding the young woman's need to escape the small country town and see at least some of the outside world.

"Yes, plenty of time. Don't worry. We'll be there as soon as possible I can assure you. Oh. You might want to keep our plans under your hat for the time being. The rumour mill can operate just as efficiently in our absence."

Beth walked back to her office where she re-read Simon's letter. Finally, glad to have a firmer understanding of the past month's events.

Simon had kept his promise.

U.S $30m she decided, if wisely invested, could return over $4m a year. At that rate it would take 7-8 years to trickle the funds back into Africa.

After that, the African people would be realizing more than they had lost in the first place. In effect, they should be better off for Simon acquiring the huge amount of money.

She'd smiled at the thought of Simon giving it all away. Maybe that had been his idea all along. The ending of the letter about Simon sailing alone had struck her.

Beth had not even known of the existence of Sarah, until she had read of her death in the newspapers, and then she'd wondered of the woman and the cost to her and Ray. She sighed as she considered the sadness of the story, as its tragic consequences once again highlighted her understanding. She now had a part to play, so the price that others had paid would not have been made in vain.

APRIL 8

Simon left the coastal town behind him and headed for open sea.

His original intention to set a course north was put aside for the moment, and instead he tacked due east until his depth sounder registered deep water. Under lowered sail, Der boat bobbed gently as some dolphin swam in close. Their seemingly smiling faces apparently accepting the good day Simon waved to them as they glided through the clear water.

He unleashed a long bag from its stowage place and removed webbing, a sail and a metal frame from it. He didn't fit the webbing and the sail to the metal frame, instead he folded them carefully, before he pushed them back into the long bag.

They would have to stay on board he thought.

When he'd finished the assembly of the craft, he tied a ribbon to it. One that had belonged to his lost love Sarah, and with little effort he lowered the shiny frame over the side of the der boat and into the sea.

Its wet shape sparkled in the sun as he controlled his feelings. Then his breath escaped as a sigh, while the hang glider slid down and out of sight to the ocean floor. He hoisted sail again, and not looking back set course for north.

APRIL 29

Three weeks after Simon had given her the account numbers and the lawyer's name, Beth read a short article in the newspaper.

Brisbane: Tuesday. Sources in the Australian Customs Service report that wreckage from a sailboat has been found by coastal fishing trawlers. It is believed the sail craft was sunk as the result of an explosion. Trawler crew members in the immediate vicinity at the time of the explosion report that a smaller motorized vessel was seen to leave the area. Wreckage from the sailboat suggests its name was the Patricia Anne. Coastal Police are investigating and believe the craft was sunk in suspicious circumstances. It is believed the owner is the same man who survived a frenzied attack which left two people dead on an outback property in Western New South Wales. It became known as the 'outback murders'. Police are still seeking a man in connection with that attack. The victim's body has, as yet, not been recovered and his name has not yet been released."

Beth put down the newspaper and wondered if Simon had finally found his peace, or is it that his story might not yet be over. Until they found his body she couldn't know for sure.

It seemed that everyone who had come in contact with the money was dead or probably dead. Her own connection with it concerned her.

She gazed for a moment out of the window of her new North Sydney office. Suddenly she startled as one of the furniture removalists dropped something onto the floor in the next room.

She would never be sure that it was over.

CHAPTER 2

On the same day a little way across the city, Federal Policeman Ben Preston was also reading the newspaper article.

He remembered the outback murders. Not only because they had been the news items of the day for a day, but also because of the small tid bits of information that had reached his desk, before the actual event took place.

Little pieces.

The first piece was in the form of a facsimile. It had been intercepted between Africa and Australia, and logged as the scam letter it appeared to be.

It wasn't hard to pick up on.

After all, in this day and internet age the lowly facsimile stuck out like a sore toe. Transmissions between the two continents were that small in number that their computer didn't even have to pick at random. It grabbed them all. Much easier now compared to the old days of five years ago, when facsimile transmissions ran at a peak hour traffic rate into Australia 24 hours a day.

The second piece was a Customs and Federal Police central computers cross reference. The computers picked up on the outback town of Bourke twice in a little over a week.

One occasioned a supposed scam facsimile to an unknown person in that outback town, and it was followed by a seemingly sudden and short trip to Liechtenstein by that same person. Liechtenstein was a major financial centre in Europe, it, and a person from Bourke were like chalk and cheese.

The action exposed the possibility of yet another scam, and the suggestion that this man Simon West had taken the bait.

But now, with the benefit of hindsight Ben knew that if the affair had been recognized for what it was in the beginning. It would have only taken twenty minutes to find the owner of the facsimile machine that West used in Bourke. Then probably another ten minutes to inform Customs that West was to be detained for questioning the moment he stepped back into Australia.

End of story.

The third piece of information that the outback murders had blatantly demonstrated, was that the whole affair had been worth closer scrutiny, but by then it was too late.

Ben had read the State Police murder investigation report. At the time there had been no actual Federal Police file on West, so any investigation was left in the hands of the State Police.

So, due to the lack of communication, the State Police had no knowledge of the two pieces of information and had only investigated the murder, not the motive behind the murder. It seemed to Ben now, that this man Simon West had just kept his mouth shut, and the 'outback murders' had in effect remained inconclusive.

Ben had also read the Federal Police memo that had accompanied the State Police file. It stated that Senior Federal management had deemed the case not important enough to warrant manpower expenditure. Although West had known the reason behind the murders, he'd obviously not committed the murders. So his part in the investigation had come down to answering State Police routine questions, relating to the murder only.

Then there was Sudovich, whose death occurred during that same period.

It hadn't come as any surprise to those in law enforcement; in fact, Ben could almost hear the champagne corks popping when it had become known that Sudovich had failed to make par.

Sudovich had been a pain in the arse. His name had always seemed to crop up at the oddest times in seemingly unconnected State Police investigations.

No hard evidence on him, just his name here and there, as if he'd had many small fingers in many small pies. Sudovich's name rarely came up in Ben's Federal investigations though, other than when State Police matters reached his desk.

Ben remembered that the intercepted Sierra Leone facsimile had been addressed to a Garry. He remembered also that he'd briefly considered the possibility of it being Garry Sudovich. It would have been the only time that anyone had ever referred to Sudovich as 'Dear' of course, unless they were making reference to the cost of knowing him. If Sudovich had been 'Dear Garry', then that in itself could be considered as a fourth piece of information. A small piece of seemingly unimportant information which appeared to have little value until he'd read of Simon West's boat explosion.

Suddenly, with West's demise, the case had new momentum and Ben felt the urge of the curious.

He glanced at the wall calendar, and after taking in its ocean view picture, he recalculated what he already knew.

Then considered the resulting fact, he was three months away from retirement and after that there would be no more investigations.

Three months.

His imagination put a bobbing boat beneath his feet now, as his nostrils sought the smell of salty air and his hands the tug of tasty fish in touch with the end of his fishing rod.

He knew that he would miss this work though.

Over the years he'd delighted in the in-depth search for answers, before understanding the motives behind criminal actions, and then finally the wholesome feeling of finished business. With that thought in mind he looked back at the newspaper. Wondering if there had been any new information on the Sudovich death, although he'd already decided it suspicious enough to be called murder.

The autopsy report had stated the golf ball had struck much too hard to be the impact of a normal ball near or at the end of its flight.

Ben turned to his computer keyboard and typed in Sudovich's name, then waited while the screen delivered to him an in-depth State Police file.

He opened it and read.

Sudovich's file went back nearly twenty years, and it appeared that with experience over those years he had learned to cover his tracks. His early years were filled with theft, possession of stolen property, possession of small amounts of prohibited drugs and assault. The assault charge was one where he had paid someone else to do the dirty work, and apparently it had been withdrawn by an intimidated victim. No charges against him at all in the last seven years, although it appeared there were many suspicions.

Ben keyed through the file until he finally come to the murder investigation. A possible suspect had booked into a motel near by the golf course under the name of Eduard Scott.

Ben browsed through a number of files. All of them based on the surname of Scott, and eventually peered into his computer screen at the face of one whose name was Edward Scott. Who was a known associate of Sudovich's, and one who was the subject of an ongoing police investigation into paedophilia.

It seemed he had dropped out of sight, as there was no credit card or passport use since his stay at the motel. Ben wondered if the man who had stayed at the motel had signed himself in as Edward or as Eduard.

There was a photograph lifted from the motel security camera film within the Sudovich hardcopy file. Ben looked back into the computer file on Scott to see straight away that the two faces were different. He wondered if maybe this man's photograph might not be on State Police files, and clicked in a search of the Federal/Customs files instead.

He didn't have to wait long.

Since the Bali bombings, there had been extensive updates to the Federal computer systems. There had also been an inclusion of information on people who had been of no consequence prior Bali.

Ben looked at the photo of the man. His reason for being on Federal files was because he was a known mercenary and hired gun. He decided there was no doubt about it, and opened the corresponding file.

There was little information.

His name was Peter Quinn who had served in Vietnam, one tour. After that he'd worked as a mercenary up until the mid 1980's, then as a personal security adviser in Kuwait and Saudi Arabia at various stages during the 1990's.

Ben felt that the man may have given the game away by now, as he would probably be feeling his age.

Quinn had no Federal Police criminal record at all, but Ben noted that he'd entered Australia three days before Sudovich's death and left the country the day of Sudovich's death.

Prime suspect Ben thought, before he made a mental note that hell would probably freeze over before he could prove it. He had no motive, no weapon and no idea of what weapon might have been used. No fingerprints, no nothing, except for a low grade photograph of a man who used a fictitious name to book into a motel.

There were some things that he did have though, and those were questions. Why the two murders in the outback? Why Sudovich's murder? Why the explosion on West's boat? Why a five-week interval between Sudovich's murder and Simon West's boat explosion? Was the Sierra Leone scam not a scam after all? Why would West go to Liechtenstein unless he was certain of something?

The one thing he knew for sure was that Liechtenstein was a tax haven. It had an international banking system much like that of the Swiss, and where there were banks there was money.

If there was money, then where is it now? The boat explosion might suggest that people were still showing an interest in finding it and that the trail was still fresh. Ben wondered about the bigger picture and decided it deserved a closer look.

It was intriguing after all.

There was also the possibility a large amount of money was somewhere waiting to be collected.

Ben had a weekend ahead of him and if necessary he could take Monday off, as he had time owed him. He thought for a moment and then called out to his secretary.

"Laura, would you book me a flight to the Cook Islands please? I need to get to an island named Rarotonga."

Laura didn't leave her desk. She'd been working for Ben for nearly twenty years now, and they were comfortable enough together to drop the formalities. When he called, she called back; after all he was less than five metres away.

"When?"

"Tomorrow afternoon if possible, please."

He looked again at the file on his computer screen and wrote down Quinn's last known address.

CHAPTER 3

Tom Lee had waited three days after he'd heard of Sudovich's death before he decided he must come out into the open. Make his presence known as Sudovich's better business half.

So on the morning of the fourth day he'd walked into the reception area of Sudovich's office, followed by his lawyer and his personal accountant.

Lee caught the receptionist's attention.

"Hello, you don't know me. My name is Tom Lee and I own most of this company. I have my lawyer here to answer any questions, and he will make any necessary arrangements for a meeting between me and any other shareholders." The lawyer introduced himself as Mr. Travers, who then opened his attaché case and extracted a letter which explained the whys and wherefores of Mr. Lees claims.

The receptionist glanced at the document.

"Would you mind waiting a moment please, while I call Mr. Sudovich's secretary?" She went to her telephone and pressed a single button before she spoke into the hand piece, "Louise, there's a man here, a Mr. Lee. I think you need to hear what he has to say."

While they waited Lee looked about the room before walking to the window. He'd never been to this building before, although he owned most of it. It was an impressive older type of structure and well maintained. The foyer was decorated in good taste which made Lee think that someone other than Sudovich had a hand in the choice of decor.

Lee had never felt the need to come to this place in the past. Whenever he had the necessity to see Sudovich, he just called and Sudovich arrived on time.

An older woman entered the room who Lee presumed to be Louise. Her eyes were red rimmed and Lee's first thought was that it may be the after effects of yesterday's funeral. On second thought he decided, her eyes were probably showing signs of rebellion against the mascara she had layered onto her eye lashes.

He introduced himself and offered his condolences at her loss before he introduced his accountant Larry Barrett and Mr. Travers. Mr. Travers then showed the letter to Louise, who read it, and then offered coffee before guiding them down a short corridor to a meeting room.

Lee waited twenty minutes quietly as Louise and the lawyer went through the necessities before he broke in.

"I'm sure that you and Mr. Travers can sort out everything between yourselves. So if you wouldn't mind, I would along with my accountant like access to Mr. Sudovich's office, all account books and financial statements. That is of course, if you are satisfied with my credentials?"

Louise put her hand to her forehead, as if there was a faint ache in there somewhere.

"Yes of course Mr. Lee. I apologize for keeping you waiting, but this has come as a shock on top of the events of the week, and I do assure you it has been a long week for me."

"I understand, and there's no need to apologize." Lee assured.

He was holding himself in check and just wanted access to Sudovich's office, not to this woman's feelings. He was here on business, not to console her for losing the fat pig Sudovich.

Lee visualized his fist in her face, and wondered if he did hit it whether the decades of make up on it might actually crack.

He smiled at the thought. Louise warmed to his smile and smiled back at him.

"Where would you like to start?" She asked.

"Mr. Sudovich's office will do. Larry will be able to find his way from there, I think. If you could bring in all records and financial statements, we can get underway with those. Oh, if that offer of coffee is still open?" Lee winced inside, unable to get over the fact that he'd actually called Sudovich Mister.

Twice.

Louise smiled before looking to the receptionist who had been standing by the door the whole time.

"Debbie, would you mind organizing coffee for the gentlemen please."

Lee watched as Debbie left the room.

They'd been here nearly an hour, and no one had come into the building, no phone had rung. What did Debbie do? Was she being paid to make coffee? Shit, he thought. He had girls who could do her job, and they could have given Larry, Travers and himself a head job as well, while they sat and listened to Louise.

Finally Louise led him into an office where he'd made himself at home behind Sudovich's heavy old desk.

Larry had gone over the books thoroughly to find the business was healthy. There was real estate in many parts of the city which was to Sudovich's credit, and rental income was high.

The next day Lee had become tired of being cooped up and had left Larry there to oversee the place, until he decided what was to be done with it.

Now, over four weeks later Larry was still running things. He ran a tight ship and business was good.

Things were running smoothly, except that Larry had a frustration and had called Lee earlier to tell him so.

Lee had had a busy morning with the arrival of a kilo of ecstasy. It had needed his attention in overseeing its distribution, so he welcomed the idea of taking an easy afternoon.

Sometimes he found gearing up for the weekend rave parties rather tiresome. Particularly now, when Larry was tied up with Sudovich's business, and most of the distribution burden fell onto him.

After parking his car and walking up to Sudovich's, now Larry's, office. He noticed Debbie's younger replacement, whom he knew from personal experience could add new meaning to receptionist.

Larry was waiting in his office. He wasn't satisfied.

"Mr. Lee, I need to find Sudovich's second set of account books. These won't stand up to an audit on their own."

The hairs on the back of Lee's neck stood firm at the very mention of the word.

"Audit, what audit?"

"I mean in the event of. Sudovich has done a pretty good job on this set, but they won't stand up under tax office scrutiny, and the end of the financial year is not far away. There's risk," he added.

Lee stared at his accountant for a moment as the implications echoed through his brain. He understood taxation risk. It had brought Al Capone to his knees and their career paths were quite similar.

"You're absolutely sure that a second set exists?"

"Absolutely positive Mr. Lee, there must be."

"You know. I'm not really surprised Larry. I never trusted that bastard Sudovich. I thought he might be scared enough of me to be very careful and now I find that I was right. He was very careful, the prick." Lee went on, "Where would the cunning bastard hide them?"

"This was his main office as far as we know, so I think they wouldn't be far away from here. I've found nothing in the way of receipts or entries to suggest a bank safety deposit box. Other than here there is only his home, and if they are there they are out of reach."

"Well we've searched this office high and low," Lee said.

Larry looked around the walls, his gaze finally resting on Lee's blue eyes. "Yes, but we haven't searched within, and I think the situation is serious enough to pull the place apart if necessary."

Lees face carried a look of amazement.

"Sometimes, Larry, I can't believe your style man."

Lee picked up the telephone and dialled.

"Louie, tell Dan the Man to go out and buy me a metal detector. The best he can get and bring it to me at Sudovich's office."

Larry listened as Lee spoke on.

"No, a metal detector, a machine people use to look for gold, it goes beep, like they use in the army to look for land mines. Fuck. Look is Dan there? Well put him on then." There was a pause before Lee spoke again, "Dan, I want you to go out and buy me a metal detector and bring it to me at Sudovich's office. Get a good one, and be quick will you? Listen, has Louie been into that shit again?"

Larry listened again while Lee listened to Dan, then Lee spoke again.

"Right, yeah I know. I think he needs a lesson. I'll talk to you about it later. See you soon, eh?

He put the phone down and turned to Larry.

"Something needs to be done about that fuck wit kid Louie. Do you have any ideas?"

Lee liked to hear Larry evade implication, while his imagination and flair that bordered on feminine amused him.

"I think we should look after him. Maybe get him into a detox program and let him have the opportunity to dry out." Larry decided.

Lee laughed lightly.

"I'd take that advice, but the nearest desert is at least a thousand kilometres away Larry." Lee's voice became firmer as he added, "Isn't the use of words interesting? You say look after him, and I say take care of him."

Larry immediately understood the difference. He knew Lee well enough to know that his infrequent word games were meant as veiled words of caution to those in his employ.

Reminders of where their loyalties should lay.

He watched as Lee sat back in Sudovich's comfortable chair and turned on its in-built massager. Partly annoyed by the steady hum, Larry took his seat behind the desk and strove to concentrate on his work.

Lee had brought a newspaper with him, so while he waited for Dan he flicked through it, occasionally reading to Larry some articles he found interesting.

CHAPTER 4

John Kane had been in Australia for six weeks. His passport stated that he'd not been in England for two years. Even though prior his arrival in Australia, he'd spent six months in his native London, where he had hired premises under the name of Henry Josephs. He'd begun a business in engineering and had put together a professional tight fitting team of welders, fitters and draughtsman. Who together, designed and manufactured five high voltage electrical transformers.

Just ordinary everyday transformers that most people accepted as necessary devices attached to power poles around any city or country.

Kane's designs were a little different. They had a special recess built into them where a small explosive device could be housed.

It would break a plastic seal and propel a deadly poison into the air. Arming the bomb was easily carried out by removing a dummy bolt and replacing it with a hollow spindle that had colour coded wires at its head end.

The business end of the spindle was a detonator. Its tapered round tipped spearhead was designed to pierce a small area of foil like metal in the top of the explosives container. Spearing its way into the explosive material as the spindle was wound into place. Alongside this recess, a small panel could be removed to reveal a clear cylinder shaped canister of a highly toxic nerve poison.

The poison had been developed by the Russians in the late 1960's and its design had been stolen from them in the early 1970's by the British. It was called 10X by them, their scientists sometimes explained to laypersons who inquired as to the reason for that particular name.

"10X? Why that means ten out of ten my friend." It would kill every human, dog, cat and rat in a one hundred and fifty metre radius within ten minutes of detonation.

The small vial of fifty millilitres that Kane had originally acquired could kill thousands of people. Three hundred millilitres which could be housed in the transformers would unleash untold horror in a densely populated city. Even Kane shuddered at the thought of the sobbing, vomiting, gagging mass of lunchtime city centre pedestrians, as they writhed and kicked their way from this world and into the next.

Kane had manufactured five of these transformers, or items as he liked to call them.

Four of the items, without their explosives and 10X and in perfect working order had been exported from Britain. One each had been imported into the United States, Canada, and Australia; these were the countries of the willing. The fourth one went to the Philippines. A country considered by Kane and his colleagues to be the most easily accessible for prospective customers to visit incognito.

The fifth had its uses in London and had been discreetly stored just outside the city centre.

Each of the items had been exported and imported without their explosive and nerve agent components. In full working order as transformers, in case they were tested by Customs agents during their transit.

The nerve agents would be placed in the appropriate housings when the items were safely in their host countries. They had been smuggled into the host countries in capsule form, while the explosives had been acquired locally.

The capsules were similar in size and shape to the pharmaceutical variety, but they were made of glass. They were strong enough to withstand rough treatment during transport, but fragile enough to be crushed between the fingers of an average strength man.

Now finally, the last item had arrived at its destination.

Its late arrival had been due to engine failure of its transport ship, and it had sat aboard that ship for some weeks while repairs to the engines had been carried out.

It had been a trying time.

The five teams of people he had in the five other countries had grown bored with sitting and waiting. Although there had not been the slightest hint of mutiny, Kane had worried that they might lose their edge. There was a long way to go, and a lot of work to be done. He had used this time well in financing another engineering business here in Sydney. The business itself was in the name of one of his henchmen, Steve Walters, who was the only team member who held an authentic Australian passport.

To the outside world it looked like a normal engineering workshop.

Its lathe was an absolute necessity, and one in use at this very moment as its operator carefully cut the thread on the neck of a detonator spindle. The sound of the lathe carried through the building and with it came a cascade of satisfaction. A welcome feeling as he looked out of his office window at the wooden crate near the rear fence of his rented premises. He listened to the lathe as he gazed through the streaky window at the wooden crate.

Unmistakable proof their transformer plan was ticking over like a well-oiled machine.

It was an ordinary wooden crate, and identical to those in four other countries. Kane had, had a number of other wooden crates manufactured. When the time came he wanted people to notice wooden crates everywhere.

Even in their sleep.

He knew that a terrorist didn't need a weapon. He just needed his victims to think there might be a weapon.

That was enough to bring out the fear.

It would also help to tie up law resources by allowing them to put their skills into practice on wild goose chases.

Kane wondered momentarily about Sudovich. He'd been more comfortable when he'd thought Sudovich's death had been by natural causes, and had felt glad the man was out of the way. Less room for complication he'd thought, but now, the possibility that Sudovich had been murdered raised issues.

Would Sudovich's removal bring its own complications? Why had he been killed, and should he, Kane be concerned about who had killed him?

Time would tell. For now, it had to be business as usual with problems disposed of as they arose.

Nothing was going to spoil his moment.

He looked out at the item crate again as a smile came to his face. It's nearly time to show my crate-ive side, he thought.

*****

Lee looked up as Dan the Man walked into the office carrying a cardboard box.

He was a big man, and most people who got on his wrong side found out the hard way why he was called 'the Man'.

His slow speech and slower facial expression suggested overall slowness, but this wasn't the case. Dan was as smart as the next man who had above average I.Q. He was also cheerful.

"Good morning, Mr. Lee. How are you going Larry, beautiful sunny day, eh?" Lee watched the big man's easy movement as he opened the carton and removed a metal detector. "I've read the instructions Mr. Lee, so I've got the basics on its working. What are we looking for?"

Lee looked at the machine. It beeped, and he saw Dan press a button on its hand piece which quietened it.

"We think Sudovich may have a safe or a hideaway in the office here somewhere. Are you sure you know how to work that thing?"

Dan nodded and Lee waved his hand about the room.

"Check out the floor. It appears to be clear, but we'll try in the corners anyway. That's where the carpet will lift easiest. Larry and I tried to lift it before but it seems to be nailed down. Try it anyway." Lee instructed.

Larry was clearing potted plants and a book shelf from the corner areas. Dan waved the detector over these without success. Lee pointed to a door which opened onto a set of shelves, where office stationery and an assortment of files were stored.

Larry started to remove these and Dan put the machine to work on the interior walls. He moved the loop over the floor boards and then waved it over some pictures which were screwed to the wall.

Dan finally turned to Lee with a shrug of his shoulders.

"It seems to be all clear Mr. Lee."

Larry chimed in.

"I've a feeling we're missing something that is staring us right in the face." They stood and looked at each other a moment, before Dan walked to Sudovich's heavy old desk and waved the detector across the front of it.

He was rewarded with a short beep as he reached the desks corner. Touching the reset button, he relocated the signal point and offered.

"Mr. Lee, I think this may be it. There's a small square of metal here," Dan said as he allowed its beep to continue for a moment to draw Lee's and Larry's attention to the particular area.

Larry walked around the desk and removed a long top drawer, before pulling from the desk a short middle drawer and a short lower drawer. He dropped to one knee to peer inside the desk and saw in the poor light a small safe. Lee walked around and squinted into the desks interior gloom, before he looked up at Dan.

"Dan, I want you to take your car and go and get Nibbles. We'll need him to open it."

Nibbles was the nick name he was given for his habit of chewing snacks while opening safes. So much so, that he'd had to take up chewing gum because the police had begun to recognize his jobs by the crumbs he left behind.

Dan left the room while Lee and Larry stayed behind. They smiled at each other while they rubbed their hands together in anticipation.

*****

Nibbles chewed his gum and quickly had the small, cheap safe open. Sudovich had obviously been so confident about his hiding place that he had forgone the need for a more expensive and less accessible safe.

Inside were thick wads of cash, being John Kane's twenty-five percent deposit. Lee piled it onto the desk top before greedily pulling at the rest of the safe's contents. It included the second set of books which he handed to Larry.

His third grasp returned from the safe's inside with a thick sheaf of receipts, a plastic coated page of silver coins, a .38 calibre revolver and Sudovich's personal diary.

Lee glanced at the papers and the coins before he dropped them onto the desk. He kept a firm hold of the diary, knowing that inside was the key to Sudovich's methods, motives and possibly access to any funds the dead man might have ferreted away.

He picked up the pistol and opened it to allow four unused bullets and two empty casings to fall to the desk top. Through force of habit he wiped it clean before wrapping in his handkerchief and handing it to Dan.

"Dan, get rid of this now. Somewhere deep because we don't know where it's been, and neither of us needs connection to it." Dan turned toward the door as Lee called after him, "Make sure it never comes back Dan. Better bring us some food too, eh? We might be here awhile."

After Dan had left, Lee turned to Larry.

"How much time will you need with that book Larry?"

"I think I'll be here most of the night Mr. Lee. There's some interesting numbers and there's a lot of them. It goes back three years to just after you refinanced him."

Lee rubbed his chin thoughtfully.

"Right, we'd better get started then. You can take the desk chair; you'll need more room than me." He then sank back into the vibrating armchair and began to read Sudovich's diary.

CHAPTER 5

In London, Geoff Letts whose job it was to act as coordinator and liaison between the five transformer teams had just arrived back from the United States, the final leg of a round tour of inspection.

Ten days earlier he'd set off from the United Kingdom and had travelled first to the Philippines. He had found their item, which had been imported in the name of a well-paid local businessman in rented premises.

One of Kane's team who held a local passport appeared to be a proud proprietor of an engineering shop.

From the Philippines, Letts had travelled on to find the situation was the same in Toronto and Washington. Each item imported in the name of a local business and housed in premises rented from that same business.

Everything was in place.

The pieces that had taken months to assemble were ready, and a discreet communications network had been set up and tested. All that was needed was Kane's order to let the game begin.

A car was waiting for him at Heathrow airport.

"Andy, you'd better do a few loops just to make sure we're protecting our privacy." Letts didn't expect a tail, but life had taught him to take nothing for granted.

Forty-five minutes later they pulled to a stop outside a small shop front which was, under normal circumstances, a direct ten-minute drive from the airport. The shop front with a 'For Lease' sign in its window was small. Wide enough for probably five doors like the one he slid his key into.

He stepped inside where dust and grit crunched under his feet as he walked through its front room. Another locked door opened to the shops office and storage room.

It was a bare room except for a telephone, and he chuckled at a sudden thought of Maxwell Smart.

His watch told him he was seven minutes early. So he brushed away some of the dust which was heavy on the floor and sat down with his back resting against the wall. He'd learnt many things over the years, and one of them was to catch naps whenever and wherever he could. Cat naps of short duration kept tiredness at bay. It also allowed him to clear unnecessary thoughts and images from his mind, and regain focus.

This was his state of his mind when the telephone finally rang. His eyes opened instinctively as his hand easily found the hand piece in the half light of the room.

"Hello. Is that you?" He said.

"Yes it's me. Is that you?" Kane came back.

"Yes, it's me," Letts answered. They were simple passwords, but effective, and without either one the men would know that something was wrong.

"How'd your trip go?"

"Perfect. I've checked all the shops. Each has its transport, lifting gear, electrical equipment, everything necessary right down to an aquarium for the office. Although over the last week it seems that each station has had some excess material stolen, which has been reported to the local authorities. Outside of that, all stations are on standby and ready to roll. They need only to hear the word from you."

Kane had been looking forward to hearing this information, and it confirmed to him that his station was the only one who had yet to report a theft. Once he'd announced a similar loss, then the hill side of snow that they had been building for nearly a year now, would suddenly show the early signs of an inevitable avalanche.

He liked the way that Letts passed on information. Every piece in a form that was easy to understand which would sound like general conversation to any eavesdropper.

"What about the sales teams?" Kane asked.

He knew there were five sales teams. He didn't know who they were, but he'd been advised by his boss Athol they would be out there. There was a team committed to each of the items. Each team well versed and well connected in the world of arms dealing and underworld black markets. Kane was not in the position to contact his boss Athol and it was more than curiosity which led him to ask of the sales teams. It was his need to know how that part of the operation was progressing, so he had something of an overall picture.

Letts was not ready for the question.

"Err, that's really Athol's area of expertise, but it appears that your shipping delay has come as a blessing in disguise. It's given the salesmen the opportunity to advertise through their contacts early, and they've reported there are two interested parties already. The salesmen in the Philippines and the U.K have learnt that although these prospective buyers don't know exactly how the items work, it seems they are willing to learn. They're chaffing at the bit to get their hands on any media that will help to make their voices heard." Kane understood what Letts meant by 'their voices.'

The people, with whom the salesmen dealt, had only one way of making their voices heard. It was usually accompanied by smoke, flame, shrapnel and the pain of innocent bystanders.

"I'll call this number on Monday at twelve noon, London time." Letts said.

Kane did a mental calculation and made note in his small pocket book, although he doubted he would forget this moment in modern history. The lives of the population of the world were about to be turned upside down, and although they didn't know the moment they would most certainly not forget the day.

"Let our people know it should be green light time early next week. Tell them to relax a little for the weekend, and then to gear themselves up for mid-week. Remind them that they need to be sharp." Kane said.

Letts promised he would before Kane inquired.

"I'm pretty sure you could do with a bit of rest, eh?"

"Yes, I am tired. I'll let the people know, and then go to sleep somewhere for a day or two."

"Good. Do that and I'll talk to you on Monday."

*****

Lee had read from A to Z in Sudovich's diary. He'd stopped once to go to the toilet during its digestion, but even then he'd read the diary while he walked to the toilet door. It certainly made interesting reading, and at times Lee wished Sudovich was still alive, so he could kill him again.

His way.

There were two things on his mind when he finally looked up from the last page.

"Larry, have you noticed anything in your book about someone named John Kane?"

Larry stopped reading and turned back some pages looking for a particular entry.

"Yes, Mr. Lee. There's an entry where Sudovich was paid a down payment of fifty thousand dollars for something or other. More recently there are payments made for import duties, shipping costs and land transport." Larry stopped looking at his ledger and while allowing the pages he'd held to fall back into place he said, "There is also an entry in the correct ledger. It seems this Kane fellow rents one of your buildings."

He stopped a moment to flick through the pages of this ledger, until running his fingers down a page.

"There are receipts for the rental of an industrial building in Grey Street, Alexandria. It does appear the goods associated with the import duties were delivered there." He paused a moment, "Number 16, Grey Street."

"Can you tell me what the imported goods were?"

Larry looked through the pile of receipts they'd found in Sudovich's safe until he read from one.

"This shipping con note says it was an electrical transformer."

Lee looked at him.

"What's that?"

Larry wondered a moment.

"Sounds like one of those big things that looks like a radiator hung up on the top of power poles, I think. I've never thought of what they're for. I've seen them, but they seem to be the kind of things that are just there and we take it for granted there is a reason for them to be there."

"I think I know what you mean. At least Sudovich wasn't importing transvestites in my company's name. I think Lou Reed was a transformer, wasn't he?" Lee said with a smile.

Larry saw the joke and chuckled.

"Yeah, well he seemed to go out of his way to suggest so anyway."

Lee stood and walked to the electric kettle.

"More coffee?"

Larry nodded.

"Tea I think, thanks. What do you make of it Mr. Lee? I mean anything other than the obvious?"

Lee was a rarity in this world, he was an expert listener.

"What do you think is the obvious Larry?"

"I think that Sudovich was paid too handsome a deposit for his part in importing this Lou Reed thing."

"I have a feeling you're right. Now we have to wonder why? What is so important about it? Or maybe it is only the packaging for what may have been inside it."

He handed Larry his tea.

"If its drugs, then I don't need the competition and I certainly don't need people operating out of my buildings. It's a little too close to home. When other people's business gets too close to me, then I need lawyers and they'll bleed you dry if they get the chance. You know that anyway, you pay my bills."

Larry remembered Lee's bills and of course, his own divorce.

Lee drained the last of his coffee as he turned to Larry.

"By the way, where the hell is this place called Bourke? Didn't you mention to me some time back that Sudovich had used my plane?" He stopped suddenly as he thought of something. Larry waited as Lee leant to the shelf below the small coffee table and picked up the newspaper he'd been reading the previous afternoon. Lee leafed through it until he came to the story about a boat explosion, and its possible connections to Bourke. He read it out loud as he picked up the diary and pointed to a page.

"Read from there on."

Larry absorbed Sudovich's last entries. "Do you know any of these people, Scott, Quinn or Horton?

Lee thought a moment.

"I know of Scott. I sacked that arsehole."

Lee stared at the wall for a moment, and then as if he broke free from a distant memory he turned to face Larry.

"You've met Peter Quinn."

"Yes I remember now. He was the one who liked to pick and choose his work wasn't he?"

"Yes, a holier than thou type of bastard. He's probably killed more people than he could count, and yet he still pulled the conscientious bullshit." Lee was silent for a brief period before he posed the question, "I'm surprised Quinn would take on work offered by Sudovich. Scott yes. Quinn? No. Not if he had a choice. Sudovich must have had a hold on him."

Lee looked Larry in the eye and held his fore finger up in the air before him, like a teacher might do when proposing a theoretical answer to a student. "Which might be reason enough for Quinn to be rid of Sudovich?"

Larry shrugged.

"Weston's name is here also," Lee continued, "but going by the question mark behind it, it would appear that he might not have been used. He's very much in demand and would be hard to get hold of at short notice. It appears by the diary and my plane's use, that something had gone wrong with Scott and Quinn. Sudovich was running out of time and clutching at straws."

Lee asked, and then answered his own question.

"Who was the other one? Horton. Never heard of him, but there seems to be no doubt he was the last straw." Lee suddenly changed the direction of his conversation, "They're of no consequence anyway. The main thing at this moment in time is this boat explosion. When was it?" He looked at the date of the newspaper. "The boat explosion was on Tuesday, only two days ago." His watch told him it was now two thirty-five on Friday morning and he corrected, "Three days ago. Which suggests to me that the hunt for the money is still on and it may not be far away?"

Larry looked a bit uncertain as Lee grinned down to where he sat behind Sudovich's desk.

"Come on Larry. Long shots are part of the fun in life, and thirty mill is at least worth a look." Larry was tired and his eyes ached, but he managed to call on reserves and conceal his uncertainty. He grinned back at Lee while at the same time a mental neon sign 'wild goose chase' flashed in his brain.

"Right, this is what we'll do." Lee advised. "Get Dan on the phone and tell him he's driving to this Bourke place first thing in the morning. He mightn't like the idea much at short notice, so let him whinge a bit, and then tell him he can take Mika with him. She'll keep him happy, and she'll know how to loosen the tongues of those bush yokels. She might be a bit unsure at first, because she has never been out of the city before, so I'll her know she'll be safe from the wild kangaroos with Dan." He chuckled to himself as he paused for breath and then continued, "You know what we want Larry. Make sure he understands. Tell him to do it quietly and not draw any undue attention. While you're doing that I'll let Mika know she's going for a ride in the country, then I'll find Nibble's boys and get them ready to keep an around the clock watch on 16 Grey Street."

He turned toward Larry from the doorway.

"One more thing," Lee said, as he pointed to the thousand dollars of Sudovich's money he'd left on the corner of the desk, "You've done good work today, so I have left you a small bonus. When you've made the calls, knock off for the night and I'll see you here around two o'clock tomorrow afternoon. We'll go around and see what this bloke Kane has to say for himself O.K?"

They bid each other good night, before Lee left the building with forty-nine thousand dollars of Sudovich's money tucked under his arm.

He'd had worse days.

*****

Friday morning saw Ben Preston working through the papers from his 'in' tray.

Since Saddam had been toppled, Ben's office had been assigned the task of carefully screening, and in general keeping an eye out for people who were of interest. Those people whose names rang faint bells, as the Federal Police computers and the Australian Customs Service computers held their own private conversations.

One man's passport had rung a faint bell, but as he was seen to be of very low interest he'd been put on the back burner. With these low interest subjects, Ben's department usually waited until they started their own paper trail. Then after a week or more, Ben's people would look into where their credit cards were used. More about where a card was used, not necessarily how often it was used. Unless the card was used very frequently in hardware stores or electronic spare parts outlets, then another bell would ring. Frequent use at these outlets was considered unusual for people who entered the country as tourists.

Ben's department had no access to any person's card, or how much was spent, just whether and where it was used. This particular person had been back in Australia since late February, and had registered a small engineering business in Alexandria. There was nothing unusual about this of course. The unusual part was that the man had left no credit card trail at all.

Ben read the slim file on the man.

Steve Walters was aged 35, and questioned in connection to insider trading on the Australian stock market before his rapid departure from Australia to England in 2000.

He remembered Walters the yuppie, his life of fast cars and expensive suits of clothing. It was a big jump downward from stock exchange player to a small engineering shop. The possibility he'd learned a lesson and had found his true purpose in life was one Ben was prepared to entertain, until he found facts to prove otherwise.

Ben wrote the address of the business down on a piece of paper before putting the file back into his in tray. Deciding he would drive past the engineering shop on his way to the airport. Experience reminded him that it didn't hurt to take a look, and after all he had to drive right by the place very soon.

He'd packed a small case the night before so he could drive straight to the airport from his office. It gave him the advantage of being ready to cut time, if for any reason he was held up at the office. As it was he had miles of time, and was in no hurry when he drove down Grey Street looking for the engineering works.

He didn't have to look very hard. A large, new sign stared out at him as he pulled to the side of the road and allowed his policeman's suspicious eyes to rove about the place. It was a big colour bond shed with a brick and glass façade and it stood condemned to ordinariness in its similarity to many others like it in the street. Large windows gazed out toward the street, each of them wearing reflections of the few near dead shrubs that lined its high meshed front fence.

Ben noted nothing alarming about the place. Some men worked in the rear yard near a cube shaped wooden crate and the blue fluttering flash of an electric welder highlighted a double door side entrance to the building.

He looked up at the high front wall of the building and his gaze steadied on a small sign as he lifted his mobile from his jacket pocket.

"Laura, it's me, Ben. Yes, I'm on my way there now. Listen, would you get in touch with a Clyde Stone Real Estate please?" He read to her the real estate telephone number from the wall sign.

"Find out from them who owns the buildings at 16 Grey Street, Alexandria, will you? No, that's all. I'll find out from you on Monday. Yes, you have a good weekend too."

Ben glanced at the building and its activity once more, before he continued his journey to the airport.

CHAPTER 6

Nibbles' three sons were all over twenty-one and old enough to choose their direction in life. They'd not always made the best choices, but they were surviving alright. Getting by on the proceeds of small time crime and dealing Lee's illicit products.

This morning they'd driven past the engineering shop in Grey Street, where each of them had the opportunity to see the wooden crate Lee had appointed them to watch. They'd arrived in two cars and had left one car in the next street before cruising Grey Street in the other to get an idea of the lie of the land. After the brief excursion they parked where they had a clear view of the engineering shop's side wall. Shane, who was the oldest of the three and the car's driver could see a small corner of the wooden crate.

Dion was the youngest of the three.

"How long's this gunna take?" He whined.

Shane answered in a quiet voice.

"Lee just said to watch, that's what we're gunna do. Don't start whingin' Dion or I'll loosen yer. Now shut up, I'm trying to think."

"Fuck Lee," Dion cursed before he lapsed into a sullen silence.

Shane threw a small plastic bag over his shoulder.

"Here, get some of this up your big nose, it might quieten yer a bit."

"Shit where'd you get this. There's a lot?"

"I want a lot back too, so go easy on it. It's got to see us through this watch job."

It was quiet for some moments.

"What do you reckon, Charlie?"

"Drive back around the next street Shane." Charlie said as he pointed in the direction he wanted to go.

Shane pulled out and onto the road, driving slowly for fifty metres before he turned right. Charlie then directed him to travel some fifty metres into the street.

"Pull over here."

He paused for a moment as he looked at a building which was set back from the road where they'd parked. It was a long building with all of the area between it and the road taken up by a large apron of concrete.

It looked vacant and appeared to have been so for some time.

The only lively thing about it was a single tube fluorescent light burning over a doorway.

"It looks like it might have been a car repair place or something, eh?" Anyway it backs almost right onto the big box yard. I reckon we bring our camping gear and move in. Tonight we'll turn up with the bolt cutters, take the lock of that gate, break into the place and move in, piece of piss." Charlie decided.

Dion leaned forward suddenly showing interest.

"What do you mean? Like a camping trip?"

"Yeah that's it boy, a camping trip. We'll bring plenty of munchies. We've got plenty of dope, the powers on going by that light and there'll be a dunny in there too. Camping with all the comforts of home, and we can even bring the little T.V."

Charlie scrutinized the building with his observant eyes.

"We'll have to bring another padlock though, because those cards by the gate tell me that a security man is still checking the place. He won't notice a different lock and we'll have a key to let ourselves out. If anyone springs us, then what's the penalty for squatting? People are doing it all the time."

A little after four o'clock Tom Lee and Larry drove through the double gateway and into Kane's engineering workshop yard. Lee had called Shane before he'd left Sudovich's office to ask if Kane was still at the workshop and as they entered the yard Lee saw what must be Kane's car. It was parked alongside another older vehicle, which suggested there might be at least two people at the site.

He drove in and parked beside the older vehicle, before he and Larry walked over to the open doorway which led into the workshop area proper. As they approached there came from within the humming sound of machinery.

The lower light level inside the building halted them in their stride for a moment while their eyes adjusted. They saw that the humming noise came from a small lathe.

A man was leaning over it making an adjustment to the job he was working on. A long slender spindle shaped object with a bolt head and threaded neck. Lee looked at the man for only a moment before he walked toward the office end of the building. He was halfway there when the lathe man looked up from his task.

"Can I help you?" He called.

Lee didn't like the tone of the man's voice, but discounted any suggestion of his feeling from his own.

"I'm looking for a man named Kane."

The lathe man turned off the lathe and it whined a little as it slowly began to lose speed.

"Mr. Kane is in his office. If you'd like to wait for a moment, I'll go and let him know he's wanted. Who should I say is calling?"

"My name is Tom Lee. I own this building." The lathe man walked through a doorway, and turned down a narrow corridor, to where he knocked on an office door lightly before entering.

"Mr. Kane, there are two men in the workshop asking for you. One of them says that he owns this building, says his name is Tom Lee."

Kane looked up.

"Is there anything lying around they might see?"

The lathe man assured Kane there wasn't.

"No Mr. Kane. Except that I was working on the spindle and they've definitely seen that." Kane looked down at his desk and began piling some papers, which he quickly stowed into a desk drawer before locking it.

His mind was in overdrive. Upon learning of Sudovich's demise, he had considered the possibility that someone would make themselves known as the new owners of the building. He hadn't expected an unannounced surprise visit. He immediately became wary and suggested the lathe man do likewise.

"Show them in here, then double check the workshop. Make sure there's nothing lying around."

"What about the spindle?"

Kane looked at the lathe man.

"Go back to work on it. It's too late to hide it now. Bring them in, quickly."

Some moments later Kane heard footsteps in the corridor. They stopped outside his open doorway where two men in expensive suits stood looking in at him.

"Mr. Kane?" One of them asked.

Kane walked toward the doorway to greet them.

"Yes. My name is John Kane."

Lee stepped forward and reached out his hand.

"My name is Tom Lee. This is my associate Larry Barrett."

Kane shook Larry's hand and then addressed Lee.

"What can I do for you Mr. Lee?"

"Mr. Kane, I was Garry Sudovich's business partner and since his accident I've had to take over the general day to day affairs of this part of our business. Larry and I have been taking stock of my real estate assets. In the course of this we've taken the time to visit my holdings. Mainly to assess their value and maintenance standard, but we will of course take the opportunity to meet those who rent or lease them."

Kane's mind was moving fast, but he never allowed himself to panic. He knew also there were paragraphs in the lease agreement about land lords approaching without notice.

"I see," he said as he gestured to the two chairs which faced his desk, "Would you like to sit down? Coffee?"

Both Lee and Larry declined the offer as they seated themselves.

They stayed for half an hour, during which time Lee talked as much as he'd listened, and as he expected he learned little. His main aim in the visit was just to have a look around the workshop and eyeball the wooden crate that stood proudly alone in the rear yard.

After their interview they remained quiet during their walk back to the car, until they became seated in it.

"What do you reckon Larry?"

"The workshop looks a bit thin on the ground, but aside from that it looks normal enough," Larry answered as he clipped up his seatbelt.

"Yeah, on the surface it looks great, but did you see the third bloke?"

"Yes I saw him; he looked like he was filling out job cards."

"That's was my first thought on the way in, but when we passed his office on the way out I saw him pull off the top docket, the customers copy, screw it up and throw it into the bin."

Larry looked impressed.

"Nicely picked up Mr. Lee, you're very observant."

Lee looked back towards the workshop as he wished he was a fly on its inside wall.

"So Kane is cooking the books, eh? That means he's either trying to build them up with the idea of selling the business, or he's laundering money."

Lee looked to the yard area.

"Yes, but where does the transformer fit in? Sudovich was paid fifty grand as a down payment, and that payment was in some way connected to the transformer. Or the box it came in." He started the car and drove to the intersection at the end of Grey Street. "If the transformer is the important part of whatever is going on, then maybe he's cooking the books to justify his being there. I mean, maybe the need for a front is as important as the reason for the transformer."

Lee's mind was doing what it did best, seeing beyond the trees. He could not and did not hope to see the future, but he saw real life as a chess board and used what facts he knew to assume his opponent's next move. Most people did that, but Lee had a natural instinct for it, which was good for him because his survival depended on it.

"There is one other thing Larry. If whatever Kane is doing is illegal, and it revolves around the transformer. Then he's doing it on my premises, with a transformer which was imported into the country in my company's name." Lee slapped his hand onto the steering wheel and lent weight to his next sentence, "He's up to something Larry, and it's bigger than the two hundred grand he was going to pay Sudovich. My worries are, how big, and if he gets burnt how much heat will I feel? The bastard is doing dirty deeds in one of my buildings and under my company name. He's like one of those pricks who steals your identity." The more Lee thought about it the more incredulous and angry he became, "Shit, and I can't even shoot the bastard." He went quiet for a moment as he dialled his mobile phone, and as it made connection he added, "Well not yet anyway."

Shane answered the mobile phone Lee had given him.

"Yeah, we saw you there Mr. Lee. We're in the car yard building behind the big box. We just have to look out the back window to see it."

He listened as Lee spoke and then put forward an idea.

"I think the best way to have a look without it being noticed would be to drill a couple of holes in it, rather than breaking it open. Then just glue some paper over the holes. That'd be enough to see what's inside of it."

Shane listened for a moment and then replied.

"Yeah Mr. Lee, I'll call you as soon as we've had a look. Tonight yeah." Shane closed the phone and turned to Charlie.

"Lee wants us to go in there tonight and see what's in the box. I told him we'd drill a couple of holes and he reckoned that would do. He said there'll be a bonus."

"There'll be a brace and drill bit in old Nibble's carpentry stuff at home," Charlie reminded.

It was decided.

*****

Kane looked up at the lathe man who was leaning in his office doorway. "Look Barney, there's nothing to worry about. If Lee suspects anything, which I am sure he does, there's nothing he can do. He can't go to the police because he's involved. We used his company name remember. He needs to find out more about what's going on, and I doubt he can. Not before our start time next week anyway, after then it doesn't matter what he finds out. No, the next time we see this fellow Lee, he'll be expecting to be paid off. We've just acquired another expenditure that's all, and we've enough capital to cover these unexpected expenses."

He extracted the papers he'd hurriedly thrust into the desk drawer upon Lee's unexpected arrival.

"How long do you need to have the spindle finished?"

"Probably two to three hours," Barney replied.

"You'd better get on with it then. Is Steve still out there?"

"He was in his office a moment ago."

"When you've finished the spindle, give it to Steve. I'll give him his instructions. Send him in on your way out will you."

"Yes sir." Barney said automatically.

Kane looked at him.

"Be careful Barney. It's Mr. Kane remember?" Kane noted Barney's agitation as he watched him go and he understood.

The transformer with its delay due to the ships breakdown had put their plan back some weeks, and it was becoming apparent that his people were showing some initial signs of stress.

They will get plenty of opportunities to off load some stress he thought.

Within the next week they'd load it on to the shoulders of the populace of five countries.

*****

Shane and Charlie used their key, leaving Dion with the promise of fast food on their return. They borrowed the brace, drill bit and a small torch from Nibbles.

Nibbles didn't mind them using the brace and bit, but he reminded them to return the torch. It was part of his professional tool kit, and he had a job on the next night.

Their return was welcomed by Dion who was suffering a severe case of the munchies. His needs were met, and then after a couple of cones they settled in and waited for midnight. Watching as the security man left another card in the front gate, before they moved on the wooden box. Shane reckoned it was a good time, and Charlie and Dion as usual went along with what he decided.

Fifteen minutes after midnight they went over the security wire which separated the two premises. In a minute they were out of sight from the road, crouched in low light behind the wooden crate. It was an ordinary crate of timber and ply wood Charlie discovered as his fingers touched its rough surface. He searched for a moment before deciding where to begin winding the drill bit into it.

Shane held his open hand under the tip of the bit and caught wafer thin shavings of wood before they fell to the ground.

Charlie finished the first hole, and then began to drill another about two hundred millimetres lower. In a short time, he laid the brace upon the ground and pulled the torch from his pocket. Pressing its glass end to the bottom hole he turned it on while he peered in through the top hole.

He motioned with a sideways nod to Shane who leaned forward to peer into the box. Some seconds later Shane sat back on his haunches and grinned at Charlie who let out a low chuckle.

Shane cut two very small pieces of duct tape and placed one over each hole. Then reached into his pocket and pulled out a small plastic fruit juice bottle.

He removed its lid and tipped out two beer bottle labels. They fell to the ground in their wet curled up form and both Charlie and Shane picked one up each. Soon the labels were stuck at odd angles with their own glue over the small pieces of duct tape.

Charlie reckoned you couldn't get more normal than beer bottle labels stuck in odd places.

Fifteen minutes later Shane called Lee on the mobile phone.

"Mr. Lee, we've been in and the box is empty."

CHAPTER 7

Ben decided to catch a small charter boat around the island to where he expected to find Quinn. A decision he felt glad of, as he enjoyed and breathed deep the cool sea breeze which carried the cries of gulls to his ears. He was tired from the flight from Australia, and was content to sit in the warm sun and listen to the low moan of the boats motor. It almost, but not entirely drowned out the sound of the small waves as they pummelled the crafts bow.

The laughter and small talk of the deckhands broke into his rest at times, as they made fun while they carried out their onboard duties. It seemed to Ben that life here was probably uneventful. Definitely very slow, but as he dozed he thought to himself, who needs events and who needs speed?

Once he'd alighted on the old jetty he asked directions and was soon taking a slow soothing walk along an almost deserted beach. The wet sand massaged the soles of his feet and offered an unusual sensation of freedom, while the skin that spent its life in socks, soaked up the warmth of a gentle sun.

After ten minutes or so he looked up to higher ground, where coconut palms waved in a slight ocean breeze. Almost as if their movement was designed to draw his attention to the small bungalow style houses that failed to blend into the green landscape.

There were five of them and he changed course to approach the middle one that the woman on the jetty had directed him to.

He was still some twenty metres from it when he saw a man sitting on its small veranda observing his approach.

Upon seeing the man Ben put down his shoes and pulled off his suit jacket. More to let the man know he was unarmed than to show discomfort at the warmth of the day.

He approached and looked up at the man.

"Hello. I think that you are Mr. Peter Quinn?"

Quinn looked down at the perspiration on the man's forehead, and a greying lock of hair that seemed to hover over it in the breeze. He made mental notes of the man's face before he peered inquiringly into his light blue eyes.

It was obvious what the man was; he had authority written all over him.

The question is. What does he want?

"Why do you want to find this Peter Quinn?"

"Firstly, I would like to point out to him that I am not here to harass him. Secondly I have no authority here. Thirdly I have no evidence whatsoever that he has committed any crimes and last of all. I would like to ask him if he might be able to help me with enquiries into other matters."

"What are the other matters?" Quinn asked.

"It's about thirty million dollars that seems to have gone missing? It's about two murders? It's about a man named Scott who seems to have disappeared? It's about a yacht explosion? It is also about someone named Garry, whom I suspect may have been the late Garry Sudovich. If so, then it's also about his possible connection to all these questions."

"Is your interest in this missing money purely professional or personal gain?" Quinn queried.

"I've been a detective for most of my professional life Mr. Quinn. It's in my blood, but for the last ten years I have run a department where our operations are mainly gathering intelligence. Much of it is gathered electronically, so we don't get out and into the street to investigate a real life mystery very often. Nothing through the proper channels anyway." He paused for some seconds then continued, "Sometimes, every now and then, an interesting case comes up through indirect channels."

"Mr. Quinn, my job is getting paid for doing what I love doing and like anyone else, I like a good mystery, and this one appears to have a certain quality."

"I'm not really concerned about the money. No doubt it will be an important part of the investigation, but I don't want it. Unless of course it's found to be in the hands of someone like Sudovich, then I would have to revise my options. There would be better places for it to be. I'm not on a treasure hunt. I want to know what the connection is between the man who is apparently dead by way of boat explosion and a double murder near a town named Bourke."

Quinn drew a breath.

"Tell me about these murders at Bourke?"

Ben had noticed a slight change in Quinn.

"The two murdered people in Bourke were a Sarah Richardson and a man named Ray Davis. The person who owned the boat which was blown up, and who has not been seen since was a man named Simon West.

"When were these murders?"

"Nearly a month ago," Ben answered.

"When did the boat blow up?"

"Last Tuesday."

"Have you any idea as to who was responsible?"

"The only description was of a man with a badly scarred face. It's certain he committed the two murders, but we're in a grey area as to whether he was directly responsible for the boat explosion. My gut feeling puts him on top of my suspect list."

Quinn looked Ben in the eye and almost to himself breathed.

"That sounds like N.C.O."

"Who?" Ben asked.

"I don't know his real name. I've never met him either, just heard about him, nothing good."

Quinn looked out at the sea for a moment before making his decision. He was surprised at the shock he'd received when he'd heard of Sarah, Ray and Simon.

He'd not really known them at all.

"What is your name?"

"Ben Preston."

Quinn reached out and they shook hands.

"My name is Peter Quinn. You'd best come on up Ben. You look like you could do with a drink?"

"Yeah, I spend a lot of my time air conditioned these days."

Quinn pointed to a set of steps, and as Ben stepped up to the table Quinn emerged from a doorway holding a long neck of beer. It was in a holder and Quinn held in his other hand a frosted glass which Ben could see had just come from the fridge.

Quinn motioned with the beer bottle.

"It's a New Zealand brew they call swamp water." Then with the bottle again, "Take a seat, relax, enjoy the view."

They sat looking out to sea.

"You knew the people out at Bourke didn't you?" Ben began.

"Yes. I met them briefly." Quinn paused, and without shifting his gaze from some distant spot on the horizon asked, "How did they die?"

Ben's mind's eye viewed the police photographs whose bloody details seemed to spring out in raw clear colour.

"They died hard, and as savage as I have seen in over thirty years of service. It would seem their killer was not a lover of women, so the one named Sarah suffered before her end. The autopsy report stated that her attacker carried out his knife work in a rather frenzied manner." Ben had spoken quietly of the matter and then lapsed into silence. For some time he too gazed out, as if in search of the fine line that indistinctly divided the ocean from the sky.

Both men's thought patterns were interrupted by the opening of the sliding glass door. Ben looked around to see a beautiful young woman who seemed to glide on bare feet from the doorway.

Her face was calm, but a troubled look in her eyes gave Ben an immediate cause for concern as he wondered at its reason. He watched as she moved to Quinn's side where she rested one hand gently on his shoulder. After a brief, seemingly nervous like glance at Ben she looked down at her man's face.

Quinn looked up at her and smiled.

"I am glad to see you. Your sense of timing was perfect. My mind and my friend Ben's mind were in a dark place and your presence released us like a ray of sunshine." She smiled uncertainly before Quinn saved her by beginning an introduction. Ben stood in acknowledgement and smiled his best smile as he extended his hand. The troubled look still dwelt in her eyes.

"You are a friend, Ben?" She asked lightly

Ben looked her in the eye.

"Yes. I am a friend Justine," he offered. She gazed into his eyes steadily for some seconds as if reading a sign. Suddenly the troubled look lifted from her eyes, and was replaced with the light of a genuine smile which strove to take Bens breath away. He realized then the reason for the troubled eyes. She'd feared his presence as a potential threat to her domestic bliss.

She once again stood by Quinn's side, now with both of her hands resting on the shoulders of the reason in her life.

"Will you be staying long, Ben?" Justine asked. Ben felt the need to reinforce her security.

He'd noticed fishing rods against the wall at the far end of the veranda and clutched at them for support.

"I have to be back in Sydney on Monday. I'm only on a short weekend trip to research possible fishing potential. My retirement comes due from my job in the public service in three months' time."

"Oh. You've come to the right place for fishing. Peter spends much of his spare time on the water. In fact, we are eating this morning's catch for dinner tonight. There's plenty if you would like to stay and eat with us? We do not have many guests."

Ben looked to Quinn,

"You're more than welcome Ben."

"In that case I would love to. Thank you."

"Good. That's settled then. Now if you'll excuse me I have things to attend to, so I'll let you two get back to your men's stuff." She laughed with content as she turned away and disappeared into the cool darkness behind the glass sliding door.

Quinn drank from his glass and after licking his lips he turned to face Ben.

"Thanks for the public service story. It put her mind at ease. She worries for me when strangers appear."

"It was mostly true. I will retire from the public service in three months and when that time comes I will most certainly be spending plenty of time on the water fishing. In fact, I've been viewing brochures on the new range of Bayliners. There's enough room on one for me to live on and big enough to drive over here to go fishing."

"Sounds as if your public service offers a handsome retirement fund?"

Ben was sipping his beer as the question caught him off guard and his involuntary laugh caused him to choke. To the extent he had to quickly put down his glass and retrieve his handkerchief.

He wiped his lips and the small splash points on his shirt front as he looked back at Quinn.

"I'm afraid that's a misconception. The fact is, if I may speak personally? My wife passed away a short while ago, and the house we'd had in Sydney suddenly became too big for me. Fortunately for me, my decision to sell happened to coincide with a small housing boom."

"Were you married long?" Quinn queried.

"Just over forty years to Marie and just over thirty years to the service, although sometimes it felt as though the service was more of a mistress."

The two men were silent in their thoughts for some moments.

"Speaking of misconceptions? There must be some associated with the word mercenary?" Ben asked.

Quinn looked Ben in the eye briefly as his fingers massaged his clean shaven chin.

"There are and there aren't. It depends on the individual soldier. Some are just born killers who'll join any war to satisfy their need, while the rest of us mainly involve ourselves in basic security for people who can afford it. It's probably similar to your service. If one of your people goes off the rails and performs a criminal act, then the public and the media will tar you all. The media will beat up a story and the public will believe what it reads in the newspapers." He shifted his gaze, and looked Ben in the eye, "I should add that my example criminal act was not meant as an insult to you or yours. It exists in all professions, from the highest to the lowest. That's why the world needs your profession to find out who was behind the act, and my profession to make sure that the act doesn't occur in the first place."

Quinn sipped his beer and gazed out over the small white tipped waves for some moments until he turned his face again towards Ben.

"It wasn't your question that stirred me Ben. It was the reminder of the stigma attached to my profession. Much the same as when those hippies labelled us as baby killers when we came home from Vietnam."

He changed the direction of the conversation.

"You know that Simon's mate Ray was over there? In Vietnam. I travelled all the way out to Bourke on Sudovich's behalf and I come across Ray, who I've never met before. He must have been within a hundred yards of where I was stationed during a major offensive by the Viet Cong."

Ben chose his moment.

"Was he in on the theft of the thirty million with Simon West from the beginning?"

"I don't think theft is the right word Ben." Quinn advised before he drank from his glass, "How about I start the story from the beginning, as Ray told it to me?"

Quinn looked toward the top of one of the palm trees; it waved in the sea breeze as if it might orchestrate the stories opening lines.

"It appeared to Ray that Sudovich was in cahoots with an African Government official who was skimming his Nation's treasury. Sudovich's part in it was to make available false documents that the African official would guide through the right departments. Initially the Government official would provide Sudovich with a sample letter. It detailed the correct government contract numbers, and was to be copied exactly before being delivered back by normal mail. The letter from the Government official to Sudovich must have got mixed up in the mail and delivered to Simon by mistake. So Simon decided to make up his own documents based on the sample letter and impersonate Sudovich."

"The temptation must have been great." Ben thought aloud.

"Yes. Very great, but not for the reasons you probably believe."

"I have a feeling you are going to prove my reasoning incorrect."

"I think I'll let you make up your own mind on that issue." Quinn suggested before he continued the story, "Ray and Sarah didn't know anything about what Simon was up to, until one night someone by the name of Scott turned up. He bounced something heavy on their skulls and tied them up. Apparently Simon wasn't there at the time. When he did turn up Scott tried the same thing on him, but he slipped on the swimming pools concrete surround and died in the pool's water. I think you'll find him buried on the property somewhere, but you'll have to dig deep because Ray mentioned a back hoe when he captured me."

"I've read the police file on Scott. I doubt that I'll go looking for him. I doubt that anyone will miss him either."

"Pretty bad, eh?" Quinn enquired.

"Paedophile." Ben answered.

"Interesting you should mention that. Ray told me he'd found his niece's address in Scott's pocket when they fished him from the swimming pool. She worked at the local roadhouse. "

"Scott must have worked for Sudovich then, did he?"

"Ray said they'd also found a document on Scott's body, linking him to Sudovich. That was something that surprised me. I was sure, and still am that Lee sacked Scott some time ago..."

"Lee?" Ben asked suddenly, as he sat up in his chair and leaned forward to receive the answer.

"Yes. Tom Lee."

"You mean the Tom Lee. Underworld figure and one of Sydney's drug lords?"

"Yes. That's him." Quinn replied before he too leant forward in his chair, by now with a surprised look on his face, "Do you mean your people didn't know that Tom Lee owned Sudovich lock, stock and barrel?"

Ben wasn't listening. He appeared to Quinn to be lost in his own world as he stared steadfast out to sea. Some moments later Ben relaxed in his chair with a thoughtful look on his face.

"Do you think it may have been Lee who was looking for the thirty million? Ben asked.

"That's what I thought in the first instance, and that's why I felt I had to go to Bourke. I thought Sudovich was working on Lee's instructions. It wasn't until I learned of Scott's involvement that I was almost positive Sudovich was working freelance."

Quinn paused as if something had occurred to him and Ben waited impatiently for him to divulge this new information.

"I'm sure Sudovich was working alone," Quinn finally offered, "but since he is now dead, then Lee may have by now made himself known as the owner of Sudovich's assets. If so, then he would have most surely gained access to Sudovich's office, his books and diaries and such."

Quinn drained his glass and then left Ben deep in thought as he disappeared into the house, before returning some minutes later with another bottle of swamp water.

"You said you felt you had to go to Bourke?" Ben inquired as his eyes followed Quinn's to the top of the palm tree and watched its movement in the wind while he waited.

"Ben. I saw a lot of drug use in Vietnam, and a cousin of mine died of an overdose in north Queensland about two years ago. When Lee first approached me for my security services I refused to work for him and told him why. You know what he did?"

He didn't wait for Ben's reply and as his hands curled into fists he spoke. "One day I came home to find a facsimile from him that contained the names and addresses of all the members of my family. Since then I've been there when he's called, but he has only ever hired me for legal purposes, like when he's in need of extra bodyguards. He won't use me for his drug work because he doesn't trust me to know too much. It's a rickety relationship, but I sleep O.K at night, knowing my family in Sydney is safe."

Ben changed the conversations course.

"Do you know how Sudovich got involved with Lee?"

"The word was that Sudovich lost heavily on the stock market and the banks wouldn't look at him. Lee it seems was good for the cash to get him out of trouble. Sudovich, the silly bugger, should have known that it would have been safer to ask the devil himself."

"From what I know of Lee, I feel compelled to agree." Ben said as he raised his glass. Quinn smiled in return as he raised his own glass.

The sun was lower in the sky now. Ben looked forward to watching the sunset which he was sure would show colour. A thick layer of cloud had grown, and it sat heavy on the horizon a long way out to sea.

"Rain, do you think?" He asked.

Quinn looked closely at the clouds.

"No, I don't think so. That cloud formation, if it lingers, might make your plane ride tomorrow a bit bumpy though."

Ben had learned more than he'd expected through his conversation with Quinn. He felt content with the knowledge he'd gained. Although that contentment was confused by the un-provable fact that he was sitting enjoying a beer, and a potential sunset with a man he firmly believed murdered Sudovich.

"What was Sarah Richardson like?" Ben suddenly asked, almost as if he needed shelter from the knowledge,

Quinn remained thoughtful for a moment.

"I didn't see much of her, but enough to say that she was a beauty. The fact she travelled the world to take part in hang gliding championships should give you some idea of her fitness. I had the feeling she was not really comfortable with what Simon was doing, but she knew him well enough to trust him."

"What was he like?"

"I think he was basically a good bloke. Like most of us baby boomers who've lived our youth in the best country in the world. During a period when you could play cricket in the street and leave your car and house unlocked. A time when you could walk the streets at night and a major crime syndicate was the local S.P bookie. A time when a copper would give you a kick in the bum and send you home if he caught you playing up. Policemen were much tougher then, as many had played their part in the war, and may have been kicking the bums of Germans and Japanese before they were kicking ours. What do they call it now? Police Service?" Quinn stopped talking for a moment to drink from his glass before he continued in his matter of fact tone, "Before justice was replaced by law. Before the countries youth became dependent on dope and American television. We grew up in paradise, and then suddenly we turn around one day and it's all gone, replaced by drugs and the crime associated with them. Not to mention a slow invasion by people, who believe we should believe what they believe, because they believe they're right. I think Simon was a little lost in this new world, and probably also a touch naïve in believing that he'd get away with the thirty million without a scratch. He was a good bloke whose heart was in the right place. One who found himself surrounded by the darkness of today's world and went out of his way to try to create some light."

Quinn turned in his chair so that he faced Ben.

"You see Ben. Simon didn't steal the money for himself. He intercepted a shipment that was in transit between thieves. His intention was to import It Into this country, invest it so it would grow, and then export the profits back to the country of its origin. To the people that it truly belongs to. That's why Sarah and Ray went along with it. They weren't thieves. They believed in Simon, and Simon believed that he was doing the right thing."

Ben allowed all he'd heard to sink in.

"By the way, you were right," he said.

"Pardon?"

"You've proved my reasoning incorrect, and I apologize for assuming the worst of Simon West."

"I'm glad you understand Ben, because it allows me to ask a favour of you."

"If I can," Ben said.

"If you would, I'd like you to use every means at your disposal to find the money and make sure it's where Simon intended it to go. So that when you pull up in your fancy boat for me to show you where the best fishing is, you'll be able to tell me that Simon, Sarah and Ray were successful in their mission, and that they didn't die in vain."

"I'll do what I can," said Ben.

"That's good enough for me. Come on. Finish your beer and we'll go and I'll cook these fish. Are you hungry?"

"Yes. I am looking forward to it. Do you like cooking Peter?"

"Love it. I was nearly finished my third year apprentice chef when my draft card turned up for Vietnam. Didn't tell the army though, they would have had me peeling potatoes the whole time. Although looking back on it, I suppose that even those who peeled the spuds played their part in winning the war."

Ben's mind shot off in the direction of confusion, and the thought telegraphed to his facial features where it adhered while his uncertainty grasped for a response, "I thought..."

"So do many other people Ben. I see it that we went off to fight the war against communism. To me, Vietnam was a battle in that war, and finally when I saw the fall of the Berlin wall and perestroika I knew that we were winning the war. And now that China has to embrace capitalism to survive. I'd say that our side, the West, won the war. Wouldn't you?"

Ben was unsure what to say. Or more so, he felt that not having been there, he didn't have the right to make comment. He tried to remain neutral in his reply.

"I believe that it shouldn't have happened," he said.

"I'd like to be able to say that," Quinn decided, "but I can't, without the benefit of hindsight of what the world would be like if it hadn't happened. Better, do you think? I mean you never hear the term 'Mutual Assured Destruction' bandied around like it used to be."

"I don't know. Even now there's room for improvement," Ben suggested.

"Well, you've three months in which you can make life a lot better for those who Simon chose to help anyway. That'll make for a little less room."

Ben felt himself unable to disagree.

CHAPTER 8

Ben touched down at Mascot airport late on Sunday night. He felt tired, but not weary enough to call it a day, so after picking up his car he made his way directly to his office.

The security man on the building's door waved him through, as he had waved him through for over ten years now. He was used to Ben being around at odd hours, especially over the last three months since his wife had passed on.

Ben had little to do at home, and no one to greet him if he went there. It was also a different type of quiet here at the office, and an easier quiet to cope with.

At his desk he typed Sudovich's full name into his computer. It took some time for the search to progress, first through the Federal Police files, State Police files, Customs files, aircraft registration and ownership, business registration and others. There was Sudovich's pilot's name to consider too, he thought.

He wondered a moment before deciding he would give Stanley a call. Stanley worked for the Australian Taxation Office, and could track down anybody at short notice, quickly and quietly.

After he had finished with Sudovich's full name, he entered the company name Sudovich had operated under.

Then it was time to do the same with Tom Lee.

Every file accessible was searched, from traffic fines and up. It was a neat pile of papers that Ben carried away from the printer.

This might take some time he thought, so he rang the security man at the front desk and told him to expect takeout food. He made fresh tea, sat down and began to read.

The only Customs document read of a shipping delivery, which may or may not mean anything, other than to inform that imports by Sudovich Holdings were rare.

As well the rest of the documents gave up little information. They confirmed that Tom Lee was a Sudovich Holdings director, and that Sudovich Holdings owned a small aero plane, as well as extensive real estate throughout Sydney.

Ben wondered at the possibility of Tom Lee having the thirty million dollars, and his hand closed to a fist at the thought of it.

Simon's idea about the disposal of the money was preferable, and as Quinn had said, *"Better there than in the Sudovich's pocket."*

Better there than in Lee's pocket too, Ben thought.

Unsure of what to do next, he reminded himself that he must find the pilot, but that task could not be performed until the next day.

The papers fitted neatly into a thick file folder, and he dropped it into the lower drawer of his desk. He was preparing to leave when he noticed a thin file folder on the top of his in tray. It had the word 'query' written on the front of it in Laura's neat handwriting. Ben picked it up and opened it; inside was just one sheet of paper.

Written on it was the address.

16 Grey Street, Alexandria.

Below the address was a short, and to the point message. Owned by Sudovich Holdings and leased by a man named Steve Walters. Ben smiled to himself as he thought aloud.

"Surprises! Like arrows out of the darkness."

A short time later he drove through puddles of coloured reflected light, on a deserted, wet city street.

He was feeling far from tired after his long weekend, and the quiet traffic urged him to drive the long way home. 16 Grey Street stood out brightly in his headlights as he gazed momentarily into the rear yard of Kane's engineering shop.

There was nothing out of the ordinary to be seen, but for some unknown reason that bothered him.

*****

Monday morning saw Lee sitting at one of the tables in his restaurant bar. He had Sudovich's diary, and he flicked through it as he waited for Larry to bring him the Sunday night figures.

He didn't like the smell of this place first thing in the morning. The strong odour of cigarettes and stale beer overpowered the sensitivity of his nostrils. Two people broke into his thoughts as they entered the room.

Dan, big boned, strong and in good shape and Mika who was small, lightweight and well formed.

They walked quietly across the floor.

"How goes it, Mr. Lee?" Dan called ahead.

Lee looked at the big man and smiled, realizing that Dan had obviously and recently seen an old English movie. He could always tell what movies Dan had been watching by the way he acted and spoke for sometimes days after the event.

Lee played along as best he could.

"It bodes well Dan. Is your arrival to be announced with glad tidings?"

"Yes Mr. Lee, glad tidings abound. We found out as much as we think available, although it would seem that most of the local folk out there knew little until the story hit the newspapers. Mika discovered the most interesting part of the puzzle, so maybe she should tell." Lee looked to Mika and noticed she was tired. It showed around her eyes for a second, before being lost beneath her smile as she shook off her weariness and got down to business.

"It appears that Simon West was involved in some way with a local accountant in Bourke. It's not clear whether this involvement was business or pleasure, but within a month of the murder she left the town and moved here to Sydney. People who knew her told me she just upped and left the town very abruptly. She brought her secretary with her, so it would seem she might have more than job prospects in mind.

"What do you mean by more than job prospects in mind?"

"Well, no townsfolk knew of any personal relationship between the two women. The two of them leaving abruptly as they did, had caused some rumour, particularly as the secretary left a boyfriend behind. I can't see an accountant looking for a job in the city with her own personal secretary in tow. I'd say that they had a job, or a private practice waiting for them on their arrival."

"Did you have a chat with the boyfriend?" Lee asked.

Mika looked at her hands and smiled briefly.

"He was, and still is pretty upset about being left behind. He told me his girlfriend just came home one afternoon and told him that she was going to Sydney with her boss. He also said the decision was sudden. There had been nothing to suggest prior her announcement a career move, let alone a move from her home town. Although having seen the town myself, and then meeting the boyfriend, I can understand her decision."

Lee sat back in his chair and sniffed before he called to the bar manager. "Bo." Bo stopped what he was doing and turned to listen to Lee.

"Bo, I want you to buy some of those incense sticks like the hippies use. Get a couple of packets and leave them here for me to light whenever I come into this place. I'm never going to get used to the stink of cigarettes and stale beer, so I might as well try to mask it a little."

He looked back at Mika as she took a perfume spray from her handbag and waved it through the air above all their heads. Lee's nostrils invited the expensive aroma.

"What about the two women now? Where are they?" Lee asked.

"I got a forwarding address for the secretary from the boyfriend," Mika offered, "It's a Post Office box in north Sydney."

"I got the same number from one of the accountant's clients, Mr. Lee," Dan chimed in, "It would seem that the two of them, the accountant and the secretary, are both sharing that postal address."

Lee looked at Dan.

"When did you two get back?"

"We drove through the night and came straight here."

"You're confident these two women might know where the money is?"

"It's the best lead available," Mika answered. "Both Dan and I had a strong gut feeling after talking to locals around the town. Something unusual seems to have caused the two of them to take off from the town. We wondered if maybe they might be involved in a sexual relationship, but the suggestion of that possibility seems to have only come about after they'd left town."

"The accountant spent some time with Simon West. The two were seen together just before the two murders, and she left town shortly after the two murders. My gut tells me that she's definitely worth following up," Dan added.

Lee considered this new information.

"Larry and I will watch the Post Office box today and follow anyone who visits it. If we don't have any luck, then I want you and Mika to work on it tomorrow. They haven't been in Sydney long, so they mightn't be expecting mail yet, but the accountant will have to keep in contact with her clients in Bourke. She'll have to turn up at some time. We'll keep watching until she or her secretary does. I want to know where they are working and where they both live." Lee looked at his watch before adding, "In the meantime the pair of you had better take today off, rest up and start early tomorrow."

"You've both done well. Thank you." Lee said as Dan and Mika both turned to leave.

Lee knew the value of a little gratitude. A sprinkling here and there worked wonders for morale, and if morale was high then he got better value for his dollar. Better value for his dollar made Lee happy, and if he was happy then everyone around him was happy.

Mika and Dan had brought good news, and he was feeling elated that the thirty million might be within reach. The thought of the money nearly outweighed the worry about the dirty deeds he was sure that Kane was up to.

Lee sat back in his chair as Larry walked into the room. They were about to talk business when his mobile phone demanded his attention.

"What time this morning, Shane?" Lee said before he listened, and then spoke into his phone again, "Next time something happens, I want you to call me straight away, right? It doesn't matter what time in the morning. If there's movement, I want to know. Do you understand?" Lee knew that Shane was covering for one of his brothers and said so, "Make sure that the other two understand as well."

He closed his phone and looked at Larry.

"You're early?"

"Yeah, one of those overseas call centre's woke me up at nine o'clock and I couldn't get back to sleep again. I have too many of Sudovich's numbers in my head. What's happening here?"

"It would seem that someone else is interested in Kane. Shane says that a car pulled up outside the engineering shop at about one thirty this morning and had a look at the place for some minutes."

*****

In the old days, Ben would have been more economical with his man power. Now in the twenty first century he could put people on the street who could take their office with them. In this case, today, he would put Anderson out on a loose tail to follow Tom Lee, while Rodgers would find out what he could about the transformer crate.

"Laura?"

"Yes?"

"Will you find out where Anderson and Rodgers are please? If they're in the building, have them come to me as soon as possible."

He watched as she lifted her desk phone and cradled it on her shoulder as she continued to work the keyboard of her computer. At his own desk, he wrote two names on a sheet of paper along with some instructions.

As he finished scribbling in his awkward handwriting Laura called. "They're in the building, and they will be here in five minutes or so."

"Right, thank you." He replied as he walked out to her desk and waited some seconds before he presented her with the sheet of paper.

Laura viewed its written contents carefully. She scanned each word before she looked up at him, ready as she had been for nearly half of her life to hear his instructions. There was of course the decryption of his written word to discuss.

"As soon as you are able," he said, "I'd like you to find access to British army records. See if there's any information on a mercenary whose name is Horton. He served with the British army in the early 1970's, and I think he was dishonorably discharged by the mid 1970's. If you can find out his full name, will you put in a request to Interpol for any up to date information they might have on him? I've written the best physical description available to me," he added as he pointed to the sheet of paper in her hands.

She looked back at him as a lightly dimpled smile touched her face. "Well there couldn't have been too many people in the British army at that time named Horton."

Ben smiled back at her as he thought; she's doing it to me again.

At various times during the eighteen years she'd been his personal secretary, she'd deliver what sounded like a carefully crafted sentence, while at the same time showing a sweet smile. Ben never knew if the smile represented a small amount of sarcasm, or whether it was that she really did see everything in the light of simplicity. He was certain he'd go into retirement without ever knowing.

Some minutes later Anderson and Rodgers arrived to stand before his desk; Ben greeted them, suggesting they sit.

"Rodney, do you remember a man by the name of Steve Walters?"

"Yes, Sir. He was questioned in connection with an insider trading investigation. Stock market corruption, wasn't it?"

"Yes, that's him. Well he's back in the country, and he's the new owner of an engineering shop in Alexandria." Ben paused to sip his coffee before adding, "He may have no connection to what I'm about to tell you, so we'll put him aside for now and I'll come back to him in a moment."

Ben took the conversation off in another direction.

"About five weeks ago, there were two murders near the outback town of Bourke. The two people killed, were friends of the man presumed dead after a boat explosion at sea last Tuesday. This yachtsman's name was Simon West, and I've learnt over the week-end from an informant, that he intercepted over thirty million U.S dollars that was destined for..." Ben smiled at the two men before finishing, "Garry Sudovich."

Alan Rodgers repeated the surname in a way similar to Seinfeld when he spoke of Newman.

"He's never going to go away is he Boss?" Anderson reflected.

Ben grinned at him.

"Well at least he lingers in name only." Ben joked before he got back to business.

"The story goes that Sudovich had a thing going with a crook in the Sierra Leone Government, who would ensure payment for bogus bills supplied by Sudovich. Apparently West got into the act somehow and ripped the pair of them off, at the cost of two of his friends, one of them being his girlfriend. West's death on Tuesday is being treated as a homicide, and if he was murdered because of his connection to the money; it suggests to me that the thirty million is still about and maybe even close at hand."

He sipped more coffee.

"I also learned over the weekend, that Sudovich had a silent partner in the form of one Tom Lee."

"Makes you wonder which one was slumming doesn't it?" Anderson mused as he lightly punched his other open hand.

"Well the partnership has been broken now. The thing is, my informant told me what plans West had for the money, and I would like to know if it got to where it was supposed to. If it didn't, then who has it? That's my unofficial question. If Lee, who we now know was Sudovich's financier, happened to get his grubby paws on it, he may have left a paper trail. If so, we might get a chance to knock Lee off his perch. My official question is, is Sudovich Holdings a working enterprise, or is it just a means by which Lee launders his drug money?"

"There might not be anything at all in this," he continued, "But there was a probable murder last Tuesday which may be connected to the thirty million. Sudovich was definitely connected to the thirty million. Tom Lee is connected to Sudovich, so he might also be connected to the thirty million. If Lee is connected to the thirty million, then it might be considered he's also connected to the three murders which came about during the acquisition of that money."

"There's a lot of ifs and maybes, Sir." Rodgers stated the obvious.

"I know there's a lot of ifs and maybes Al, but when it comes to Lee, I'll take any clue however slender it may be."

"Where do you think Walters fits in boss?" Anderson asked.

"I'm not sure he does, Rodney. It may just be by coincidence that he's operating his new business venture out of a building leased by him from Sudovich Holdings. Walters may, or may not be in league with Lee, I don't know. If he's not, then we'll find out about it as we go along. If he is, then I'd like to know how he is connected to Lee. Walters arrived in Australia about four weeks before Sudovich's death, and he's in one of Sudovich's buildings. It might all just be coincidental and not come to anything, but you never know until you've had a look, and that's what I want you to do."

Ben drained his now near cold coffee and picked up a copy of the customs sheet from his desk.

"There is also this."

He handed the paper to Rodgers who viewed it before handing it onto Anderson.

"It's a high voltage electrical transformer and the only thing imported by Sudovich Holdings in the last five years," Ben continued. "Well the only legal thing anyway. Walters spent the year prior to his arrival back in Australia in England, and this transformer was imported into Australia from England. More coincidence? Why would Sudovich import a transformer, surely there are manufacturers within Australia?"

"Alan, I want you to check out this transformer. Find out the carrier who picked it up at the shipping yards and where they delivered it to." Ben handed him a photocopy of the customs sheet. "I think we might assume it went to Grey St. If so, did it go there directly, or was it off loaded somewhere else first? It might be that there's no connection to Walters at all, but if it's a new way they are using to import illegal shit, then we might just gain one more nail to hammer into Lee's coffin. You'd better get onto Customs too. Ask them to tie a bell onto any future imports by Sudovich Holdings, or Walters and keep us informed. It might be good idea to do the same thing with the State Police. Get them to tie a bell to Walters and Lee's names and any of their known associates. I want to be informed of everything from here on in, even if it's just a traffic fine."

"Rodney, find Lee and stay on his tail for today. This might be a good time to get an idea on his movements these days. I've noticed his file hasn't been updated for a while. You might also give the police in Bourke a call. Find out if there have been any new developments. While you're speaking to them, ask them if there is a swimming pool with a concrete surround on the site where the outback murders took place."

"I assume you'd both be interested in some overtime?" Both of the men nodded as Ben continued, "As I said, there may be nothing in this, but I have a feeling there is certainly something afoot."

The two men turned towards the door to leave.

"One other thing," Ben added, "For the time being there'll be just the three of us in the unofficial loop. If anything turns up, then we'll make it an official investigation. Until that time, just poke along quietly."

Rodney Anderson's first task was to check vehicle registrations to find out what type of vehicle Lee was driving. Then after gaining a telephone number for the Bourke Police, he drove to Kings Cross where Lee's club was located.

The street outside the club was busy and he drove through it a few times trying to locate Lee's car. Having no luck, he drove the back lane behind the club.

He found the vehicle easily enough, but while he looked around for somewhere to park his own to discreetly view it, Lee's car began to move off down the lane way.

Anderson couldn't believe his luck; he'd expected a long wait and was happy at the surprise as he turned his car around and followed. Hoping it was Lee who was driving the car, before a frown creased his forehead as a pessimistic thought entered his head, and through it he thought aloud.

"It's probably his bloody mechanic taking the car to the garage or something." It was a thought that proved groundless, unless the garage was on the north shore. The path the car's driver was taking could only lead to Sydney's Harbour Bridge, and very soon Anderson was paying the bridge toll.

A space of four cars behind Lee was good for surveillance and he stayed at that distance until Lee reduced speed. Finally motoring slowly, as its driver searched for a parking place near a North Sydney Post Office. Anderson found a parking space nearby. It was not the best of places for observation he thought, before he decided he would venture a little closer on foot. Walking to a small coffee shop whose window gave a clear view of Lee's car.

Shortly after he'd seated himself with his coffee and a cake, he saw a man alight from the passenger side of Lee's car and walk across the road to the Post Office.

Anderson reached into his coat pocket and brought out his camera. The light of the day ensured a good photo opportunity when the man returned to Lee's car.

It may take some time he thought. The man loitered around the Post Box area, where it seemed to Anderson he watched every woman who entered. He paid little attention to the men who went in to check their mail, and no attention to the people who went into the Post Office itself. It appeared the man was waiting for someone to turn up, but wasn't sure if he knew who he was expecting.

It finally occurred to Anderson that the man was watching to see who would open a particular Post Office private box. A suggestion the man knew the box number, but not the person who owned the box

Upon finishing his light meal, he left the coffee shop, crossed the road and entered the Post Office.

He considered his police business important enough reason to disregard the ropes on chrome poles, and proceed directly to the counter. Some moments later a staff member approached him. She began to speak, but went silent upon seeing his Police identification open on the counter top between his cupped hands.

She looked at the I.D wallet as he spoke quietly.

"My name is Rodney Anderson, and I'm a detective with the Australian Federal Police." The woman looked up from the card as he went on, "I need to know if you have a security camera that views the Post Office private box area?"

The woman looked him in the eye.

"Yes, we have," she said.

Anderson looked back at her and asked if he might be able to see the Post Master.

"Of course, you can use this door," she replied as she walked to the access door and unlocked it, "I will take you through to him."

Anderson waited a moment before the locked door opened. He followed the woman to an office, where a round man with a shaven head, smiling eyes and an intelligent looking face sat behind a much cluttered desk. After introducing himself to Mr. McGirr, he explained what he wanted. Five minutes later he saw through the lens of the security camera, the man he'd followed who was still loitering around the private box area.

As McGirr showed him how the camera could be zoomed in, Anderson found he could read the box numbers quite clearly, and he began to note the people associated with them. Zooming in on the number first, and then closely observing the person's face. He would not know if the right person had turned up, until the man he'd followed gave him some sign of his own success.

The security cameras tape would accompany him when he left the Post Office as Ben would want to see it, and the Federal technicians would want to lift some still photographs from it.

About an hour later the man left the private box area, and Anderson felt a feeling in his gut that he had missed something. The feeling passed some moments later when another man arrived in the post box area. Anderson relaxed a little as he zoomed in on the new man's face, immediately recognizing Tom Lee.

He zoomed out, and watched as Lee walked halfway along the private box room, to where he stopped and looked carefully at the black doors of the post boxes. Anderson could not know which number Lee had looked at, but he had a fair idea of the area of the wall where Lee's attention had been directed. As Lee walked slowly back to the entrance way and looked out into the street. Anderson took advantage of the situation, rotating the camera so that its lens was pointed to the area where Lee had shown interest.

His first attempt at maneuvering the joystick was a little heavy handed and the camera moved too far. When he moved it back to the right again, a strip of the mesh cage the security camera was housed in, imposed a dark shadow down the centre of the screen.

With one more slight adjustment he was satisfied, and zoomed into a point where he could read the numbers clearly. It quickly became obvious that these particular boxes were the larger type reserved for businesses who expected volumes of mail.

Anderson was on the verge of zooming back out, when suddenly a hand with a key in it appeared in the lower corner of the screen. It moved to a box, and hovered momentarily before the key it held slid into the keyhole of number 169. Anderson quickly zoomed out, and saw clearly a young woman on the black and white screen.

He was a little disappointed that he could not see her face clearly, but almost at the same time he felt a sudden elation. Lee, who was silhouetted in the entrance way by the outside daylight, left the room.

Anderson waited until the woman had also left the room. He pressed the STOP and the EJECT button on the video machine, and with the tape in his hand he walked quickly to the Post Master's office.

Mr. McGirr was behind his desk and looked up from his work as Anderson appeared at his door:

"Mr. McGirr, I need all the information that you have on the business, and anyone associated with the business box number 169. If you can get that for me, I'll be back shortly."

He made his way to the locked door at the end of the Post Office front counter and let himself out. Doubting he would attract any attention from the customers. To them he was just another postal person, but he felt the eyes of the Post Office staff on him as he walked to the glass entrance doors and stopped before them. Anderson wasn't sure which way the young woman had gone, but he knew that Lee and his partner would unwittingly give him directions.

He looked down the street; sure that Lee would be back to his car by now. His thought was confirmed by Lee's partner, who was at that moment passing the Post Office and walking up the street.

Anderson halted his progress in order to open the door for a lady with a pram, who wanted to exit the building. Glad to have a valid reason to let Lees partner get a little further ahead. He helped carry the pram down the front steps, and by the time he had done so, the partner was about ten metres further on. At the same time, a quick look down the street showed that Lee was having trouble breaking into the traffic. Anderson could see his turn indicator flashing, and knew that even when Lee got into the traffic he would still have to do a U turn.

He set off after the partner; sure that Lee would be occupied for at least the next five minutes.

After some minutes walking, the partner slowed to a halt and dawdled momentarily outside an office block, before moving towards the street to stand on the edge of the roadway.

Anderson moved toward a council footpath bench, where he waited until Lee's car came into sight, and for the partner to quickly cross the street on its arrival. As Lee's car slowed down, he opened its passenger door and hopped in.

Then Anderson watched as Lees car passed down the street, waiting some minutes before it came back into sight on his side of the road. Its turn indicator came on, suggesting that a parking place had been found just near the office block. He was sure the two of them would bide their time and watch for when the woman finished work for the day, in an effort to find out her home address.

Anderson was sure he had that already, and her name.

Both pieces of information would be on the Post Office box application form, along with address of the office block that the woman went into.

As he walked back to the Post Office, he decided he would go to the woman's address and just wait for Lee to follow her home. While he was waiting he could call up the local police at Bourke, and get them to forward any new information they had on the outback murders.

The girl who escorted him through to Mr. McGirr's office was younger than the first. More his own age, and proof that a good day could get better.

*****

Beth and Lynnette emerged from a residential car park below a small block of flats in a quiet suburban street. Lee waited until the two women disappeared behind the closed door of a first floor flat before he left his car. He crossed the road, and Larry watched as he made his way up the stairs to knock on the door they'd disappeared through.

The older woman answered the door, and Larry wondered what Lee had said to her, for her jaw seemed to drop before Lee stepped through the doorway forcing her to step back and out of Larry's sight.

Lee turned and beckoned to Larry to follow, and as Larry left the car to walk across the road, he hoped to himself that this wasn't going to go badly.

He knew Lee's temper.

*****

Anderson saw the two men go into the flat. Something of the gentleman in him shouted loudly in his mind to go and help these damsels in distress, but the detective in him shouted louder and he waited.

He knew from Ben's informant that Lee was after the thirty million dollars. There was no way that that amount of money was in the flat, so the women's lives were not at risk, as Lee would need them to help him retrieve it.

It's probably in the Sarah-Ray Foundation he thought, it was where the Post Office box was addressed, and Lee would have to devote a bit of time to acquire it. He would be up in the flat now, bullying, and probably frightening shit out of the two women in an attempt to find out the best way of going about it.

While he waited he called in the registration number of the B.M.W the two women had arrived in. He was not overly surprised when he learned the vehicle registration carried a Bourke address.

Anderson waited for a half hour, and as the seconds ticked by he was plagued by the thought that his reasoning might have been wrong.

Finally the flat door opened, and the man he didn't recognize stepped out. Lee followed, and with raised pointed finger, threw some final words through the open doorway, before he walked toward the stair way to the ground level.

Some minutes later, after Lee's car disappeared down the road Anderson climbed the stairs and tapped on the flat door.

He'd dealt with enough scared people in his time to know, to stand well back from the door and not crowd them.

This he did, while at the same time holding his warrant card forward towards the lens of the peep hole in the door.

A moment later the door opened, although this time held by a security chain. The younger of the two women, the one who had retrieved the mail from Post Office was a natural beauty. No makeup and her brown eyes flashed like polished bronze as she looked out into the afternoon sunlight.

"Who are you?" She asked.

Anderson held his identification card closer, and was fascinated as he watched her face as she viewed it.

"My name is Rodney Anderson," he answered after some delay, "I'm a detective with the Australian Federal Police. I'd like to, if I may, come in and talk to you about the two men who just left here?" She looked a little unsure as she glanced at his I.D card again, before she released the security chain to allow the door to open fully.

Anderson walked through a small hallway to the sitting room where Beth was seated. She held a handkerchief in her hand, with which she dabbed her eyes. He reckoned her to be thirty years old, but she looked a little more than that at this moment.

"Are you alright? I mean, other than that you are obviously upset?" She looked up at him at the first part of the question with a look of incredulity. It lasted until he finished the second part of the question, at which her face softened and she nodded.

He looked at Lynette. Her face was set with a determination that suggested to Anderson, she was not going to allow herself to be upset. Strong girl he thought, or maybe she'd been down similar roads before at the hands of men.

Beth was bringing herself back to composure and he introduced himself before he asked:

"Those two men, was their visit connected in any way to a man by the name of Simon West?" Anderson felt almost at a loss as the older woman suddenly convulsed.

A single sob, which sounded to him like it escaped from her very soul. She seemed to quiver a moment, as she hunched over with the handkerchief pressed firmly to her eyes.

The younger woman's look of grim determination was suddenly replaced with a softer sadder face, as she moved to the older woman's side to console her.

He knew then, that whoever Simon West was, he had touched both of these people, and that the time since his death had not been long enough for them to get through their grieving.

Now he did feel at a loss and the unusual feeling of uncertainty stayed for some seconds, until he reached into his pocket and retrieved his mobile phone. He glanced at the women again as he waited for an answer, and then turned away from them to talk quietly.

"Boss, I am in the company of our link to Bourke," Anderson said as he walked into the women's kitchen, feeling better able to speak freely there. He spoke for some minutes, explaining briefly the events that led up to this moment before asking, "Shall I bring them in?"

Anderson listened as Ben replied, and then finished the conversation. "O.K, I'll expect you then."

He returned to the sitting room where the two women were seated. "I've just spoken to my Boss and he wants to speak to you personally so he's coming over here. We may have to wait an hour or so, as the Bridge traffic will be heavy by now." Unsure as to what to say next he asked, "Can I make you a cup of tea or coffee?"

A short time later with three coffees he returned to the sitting room and made small talk in an effort to try to calm them, so they'd be easier for Ben to question when he arrived.

The pleasure was his, when after he'd seen fear, anger, determination, softness and sadness on the younger woman's face; he was finally able to witness the slight smile which at last crept to her lips.

He sipped his coffee and was content in his waiting.

CHAPTER 9

John Kane and Barney had spent their Monday afternoon in an old warehouse overseeing the erection of a newly purchased prefabricated room.

They, and the other members of their Australian team referred to it as 'the room', mainly because of the reason they'd given to its manufacturer. A small prefabrication company in Hurstville, who believed they were manufacturing a dust room, a clean, dust free enclosure for rebuilding electric motors.

'The room' automatically became its code word.

It measured three metres by three metres and one point nine metres high. It had enough floor space inside to house the transformer, a small table and ample walk space between the two.

The bottom half of each wall was made of light weight timber paneling, while the top half of each wall was filled with windows of clear Perspex sheeting. It was designed to give a visual access of three hundred and sixty degrees. Each wall was made up of three panels whose rubber lined edges slotted together. A folded hinged roof was easily lifted by the two men over one wall, and unfolded in place on the top of the room. A smaller panel of Perspex was designed to be the doorway.

The two members of the Australian team, who were to transport the room and erect it at its inspection site, had been living in Sydney for some weeks. Kane had instructed them upon their arrival in the country, that due to the unexpected delay they should find work and live in the immediate area close to the transformer storage building.

His reason being they stood more chance of going unnoticed by being obvious. Already they were being recognized in local shops, fuel stations and of course the local pub.

To the locals in the pub they were known as the pommy bastards, while the people in the stores and on the street identified them as Rob and Robert. These were the names on their forged British passports. Names chosen with the idea it might confuse anyone investigating them, if of course, that situation ever arose.

They were big men who handled the panels with ease. Their first attempt in the room's erection had taken them nearly thirty minutes. Then they'd decided between them to number each panel with a small brush and white paint.

Dismantling the room, they erected it again and then repeated the process three more times. Deciding that in placing the roof onto the wall top at one end before installing the wall in the other end, its erection was made easier and somewhat quicker.

For the fourth erection they were instructed by Kane to load the room back onto the truck, and then unload it again. Carry it back to its erection site where, with their previous practice and the numbering system they put it together in less than twenty minutes.

These practice sessions were necessary for when the time came for the room to serve its purpose, neither of the two men knew where the actual event would take place. Any given location could change at a moment's notice.

So each of the practice runs were carried out with that knowledge in mind. When the real time came, they might be working at night, under poorly lit conditions, in unfamiliar surroundings and possibly against the clock. Although it was understood that if everything went according to plan, then this warehouse was the ideal location. Everything needed for a successful outcome was in this one place, and in one place was the safest place.

Kane knew that moving the transformer truck outside this warehouse even once risked being observed, and it was a risk he'd rather not take. He'd held a similar view about himself and Barney.

They had restricted themselves to routine and had stayed within the boundaries of that routine. Today they had stepped over the boundary by coming to this building, but when they left this place today they would never return.

Kane knew that when the advertising campaign began, his own and Barney's movements could be under close scrutiny. Knowing this, gave him the power to lead whoever was assigned to keep him under observation to wherever he wished. He understood that in the days to come, there would be many people invested in the search for the transformer. and those suspected of association with it.

If he and Barney were to be under a twenty-four-hour observation as he suspected, then he would be in the position to lead at least six observers away from the transformer building.

In that case, it should follow that if he and Barney split up, then the two of them should be able to tie up twice that amount, maybe more.

The same would also apply to Steve Walters.

All they had to do to tie up valuable police resources was to stay at home and watch T.V.

The transformer was still loaded on the first truck which had received it outside the Liverpool building site. It was easy to quickly unload with the fork lift truck which was at the rear of the load tray. The space between the transformer and the fork lift truck was enough to accommodate the timber and Perspex panels. A steel tool box had been welded to the underside of the truck to contain the aquarium.

Barney had marked out an area the exact size of the transformer on the floor inside the room with a piece of chalk. He now watched as Robert was in the act of placing a small fold up camp table on the floor close by the nearest chalk line.

With the table in place Robert walked around it and decided there was ample room to move.

Walk space was an absolute necessity when the demonstration took place, as the person inside the room would be restricted by a bulky HazChem suit.

Rob took a cardboard carton from the trucks tray top and carried it into the room. He lifted from it a medium sized glass indoor fish aquarium which he placed onto the table. It was a normal everyday fish aquarium, similar to any other that might be found in schoolroom, office or home except for three rather indistinct changes.

Its Perspex lid was fixed in place with adhesive, which undoubtedly made the act of inserting fish impossible.

Accommodation for this was made with the second change in its design.

That being a ninety millimetre hole cut into the affixed top. Over this hole there was glued in place a ninety millimetre inside diameter threaded flange. It was through this flange that wildlife of choice could be inserted. A threaded bung was then to be screwed into the flange, thus leaving them alone in an air tight environment.

The third change was a smaller hole of perhaps four millimetres in diameter. It had a patch of Latex pulled taut and set in place over it. He tested the table's stability by holding the aquarium by two of its corners and rocking it gently back and forth.

Satisfied with its support he reached into his pocket and produced a child's plastic pencil case and a tube of super glue.

There was difficulty in removing the tubes cap because of the leather gloves he wore, so he removed them and pulled on close fitting surgical gloves.

Kane watched as Rob glued the plastic pencil case to the aquariums lid, where it would hold a set of two Pasteur pipettes. One was for immediate use during the demonstration and a second for use as a spare.

Pasteur pipettes are a common piece of equipment used in laboratories and are similar to the everyday eye dropper. They are designed for disposal and are around two hundred millimetres long.

Barney brought the pipettes to the table, where Rob, after accepting them, placed them without their rubber caps into the pencil case. He then took from Barney a small tin with a hinged lid, and with the aid of more adhesive, he glued it onto the inside base of the pencil case, so it sat with easy availability with the pipettes.

Some minutes later he lifted the tins lid and carefully removed one of the rubber caps. It took effort to fight off his basic human impulse to squeeze it, like it might when pressing an OUT OF ORDER button or touching a wall beside a WET PAINT sign. He held back the temptation and instead lifted each of the rubber caps in turn to eye level. Content with what he saw inside of them, he carefully placed the two of them back onto their bed of cotton wool. Finally, he placed a wad of cotton wool over the contents of the pencil case and snapped the pencil case lid closed.

A small hole had appeared in one of his surgical gloves where the glue had burnt through. He removed it and stuffed it into his right side pocket, before tugging a replacement from his top pocket.

The four men had all been wearing overalls, gloves and stretchy beanies since getting into their truck at lunch time. Now as the day warmed they all felt the heat. The gloves were an attempt to remove the possibility of leaving finger prints and the overalls so to not leave traces of clothing. Beanies covered their hair so they'd not leave anything that could be used in D.N.A sampling.

After Robert and Rob had loaded and lashed the panels onto the transformer truck, Kane stood back to view their handy work. He liked what he saw; the truck was light, compact and mobile.

There were only four other trucks like this in the world. One of them was in the Philippines, one in the U.S, another in Canada and one in the U.K. Each one was identical to the others, with its own transformer, forklift truck, room panels and aquarium.

There were four other items necessary for a successful outcome and they were not on the truck. They would remain under wraps until either Robert or Rob brought them to the room at demonstration time.

Three of the four items were definite proof they were conspiring to commit a crime.

As it was now, conspiracy to commit a crime would be hard pressed to prove when the only facts were a transformer, a fork lift truck and a pre-fabricated room.

Kane had always been an extremely careful man. Evidence of this was made apparent once more to Barney, and yet again it reinforced his faith in his boss. Kane's order that the three items only be brought forth just prior to the viewing by potential customers allowed him to feel more at ease. The knowledge, they were as far removed as possible from critical consequences if things went wrong allowed Barney's morale to soar.

Barney had only seen one of the three most important items. That being the spindle he'd made. He did know the other two items were a three hundred millilitre 10X container and an explosive charge.

The detonator spindle had demanded his complete attention with its invention on the lathe. Outside of that experience, explosives were not his business and he didn't like poisons.

Like poisons, the forth item was not dear to him. It being a small cage of inquisitive whisker twitching rats, but he understood they had an important part to play.

Kane had not mentioned to Barney the exact time the campaign would begin, but Barney knew it would be very soon. He could feel it in his gut, and as the thought of it crossed his mind he unconsciously licked his seemingly dry lips.

Kane's voice jerked him back to the present.

"Barney." Barney's train of thought derailed, and he looked to where Kane stood by the side of the transformer truck. "It's suddenly dawning on you, the enormity of what we're about to undertake is it?"

Barney stood silent and gazed at Kane for a moment before he said with a nod of his head.

"Partly I think Boss, but more so the fact that it's about to begin. You know. It's like the first parachute jump. You do all the routine on ground training without any thought about the real event, and then suddenly the day arrives and you're about to board the plane."

"And when you boarded that plane Barney, what did your jump instructor tell you?"

"He said, "Relax and to keep your mind on the business at hand. If anyone wants to change his mind at the exit door, just remember that when you turn around, the first thing you will see is my look of amazement."

As he finished the sentence Barney saw an intrigued look on Kane's face and he laughed as he answered Kane's silent question.

"The story went that Sergeant Smith's look of amazement only came about when someone thought that seeing it would be easier than doing the jump."

"Did anyone ever see this look of amazement?" Kane asked.

"Not that I ever heard, boss."

"Then it would seem to me that what Sergeant Smith was in effect saying was: Relax, keep your mind on the business at hand and remember your fear of the unknown is all in your head."

Barney rubbed his chin and with a thoughtful expression on his face replied:

"You know boss, I never thought of it like that. But now you mention it, it's clearly correct isn't it?"

"I think so Barney." He looked at Robert and then at Rob to make sure they heard what he was to say next, "Keep it in mind because we'll be jumping within the next twenty-four hours."

******

Monday Afternoon

Lee and Larry Barrett were biding their time in traffic which was moving slowly towards the toll gates on Sydney's Harbour Bridge.

Barrett was nose deep in his lap top, while Lee was wondering if he should ring Dan. Ask him to go and keep an eye on the two women in Lane Cove just in case they decided to try to leave town. It was a thought that only lasted a moment, until his eyes rested on the older woman's address book on the dash of his car.

He'd discovered it in the woman's hand bag, and it stated clearly that her mother and her sister lived just a few suburbs across town. Facts which gave his supreme optimism surety that the woman would keep her place.

Lee had learnt at an early age that women kept a lot of interesting bits and pieces in their hand bags. He'd found out then, that a handbag could give instant access to their lives.

It pleased him to be in possession of the keys to other people's vulnerabilities.

He'd been deep in thought about what he had discovered from the older woman's handbag when his mobile phone suddenly rang. It startled him back to a traffic queue reality and he spoke almost absent mindedly into the phone.

"Shane. What's news?" He listened for a moment before saying, "Right mate. Keep on it."

"It would seem that maybe someone's keeping tabs on the engineer's work shop in Grey Street."

Larry looked up from his work.

"Same people who were in the vicinity the other night, do you think?"

"Who they are doesn't concern me as much as, what it is that Kane has that warrants inspection, or even surveillance? I feel sure it has something to do with that wooden crate in his backyard, correction, my back yard." Lee couldn't help the passion that controlled his tone as he rasped out those last three words, "I've got to tell you Larry, I'm a bit worried about where this might go. Damn Sudovich. I hope he's frying in hell right now." Barrett didn't answer and quietly looked at his lap top.

He knew that Lee was mainly pissed off because he needed to be in control. Where Kane was concerned, Lee was far from being in control. He kept his thoughts to himself, because now was not the time to be too talkative to Lee.

Silence is golden, but sometimes silence is just plain safe.

Personally he wasn't worried about Kane, or the wooden box. He could keep himself at arm's length from the whole affair.

On the other hand, he was concerned about who those were who concerned themselves with Kane. If it was the law, then they were as close to Lee as they had been for some time. Not because of their own doing though, he thought. It appeared that they may have had a stroke of luck.

If Kane's business dealings at Grey Street were going to be investigated, then Lee's association with the business premises would probably be enough to warrant legal access to Lee's affairs. If that happened, then even if the law didn't find anything on Lee, they could create so much turmoil that Lee's business operations could go into free fall over night.

Larry liked to fly high on Lee's wings, but he did some serious thinking when, at times, it appeared some feathers might be working loose. He made a mental note to get in touch with Moot the forger and have him bring his second passport up to date.

Twenty first century transport held the key to keeping most affairs at arm's length.

CHAPTER 10

10pm Monday

John Kane slid a single phone card from the small pack he carried with him at all times. He reckoned with a cursory glance he still had about six hundred dollars' worth of credit.

As he stood by his choice of public pay phones, he dragged his fingers across the end of the pack. Listening to a memory, as the sound reminded him of his childhood, when the small piece of cardboard clipped to the frame of his push bike brushed his bicycles spokes as he rode along. His thoughts were interrupted by a group of young people who were walking down the street towards him. He saw they shared a bottle of alcohol and two of them carried a coke bottle each. He hoped they weren't looking for trouble.

Kane had been missing his martial arts training due to his current work program. He might be a little rusty, but he didn't want to hurt anyone and after all there were only five of them. As it was, their talk and friendly banter went silent as they approached and they passed in silence. There came a mutter from one of them, and there was laughter at the obvious joke.

More than likely at his expense Kane thought. He watched them go before pulled at his shirt sleeve and checked his watch.

It was time.

He turned into the phone box, and after inserting a card he keyed the number, then waited for some thirty seconds before he said:

"Hello. It's me. Is that you?"

"Yes, it's me. Is that you?" Letts replied.

"Yes, it's me."

"How's tricks?" Kane asked.

"All's well. The blueprints and the evidence will be placed in the workshop at two thirty tomorrow morning my time. The copies of the blueprints and the design documents are ready to go out to the media."

"Good. Everything's moving smoothly here. Our excess will be moved tonight and the losses will be reported to the proper authorities at ten o'clock tomorrow morning our time."

"O.K. I will see to it that the authorities here are notified about the workshop. The documents will be delivered at ten o'clock tomorrow morning our time. I think that will work out alright. It should make Wednesday morning's newspapers, your time. I will also enlighten our colleagues that zero hour is 10am May seven, Sydney time."

That was it, the culmination of all their work had finally come about. There seemed to be little else to say and the two men lapsed into silence, each for a moment alone with their thoughts.

They'd both been here before. They'd seen war and they understood perfectly the darkness before the dawn and the quiet before the storm.

"Feels like up country work, doesn't it?" Letts broke the silence.

"Yeah mate. I'll see you on the other side." Kane answered.

"Will do." Letts agreed.

Kane put his hand piece down and stepped out of the phone box. Barney waited in the driver' seat of the car and Kane brought him up to date as he slid into its passenger seat.

"Well it's go time Barney. We report our loss to the police at ten o'clock tomorrow morning," he said as he buckled his seatbelt. "Get in touch with Jerrod will you? Tell him we'll need the little van on site at 0300. Remind him that the security man does his last round between three and three thirty, and that he should wait out of sight until he sees him leave. You might suggest to him it would be a good idea to put the winch battery on the battery charger until he's ready to leave, just in case."

Barney started the car and pulled it into gear.

"What do you want to do now, boss?" He asked.

"I think we might pull into the Chinese restaurant near our digs and have a feed eh? There's a phone there and you can contact Jerrod. While we're there we'll get something to take away. We might find ourselves a little peckish by three o'clock. After that we should get some shut eye. We've a long night ahead of us, and we need to be in good shape when we turn up at the workshop at nine o'clock in the morning."

*****

Letts stayed with the telephone and made calls to each of the operational team leaders in Washington, Manila and Toronto. His last call was to a local London number.

Quietly and directly, he informed each of those who answered the phone that 'zero hour is ten hundred hours May seven, Sydney time.'

After listening for the time and date to be repeated back to him, he terminated each call without any more conversation, other than a brief good luck. He then delved his hand into the carry all bag which sat on the floor beside him and withdrew from it a satellite phone. While he allowed it to rest in his lap he lifted the carry all itself and turned it inside out.

His fingers slid easily under the stiff loose flap which gave the bottom of the bag its packing base. With lifted flap he could see with the aid of a small torch a list of numbers written on the flaps underside. Beside each of the numbers were code words which should correspond with those given by the sales rep who answered his call.

The first number was to the sales rep in the Ukraine, the second was answered by an accented man in Saudi Arabia, the third Syria, the fourth in the Philippines, the fifth in the U.S., the sixth in Canada, the seventh in Egypt, the eighth in Pakistan, the ninth in Lebanon and a tenth to the sales team leader in the U.K.

To each of these sales team leaders he gave the time and date of zero hour. After hearing them repeated back to him he terminated the call without further conversation.

Letts had no idea who the people were he'd spoken to. His knowledge that Athol had chosen each of the sales teams personally for these in country tasks was all he needed to know.

He was content with that.

*****

The sales team leader in Syria had been, like most of his colleagues, in country for ten days and he'd been successful in his advertising campaign. A success partly due to the fact that he, like most of his colleagues had lived and worked in, or In some cases had been natives of the countries they were now working.

He'd emigrated from Syria to the U.K eight years earlier, had completed a University degree and experienced the Western lifestyle.

Now he was back in his native country. In a city he knew well and using a language which flowed easily from his lips.

His present occupation was not one he could possibly have envisaged as the young Syrian. He'd fled to the West and a better life all those years before, and had learnt the meaning of freedom of choice.

That freedom of choice had, in a roundabout way, brought him home again. Not as a holiday maker, or even as a prodigal son, but as a salesman for a weapon of mass destruction.

He'd hit the ground running on his return and it had not taken long to look up contacts from the old days, where some of whom offered contacts of their own.

It took little persuading to draw in those with extreme views, even less when they understood their chance to gain a weapon of mass destruction. Particularly one which would be ready to fire off at their will once they had paid the auction price, and to date he'd snared three interested parties. Each had demanded proof of the existence of such a weapon, and he had been expert in his gentle persuasion. Allowing each of the parties to understand he would soon bring them proof. Inform their servants, his contacts, and they would bring to their masters the news that enlightenment was close at hand. He had wondered at the limit of their patience. Not as yet to the point of worry, but now as the call had come from Letts, he felt a sense of relief, and security in the knowledge that the hardest part was over.

Under normal circumstances the hardest part would be to relieve them of the weight of their purses, but he knew that on this occasion he had something their passion demanded. A light smile played about his lips as he made the first of three calls, and it lingered briefly until he got down to business.

"Yes, my friend, it is me," he spoke quietly, "It is time to take news to your master. Tell him he should watch the B.B.C news tomorrow morning. He will have the proof he seeks."

*****

Tom Lee was in a restless sleep at three thirty on Tuesday morning. Thoughts of the man Kane had clouded his usually clear mind, and had overcome his quiet jubilation at the prospect of access to Sudovich's lost fortune. Lee, like most humans when they worried about an issue, envisaged a worst case scenario. The worst case scenario for him at this time was the downfall of his empire, or imprisonment.

Or both, he thought wearily as he pulled the palm of his hand across his furrowed forehead. This worry regarding Kane was not the whole reason for his restlessness though.

If it had been he would have used his discipline and simply put it out of his mind. Like any other problem that might arise during the normal course of his working week. The main reason was the crate, or rather, what had been in the crate.

His frustration at not knowing the contents of the crate, and his inability to scratch its itch of curiosity pulled at him. His feelings of helplessness seemed to forge together against him. Until his mental fabric was torn to shreds and his incomplete thoughts churned into chaotic confusion. He got out of his bed and walked to the kitchen in search of something to drink. As he opened the door of the refrigerator, his eyes came into contact with one of the advertising pamphlets which hung behind magnets on the outside of the door.

As the door swung out and past his face he registered the words TAKEAWAY & DELIVERY.

Lee closed the door and looked at the pamphlet and spoke to himself as he stared at the words.

"Takeaway and delivery, takeaway and delivery." He thought a moment before saying the words again, this time swapping them around, "Delivery and takeaway." Of course, he thought. That's the answer, and to hell with Kane. "The crate was imported by Sudovich Holdings and I am Sudovich Holdings. Which means that the box belongs to me and what belongs to me I can take away. So tomorrow I'll drive into my yard at Grey Street, pick up my box and take it away. If nothing else happens, I should at least get a reaction from Kane and force the issue. He won't be in a position to go crook about it. He can't call the police because he's up to his neck in something and he won't want to draw attention to himself. All he will be able to do is negotiate and we'll negotiate on my terms. It's brilliant."

Lee was suddenly happy with the relief he felt. Once again he was in control and he danced across the kitchen as he laughed out loud.

"It's my box John Kane, so stick that up your big nose."

His frivolity had woken his young wife from a private dream. Lingering images left her body warm within and she felt an urge to fan the flame.

Lee entered the bedroom and she sat up in bed and watched him. He stepped a dance step across the bedroom's carpeted floor, singing as he went:

"It's my box, cha cha. It's my box, cha cha." As he came to the edge of their bed she moved over to his side and met him.

She'd learnt through her experience with him, that when he was in this mood, it was the best time for her to put forward a physical proposal. This was the man she'd married for her convenience, and as he smiled at her she felt the warmth become more heated deep down in her belly. She reached out her hand to where he stood beside their bed, and cupped him through the loose soft cloth pajamas. As she did, she felt the weight in the sack begin to rise as its excess skin was drawn up to accommodate the expansion of a slowly heating erection.

As it did, it escaped the pajamas open front. She watched, fascinated as it pulsated and grew not six inches before her wide open eyes. She didn't have to touch it, not yet. She leaned forward until it was near the tip of her nose and she could see clearly, the taut, stretched rose-red skin.

Finally, when it seemed that it was fully erect, she gave its head a quick flick with the tip of her tongue and it gave one more spasm like jump. She knew then it was as pumped as it was going to get. Until it gets into some place a little warmer, she thought.

She gave it another quick light flick for good measure, and as she rose up on her knees she allowed one of her breasts to brush its blood engorged end and it gave another spasm. Slipping down her panties, she lay back on her bended knees. They parted and she became even more excited when she realized how wet she was. She was hungry for the pleasure shaft which stood erect before her. The heated, hard stem her pussy was begging her to take, to envelope and drain its loving spoonful. She slid a finger between her open and ready vulva.

Touching gently her blood engorged clitoris. Just once, before she had to make herself stop. Too much would surely take her over her orgasmic edge. Instead she ran her fingers through her matted growth of pubic hair and looked up at Lee with slitted glowing eyes as she purred to him:

"This is your box Tom, my man. Come to me."

Tom Lee was ready to oblige and he reached down to his bedside table to unload the glass of water. As his hand left the glass his mobile phone suddenly rang out.

A split second after the phones first bleating sound she whispered with a pleading tone.

"Don't answer it Tom, I need you now. Please.

Lee had automatically picked up the phone by the time it had made its third sound.

"Shane. What's happening?"

Shane spoke to him with a voice coarse with the sound of exaggerated whisper:

"Boss, it's the big box. Someone's stealing it."

Lee's voice sounded loud as he demanded.

"What?"

Sally watched as the colour of the hardness slowly faded and the shine of the stretched skin began to disappear. She moved toward it and took it into her hand, trying to massage it back to life, but she felt disappointment spread to her belly when it began to soften.

"No, no, no," she cried quietly to herself.

"Boss, a small van pulled up outside the gate a few minutes ago. A bloke got out of it and used bolt cutters on the lock. Then they drove in and reversed up to the big box. They're winching it into the van now."

Lee couldn't believe what he was hearing. No words came from his lips which moved until he clutched at the only straw available.

"Follow it."

"But boss, we're locked in and our car is a street away. By the time..."

Lee interrupted him.

"Well, follow it on foot then, at least to the highway. See whether it heads out of town or back into town. Do bloody something." Shane broke the connection and for a moment Lee stood staring at the far wall with his dick hanging out. Slowly his face screwed up in fury. He cursed loudly until he turned and punched the wall at the head end of the bed.

He looked around for some clothes and quickly pulled them on, even though he had no idea what it was he could do. As he left the room he called to Sally:

"I've got to go."

Sally didn't look at him. She opened the drawer by her side of the bed and withdrew from it her vibrator as she called after him with a snarl.

"Piss off."

Lee heard her and through his confusion he whispered, "Women."

Sally lay back in her bed and inserted the thick end of the vibrator. Her own wetness allowed a smooth entry and she welcomed its presence. She found the power switch and suddenly felt a muscle-tensing urge to scream when the machine whimpered as it dragged the last of the energy from its batteries.

The moment had passed. There would be no satisfaction this night and she withdrew the plastic utensil. It held her gaze for a short moment before she told it scornfully.

"Fuck you too!"

She threw it onto the carpeted floor where it bounced once before ending its travel against the painted skirting board. A final glance at it gave her at least a small sense of gladness in that it didn't break. Her fingers curled into small fists as she buried her head into her pillow and tried to cry. Hoping that that emotion might at least, lessen her heated frustration. Thoughts that came to her from nowhere spun uncontrollably through her head, and for what seemed to be a long time she was wide awake and aware. Suddenly a picture formed in her mind and she mentally relived moments of only some days past that were still warm within her memory.

An X rated memory, she thought. Visions of a big man with a big heart and a big manhood became the focus of her mind's eye. She visualized the memory she had of his extended organ. Remembering clearly the moment when she had looked down between their two bodies. Seeing what was about to invade her, and watching its glistening head disappear. The shaft growing gradually shorter as it slid up and into her.

The thought of it hastened her hand, as it automatically and seemingly with a mind of its own moved down and across her belly. She felt a tingling sensation which announced the contact of her fingers with her downy pubic nest. She knew then, that all was not lost. Soon she would have cause for, and would claim the sleep that was deservedly hers.

Soon after she'd used her fingers to exorcise the demon frustration from her loins she would sleep, and in that sleep she would dream of the big man who'd promised her he'd sever her bond to Lee. Sever the bond to the man who could give to her what she materially wanted, but failed to deliver what she physically needed.

Sally's idea of the perfect man was one who didn't belt her around. One who also had enough money to support her in the manner to which she'd grown accustomed. At the same time, he had to be ready to deliver to her physical demands when her need arose.

She didn't love men; only saw them as a necessary evil. Like an accessory which is designed to make life easier. They were all much the same, with their only difference being their bank account and their performance in bed. She didn't care much about what they looked like, or their age. Life was short and you grabbed whatever you could get your hands on. As a woman's body was only supple and firm for so long, one grabbed as quick as one was able.

The big man was a gentleman and he was considerate in her bed. Unfortunately, he lacked somewhat on the financial side, but he had promised her that there was a big plan about to come to fruition, and when it did he would sever her ties with Lee. It was a promise she didn't cling to. She'd heard every promise known to man and had learnt that promises were just words. Words were worth nothing until with time they became real enough to be seen and touched, and of course spent.

Her father had taught her early in her life that promises were just words. Used by some men as a weird form of self-justification after they had taken what they wanted, and were unable to apologize because an apology was an admission of guilt. So they offered promises instead. As time went by the promises stopped and they were soon replaced by threats. These were better in a way because they were, to her, closer to an apology.

The threats were most certainly admissions of guilt. The fear she'd held at the time because of those threats, at least took away from her the thoughts that she was a guilty party.

Sally had reminded herself many times in her life that she was the innocent victim and that her father was the only guilty party.

Many years after the event he had found her and had sought reconciliation. She had watched his shoulders fall and the wretched look in his eyes as she made a promise to him.

"I will promise you one thing. When you die I will come to your funeral and piss on your grave." Sally still found it amusing when she remembered that particular funeral. She'd used a syringe to transfer her urine from to an empty perfume bottle. It carried easily in her hand bag to the cemetery, and while she waited until the service was almost over, until the time when the odd few members of the family threw small handfuls of dirt into the gaping hole in the ground. Then she'd walked to the edge of the grave and held up the small bottle up for all of them to see, before she unscrewed its lid and began to sprinkle its contents onto the satiny lid of the timber coffin.

It had seemed to her at the time that an age passed while the yellow liquid dribbled and spat from the small orifice in the bottle.

When no more liquid would come, she held the bottle up again, and looked into the faces of those who stood near to the grave. Some had smiles of appreciation for the way Sally was showing respect for her father by sprinkling what appeared to be expensive perfume onto the grave.

The small bottle had held their attention for a long moment before she'd spoken out in a clear voice:

"This morning I filled this little bottle with my own urine, because the last time I saw my father I told him I would do for him the same as I would do for any low life paedophile, and piss on his grave." Funerals are usually quiet events, and this one was too until this point in time. In just a short moment, Sally had proved that even quietness can be hushed.

For a short period of time she'd looked into faces which reflected physically the inner feeling of anguish, anger and shock. The silence was finally broken by a sound which brought an expression of surprise to Sally's face. She'd looked aside to see that it was her cousin Jenny who was clapping her hands together. It was followed shortly after by cousin Ruby who clapped harder and faster, as if the act might encourage the demons to leave her with haste. Crest fallen looks appeared on both of her cousin's parent's faces, as the realization hit them of what had gone on before them unnoticed.

Sally had looked down into the hole in the ground before she'd let the small bottle fall from her fingers. It bounced off the lid of the coffin, until it, and its hollow sound disappeared into the darkness between the coffin and the dark earth.

Turning from her father's grave, she had only walked a short way to her car when she had been overtaken by her cousin Jenny. Who with tear laden eyes had thanked her for letting the truth be known. It was at that time, while the two women spoke, that poor Aunt May's knees buckled under her as she fainted and had to be helped back to her car.

Sally's only regret for the day was poor Aunt May. She'd called her by phone after the funeral, and was told by her Uncle Joe who answered the telephone.

"She'll be alright Sally; she's a tough, old bird. Just a bit much for her in one day, I think."

Sally had been unsure as to whether there had been a touch of humour in her Uncle Joe's voice. She had no way of finding out before the phone had been handed to poor Aunt May, who confirmed Uncle Joe's report. She'd not been in search of sympathy from poor Aunt May. Nor did she receive any. She'd come away from the conversation with the feeling that poor Aunt May's lack of understanding, would cause her to push the events of the day deep into the closet. Maybe causing crowd conditions for any other skeletons who might reside there.

Promises were lies, and lies tore at the protective coating of trust.

When the protective coating was tattered, then its inner core became tarnished and lost its lustre. For those whose trust in others had lost its lustre, they became emotionally alone in an effort to find protection against further betrayal.

Alone against the world is how Sally saw herself. She had learnt from experience that anyone who was alone against the world was in need of tools with which to sculpture that cold, hard reality. Sally's most effective tool was her body. A second and almost important tool was the man who wanted her body. Once he was under her spell, he acted as her apprentice, and carved her sculpture for her.

If the big man's plan was successful, then she would hear his bid. After all, his promise to her was only an announcement that he considered himself to be in the running. If his bid was high enough, then she would consider the best way to tackle her only option. Divorce Lee, and take him for what was legally hers.

Thank God for matrimony she thought, surely the surest fire, tax-free investment.

There was one thing that deserved serious consideration. That was the fact she would need protection during the period leading up to the conclusion of that divorce.

Sally felt confident the big man could offer her that. It was a factor in his favour, and it would support him in his bid.

She didn't know the big man's plan, but she knew that even if it didn't come to fruition, then there were other men out there who would be prepared to take his place. It would only be a matter of time before one came forward to offer promise.

Sally reached her peak and came in her hand. The sensation engulfed her, highlighted her body to a state that overwhelmed her mind. To the extent she ceased to exist for some moments. Shortly thereafter she opened her eyes and looked up at the ceiling. Due to its colour in the low light it seemed to be far away, and she made a decision.

Tomorrow she would take Lee's credit card and satisfy her need for revenge by going shopping. It was most certainly her most satisfying form of revenge. A form of revenge she still found profoundly amusing. It proved to her again and again, that no sex cost Lee much more than many men paid to have sex. Sally felt a little thrill. She decided that not only would she go shopping, but she'd also stash a little of Lee's cash into her rainy day account.

Tomorrow she would also make contact with the big man and coyly remind him that promises were made to be kept.

She understood men enough to know that a woman only had to pretend to listen, and a man would talk himself into a corner without any coaxing at all, particularly if he was driven by desire.

"Men!" She said out loud to the ceiling, "Their stupidity is the only thing I can count on." She nestled into her pillow and drifted off to sleep.

CHAPTER 11

Tuesday 4 am.

Lee's mood was just plain rage which prompted him to command his motor car aggressively. It bounded out through slowly opening electrically operated front gates and onto the quiet suburban street. Where its tyres squealed loudly, almost competitively, with its howling high revving engine and offered a combined noise, which would without doubt leave Lee's neighbours less than impressed.

It also alerted an old ginger cat that had been scrounging about the street. The headlights of the fishtailing vehicle, along with its screaming roar confused it to the extent it scratched at the tarmac surface of the road in its effort to get to safety.

The cat's quiet life was suddenly interrupted, and its experience in dealing with the hazards of life in the city had not equipped it with the exercise needed to avoid a fishtailing vehicle. Its tried and tested method of evasion was, *avoid the lights, avoid the car.* A basic manoeuvre that was popular with cats and usually easy to perform. The vehicles headlights swept back and forth, almost in time with the cats indecision. As it scratched the tarmac a second time to change direction, it realized it might be about to use up another of its nine lives.

A split second later it discovered it may be its ninth life, as it bounced off various mechanical automobile parts before being thrown out from under the rear of the vehicle.

Lee saw the cat too late and shortly after it disappeared from his view he heard a thump as the animal passed under the car. His troubles with Kane and the wooden crate began to pale in significance, compared to the scary ordeal of dealing with Mrs. Brown.

Lee slowed the car and pulled to the side of the street, parking close to the kerb whilst trying to put his thoughts into order. He felt sorry for the cat for a while, until he remembered the few contacts he'd had with the animal in the past. As he sat in the darkness he considered the times he'd cursed Mrs. Brown's cat for its tomcat stink and its noise.

The cat had certainly interrupted his sleep at times with its late night wailing. There were also the mornings when he'd decided on breakfast on the back porch only to be met by its eye watering stink. As he considered the cat's demise and his part in its end, he felt less sorry for it. After some minutes he felt almost glad he'd *done it in*. He laughed out loud as a thought occurred to him, and he visualized a newspaper headline, 'Underworld figure whacks neighbours cat.' He laughed uncontrollably as his frustration began to lift, and as he wiped away his tears of mirth he looked around and over his shoulder. The houses in the street were quiet and there were no lights visible.

Anyone who had woken to the noise he'd made, would surely, after a brief look into the street, be back in their beds by now he thought. He looked at his wrist watch and decided the 'crime' he'd committed was only five minutes old, so the crime scene was still fresh.

He'd turned off the cars headlights when he'd parked. Now as he pulled the car into gear he left them as they were and turned the car around towards where the cat lay in the middle of the road.

Pulling up beside its body he left the car to pick up the cat by its tail, then walked around to the boot, lifted the lid and dropped the cat inside. He was still chuckling lightly as he quietly closed the boot lid and returned to the driver's seat. Safely inside and hoping he'd been unobserved. He again pulled the car into gear and cruised slowly to the next side street, where he turned left towards the main highway.

As he went he said to himself.

"There you go Mrs. Brown, no body, no motive and you can only guess at the weapon. Tom Lee has whacked your stinking cat, and if you accuse him he will admit to it and say that he took the cat from the road in an attempt to find a vet. I'm very sorry Mrs. Brown. It was a terrible accident, but you have to admit that it was an effective way of stopping it from pissing on everything. For that reason, its passing will more than likely be celebrated by everyone in the street." He'd travelled a short way down the highway with his mind still totally involved with Mrs. Brown's cat when suddenly his mobile phone called for his attention.

"Shane. What's happening?"

Shane voice came to Lee with a rasping sound, breathless from his early morning run.

"Mr. Lee. I ran down the road as quick as I could, but I missed seeing which direction the van went."

"Did you see its number plate or anything?

"No. Just a dark coloured van with no lights. The three blokes in it looked like they knew what they were doing. They were in, loaded and back out again in short time, pretty smooth."

Lee was silent for a short time before he instructed.

"Right. Look, there's nothing that we can do about it now. I want you to sit tight for the rest of the day. Keep me informed as the day progresses. Let me know everything that goes on in there today. Who comes, who goes, delivery trucks whatever. How are the boys getting along?"

"Dion's a bit fidgety, but Charlie's keeping him in line. I'll tell them we might be out of here tonight sometime that be alright?"

"If you want, you can tell Dion he can leave. You and Charlie can handle the job, can't you?"

"No Mr. Lee. He won't go on his own. He needs me or Charlie with him or both of us. He doesn't like being on his own."

"Alright Shane, you know him better than I do. Whichever way you do it, just keep me informed, eh?"

He rang off, and immediately dialled Larry Barrett's number.

"Larry. Time to get up son, there's work to be done."

Lee waited a moment for Larry to wake before he continued.

"It's nearly four thirty and time for your early morning run. Ha. Ha. Listen, I've just talked to Shane and he tells me that three men in a dark coloured van have broken into Grey Street and stolen the wooden crate. I don't want to talk about it over the phone, so I'll see you in the club as soon as you can make it. Be quick Larry, I'll be there in twenty minutes and I want you there soon after, right?" His next call was to Dan the Man, and shortly after he placed a call to Mika.

Lee had fifteen trusted troops in his employ. He gave instructions to Dan and Mika to make sure that all of them understood they had work today, and that he expected no excuses from any one of them. After he'd broken the connection and put the phone into its battery charger receptacle, he considered the work that had to be done on this day.

Dealing with the reasons behind Kane's existence, and whatever it was he had going on in Grey Street was one thing, but what crazy idea could be behind the theft of an empty wooden box. He considered the problem for some minutes more before he compiled his thoughts.

"Point one; the wooden box is, correction, could be, a serious threat. There's nothing I can do about it outside of killing Kane, and even that mightn't solve the problem, particularly if Kane is only the front man."

"Point two; what is it that can be so important about a bloody transformer, to Kane or his employer, that they'd be prepared to pay Sudovich a fifty thousand dollar down payment just to import it for them. A two hundred thousand dollar import they could have imported themselves for a tenth of the cost."

"Less." He corrected himself.

Lee consoled himself, even though he was uncertain about Kane and his mysterious wooden crate, he was certain about the work that he and his people would carry out on this day, and the next if necessary. He would take out insurance. After all, that's what most people did if there was a hint of a threat to their goods and chattels. As there was no insurance company that would cover this particular problem, then he would cover it himself.

The first thing he would do would be to have Larry bag all of his assets. Business, real estate, everything he could safely strip from Sudovich Holdings and transfer offshore, just in case this mild form of hiccoughs became a serious influenza. While that was happening, Dan and Mika and the rest of the troops will be out on the streets calling in all loans. Sell off as much stock as possible. Bring in as much cash as possible in the shortest possible time, and most importantly, as quietly as possible.

Lee knew he would have to work quickly, because as soon as the story hit the street that he was pulling in stocks, it might appear to some that he was in trouble. Once his competitors had a sniff of that possibility, it wouldn't be long before they started to infringe on his turf.

They'd dip a toe in at first just to test the waters, and if he didn't react then they'd try to move in permanently. With too many people crowding the starting blocks they could find themselves confronted with a trade and turf war. If that happened, then a lot of people would get nervous, and Lee knew from experience the complications that could arise when criminals got nervous. He knew it eventually boiled down to shoot first and ask questions later, which in turn, only made people more nervous.

It could get a little tricky, he thought. But he was trying to cover his arse here, and if it upset anyone else then that was just too bad. They'd just have to look after their own freckles.

Lee had direction. He had a plan, and he felt good as he drove towards his club. There was a new day about to begin, and by the end of it he was sure he would feel a little more secure than he had in the most recent past.

It was funny, he thought. It seemed he had turned a corner with the wooden box problem. His thinking had become clearer and more positive since he'd whacked Mrs. Brown's cat.

"Should have killed it a week ago," he said out loud as he pushed his foot down hard on the accelerator.

Tuesday 9.30 am.

Tuesday morning saw Ben Preston in his office. Having risen early he'd made his way into work before sunrise with a heightened sense of excitement. The feeling in his gut made him feel more alive than he'd felt for some time.

Being close to Lee, as close as anyone had ever been, had caused his blood to flow more readily. Now he needed Lee to make his next move, and as Lee had made initial contact with Beth, Ben knew he would visit her again.

He also knew, or was quite sure anyway, where that second visit would take place. Lee would probably not return to her place of residence, he thought. He would go to where he expected the money to be, and that was at her office.

His overbearing arrogance would carry him there, where he would most likely waltz into her office unannounced as if he already owned the place. Ben would have both places wired to make doubly sure and enhance his chances to pull off the perfect ambush.

He was in an interesting position. It was not often that people in his profession had knowledge of a crime before it was committed. It did happen at times, but usually it was based on information gained from informants whose advice may or may not be accurate. This information was accurate to the extent he had the *where, why* and *how*.

With a little patience he'd have the *when*.

While he waited for the *when* he'd have the *where* wired for audio and visual. A few secreted electronic accessories would record each footfall of Lee, and with these in possession would come the power to legally turn the world upside down for the crime boss. Give it a few extra shakes too, he thought. There was one drawback though, and it almost hurt him to think about it.

He needed Beth to help him, and this she was prepared to do, but in doing so she would be the one out on a limb, and Lee would be the arsehole who held the saw.

Ben wanted Lee badly, but he felt an awkward need to keep the limb intact. Not necessarily only for her sake, but also for the thirty million dollars and the plans she had for its disposal. The two reasons which his humane side used in its plea for a small justice.

Thirty million dollars he reminded himself.

It was a lot of money, and indeed it appeared to be the reason for at least five deaths already. That is of course, if he took Sudovich and the missing man Scott into consideration.

Ben knew he was officially obliged to investigate the circumstances surrounding the deaths of all these five people. He also knew he could officially put that investigation aside for the moment, if he had reason to believe another investigation held priority. Tom Lee held utmost priority at this time, and his gut feeling emphasized that belief

He glanced at the clock on the wall, and as he noted the time he saw Anderson and Rodgers enter the operations area. He'd summoned them earlier and was pleased to see they were punctual. He asked for the door to his office to be closed, and as they neared his desk he invited them to sit, and then asked Anderson,

"Rodney, you've brought Alan up to speed on your outing yesterday?"

"Yes Sir. Up to the point when I left the women's flat upon your arrival," Anderson replied.

"Good man," Ben said.

There were two brochures on his desk. He handed them one each and then sat quietly while they read.

The brochures were outlines of the Sarah Ray Foundation. Much the same as the charity brochures that ordinarily turned up in most people's mail boxes, with pictures of skinny African children and drought ravaged crops. They also displayed the function of the Foundation, and the way the profits were to be dispersed.

Beth had, had them printed up, for even though Simon's money offered a firm base fund for the Foundation, she would still advertise for private and public donations.

Rodgers spoke first.

"Is this where the thirty million went, Boss?"

"Unofficially Alan, yes. It seems that West stole the money and then hired Beth Cooper to manage it. She has documents in her possession that should, unless under very close scrutiny, prove she accepted the job from West without any knowledge of where the money came from. West was careful on her behalf, and set it up so if anyone ever asked any questions then she'd be in the clear." Ben drew a breath before he continued.

"The situation now is that Tom Lee, being Sudovich's silent partner, has turned up on her doorstep. He's demanding what he calls his share of the money. I've spoken in depth with Cooper, and I know that she, being the one responsible for the Foundation will be scrutinized and audited like any other charity. Hence I believe the money is in good hands and will be used as the brochure states, so I'm prepared to let it be." Ben let what he said so far sink in, as he studied carefully his two apprentices' faces.

"This is where there's a slight problem. I want Lee, but I also want to keep the Foundation aside of that investigation. So, I might want to steer the investigation into Lee in ways that may not be totally by the book." When no question of dissent seemed evident, and with no sign of fresh questions from the men, he persisted,

"In regard to your question Allan, I said unofficially because I wanted to keep you both in the loop, and let you both know where I would like to go with this. I will be retiring from the job in seventy-two days. You two both have your whole careers ahead of you, so if any shit hits the fan, then I'm totally the responsible party. If anything comes up at all in the future, then all the two of you know is what you knew before this briefing started. If you agree to do it my way, then this conversation never took place."

Ben sat back in his chair and looked at them in turn.

"If you decide we must do it by the book, then the thirty million could end up in the politicians' and lawyers' pockets." Now would be a good time to go and make a cup of tea he thought. Give the two men a chance to talk.

"Tea or coffee?"

"No thanks, Boss." Rodgers said as Anderson asked for coffee.

Ben returned some five minutes later bringing two cups. He seated himself and looked at each of the two men in turn.

"O.K then, what's happening?"

"We're in agreement with you Sir, but I reckon that Lee, if we can get him, will spill the beans on the Foundation at his first chance anyway. So what's the point in hedging around? We want Lee, but if we get him this way, through Cooper, then the Foundation is going to be in it up to its chin isn't it?"

Rodgers was the younger of the two men, and even though Ben knew he was going to become an excellent detective, it was yet to come with experience.

Ben looked to the more experienced of the two.

"What's your feel of the situation, Rodney?"

"Under normal circumstances I'd agree with Alan, Sir. By normal I mean, if we were dealing with a smaller time criminal rather than Lee. On this occasion I'd bet that Lee won't spill the beans, because it's in his own interest to remain quiet. He'll know as well as we do, that if the Foundation is investigated then the money will disappear into the system. Probably into Government coffers, and if that happens it's lost to him forever.

If he stays quiet about it, he can hope it is still within reach and he can try for it again at a later date. I think that even criminals rely to a certain extent on hope."

Ben looked Alan in the eye and followed up Rodney's statement.

"Lee will also keep quiet because he'll believe he's the only one who knows where it is. I think he'll want it to stay that way for fear of someone else stealing it away before he can get to it himself."

He watched as Alan slowly nodded his head and was delighted in the sight of the young detective learning another facet of his trade.

"There are books available on Criminal Psychology," he added for Alan's ears before he got back to the business at hand.

"Rodney, I want you wire Cooper's office and her flat for audio and visual. Get the technicians to install something that either she or Booth can safely activate when it's needed. Ask them about that new one they have which automatically dials a mobile phone the moment the tapes are turned on. When they're finished setting it up, see to it that I get one of the mobile phones please."

Technology had come a long way since the old days when officers sat around waiting for the tapes to roll. These days the tape recording system would automatically dial the operating officer via the mobile network the moment the tape was turned on, by either Cooper or Booth.

The operating officer, when alerted by the mobile phone call could then listen in on the conversation while it was being recorded. It played an important part in allowing him to keep pace with the situation while he was travelling to where the taping system was placed.

It saved on man hours, and cut out the tedious boring hours of waiting for the target to arrive, if of course he arrived at all.

In this case Ben would answer the phone and do the listening. If things got out of hand for the two women, he could have back up people on the spot in minutes.

"Now Lee is bound to mention to Cooper about where the Foundation's money came from. I want the tapes hot of the press, delivered to me personally, by either one of you. Don't let anyone else hear them. You might explain to both Cooper and Booth that they should communicate with one of us three only, and for the time being I think we'd be well advised to restrict the loop to just we three."

Ben looked at Anderson, and then to Rodgers.

"Any questions?"

When neither of the two spoke, and each nodded their heads he moved on to the next issue.

"Alan, what did you find out about that box in Grey Street? Alan had his note book open and he began to deliver his report, at times reading from his notes an outline of his previous day's activities.

"Sir, I checked out the carrier and he gave me the address that he delivered the transformer to. It was a building site in Liverpool. I asked him why he didn't deliver it to the delivery address on the consignment note. He said that as far as he knew, instructions had been given by phone to the carrier company asking if the crate could be delivered to the Liverpool address instead."

"The driver told me that when he arrived at the Liverpool address, there was a truck carrying its own fork lift. They transferred the crate to that truck on the street outside the building site. The driver also said he thought the people with the second truck had no connection with the building site, because he was still there when they drove off in a westerly direction." Alan stopped a moment and looked up in silent apology as he was suddenly faced with a blank page in his notebook. He quickly turned the page and continued.

"I checked with the carrier's office, and it was signed for, by the side of the road, by someone going under the name of Turner. The name on the side of the second truck, as far as the driver could recall, was the same name as on the con note. That being Sudovich Holdings."

"My request to customs and the State Police for alarm bells to be placed on anything connected to Sudovich Holdings, Walters or 16 Grey Street is in process. If there's as much as a parking ticket, then we'll know about it."

Ben was thoughtful for the moment after Rodgers report. He'd listened without interrupting while the young detective had delivered it before he made an observation.

"It would appear our suspicions about the crate may be correct. The fact that the crate has gone the long way around certainly suggests we may be on to something. Now we have some idea as to what we might look out for in the future." His voice trailed off as a thought from another angle struck him. Both Anderson and Rodgers watched their boss as he suddenly appeared to reflect deeply, his teeth clenched and his fingers pulled at his chin as if there was an invisible beard beneath it.

He finally spoke the thought out loud.

"I've been looking at this box thing as maybe an import device for smuggling drugs, or that was the first thing that I thought of when I learned it was connected to Sudovich."

"What else could it be, Boss?" Anderson asked, "Unless of course it's weapons, there's a strong market out there for hand guns."

Ben looked to the younger of the two.

"What springs to mind for you Alan?"

"Well, Sir. It could be a terrorist link. It sounds unlikely, but times are changing."

"I agree on all three possibilities Alan. I've just had to remind myself that this is the twenty first century and the criminal climate has changed. Is this crate any different than an unattended backpack or suitcase at a transport terminal? That's the problem with terrorism, you never know, and even the least hint of suspicion must be evaluated."

Ben paused and sipped at his now cool tea before issuing an instruction.

"Alan, I want you to write your report on the box right now. Everything we know so far and have it to me within the hour. I have a meeting scheduled with the Commissioner at nine thirty, and Commander Rusty Bates of the new Terrorism Task Force will be there. I think they should be brought into the picture. I'll pass it on to his Task Force people just to be on the safe side. If it comes to nothing then I'll just have a little egg on my face, but I'd rather that than the possibility of living with regret in the future. If they come up with something that lends to Lee's involvement, even if it's only that the crate is on his land, then he'll hit the ground harder under the new terrorism laws than he will for his attempted extortion on Cooper's Foundation."

He sat back in his chair and rubbed his hands together unconsciously, as Scrooge might do, when he envisaged a new financial plan.

Ben was quiet for some seconds before he said, almost to himself,

"It would seem that we may well have two ways to crack Lee's golden egg. With a little bit of luck, either way will be suitable."

Rodgers and Anderson both stood to leave Ben's office. Anderson holding the door as Rodgers walked through the doorway before Ben caused the two of them to turn when he offered a final word.

"By the way, I asked Cooper what she knew of West's reasons for stealing the thirty million. She told me she asked him the same question during the last conversation she had with him. It seems that his answer to her was that, he thought that it was the right thing to do."

"One other thing," Ben said before the two men left the area, "What did the Bourke Police say about the swimming pool?"

"Oh! They confirmed its existence, Sir."

Ben noted the inquisitive look upon Rodney's face and felt it deserved some form of explanation.

"Just adding backbone to my informants' credibility Rodney, that's all."

CHAPTER 12

Tuesday 9.45am

Lee was content to the extent he felt relaxed. With this feeling of small comfort came the ability to make clear and concise decisions born of organized thought patterns.

In the days prior he'd had thought patterns, but they had been far from organized. He'd read somewhere that jumbled thoughts and indecisiveness were known to be symptoms of depression, and for a short time he'd wondered if he was a victim of what was known these days as an illness.

The thought had been put aside because he believed that depression of any sort was stupid.

There was no point to it. If things got so bad they might cause depression, then there was a good chance those same things were as bad as they were going to get. So if things weren't going to get any worse, then there was no point in being depressed. If a person was already at rock bottom, then things can only go one of two ways.

The first way, was that a person stayed on the bottom because they were too slack to get off their arse to do something about their problem.

The second way, and the only one left, was that they could only go up. If things were going to get better, then it was time to be enthusiastic.

In a nutshell, being at rock bottom was a time for optimism.

Lee liked his little forages into the world of philosophy, and had wondered at times in the past whether he might have been monk material. Other times he visualized himself sitting in a cold cave high on a mountain, where he tore pages from a book of wisdom and burned them on a small fire.

Conceding to himself that one did not have to be wise to know that a book of wisdom would be of no value at all if you're frozen solid in your cave. He sat back in his chair and sniffed the air, unsure whether the incense sticks did enough to alleviate the smell of the bar room.

The office where he and Larry were seated was separated from the bar area by a paneled wall, but like the smell of the incense which crept into the room, so did the sickly odour of spilt beer and stale cigarette smoke.

He suddenly laughed out loud as a memory of Mrs. Brown's cats stink flashed through his head. Larry looked at him from behind his desk, but refrained from comment as he sat in silence with his telephone to his ear.

Lee was not sure if Larry was listening to someone as they spoke to him over the phone, or whether he sat quietly while he waited for someone to answer the phone. A short time later Larry spoke and it sounded to Lee that the call was coming to an end.

"Yes Adam. Yes, if you can get it under way, that'll be good. I'll print up the documents and E-mail you the necessaries. Yeah, that'll give us a head start. Good, I'll expect it by courier. Right mate, see you."

He put the phone down and spoke across the room to Lee.

"Adam says he should be able to organize a shelf company in New Zealand. It'll take at least twenty-four hours and he'll send us the product by courier as soon as he has it done."

"You're an accountant, how come you don't do it yourself?" Lee wondered aloud.

Larry picked up some papers from the desk top and sat them in a pile at the side of his computer while he answered.

"Time mainly. There's a lot involved in what you want to do. Most of it I can do from here, and while I'm busy organizing this end, he'll be getting his end done. Hopefully this way we'll have everything ready for your signatures by tomorrow afternoon. Will that be early enough?"

Lee looked thoughtful for a moment.

"To tell you the truth, I thought it would take a week or something."

Larry looked at his computer screen, and then tapped his keyboard a few times before he responded.

"No, not anymore, we're in the days of I.T." Lee didn't know what I.T meant, outside of knowing it was to do with computers. He knew little about computers, and was uncomfortable to some extent when in the company of people who were accustomed to them, particularly when electronic terminology was bandied about. They may as well be speaking in Russian as far as Lee was concerned, and sometimes he hated Larry for his knowledge of them.

Or maybe it was that he hated Larry because of his own lack of knowledge of them. A hatred born out of the frustration Lee felt when considering the fact, he was being left behind by this I.T thing. He felt uncomfortable now, and he stood to make ready his departure from the room.

"Do you need me here for anything?"

Larry tapped his keyboard again before he looked up at Lee.

"Sorry, Mr. Lee. I didn't mean to ignore you, but this set up demands all of my attention and will do so for the rest of the day." He paused for some seconds before he asked, "I do have a couple of questions for you though, if we can do that now?" Lee sat back down again and waited a few minutes until Larry spoke.

"I just need a few points clarified, but first I should run through what's happening. New Zealand is not far enough away for what you want. I mean, knowing as I do the reasons why you're setting up off shore, New Zealand is too close and Vanuatu would be better. We have the time factor to consider so we're restricted in our options. Things move slowly in Vanuatu, and as you said before, it could take a week. If we move to New Zealand first and can get it established by tomorrow afternoon, then, even if the shit hits the fan here tomorrow, it could take weeks or more before any investigation into your business affairs here can affect this new offshore company in Kiwi land."

Larry paused to drink from his bottled water, and as he re screwed its lid he continued.

"Once you're based in New Zealand, you'll have the time available to you where you can wait to see which way the winds blow here in Australia. As soon as Adam has New Zealand organized, I'll get him on to Vanuatu. In a week's time you'll be able to move easily, and at short notice from New Zealand to Vanuatu. In effect, New Zealand may well be only a temporary staging point with Vanuatu being the final destination. Depending on your decision when you know which way the wind has blown."

Larry followed up with a question.

"Have I explained it clearly enough?"

Lee was happy enough with the explanation.

"Yeah, what you're saying is. I might be going to Vanuatu, but I'll be using New Zealand for a brief stopover to catch my breath." He added, "If necessary."

Glad to have made his counsel clear, Larry moved on to the queries he had. They spoke together for another five minutes before Larry brought the briefing nearer to its end with some final, but necessary questions.

"When you say that you want all your assets under the off shore company's umbrella, and I apologize if I sound impertinent, but does that include your residence, and if so where does your wife, Sally, fit in? I ask because, she being your spouse is entitled by law to fifty per cent of that asset, so you won't be able to include it unless she is prepared to sign it over."

"I doubt she would be prepared to do that." Lee said.

"She may do so if you were to offer her a directorship of the company. What I mean is. If you made her a director, she might be prepared to put her half of the residence under the umbrella, especially if she understands that if you are investigated she might lose the whole house. If her half of the residence is under the umbrella, then it may in turn protect your half of the house. I make the point of her directorship so you'll have someone close to you to make sure that the company is run, and decisions can be made if for some obscure reason you are incapacitated." Larry watched Lee and realized that he had confused the issue. "I should point out to you that companies are owned by the shareholders, and in this case you will be the only shareholder. Directors own nothing unless they are shareholders. They are only there to make sure the company is run to the best of their ability, on behalf of the shareholders. In the event of the only director, you, who is the major shareholder, being incapacitated then the company will stop in its tracks, because no one will have the authority to even pay the phone bill. If Sally is a director and not a shareholder, but is the wife of the major shareholder, then she is in the position to direct, and sign documents on the behalf of her husband and the company, but she will in effect own no part of the company."

"Mr. Lee, forgive me if I'm out of order, but if it is your wish, you might not include the residence. Leave it as it is and hope for the best, but remember that the sole reason you are setting up this offshore company is to protect your assets. The way Australian law stands at the moment, is that any assets which may have been paid for by monies criminally attained can be confiscated by the authorities. Now the reason you are trying to protect your assets is because of the possibility, and I emphasize possibility, of an investigation being launched into you because of Sudovich's stupidity with this wooden box thing. If you decide to forget the residence, then so be it. I am your employee, and your directions are my orders. I will carry out those orders to the best of my ability, but my advice to you is that you should have Sally as a second director, because if there is an investigation, then there is the possibility ..." Larry paused momentarily, his mouth was open, but it seemed that he had some difficulty in spitting the words out, "Of you being arrested and you won't be able to pay the phone bill in hand cuffs or direct anyone else to either."

Lee was quickly on his feet, and he stood before the paper strewn desk. His hands had become fists and his eyes sparkled with menace as he glared down at his accountant.

"Larry whenever you have a point to make, make it, but never drive it home. Understand?"

Lee sat down again and shuffled his shoulders under his coat until he was comfortable, and then sat with his fingers pinching his lips while his eyes stared at the small pot plant in the corner of the room. He held that pose for some minutes deep in thought, until he moved his fingers to the underside of his chin and kneaded the loose skin that became available due to his head being tilted downwards.

Larry listened as Lee's breathing slowed, and as it did he felt the stiffness leave his jaw muscles as he unclenched his teeth. He wiped his hand across his fore head, noticing as he did the small beads of perspiration that had leapt from his skin a moment before. He was glad for a reason to stop talking as he reached for his bottled water.

Lee sat back in his chair and exhaled.

"Do whatever you can with the house, better still, include it in and I'll bring Sally around. I'm pretty sure she'll see reason. As far as the directorship is concerned, there's no way that she'll become one. I may have to give her a share of the company just to make her comfortable in signing the house over, but it will be the smallest share as possible, I can assure you."

Both men were quiet. Larry waited while Lee wandered through his mental decision making factory. His next question suggested to Larry that he was on the verge of an outright decision, but needed a little encouragement.

"What power would this second director have?"

"They'd have no power at all. You are the major shareholder, so they would have to follow your directive and carry out your instructions to the letter. If for some reason you were incapacitated, for example if you were forced to, or decided to leave the country, then they could still only carry out your instructions. Instructions issued by you would have to be in the form of a letter of authority signed by you." Larry went into wait mode again as Lee contemplated his finger nails. For a moment he contemplated Lees finger nails too, until he looked away and watched the virtual geometry on his computer's screen saver. The question that he had been waiting for finally came.

"What about you, Larry?"

"Sorry, Mr. Lee, what do you mean?"

"What about you as the second director? You know the business as well as I do, and there will be no pressure on you because all the decisions will be mine."

A look of surprise came over Larry's face as he tried to find the right words without sounding too enthusiastic.

"I don't know Mr. Lee. I, err...

Lee read Larry's indecision and believed he understood the reason behind it.

"Are you unsure about being connected to a known criminal who might be about to be subjected to an intense investigation?"

Larry was cornered, and there was only one answer available to him, "No, Mr. Lee, that's not entirely correct. I mean, yes. If that suits you, if that is your wish, then I will be the second director." He paused for effect before saying with as much sincerity he could muster, "Thank you for your faith in me."

Lee grinned as he stood up to leave.

"My pleasure Larry, now do you need me here anymore? There are other things I should be getting on with, and I know you have a busy day ahead of you. If you need me, I'll be on my mobile."

Lee walked to the door and let himself out of the office. As he did, Larry looked up at the door as it closed behind him.

The slight smile that touched the corners of his mouth slowly turned into a fully-fledged grin as he marvelled how bullshit baffled brains. It would have announced to anyone who could have seen it, complete satisfaction.

He turned to his computer and touched the Y key to remove the screen saver as his own whispered voice registered in his ears,

"It's my pleasure, *Mister* Lee.

CHAPTER 13

2.30 am Tuesday London time

Geoff Letts walked a quiet and dark street in an inner London suburb.

It was a cold night, and he dug his hands deeper into the pockets of his woollen coat. For even though he wore gloves his fingers still felt the chill of the Northern Hemisphere. To be expected he supposed at two thirty in the morning.

He was glad the street was quiet, because the work he had to complete was better carried out without unnecessary observation.

A lone car passed. Its tyres making a squishing noise on the asphalt which had been left wet by last evening's rain.

Arriving at his destination he unconsciously looked about behind him to double check his surroundings. Seeing nothing to arouse his senses he turned to the lock and inserted a key.

He could see the outline of the steeply sloping roof of the engineer's workshop. It appeared to be plastered to the electric light pollution which shone upwards from an unusually quiet and apparently sleepy city. Letts used a second key to gain entry through a Judas door, and into the workshop area. The Judas door was within one of the two large sliding doors, which gave easy access for the movement of transport to and from the workshops loading bays.

Now he was inside the building and with the Judas door safely secured behind him, he lifted a small bright beamed torch from his coat pocket and used it to guide his feet.

Its beam brought with it surrealism as shadows of miscellaneous pieces of workshop equipment flitted and danced around the room.

A sudden sound caused him to stop in his tracks. He turned off the torch while he stood motionless in the pitch blackness, straining his ears against the silence towards the suspected direction of the sound. Possibly a rat he thought, and he hoped to hear the noise again in order to substantiate that thought. None came, and he flicked the torch once more to life. Dismissing the sound as unimportant as he again stepped his way carefully over the oil stained concrete workshop floor.

The cold wind outside whispered as it gained entry into the building through gaps in its iron walls. Its sound accompanied by the distant rattle of a loose sheet of iron, whose beat rose and fell on the intensity of the undulating wind. Letts climbed a set of welded steel stairs. They elevated him from the workshop floor to the top of a concrete loading bay, from where it was a short walk of five paces to an office door. It had been known to him as the draughtsman's office when he had visited the building during the time of the transformer's design and manufacture. One man from the design team had indeed been a draughtsman, and it was here in this space that he'd drawn the basic design of the transformers. Those drawings and blueprints were part of the reason why Letts had to carry out this late night mission.

He followed the beam of his torch to a small safe in the corner of the room, where he played the combination until its door swung open. Under the bright beam the safes contents lay open to his gaze.

Letts reached into the safe and removed an envelope.

It was addressed to a London newspaper and he recognized the handwriting as his. He'd prepackaged the envelope personally some weeks earlier, and had left it here reckoning it to be more secure than if he'd removed it to the outside world.

He looked at the handwriting which resembled a scrawl. A crude and to the point inscription that might appear to be from the hand of a very old person, and not due to the finesse of his own left hand. Addressing the letter had been the first time in his adult life he'd tried to write left handed. He'd been surprised at the difficulty, and it reminded at the same time that he'd be stuffed if anything ever happened to his right hand, because he was far from ambidextrous. The envelope itself was in a clip top plastic bag, and he folded it loosely so the inside of his coat pocket could accommodate its bulk.

The envelopes contents were a letter and some photographs of the transformers blueprints. Not a lot of information for the press, but enough to most certainly whet their appetite.

They also gave details of the work carried out by the said terrorists, along with the address of the engineer's workshop where their diabolical deeds had transpired. Once the press had an inkling of a possible story, they would use their own resources to ferret out more than enough information.

Given a few days of leaks, comments from reliable sources and experts evaluations, they'd not need to speculate, for they would have more information than they could put to use.

He reached again into his coat pocket, and lifted from it a small tin with a hinged lid, opening it to see a single glass capsule lying in its bed of cotton wool. He closed the lid again and took from the safe another envelope. This one was empty and it had written on it in the same left handed scrawl. 'TAKE CARE. THE CONTENTS OF THIS CONTAINER ARE EXTREMELY HAZARDOUS.'

Letts knew that the people who opened this safe tomorrow morning would more than likely be wearing HazChem suits, but just to be on the safe side. The warning clearly pointed out the capsule was to be handled with extreme care.

For a moment he considered leaving the safe door unlocked, to give the person who opened it in the morning easier access. Then decided that too many things could happen between now and the moment the police cordoned off the whole area in the morning. Having made his decision, he spun the combination dial, and with his torch in hand, he checked the floor around where he had been, before he moved off toward the office door. It closed quietly behind him as he reached again into his coat pocket. Withdrawing a battered booklet that he'd bought some months ago from an underground bookshop.

While he knew by the pictures on its grubby pages that it was a terrorist's hand book, he had no idea what the booklet was called. He couldn't read Arabic.

Just a little deception to confuse the issue he thought, as he dropped the booklet on the stained concrete by the welded steps. Five minutes later he was back on the street walking towards the place where he'd parked his car.

He checked his wrist watch; it was five minutes past three.

A quick mental calculation allowed him to conclude that Kane would probably be having his lunch about now, after spending part of his morning making known his lack of knowledge about wooden boxes.

Letts drove to a local park he had visited some days before and easily found from memory, the steel grilled storm water drain he'd discovered on that occasion. He leaned from his open driver's side door to drop the keys he'd used to gain entry to the engineer's workshop. Content with his accomplishments, he drove towards his rented apartment.

There were two more things to do. One was to change the number plates on the car so it would be ready for use in the coming morning. The other, he muttered through a yawn.

"Time for bed."

CHAPTER 14

It was two thirty-five in the afternoon when Alan Rodgers walked hurriedly into Ben's office. He was excited as he said to his boss.

"Sir, I've just had a call from our cousins in blue. It seems they were called to investigate a break and enter this morning at 16 Grey Street."

Ben looked up him from his office desk, and saw that no more would be forth coming until he made a request.

"Well spit it out, Alan. What happened?"

"Well according to the investigating officer the only thing that was taken was a wooden crate, Sir." Ben looked away from Rodgers and stared at an invisible spot on the wall opposite. Rodgers could see that his boss's mind was in overdrive and he watched as Ben's fingers drummed a short beat out on the wooden desk.

After a short moment the spot on the wall lost its significance and Ben looked back at Rodgers.

"Did the investigating officer say the name of the person he questioned?"

"He said that there were two men there, Sir. A man named Barney Wild and a bloke by the name of John Kane, who seemed to be the man in charge." Rodgers read the second name from his notebook.

"No mention of Steve Walters at all?"

"As far as I know he didn't mention that name, Sir."

"Where's Anderson?"

"I think he'll be finishing up at Cooper's office, Sir."

Ben thought for a moment.

"Well call him and let him know where we'll be. Then let him know that he's to call me as soon as he's finished up."

"Sorry Sir. Where will we be?"

"We'll be at 16 Grey Street."

"Yes Sir. Ah! Sir, do you mean that you are going to look into it personally?"

"Yes, Alan. I know you are used to working for me, but do you think you'll mind working with me?" Ben asked with a look of feigned indignation on his face. It lasted only until he smiled and let Alan know that he was toying with him.

"Yes, Sir. No, Sir."

"Right, ring Rodney and let's get the show on the road. We'll take your car."

There was midday traffic and a trip of a little over half an hour preceded their entry into the workshop yard. Five minutes after that, they were directed through a well-equipped workshop area to an unadorned office, by the man whose name was given as Barney Wild.

They introduced themselves to the man who had been, upon their unannounced arrival, seated behind a lightly cluttered desk. The man rose to his full height and greeted each of them with an outstretched hand. Ben noted, as he was forced to do at times, that his size was matched, although the man who introduced himself as John Kane was leaner, and Ben decided, much more fit than himself.

Even when Kane was seated he radiated a confidence usual for most well-built men. He also gave a high measure of modesty, and as Ben was to learn, he was sure footedly quiet spoken with his words. He read the man's tan. It told him that Kane was most likely an outdoors man whose lightly tanned forehead suggested he sometimes wore a hat or a cap.

Their interview lasted about twenty-five minutes before Ben and Rodgers walked back to their car.

"What do you make of him, Sir?"

"I think there's more to him than meets the eye, Alan. Call Rodney and tell him to meet us at the office as soon as he can, earlier if possible."

After a half hour drive back to their headquarters they entered Ben's office, where they found Rodney Anderson waiting for them.

"What's happening boss?"

Ben greeted Rodney with a question before he offered an explanation. "Gidday, Rodney. Is Coopers place all sorted out?"

"Yes Sir. There are two cameras in her immediate office area and two microphones. With an extra microphone in the toilet in case Lee needs to use his mobile while he's there. We could have his calls intercepted, but that would have required some explicit explanation, and of course more paper work which wouldn't suit our needs."

Ben understood. The less said about the Sarah Ray Foundation the better. He knew that the law stated it was illegal to intercept a call without the legal paperwork, whereas it was permitted to tape a person who was making the phone call, if that persons conversation was connected to a crime that was being, or was about to be committed.

They had permission from Cooper to wire her office, and any conversation that took place within her office was deemed to be her property. She would give her permission to record a specific conversation simply by switching on the recording equipment.

Rodney produced two mobile phones from his jacket pocket.

"I organized an issue of two of these little puppies, Sir. One is a backup, just in case. Should I hold on to one of them?" Ben nodded his agreement as he held his hand out to accept one of the phones. He looked at it briefly before he looked again at Rodney in silent request for operating instructions.

Rodney came to his aid and Ben was reminded again that he was a copper from the old days, who was operating on new ground with an even newer technology.

"Just slide the button on the side and she's operational. There's a battery charge indicator in the window and the battery is good for seventy-two hours."

He paused for a moment to pull a length of wire from his other pocket. "Here's the battery charger. Now that you're turned on, all you have to do is wait for Cooper. When she switches on her recording gear each of these phones will be automatically dialled. When it rings you press this button and you will hear everything that is being recorded by all of the microphones. In this case we will both have access to the conversation being recorded, and on top of that we will be able to communicate with each other.

Rodney held his phone up to show Alan, like a kid might do with a new toy.

"Brilliant, isn't it?" Ben would like to have shared in the young detective's enthusiasm, but he found it difficult to be enthusiastic about a technology that was leaving him behind.

There were also other things to occupy his mind at this moment. He brought the briefing back to the business at hand as he gave the mobile phone one more glance before putting it in his jacket pocket.

He directed the conversation by saying to Anderson,

"Alan and I have spent some time over at Grey Street this afternoon. The people there have reported a break in, and it appears that someone has stolen the wooden crate."

Ben looked to Rodgers and pointed towards the young detective's notebook.

"Will you bring Rodney up to speed please Alan?" He believed that Rodgers shorthand expertise should cover the whole interview.

"When we arrived at the Grey Street premises, we were directed to a man whose name is John Kane by a second man

who gave his name as Barney Wild. Wild, it seems, is the hired help, while Kane appears to be the man in charge. John Kane stated he is Steve Walters's partner in the business and that Walters was over town somewhere quoting on an outside job. Other than this comment there was no other mention of Walters."

"Kane's story is that when he and Wild turned up for work this morning at nine o'clock, they found the front gate open. Its padlock had been cut, probably with bolt cutters. They both checked the building for break in, but found that no entry had been made. It was Wild who noticed that the wooden box had gone missing."

"When we asked Kane about the wooden crate, he said that neither he, Wild or Walters knew anything about it. The box, as he referred to it, was owned by Sudovich Holdings, and it was as far as he could remember, delivered by a man named Turner who unloaded it from a truck which had a Sudovich Holdings sign on its side."

"Kane said that he and Walters rented the premises from Sudovich Holdings and no one at Grey Street saw anything untoward about the wooden box. Other than the fact that it arrived one day without any notice from Sudovich Holdings, which he, that is, Kane saw as bad manners. Other than that it's been sitting in the rear yard since then."

"One significant item that Kane mentioned was that he received a visit from a man named Tom Lee who introduced himself as Sudovich's business partner. Lee pointed out to Kane that the reason for his visit was to familiarize himself with a side of the business which was usually left in the hands of Sudovich."

"Kane said that he could have brought up the matter of the box with Mr. Lee, but it had slipped his mind at that time." Alan looked at Ben and as he concluded. "That's about it, Sir."

Anderson looked thoughtful for a moment.

"What did you make of this bloke Kane, boss?"

"Well it appears to me, that the he is what he suggests himself to be, that is, a businessman operating his business. If not, then he is very well rehearsed. The thing that I noticed while we were in his office was the quiet. No sound of equipment, not even an air compressor, not a sound. Maybe that is normal at times. My noticing it may just be my suspicious mind not discounting anyone who's been in contact with the wooden box. When I entered his office I felt almost as if I'd been expected." He continued. "There was a pile of books and papers on the floor by the door, and the book that was in touch with the floor was about the size of the dust mark on the chair that I was offered. It suggested to me that he'd prepared the chairs with the expectation of two visitors."

There was one other thing that Ben had noticed. A critical point if looked at with a suspicious mind and it posed a question which was in dire need of an answer. Why was it that Kane had not even shown the slightest interest as to why the Federal Police would be interested in a seemingly minor crime like a break and enter? In his experience, just about everyone who'd had a crime committed in their backyard usually had a comment, or question which they made or asked of the investigating officer.

This sort of complacency might be found to be more evident if the investigating officer was ordinary everyday State Police. If the investigating officer was identified as Federal Police, then Mr. General Public had a tendency to sit up and take notice. He'd certainly be more inquisitive.

He let this observation lie for the moment with the intention of finding out if Rodgers had picked up on it.

"What about you, Alan? Did you draw any conclusions?"

"Yes Sir, a couple of things. The one called Barney had very clean hands. Not only clean, but they appeared to have no ingrained grime. His fingernails were also very clean, even the edges and the cuticle. My father was in the same game and even with industrial crème cleaner he couldn't get his hands as clean as Wild's were. Maybe Wild is very committed to his personal hygiene, which might explain why the workshop hand basin was spotless, unusually clean for a workshop. The other bloke Kane didn't have a computer in his office which struck me as odd. There was a computer in the open office area that we walked through to get to Kane's office, but it had no printer. It looked to me like an old Apple which I doubt would be fast enough to run an M.Y.O.B program. The oddest thing I thought was that Kane showed no interest at all in why Federal Police would be interested in a small time break and enter. Not much to go on, Sir. Maybe I'm thinking like you, with a suspicious mind. I agree with your earlier observation that there may be more to Kane than meets the eye."

Ben smiled lightly. Glad to have heard what he'd been listening for and he raised another point.

"Kane seemed to be extremely forthcoming with information. He looked to me to be glad of the opportunity to be able to mention Lee, and of course he slipped Sudovich's name into the conversation. In my experience people who are being interviewed by the police usually only mention someone else's name in an attempt to redirect police attention. Anyway all this is supposition, and the only real facts that we have are. There was a wooden box that we felt warranted close scrutiny, and now suddenly, it has disappeared under suspicious circumstances."

"So we are where we were, other than the fact that we are in possession of more supposition." Anderson announced. When there was no response from his two colleagues he asked, "Boss, what did Commander Bates say about the crate at your meeting?"

"He read Alan's report. When I explained our interest in Lee, he welcomed my request that we give the wooden box close scrutiny. He asked if we would keep him informed if we found that it is connected to any known 'names' or radical elements, and that means I owe Rodney an apology."

"Apology, Sir? What for?"

"Well Rodney, seeing that I was the one who requested we follow up on the wooden box, then I'm the one responsible for the fact that you are going to sit through hours of speed camera tapes searching for the truck that carried the transformer away from the building site in Liverpool."

Ben waited a moment until the groans had subsided before he chuckled at him and continued.

"Come on. Who else gets paid for watching T.V? You know the trucks departure point and where the cameras are situated. You have a description of the transformer truck and the approximate times."

Ben then turned his attention to Rodgers and gave him directions.

"Alan, I want you to have another talk to the transport driver who made the delivery to Liverpool. Have him concentrate on the fork lift truck, then test the memories of the people at the building site itself? Find out if anyone in the houses or buildings opposite remembers anything of it? Those who are behind this venture must have bought it from someone; it may even have been registered. Check out fork lift truck registration transfers back as far as a month before Walters's arrival in the country."

The two detectives turned to leave Ben's office and then stopped. "Rodney."

"Yes, Boss."

"Is Cooper's mobile turned on?"

Rodney Anderson reached into his jacket pocket and lifted out the surveillance phone. He looked at it, and then slid the switch at its side into the 'ON' position.

"Sorry, Sir."

"Stay on the ball Rodney. After all, if those two women need back up, I'm sure that you would want to be the first on the scene wouldn't you, and act on Miss Booth's behalf maybe?" Ben suggested as an almost undetectable smile touched his lips.

"But Sir, I'm a happily married man." A slightly embarrassed Rodney Anderson replied before he joined Rodgers. As they went, Anderson quietly said to Rodgers, "He doesn't miss a thing Alan, doesn't miss a thing."

CHAPTER 15

Tuesday 2.45 pm

Sally had just finished carrying the product of her shopping trip into the bedroom she shared with Lee, leaving the parcels in a careless pile on their bed.

The prizes were left in their respective packaging. She would return later and forage through and admire each of them. Like a Viking might do with his booty after the raping and drinking was done.

She sat down on the small available space at the corner of the bed and kicked off her shoes, then discarded her clothes before stepping naked to her bathroom to shower. After she'd dried herself, she paused in front of the large wall mirror with the oversized fluffy towel wrapped around her. She needed large towels, and this one suited her as it covered her body from the base of her throat to her knees. She inspected her chin, looking for the telltale signs of doubling by tilting her face upward toward the ceiling and slowly lowering it down again.

Finding that part of her seemingly in order, Sally held out her arms and viewed the muscle that ran from shoulder to elbow at the back of her arm. First one and then the other, giving each a little shake in order to test for firmness.

After lowering them back down to her sides, she moved her hands to the hem of the towel. It hung just below her knee caps, and clasping the hem she very slowly lifted it to expose her legs. As she did, she twisted her upper torso in order to inspect the rear of her evenly tanned and toned thighs.

Sally almost breathed a sigh of relief, when after close examination she discovered no sign of cellulite or burst capillaries. Standing full frontal to the mirror she dropped the hem of the towel and loosened the fold at its top. Allowing it to slowly fall away to reveal her upper body in centimetres, like a card player who inspects the set in hand one card at a time.

It was not that she was trying to tantalize herself. Her reason for slow revelation was due to her fear of discovering a blemish. Almost as if she would rather not look, but like a miser she was forced to uncover her treasure and count it for reassurance.

Sally feared aging, hated the invisible sadist whose signature of torture and torment was etched into the bodies of most of those around her.

There was evidence in the street, and she saw it through her window as people shuffled by. It didn't matter which way on earth they went, these wrinkled sagging victims. They all travelled in the sadist's direction and to the same ultimate destination.

His prowess was even displayed on the screen of her colour television set. On the faces of models and film stars who slowly progressed through their prime.

After some long moments she allowed the protective covering to fall, laying herself open to whatever mercy total exposure supplied.

Turning side on, she ran a caressing gaze from her hip to her shoulder and was reminded once again why men wanted to play out their fantasies with her.

Or rather on her, she corrected.

Having discovered nothing to cause her concern, she ran her hands down over her hips and finally her thighs. Feeling for natural desecration like burst capillaries, and upon finding no evidence she returned her attention to her breasts.

She held them gently in her two hands before giving each of her nipples a light tweak. They rose up to the point she preferred when she went braless under the soft caressing material of her favourite blouse. After releasing them she watched their proud stance before giving her body a little shake.

Thrilling at the wobbling graceful dance they gave, as if they were glad to be able to perform for her.

Sally picked up the towel from the floor. Looking to the mirror as she bent over to take careful consideration of her buttocks, and then kept them under close scrutiny as she stood up straight again. She hated to take her clothes off for fear of finding fault, but by the same token she loved to be naked. Particularly after she'd carried out a thorough visual check and had passed inspection.

She loved her body, and as she stood before the mirror admiring it the telephone interrupted her, forcing her to drag her attention away from her firm form. With a feeling of disappointment, she turned to the doorway and walked across her bedroom to answer it.

Lifting the hand piece, she purred.

"Sally."

It was the big man and she immediately felt uncomfortable.

"Dan, I asked you not to call me here on this phone. What if Tom were here and he answered it?"

"Please Sally don't be hard on me. I really needed to hear your voice and I know that Lee isn't there because I can see him over near his office here at the club."

"Damn it Dan!" She began and changed her course and asked, "What's he doing?"

"He's busy talking to someone on his mobile. That's why I took the opportunity to call. He's had everyone busy all day running left, right and centre. Something's going on. I'm not sure what. He's calling in loans, moving stock and cranking up the meth lab's production, like we're preparing for a siege or something. But enough of that baby. How're you going?"

Sally was still a bit edgy, but she answered him with the words she knew he wanted to hear.

"I'm good Dan my man. I've just had a shower and I'm standing here naked. My nipples are hard and I've put a light spray of perfume on my pussy's bush. I'm a little hot and thinking about that big pussy tickler of yours." She paused for some seconds before she added teasingly, "How are you going Dan?" She listened as Dan suddenly drew in breath and heard what sounded like a tongue moistening lips.

"Oh baby, my bloods pumping."

She teased him again.

"Maybe you'd better sit down Dan. By the time that organ of yours fills with blood you're bound to feel a little light headed." She chuckled down the phone to him and his ears welcomed the musical sound. He laughed out loud at her joke before she turned the conversation and steered it towards business.

"How's your plan Dan?"

"I'll probably be moving with it in the next day or so Sally. Things are nearly set, so it won't be long before you're free."

Sally listened as she heard Dan's name called out by someone in the back ground.

Dan answered it.

"Yes, Boss?"

Dan's voice came back to her in cautious whispering tone.

"Got to go Sally, things are moving here. Love you."

The connection broke before Sally could answer. She looked at the hand piece for a moment before she replaced it onto her dressing table. Deciding that now was a good time to go through her new trophies as she reckoned it would probably be some time before her husband came home.

Sally picked up a purchase bag and tipped its contents out onto the bed. As she did she wondered what it was that was going on in Tom's business, and was it something that could possibly impact on her lifestyle. It certainly explained his restlessness over the last few days, and she decided it may be a good idea not to impress on him the cost of her shopping spree. He'd learn of it soon enough when the statement arrived in the mail and maybe by then his mood might have improved.

There was one other thing that Sally had learned in her life, and that was to not to push her luck too far. Survival depended on knowing where the line was drawn and if she was nothing else other than being a beautiful woman, Sally was a survivor.

Tuesday 2.55 pm

Tom Lee had indeed been on his phone.

It seemed to him that he'd had it to his ear for most of the morning, and he suspected it would be there again for a large segment of the afternoon. He had no sooner left Larry in the office, after interrupting him yet again, that the electronic device demanded his attention.

A lot had been happening and his troops in the field called often to find out who they were to visit next, and how much they were expected to collect. There were a lot of people who owed him money and his troops were instructed to collect. Lee understood that it would be easier to have had the information they required printed out, but he preferred word of mouth.

He trusted his troops as much as he trusted anybody, but the fact remained he didn't trust anybody absolutely. Printed evidence of his business dealings in anyone's hands was a temptation he could not afford.

Although he doubted his competitors or even the law would have any use for the information, he was a believer in the old saying about the forest for the trees, although he did view the saying from another angle.

In this case he could keep an eye on the printed information until it got to the trees, but once it got past that point and disappeared into the forest then he had no idea where it could end up. He'd been surprised just how much he relied on Larry, and had decided that he should not interrupt him again. The work the accountant was carrying out, in hiding his assets, was more important than the task that he performed.

Cash collection.

He noted quickly the caller's number in the phones small window.

"Shane. What's new?"

"Mr. Lee. That car, the one I told you about yesterday? Well it's just driven in to the crate place. The two guys that got out of it flashed badges at the guy who spends all his time in the work shop. Then the work shop guy took them inside, probably to his Boss. Wait a second."

Lee was forced to hold for a moment and while he did he listened to a voice in the background which sounded like Charlie's as it issued a running commentary. It sounded to Lee like Charlie was doing the watching, and then relayed the events as they happened to Shane.

"Mr. Lee. The work shop guy has left the two other guys inside and is back in the yard again. Charlie says they're definitely coppers, but he thinks they may be Federals and not just ordinary pigs. Charlie reckons they look a bit heavier than ordinary coppers."

Lee had no comment to make and his long pause brought forth a question from Shane.

"Mr. Lee. Are you still there?"

Lee was still there, but his mind was on other things and he answered Shane without actually concentrating.

"Um, yes Shane. Just bear with me for a moment, will you?" Shane waited. The pause that followed seemed to be to him the longest he'd ever known Lee to make. He waited as long as his powers of concentration would allow before his hyperactive brain took charge.

"What'll we do Mr. Lee?"

"Just sit tight Shane. Call me when they leave, and then after that stay there until it's safe for you to leave after dark. No earlier, you understand? You've done good work and worth a little extra cash, eh?" Lee broke off and folded his mobile as he looked up and across the bar room to where Dan the Man was standing. He called out to him and then watched as Dan walked across the bar room to stand in front of him. Lee noted as Dan halted, fine beads of perspiration which glistened under the artificial bar room lighting.

Lee looked up at the man who was a good four inches taller than himself and noted a shift in Dan's normally steady gaze.

There was a lot going on around him to keep Lee's mind occupied, but he put it all aside for a moment as he was struck with the gut feeling that something was not right with Dan. As he let the pause in his speech linger, he noticed a movement of Dan's big feet which suggested to him nervousness.

Lee had been a poker player for a long time. He made use of his poker player face to hide the suspicion that he might otherwise have shown before he issued Dan with instructions.

"Dan, I want you to drive over to Grey Street, Alexandria. You know the area? Well I own the building at number sixteen, and right now there are two coppers there. I want you to drive there with haste and then follow them to wherever they go. I need to know if they're Federal coppers or just ordinary plain clothes. As soon as you find out, make sure that you call me straight away. You got that?"

Lee looked into the windows of Dan's soul and the name Judas immediately sprang to mind as Dan avoided his gaze. Lee believing that if the suspicious knew that they were suspected, they were from that moment on more guarded. If on the other hand the suspicious believed that they were unsuspected, then they would take more rope with which to hang themselves. He decided he didn't want Dan to know that he saw through him, so he tried to put him at ease.

"Come on Dan. You didn't pick up a bug out at Bourke did you and come down with a case of to-Bourke-ulosis or something?" He laughed as he patted Dan on the shoulder and turned him towards the door.

Dan laughed as best as he was able.

"No Mr. Lee. I've just a bit of a headache, that's all."

Lee had to prevent himself from pushing Dan out the door and instead advised.

"A nice drive through the city might do you good. Get out of here for a while. Go and follow the bad guys, and when you get back we'll knock the top off a few cold ones. How's that sound, eh?"

As Dan walked down the ramp at the back of the club, Lee watched him go and felt a little disappointed as he thought to himself.

"You're the last one I expected to spin around Dan and I wait with interest to see what made you turn."

Tuesday 3.20 pm

Dan the Man arrived at Grey Street. The industrial roadway tested his car's suspension as his tyres rode over an abundance of uneven pothole patches. He was reminded why it was he hated industrial areas, as he noted through his cars windows the drab visual environment. It presented itself in the form of oversized sheds in colours of galvanized iron, faded paint and rust. Each one of them with an office reception area that resembled a brothel madam's mask of makeup ten years after forced retirement. Suggesting the original designer had realized that even though he faced over whelming odds in his battle against boring, he had to try something.

It may have worked with the first one Dan thought, but in trying to beat the odds, each of the succession of designers had only succeeded in adding another facet to boring.

He drove slowly past number sixteen and saw the car which had been described to him by Lee. Then he travelled through the street, onto an intersecting road and with the aid of his right turn indicator turned onto the vacant lot where Nibbles three lads had parked some days earlier. Dan pulled over and switched off his car. He was immediately presented with another dimension of industrial area dullness.

Quiet.

Not silence. One would still be able to hear a two-inch nail drop, but a quietness which to Dan's inner city ears was akin to deafness. It was broken only by the sound of a passing vehicle, or sometimes occasional sudden sounds like a banging garage door or steel dropping on concrete. Dan's idea of industrial deafness was not being able to hear the sounds of the inner city.

The traffic as it rolled on when the lights turned green and the occasional screech of brakes. A siren as it cried of danger or heartbreak. A moment's music as one passed an open doorway of a record store, or even the thud as a wad of newspapers landed on the footpath beside a street vendor's stall.

The ever changing sounds of the inner city were the vibrations that Dan's ears lived for. He closed his driver's side window and turned to the only other option available to him. His car's radio waves saved him from the quiet and although it was soothing, it was yet another song which brought to mind Dan's only regret in life. He'd been born too late and had missed the 1960's.

His library of records, tapes and CD's at his home held most of the songs of that era. He'd heard stories from many of those who had lived that time, and their proof he'd missed a historic period was in the fact that he'd not met one person who had a bad thing to say about it.

Except of course the odd person whom he'd come across who'd been a parent of a teenager during those times of change.

Other than that, the music and the stories were all he needed. Their foundation was enough to base a belief that he'd missed out on an ingredient necessary for a full and wholesome outlook on life. He'd missed out on the excitement which had been brought about by a clear 20/20 mental vision of a Shangri-La future, and the extreme optimism that the 'all you need is love' revolution would bring about a brave new world.

Dan sat with his eyes closed allowing the music to soothe him. Suddenly his mobile phone demanded his return from his longed for dreamtime of joy to the world, and be present again in this post 9/11 reality.

He fumbled for his phone and brought it before his face. Only then, when it was the last thing to do he opened his eyes and looked at its screen.

Dan's disappointment at missing the end of the song was overcome by curiosity when he didn't recognize the caller's number.

A voice came to his ear.

"Dan Sanic?"

"Yes?"

"Two hours ago you called and requested a meeting with my employer?"

"Yes."

"Your request has been granted. Be in the front bar of the hotel which is on the corner just near your employer's club at five o'clock today. You will be contacted there. Is that understood?"

"Yes, I understand."

The caller disconnected, and Dan breathed in so deeply that the buttons of his shirt pulled at the ends of their button holes.

He held the breath for a short moment, before allowing the air to slowly be released through his slightly parted lips. At the same time, he let his whole body go limp, to the extent that he might dissolve into his car seat. With slowly opening eyes, he saw through the thin slits between his eyelids a large industrial shed on the corner of Grey Street.

Someone had painted a picture of Donald Duck, depicted in a moment in time bent over a manual air pump. Its air delivery hose led away from the painted pump to an actual air hose fitting which projected from the shed wall.

As Dan watched, a man came from within the shed and attached a length of hose to the outlet. An object dangled at the hose's end before being clenched in the man's hand. Suddenly a cloud of rust coloured dust announced the release of compressed air pressure as it ballooned from a trucks tyre rim.

His eyes were quickly torn away from the man in a reflex action. They became fixed with interest on the cloud of red dust. It swirled around the man and then away, to be collected and dispersed by the light outside breeze.

Dan blinked almost as if it were a cloud around his own eyes. Then once again he took a deep breath, letting it escape through pursed lips with a low whistle. He was not one to whom the feeling of uncertainty was usual, but he recognized its taste as it returned from where it had lain dormant for some time.

In a recess hidden away, as might be an article left unseen in an upstairs attic until rediscovered and then again remembered. He looked at the mobile phone where it lay prone, as if pretending innocence. Finally, he reached out to touch it as if to prove its existence.

"Yes," he thought aloud, "I did make the call. There had come an answer to my call and it has brought to me uncertainty." Dan's young crime life had matured under the watchful eye of Tom Lee, and he knew that he owed him. If not for Lee he might have been jailed by this time, or worse, dead.

He'd learnt much from Lee. Had sometimes stepped close to the line that defined the limits of loyalty, but now, after he'd met with Eddie Paulini he would be stepping over that line.

Past the point of no return, heading down the road to where he would betray Lee and take over where Lee was destined to leave off. He'd known from the beginning that falling under Sally's spell would lead to someone's ruin.

It was often perceived to be an inevitable outcome for any triangle relationship. There was no doubt that the probability in this party was decidedly high.

The uncertainty he'd felt on his first secret meeting with Sally had caused him to be slow of the mark. She had seen the need to take the situation in hand, guide him to the threshold and then onwards toward his initial lesson in betrayal. That same uncertainty, being a mixture of the sense of betrayal and a fear of discovery had stayed with him on each of the occasions he'd returned to her for new and more advanced lessons.

The fear of discovery heightened his sexual satisfaction.

Like a rich kleptomaniac who shoplifts for the thrill and then becomes addicted, taking greater risks in an effort to enhance the thrills. Dan knew that his mischief would end in discovery at some stage. It added to his belief that it would be better for him if he went on the offensive, and then, while he held the upper hand, remove the shroud of secrecy.

On his own terms he could display the truth. Lay it out in the open at a time when it would be too late for Tom to retaliate.

It was a dangerous game he played, and the stakes were high.

His actions could cost him his life, but Sally, along with the speed and ecstasy distribution network was a worthy prize. There was also the fact that Sally should, in the event of Lee's demise, be entitled to at least half of everything that he'd owned.

It was obvious to Dan that if he was going to strike, then now was the time. Apart from the prize, there was also the possibility that if Lee disappeared, then maybe these Federal coppers might lose interest and go sniff around in someone else's backyard. He looked at his watch and noted the time. There was still time to back out and get away.

Not much time though he thought, because in less than two hours he would discuss possible outcomes with Eddie Paulini. After that, there was no turning back.

Eddie Paulini was the Italian side of town, and as Dan had no idea what kind of loyalty he could expect from Lee's former employees immediately after his coup. He felt it would be good insurance to engage some form of back up.

It would surely cost him a percentage of the distribution networks income, but if, for that moderate cost he was assured an ultimate success then who was he to complain. In the end he would have more than he had now, with Sally and her real estate as cream on the cake.

Dan listened to the radio some more and was happy when the Stone's Ruby Tuesday came on. Another classic, he thought. Toward the end of the song he saw the car which belonged to Lee's suspected Federal Policemen leave through the engineer's front gate. He watched it as it turned left and disappeared around the corner, before he started his own car and followed discreetly behind it.

CHAPTER 16

Tuesday 4.55 pm

It was five minutes to five o'clock when Dan walked into the front bar of the hotel.

The place was crowded and he felt somewhat obvious in his dark suit.

He ordered a light beer and sipped slowly with the desire to keep his head clear. Water would have been preferable, but he felt he looked out of place enough as it was without driving the point home to this rough and ready crowd.

After no more than a quarter of the glass of beer he felt a touch at his elbow. He turned his head as he heard a voice say.

"Mr. Sanic?"

"Yes? I'm Dan Sanic."

The man was also wearing a suit and Dan immediately noticed a light gold chain which held a crucifix. It sat just below the knot of his tie and its gold sheen was highlighted by the dark materials backdrop.

"I have a car waiting, Mr. Sanic. Please follow me?" Dan had expected to leave by the front door. He was taken aback, but glad when the Italian man walked to a hallway and then through a series of doorways before stepping from the rear of the building.

The Italian man walked to the rear door of the car and held it open in silent invitation. Dan slid into the car and immediately felt the glare of the outside sunlight leave off its invasion on his eyes as the Italian man gently closed the door. Another man who was dressed similar to the Italian man pulled the car into gear and they cruised quietly out of and away from the car park.

They drove through the city centre in silence. Dan watched out of the window the hustle and bustle of the crowded streets.

They appeared surrealist as their noise was lost in the obvious sound proofing of the car.

After a short while the driver turned the car up a litter strewn laneway. Where it meandered to avoid wooden pallets, garbage bins and a street lady whose shopping cart contained the product of her homeless life.

As they had left from the rear of the hotel, they now approached the rear of another building. Although the reason for this could be given that it was easier to find a parking place, Dan suspected that it was probably more a case of discretion.

Dan didn't feel good at all.

The curse of uncertainty still plagued him. More so now that he was past the point of no return. He worried that the Italians might see his impending betrayal of Tom as suspect, maybe to the point that they might question his loyalty to them.

After all, if he were in their shoes he would most certainly view his motives, and of course his loyalty with an extremely critical eye.

Dan took a deep breath and told himself quietly.

"Take hold of yourself Dan. Shed all emotion and look at the big picture. The big picture is business. You're here to talk business Dan, just business." He listened to what he said in thought and tried hard to believe it, but he couldn't help admitting to himself that he was scared. This was a brand new adventure, where he, Dan Sanic, was going to meet a powerful man. Not as an employee or a messenger, but as a businessman to put forward a business proposal.

Dan looked about him as he was led down a very ordinary corridor, until the Italian suddenly stopped short and grasped a door handle. He pushed the door open, looked up at Dan and gestured enter with an open hand.

The Italian had been silent up to this point, and Dan was glad in a way to hear him speak.

"If you'll excuse me, just a precaution you understand." He said as he moved toward Dan and ran his hands over his large body. After the thorough pat down, Dan wondered why the buttons on his suit coat were scrutinized.

The Italian man finally stood back.

"If you would like to make yourself comfortable Mr. Sanic, I assure you that your wait will not be long. Would you like tea or coffee?"

Dan briefly surveyed the room he found himself in before he turned to the Italian man.

"I would prefer water please."

"Yes Mr. Sanic. I will see to it myself."

The Italian man closed the door quietly and left him alone in what appeared to be a conference room, equipped with an oval table which was closely crowded with fifteen padded chairs.

Although he was tempted to sit down, he instead walked across the room and viewed a water colour of an outback Australian scene. He was about to look closely at the artist's name when he heard the door reopen.

Thinking that the Italian man had returned with his badly needed water, he turned to accept it. His surprise was overwhelming when instead he found himself confronted by an attractive young woman.

Dressed in a smart dark suit, she appeared to him to be confident as she strode away from the now closed door. Her greeting was with a smile and an extended hand. He accepted both, and immediately noticed how delicate her fingers felt in his large boned hand.

He was in control enough to be sure to remember his strength as he took her hand, and he nodded to her as she introduced herself.

"Good afternoon Mr. Sanic. My name is Mary Marshall. I'm sorry to have kept you waiting."

"I take it from that, that I may address you as Mary?" She looked up at him a little surprised.

She was used to living in a man's world, and had worked hard to build her career within it. Where she was not used to being asked, how it was that she preferred to be addressed. It did happen at times, but normally men just took it for granted that she being a woman would accept whatever way it was that they preferred to address her. They had been right to a certain extent. She had given them a little lee-way, and accepted the inevitable by always introducing herself as Mary. She did at times chide herself for allowing them that lee way, but it was easier in the long run. It gave her the opportunity to get to the point without having to beat around the male ego.

"Mary will do fine, Mr. Sanic." She wondered if he was the chat up type or just well mannered.

"Then how do you do Mary? My name is Dan."

She would find out as their meeting progressed that Dan was well mannered and she would never have guessed that he'd had some of the best teachers in the art.

Dan had taken lessons from some of the best in the good manners business. Cary Grant, Bing Crosby, John Mills and a host of others who had adorned the silver screen. All of whom now lived in his extensive personal library of videos and C.Ds.

Mary invited him to sit and she understood the reason, but didn't take his action as personal, when instead he automatically turned his head toward the door, as if he believed they were still one person short.

"Dan, I'm here on behalf of Mr. Paulini. As his personal assistant I will report immediately back to him. I do understand that you expected a face to face meeting, but would you mind viewing this as a preliminary to that face to face meeting? It will take place at a later date, depending of course on the outcome of this preliminary meeting."

Dan, who was by now seated, placed his hands flat onto the top of the table, as if to begin the action of pushing himself to his feet.

"No way," he said in a quiet voice.

He was about to speak again, but was interrupted by a light knock on the door, before the Italian man entered with a tray that held bottled water, clean glasses and a bowl of ice cubes.

The two of them were silent as the Italian man placed the tray onto the table before he looked at Mary who replied to his enquiring expression.

"That will be all Benny. Thank you."

After Benny had left the room Mary was about to speak when Dan interrupted her.

"Miss Marshall. Mary." He corrected himself. "The reason I am here is to put forward a proposition that will without doubt be a major benefit to your Boss. Now please understand, you cannot know the position that I place myself in by being here, and I..."

Mary interrupted him.

"Dan please. We do understand the position you find yourself in, and if you like, I can explain to you how it is that you came to be in that position? You will see we know much more than you realize." Dan went quiet, unsure what it could be that he was about to hear. He bided his time by watching as she took a bottle of water and after removing its lid shared its contents into each of their glasses.

"Ice?" She asked.

"No thank you, no."

She sipped at her glass, and after placing it onto a coaster she'd taken from the tray, she looked at Dan as if deciding where to begin.

"Dan, as you will no doubt guess from what I'm about to tell you. We have ears in many places, and the owners of those ears inform us that Tom Lee is now at this moment consolidating his cash assets. He's collecting on all outstanding debts and is off loading as much amphetamine and ecstasy as his factories can produce. This suggests to us that he may have immigration, or in the least, a long off shore holiday in mind? We are unsure as to why it is that he appears skittish. We think it may have something to do with the fact he fears his possible connection to his former partner's involvement in something that we believe was much too big for him." She paused to sip from her glass before she continued.

"We know that whatever it was that the former partner initiated, has the focus of Federal Police attention now. Lee may in the long run prove that he has no connection with that plot, but just his connection with this former partner will prove him to be a popular aspect of their investigation. Hence it may draw plenty of unwanted attention."

"If their investigators get even just one foot in his door they can make life very uncomfortable for him, to the extent that he either shoots through or tries to tough it out. If he shoots through, then his territory will be up for grabs, and that could be a little tedious for the rest of us. If he tries to tough it out, then his competitors will attempt to crowd him out and that could create a situation of extreme danger."

She let what she'd said sink in while she looked to the folder on the table top before her and shifted a sheet or two of its paper.

"You've been with Tom Lee for a little over seven years now?"

Dan looked from her face to the folder and his tone was incredulous.

"You have a file on us?"

Mary replied in a teacher like tone as she flicked her fingers through the page corners of the thick file.

"Dan, we Italians have been in business since the fifteenth century. Part of the reason for our survival is that we've learnt to change with the times. There is one thing that has not changed of course, and that is the method we use to gain inside information, a basic necessity that ensures successful outcomes. We change with the times, these times demand information, and at a rate that sometimes I fear that our main frames will burst."

Mary went back to viewing the pages in the folder with apparent total concentration, biding her time and waiting for Dan to make his move. She knew he would. It was only a matter of time. She had led him along the garden path and now it was up to him to pick the berries. All she had done up to this point was to tell him what she knew to be fact. That was within the law and an act of self-preservation on her part in case something went askew. If she had put forward a proposal, then she would be crossing the line, so she waited for him to say what it was she expected to hear. Then he would be in the compromised position if ever he talked out of school.

Dan tugged the top button of his shirt with his hooked finger and took water from his glass as tried to bring his thoughts to order. It appeared to him that Paulini had an informant in the police department who kept him up to date with certain investigations. Most certainly he also had a pair of ears inside Tom's organization. Organization? These Italians made Lee's set up look like a side show.

Dan was way out of his depth. He felt like he had fallen into the deep end, and now had to stay afloat long enough to learn to tread water. He had come here to deliver a business proposal. Suddenly he felt like he had tendered a job application and was sitting the interview.

He tried to get back some control of the situation.

"Mary, I know these things you've explained. I can see that Tom Lee is in a position which could become precarious. What I want is to take over if the situation becomes critical. As you've pointed out, I've been inside Lee's organization for seven years and I know it like the back of my hand. My main problem is that I don't know which people on Lee's staff will be willing to side with me. The fact of the matter is, I know what must be done, but I don't see how I can carry out my plan on my own."

His words rang in his ears and he had to admit to himself that it sounded very lame. He felt somewhat dispirited until Mary revived him.

"Dan, if the situation develops to the extent that you are in need of our financial advisory services, or if you see the need to restructure the business interests from the ground up, please do not hesitate to call me." She paused for a moment to take from the folder one of her business cards as she added, "Of course if you find yourself in need of our professional staff you can be assured of our support." She didn't touch the side of her nose in a 'wink, wink say no more' fashion, but Dan understood what she meant by staff. After all, that is what he'd asked for.

Dan knew that the meeting was over when she stood up. He rose to his feet and allowed her to escort him to the door. The Italian man had been waiting in the corridor.

"Benny if you'd show Mr. Sanic back to the car please. Instruct the driver to take him wherever he wishes to go, and then return here to me."

Mary stood back from the doorway to make room for Dan to pass by. As she did, Dan noticed a small wire which ran from behind her ear to a type of hearing aid piece of apparatus. He'd not noticed it before as she had been sitting with the earpiece away from him. Did she plan the seating arrangement at the table to be free from embarrassment in being hearing impaired, he thought?

Dan felt some sympathy for her. He dragged his eyes away from her ear before he moved through the doorway, catching the intensity of her perfume as he went.

She spoke to him as he stepped into the corridor and he turned to face her. "Dan, there is a good chance that we will hear of, how shall I put it, the development of a critical situation before you do, but please let me remind you. When you feel it's necessary, call the number on my business card and all of our resources will be immediately put at your disposal." She held out her hand to him and he took it. She finished their business with the compliment, "It's a pleasure to do business with you."

Dan returned the compliment with a nod of his head before he turned away and followed Benny down the corridor.

Mary turned and walked back to the oval table to collect her folder of papers. As she did she spoke out loud like mad person might when the walls closed in.

"I think that now, after all these years you may be on the verge of acquiring all of Lee's territory Mr. Paulini. Would you agree?"

She listened as her boss's voice came clearly through her ear piece before answering, again speaking to the microphones embedded in the four surrounding walls.

"Yes Sir, Thank you. We should, I think, hear from him within a week."

Mary removed the ear piece and dropped it into her coat pocket. Her smile was broad when a knock came at the door and she looked up from the open folder to speak to Benny as he approached.

"Benny, would you mind taking this folder to my secretary, tell her that I've read through it and I'm satisfied with the figures. If she can have it prepared for lodgment with the Lands Department by noon tomorrow I'll be happy. Thank you." She handed him the folder, which Dan had mistakenly believed to be devoted to Tom Lee's outfit. As he turned away to leave she wondered about Dan Sanic. Coming to the conclusion that it wasn't stupidity that possessed him, it seemed that he was just knee deep in naivety.

Mary slowly shook her head from side to side as she spoke quietly to herself.

"Poor Dan, if we had a file on Lee's operation it probably would not more than a page long, and unless you play your cards right, your future might even be shorter."

Tuesday 9.50 pm

Ben Preston had had a long day. He poured a drink from one of the bottles which adorned his living room side board before he took a pre-cooked spaghetti sauce meal from his freezer.

Sometimes in his spare time he'd cook up a large boiler of meat sauce and a separate pot of spaghetti. Then placed meal sized portions into plastic containers to be stored in his freezer. He rarely felt like cooking when he came home late, and unless he had taken the opportunity to eat out, or buy take away he relied on the frozen pantry.

Freezers were like micro-wave ovens and automatic washing machines he thought. They were a bachelor's best friend, or in his case, a widower's best friend.

With the timer set he pressed the micro waves start button, before habitually removing himself to his lounge room to see what his television had to offer. The lounge room was small. As was the whole flat he lived in, but it was easier for him to maintain compared to the house he'd vacated after his wife's passing.

Ease of maintenance was not the main reason for the sale of his original dwelling. It was only one quarter of the reason. With one of the other three parts being that he was not staying in Sydney after his retirement.

The third part was that a rented flat would be easier to walk away from at short notice when that time came. The fourth part and by far the most important, was that there were no ghosts in this new abode. Other than the few which were attached to the assortment of photographs he had scattered about this room.

In less than three months he would leave Sydney. Accept his police pension gratefully, pack a bag and walk out to see where life would take him.

Walking away from this city would not be hard, and he agreed with Quinn. They were both alike, and like other baby boomers they'd lived through the best period of the twentieth century, until finally they noticed change. Sydney, like cities all over the world was unable to escape the change that the drug culture brought and spread through its communities, infecting all those susceptible as it seeped through to the cities soul.

It was not noticeable at first that the 'big smoke' was losing its innocence. In time it became more obvious, when offshoots of its culture began to make their impact known, like AIDS, home invasions, bag snatching, burglary and street gang activity.

Not to mention distraught parents who tried desperately to cope with untrustworthy offspring who would sell those same parents for a quick fix.

In one way or another it affected everyone, including innocent bystanders who were not surprised by anything anymore.

Ben had served the community as a policeman for over thirty years. He'd fought a good fight against the bad guys, but he'd reached a time in his life when he had to hand over the reins to the younger generation. To law enforcers of the new age, who had a better understanding of the threats that twenty first century society faced.

He sat back in his comfortable chair and used the televisions remote control to flick through a reality show and an old movie before accepting the late evening news.

A woman reporter stood in an overcoat on a windswept wet street. Suddenly the camera left her. It captured a white van in its lens and held it as it passed through a gateway to an industrial buildings yard.

Ben had only a short moment to catch sight of a large doorway in the industrial building on the far side of the yard. Its shadowed openness in the side of the building was momentarily obvious, before the delivery gate which led onto the street was closed.

He did gain a brief glance of a man dressed in a chemical hazard suit, as the cameraman tried to glean as much information from the shot as possible.

A second later he was again faced with the woman in the coat, and he turned his TV's volume up in time to catch a segment of the story.

"... it would seem from the documents which were delivered to our newsroom by person's unknown, that the building partly hidden by the gates behind me was used to manufacture the electrical component. The documents also state that the electrical component was designed to house a weapon of mass destruction. The fact that our news crews arrived at this site at around the same time the authorities did, suggests that it is those same persons' anonymous intention to bring this stark reality to the attention of the whole world. The documents also state clearly that there are five of these weapons. Four of them exported from England to countries which were known during the lead up to the invasion of Iraq as the coalition of the willing...."

The news reporter was interrupted by the noise of a truck that passed behind her. It turned into the gateway where a policeman moved to open its gate.

Ben watched, and then suddenly realized that the news story was unedited. While that thought lingered in his head, the name of the news corporation, B.B.C London flashed onto the bottom of the screen, along with the word, LIVE.

He leaned forward in his chair and stared at the screen. His ears pricked with intent at hearing every word that was spoken. Reward came with a brief glimpse of the large doorway as the truck passed through the gateway. For a second his eyes feasted greedily, before the gate was closed again, concealing from view all activity on the inside.

An object caught in his brief glimpse had sat squarely in the buildings open doorway. It registered in his brain and he saw it again clearly in his mind's eye. It was the identical twin of the one that had attracted his attention in Grey Street and he breathed words of recognition through dry lips, "Another wooden box."

The feeling he'd felt in his bones about the wooden box in Grey Street came upon him again, but now with much more urgency. Something very serious is going to happen, he thought. Suddenly his mobile phone called out for attention.

"Preston."

"Ben its Rusty Bates. It seems we've work to do. I've put the word out for a full briefing at H.Q. All hands on deck A.S.A.P."

Ben's answer was brief.

"On my way."

He'd no sooner put his mobile down, when his landline phone started its call and he walked across the room to it.

"Preston."

"Boss it's Rodney, are you watching the news?"

"Yes. I've caught enough it to understand why Commander Bates just called to let me know that everyone's called in for a full briefing. All hands on deck were his words so I'll see you there. I'll call Alan and let him know. You pass the word on to the rest of my people will you?"

"Yes Boss. It appears that you were right about that big wooden box?"

"Sometimes I wish I was wrong young Rodney. No time for talk now. It's time to get moving. Let's go."

"Yes Sir."

Ben turned about and walked into the kitchen to his now hot meal. He removed it from the microwave and placed it, still in its freezer container, into a shopping bag.

In his bedroom he put on a clean shirt and carried with him another two others as spares. Doubting he would be returning to this place tonight. He moved to the lounge room and tried for some seconds to gain more information into what was happening in London.

Reluctant to turn off the television and thus cut himself off from his only available source of information, he listened for several more seconds as he donned his coat.

The door was almost closed behind him when he remembered Cooper's phone, and he had to juggle his carried items as he retrieved it from the kitchen breakfast bar.

A few minutes later he was on the road and heading toward what he believed to be the beginning of a serious situation. The world had changed, and although he wished at times that God would come and cleanse the world of evil, he was also glad at times that God as yet hadn't done so, because he needed evil.

Evil was the fox and he, Ben Preston was the hound.

Take away the fox and the hound's life was without meaning.

As he drove hard through the city's streets he felt excitement build within him.

The chase was about to begin.

CHAPTER 17

Tuesday 9.50 p.m.

Larry had gone at it hard for the whole of the afternoon. It left him with a hollow stomach and a headache, but he finally had all the T's crossed and the I's dotted. He sat back in his chair and rubbed his fingers into his dry and tired eyes, before looking again at the neat pile of applications and lodgment forms. The fat sheaf of paper sat like a cairn, a monument which not only celebrated his hard day's work, but to the accountant it stood as a masterpiece.

Reaching forward he touched, almost caressed the screen of his computer, and with quiet voice he thanked it, and all of its cousins for allowing him to accomplish so much in such a short space of time. Then he slouched back into his chair again. Relishing in the kind of afterglow that exists between humans and the machines they know are necessary for their standard of living.

Larry looked at his watch and decided it was not too late to call Adam. He hit the speed dial and waited through a set of three tones.

"Yes mate, it's all done. What time is good for you in the morning?"

"How about I meet you in that coffee shop near your office? Yes, eight thirty is fine mate. See you then." After some minutes he stood and stretched his cramped body to its full height.

Then with the pile of papers cradled in the crook of his right arm, it was time to approach Lee for signatures. There were fifteen of them in all, and he hoped that Lee would sign quickly. If he, Larry had to go through and explain each of the documents to Lee, then there would be little sleep this night.

He made his way to Lee's office and was glad of the sound insulation it offered. Evidence of its effectiveness was obvious as he pushed the office door closed and the noise of the bar almost disappeared.

Lee sat at his desk and held in his hand the remote control which he had been using to flick through the programs on his wide screen T.V. He put down the remote as Larry sat in the chair opposite him, and Larry knew by the sounds of the news reader's comments that there had been yet another bombing in Iraq.

Larry placed the paper pile onto the only small clearing available on Lee's desk and looked toward Lee as he was asked.

"All done Larry?" Larry saw worry on Lee's face. His look of fatigue seemed to be emphasized by the five o'clock shadow which was now in extra overtime.

"Yes Mr. Lee. There are just the signatures and everything can be lodged first thing tomorrow. If you like, I can leave them with you and you can go over them. I can pick them up in the morning and take them into town." He'd hoped that Lee would read in his answer that he was mainly interested in going home and crawling gratefully into his soft bed. Lee either didn't read, or he wasn't interested in Larry's desire. He instead sought information.

"Tell me about this... Lee broke off his question mid-sentence, and Larry watched as Lee's gaze suddenly became fixed on the television. His fumbling of the remote control as he attempted to raise its volume also caught Larry's attention. He turned to see what had distracted Lee, and was greeted with the sight of a winter garmented woman. Her windswept hair sought the attention of her waving hand as she stood on a rain wet pavement.

Larry saw 'London Live' in large letters in the corner of the screen a second before his ears tuned into the commentary. Lee finally got in control of the volume.

"... an hour since all the major news outlets received documents stating that the weapons of mass destruction were in fact manufactured in the building behind me. The documents state clearly that the weapons are designed to emit a poison gas, and are in the form of an electrical transformer. Some moments ago, we were allowed a brief glimpse of the inside of the yard when the front gate was opened to allow passage for an emergency services truck. We could clearly see one of the large wooden boxes, or crates which the documents state was the type used for the export of the weapons."

The windswept woman paused for a moment as she glanced at the folder in her hand. Larry watched as she waved her microphone hand over the folder, succeeding in her attempt to turn a page in the gusty conditions.

The microphone travelled back to where it hid her pointed chin and she went on.

"We're advised by the documents that there are five crates in all. One is still here in Britain. The others have been exported, to the Philippines, Canada, the United States and to Sydney, Australia.

Larry's mouth was dry. He flashed his tongue around its inside in order to make moisture. As he did, his hand automatically laid upon his breast where he felt the comforting hardness of the cover of his recently updated passport.

He'd placed it in the inside breast pocket of his suit jacket when he'd picked it up from Moot the forger. Deciding then, that the small book would stay with him at all times. All he needed for a short notice exit was both of his passports and some credit cards. His recent divorce had made him almost possession less, so he was certainly able to travel light.

He looked back to Lee expecting some type of verbal outburst, but was surprised when Lee just quietly lowered the televisions volume. He spoke almost with an air of despondency.

"Which of these need signing?"

No words were spoken as Lee signed some of the forms. Larry passed them over and when he retrieved them, he inserted them back into the paper pile. When the last block of paper was back in order, Larry waited for some moments, until it became clear to him that further conversation between the two men was not likely. He retrieved the pile of documents from the desktop and made his way to the office door, closing it softly behind him.

It was as if Lee had not noticed Larry's departure from the room. He sat quietly as the television soundlessly displayed more pictures of the windswept English street. Lee picked up the remote once again, but decided there was no more information the news service could offer him. It had said enough.

The image of the wooden box was all the information necessary to know that the shit was about to hit the fan. He looked toward the two suitcases which stood against one wall of his office, then made his way to the office door and locked it.

Satisfied with his privacy he turned his attention to his safe. As its heavy steel door swung open, his eyes were greeted with a colourful display of money. He quickly removed the wads and carefully placed them into one of the suitcases.

As he transferred the money he felt a sullen smile exercise his facial muscles as he thought. Drugs, worth their weight in gold and then multiply by fifty. When it was full he closed it and locked it with a small padlock, before filling the second case, until the safe only contained small denomination notes. He padlocked the second suitcase, and then moved a lounge chair away from the wall to expose the corner of the carpet. It peeled away from the floor to reveal a steel door which had been set into the concrete.

It opened quietly and he dropped the two suitcases into the dark hole that had been hidden beneath it, before relocking the steel door and replacing the carpet and lounge chair over it. With his task completed he sat down lazily in the lounge chair and tried to decide what to do next.

He could visualize his options, but found it next to impossible to organize his thoughts. The television set caught his attention again, and he turned it on its swivel base so that its screen was visible from the lounge chair.

With a cushion comfortable under his head, he lay on the lounge and thumbed through pay T.V. He found the movie channel, and then settled to watch the early stages of an old Steve McQueen classic, 'Tom Horn.'

Maybe if I just take some time out and clear my head a little he thought, as Horn shot a musical minded cowpoke in the leg.

Tuesday 10.15 pm

Ben sat quietly in his car and dialled Alan Rodgers' number on his mobile phone while he waited for the traffic lights to change. Several ring tones later the familiar voice of his apprentice answered.

"Yes, Boss."

"Alan. I'm not interrupting anything critical, am I?"

"No, Sir. What's happening?"

"Have you got your T.V on?

"No, Sir. It broke down last week."

"How did you go with the truck driver who saw the fork lift truck?"

"I got on to the company and learned that he is away on a delivery job down at Nowra. They don't expect him back at his loading yard until tomorrow morning." Rodgers paused in his comment as if he was unsure whether the next thing he said might suggest a lack of enthusiasm. He covered himself by saying, "Boss, I have his home number and address. I could call him, and if he's back in town, I could go and see him now."

"Yes, do that. Commander Bates has called for a full briefing, which means everyone, but I can fill you in on the outcome of that. Go to the man's house and stay there until he comes home if necessary. Then hook up with Rodney and find out what he discovered from the traffic tapes and report to me."

"Yes Sir. Boss what's happened?"

"It seems that this wooden box thing is bigger than any of us envisaged, Alan. Switch on your radio and listen to the news while you're driving to the truck driver's house. Better still, the A.B.C is offering full coverage. You'll find out from them more than I know at this moment. I'll see you the moment you have news."

Ben put down his mobile phone and tried to listen to the radio's coverage of the story. At the same time he considered his next move.

There was a lot at stake and he had little to go on. Just the delivery truck driver, the fork lift truck and a wooden box. Of John Kane's involvement he was sure.

He was also sure that now the news had broken about the reason for the wooden box, Kane, along with Walters and Wild would expect surveillance and be sure footedly discreet.

As for Lee?

Ben was convinced that he would not knowingly put himself at risk by having a close association with the wooden box. Having it firmly planted in his own back yard, even for the short period that it had been, didn't fit Lee. He was not known to leave evidence lying around. No, Ben thought, it feels to me like Sudovich was freelancing. As he had in the Nigerian deal and hopefully because of it Lee was going to be a not so innocent victim. Ben knew that because of the wooden box, he would have access to Lee and he would go through him like a dose of salts.

Unfortunately, the wooden box and its association to terrorism would push Lee to the back burner for the time being, but Ben was happy in the knowledge that he would stew for a while. He drove through the streets of Sydney, as words like 10X, toxic, disaster, death, issued from his radio, and he cursed. Not because the world was a hard place, but because of the arseholes who made it their business to make it that way.

*****

Athol alighted from a motor car outside the front door of a country house that sat on acreage not far from the outskirts of London. He was escorted into the house by one of his subordinates, who cast a glance around the garden area before he stepped through the doorway and closed the door behind them.

Once inside he ushered Athol through a wide doorway and into a room which two weeks earlier had been the house's main dining room. It had been cleared of all its original furniture, except for the huge dining table. Its expansive polished top was now almost covered with computer consoles and key boards. Their connecting cables snaked their way to a large computer that occupied space on the floor.

Athol, who was fifty-five and by far the oldest man in the room, felt a little off balance. Not because of his lack of I.T knowledge, but by the fact that the people who occupied places around the table were so much at home with such advanced technology. They sat with an air of certainty. Like lords of their realms whose ability allowed them to be nonchalant, like a beautiful woman or a domestic cat.

Athol knew they knew their business.

The fact that they were in this room was proof. They had all been vetted by people who knew as much as they, and more.

After some minutes of watching the activity of the people within the room, Athol's subordinate, Charles suggested.

"If I might give you an in depth tour?"

"Mmm? Yes, of course."

Charles led the way to the head of the table and pointed to the console there.

"This is what we call our command console. It will be operated by Phillip here." Phillip looked up momentarily. He nodded politely at the interruption before returning with vigour to his keyboard.

Charles resumed his commentary.

"After the sales team leaders have passed on to prospective customers our web address, the operations teams will carry out the demonstrations. Then the bidding will begin. All of the bidders will come through to this console. When they do, Phillip will redirect each of them to one of his colleagues, so that each of the bidders will be handled by the operator of one of these other consoles."

He waved his hand toward and over the congested dining table before continuing.

"When the bidder has been designated to a console, the operator of that console will bring into operation a computer program. It is designed to worm its way in through the bidder's back door, and ferret out information necessary to allow us to hack in to his computer at a later date. As you can see we have thirty-two consoles and each one of them is capable of overseeing three bidders. While we have a bidder on line, our devious computer program will infiltrate the bidder's computer, gaining information on access passwords and connection numbers. Once we have these, we can hack in at a later date and search for passwords and code numbers for banking transactions and accounts."

Charles, without explanation stepped to a small table which stood nearby and offered quietly with a raised glass, water. Athol declined with a slight shake of his head. His attention fascinated by the precise finger movements of the whiz kids until Charles resumed his commentary.

"We expect a better than average outcome, but we'll not know until the fat lady sings."

"We'll have to hope for the best then," Athol added before he offered a consideration, "If we can attach ourselves to ten to twenty per cent of them, I'll be satisfied."

"Then we will suck dry ten to twenty per cent of them," Charles chuckled

They turned away from the table and slowly walked together toward the door. As they went Athol showed his curiosity.

"You seem to have a good understanding of all this high tech business?"

"Not really. I'm at virtual loss. Please excuse the pun," He chuckled again before continuing, "No. I'm pretty much out of my depth. I understand what I hear if it's well explained. I'm lucky to have amongst my band of people here, some who would make good teachers. Another thing in my favour is that, like you, I'm a good listener."

Charles stood by and watched as a chauffeur opened the car's rear door, and then again as Athol nestled into its leather seat. He waited until Athol was comfortably seated before he leaned in through the open door.

"There is one more thing," he said. "The sales teams are at this moment making known to their potential customers our web site address. The clock will start to tick, as it were, on schedule in a little under four hours." Athol offered a slight nod. A sparkle came to his eyes as movement at the corners of his mouth suggested a glimmer of a smile.

He waved as the car pulled away, and as it slid easily down the driveway towards the entrance gate. *The reasons why people as rich as Athol got involved in activities like this were secrets that only people like Athol could know,* Charles thought as he walked back to the house and his workplace.

CHAPTER 18

Tuesday 10.30 pm

Mrs. Griffin became Sydney's first victim.

After watching the late night news she'd made herself a cup of tea. Then content, she returned to the A.B.C's full coverage broadcast. To watch as events unfolded, while knowing that whatever the outcome, God worked in mysterious ways. Her pension offered small comforts in the Sydney suburb of Parramatta where she spent her days sewing and knitting amongst the Christian icons which adorned her living room.

An ancestral set of Rosary beads rested in her lap, ready for her nightly ritual of prayer for the world and its inhabitants. She'd grown used to living alone since her dear Arthur passed away. Her loneliness reminiscent of the time a young dear Arthur had served in the Second World War.

Her only wish was that her daughters and her son would visit more often. Allow her more time with her grandchildren, but she, in her understanding maternal way allowed them their reasons.

"The world is much faster now Mum. Nothing is concrete and certain anymore. We can't make the time like you and Dad did; now it's... I don't know. Different."

Mrs. Griffin picked the crumbs of fruit cake from her plate and drained the last of her tea. As she reached over to place the cup and saucer on her chair side table, she felt the first of the pain in her chest.

She knew what it was. She had been down this road before, and she quickly picked up the hand held phone. She was successful in pressing the stored 000 button, but then the pain became greater. Suddenly she lost her ability to hold onto the phone. It fell to the floor at her feet and bounced away, a metre across the carpet.

Mrs. Griffin folded down the front of her armchair. Finally, on her knees she reached out for the phone, but only succeeded in falling face down onto the carpet beside it. Facing it, but unable to lift her hand to reach it, she heard its engaged tone. Even if she had been able to perform the miracle of touching the redial button, she would need a second miracle to gain access to the 000 switch board. It was congested by those who sought immunity from the infectious alarm brought to them by their news service. Her loyal companion, lap dog, Kinkster, was unsure about this very recent event. He sniffed at his mistress's face before licking at her cheeks. She didn't respond.

He laid his lower jaw on his outstretched front paws near to, and in front of her face. There finding small comfort in her shallow breath, as it at intervals caressed his whiskers and offered at least a hint of normality.

The pity of it was, she was not to be the only one.

Wednesday 6.10 am

Ben Preston had not slept well. Visions of the probable effects of the deadly poison 10X had lingered in his head. The description by an expert at the late night briefing had also been enough to leave him with feeling of guilt. When his basic instinct had initiated a single thought in which he hoped he'd be nowhere near this W.M.D if its button was pushed.

He'd put the thought quickly out of his mind, but the fact that he'd had the thought, drew his attention to the potential paranoia. Ben saw himself as a level headed man, and realized that if he had the thought, then so would many others in this city of millions.

Once the rumours and inaccurate news bulletins were broadcast, the fear factor would most certainly rise. Reckless advertising by those who sold articles designed to give the purchaser an edge in a catastrophe would urge the fervour

Ben had read all of the police manuals on the subject, so he had a fair idea what to expect. He was lucky in having access to firsthand information. The city's citizens had to accept edited news broadcast, which may or may not be accurate and up to date. He'd considered worst case scenarios for some time, until he'd reached the conclusion that he'd be well advised to put it out of his mind. Prepare instead for the coming days and the business at hand.

It had been two am by the time he'd finally removed a small fold up stretcher from beside his filing cabinet. He felt that he should keep on the job, but he knew that sleep was necessary.

At six am he carried his fresh clothes to the locker room and its showers.

Twenty minutes later, as he refastened his watch to his wrist he was reminded once again of his old fashioned mindedness. When with a wrist watch pressure tested to one hundred metres he still had the habit of removing it to shower.

He checked its time as he recalled his enquiry with Rodney and Allen the night before. Their success with the transport driver and the traffic tapes had been limited, and before sending them home he'd suggested they get rest and report to him at seven am

He glanced at his watch again. They would be another quarter hour he decided.

He sat at his desk to fill in the time. As he did so he noted the name Horton on the cover of a file in his 'in' tray and began to read. It was a copy of a British Army document, and he discovered in the first two paragraphs that Henry Maurice Horton was a man not to be taken for granted.

Accompanying the Army document was an Interpol facsimile, but the information on it was three years out of date. Probably of no importance he thought, except for the brief list of Horton's then known aliases. He closed the file, leaving it on his desk top with the idea that the aliases could be looked into by Alan.

Ben had organized teams of his men the previous night to carry out twenty-four hour surveillance on Kane, Walters and

Wild. He'd considered full time surveillance on Lee, but the seriousness of the wooden box situation demanded he be economical with his resources.

During the late night briefing, when Lee's name had come up in connection with the wooden box. He'd learnt that the State Police were running an eaves dropping operation on Lee's home and club phones.

Their resources didn't stretch to twenty-four hour surveillance, but the phone taps seemed in their eyes sufficient. Practical, since their interest was based only on a rumour that something was going on at street level.

Ben surmised that he would have to be happy with what he could get. His fingers drummed on his desk top, more out of frustration than impatience, as he wished for something definite to get his teeth into. Maybe he'd feel better after some breakfast, he thought.

He unplugged Cooper's phone from the charger. Wondering at its necessity once Lee realised the importance of the wooden box which had been stored on his premises. His concern for the implications associated with it might outweigh his interest in Cooper's financial affairs. Unless Lee made a last ditch effort to recover from her what West had stolen before he made a run for it. The State Police Commander had assured him the previous night, that Security at the airport and other points of departure would, as of today, be on alert with instructions to apprehend him if he tried to leave the country.

Which suggested to Ben that they, the State Police, might have more than just a little confidence in their street level rumour? Maybe hope, he thought.

They did have a possible connection between Lee and the wooden box. So they had at least, a reason to hold him while he helped with their enquiries into his criminal affairs.

There was some activity about the office now as more of the troops rolled in. Much of it was passing traffic which moved with purpose to and from other offices strung out along the corridor.

He glanced over to the wide doorway which connected his teams large work area to the corridor and was rewarded with the sight of Rodney. He stepped through the doorway some seconds before the wiry frame of Alan Rodgers. The two men looked rested, and Ben noted the expressions on their faces. They normally radiated freewheeling good spirit when they arrived for work and then became more businesslike as their day rolled on.

Not today.

Today was different.

Today it appeared as though their 'down to business-like manner' had risen with them from their beds.

Even their carriage suggested downright seriousness. As they bid him good morning, the tension in their voices made it apparent that neither man really believed there was anything good about it at all.

"What's happening outside?" Ben enquired.

"Traffic seems to be a bit on the light side. It might just be me Sir, but there appears to be fewer cars on the road into town. Even for this hour of the morning. Lots of traffic patrol cars and random check points, where uniform seem to be inspecting all small trucks and vans." Allen answered.

Rodney also had little to offer.

"Talk downstairs is that all of the emergency services switchboards are in overload. It appears that people are seeing wooden boxes everywhere. At least three of the cities radio stations I tuned into are devoting all their air time to the terrorist situation. There seems to be a lot of experts around all of a sudden."

Ben wondered how many of the media commentators included accuracy in their expertise. He picked up the Horton file and handed it to Rodney.

"This is the man who most certainly committed the outback murders. He may also be responsible for West's boat explosion." Rodney passed pages to Allen as he read them. Ben waited until they had both finished studying the thin file.

"Allen, I want you to check out Horton's aliases. We might be able to at least ascertain whether he has left the country. While you're doing that, follow up on the new information you've gained on the fork lift truck. If it was purchased for this particular job, then it was more than likely advertised for sale somewhere. Find out where. While you are on that, find out what Steve Walters has been doing between the time he left Australia after the insider trading thing and the time he arrived back here. He's the only one of Kane's people who we are certain is using his real name."

"Rodney, its back to the tapes for you I'm afraid. Find out which direction the transformer truck went after it was loaded at the Liverpool building site. It's all we have to go on for the moment, so we'll have to be content with it until more information comes to hand."

Ben paused for a long moment. He sat with a clenched jaw, while his fingertips drummed heavily on his desk top. Finally, he looked up again at the two young detectives.

"I know that more information is going to come in. The fact that the terrorists have allowed the media in London access to their activities, suggests to me that they'll leak to us a little knowledge at a time. Enough I'd reckon to keep our attention diverted in a direction of their choice."

There was to have been another sentence. One that would have turned his statement into a phrase of wisdom, but his attempt to add it was blocked by the urgent call of his desk telephone. He lifted the hand piece and listened for some seconds before he used his pen to write on a scrap of paper.

When he'd finished writing he listened for some seconds more before he put the telephone hand piece down again.

"Allen, we need this web site now. We're advised not to go online, because the site itself has been advertised through the news services and it's expected that most of the country will try to access it. Fear of overload or something. Plug us into our central computer. It's already connected to the site it seems." He listened as Allen tapped keys with accurate speed, as his eyes settled onto a picture of an electrical transformer. It was obvious on the computers coloured screen, even though it was partly hidden behind a set of bright red numbers. Similar to those found on a digital bedside alarm clock, and seemingly superimposed over the transformer.

The three men, along with most of Australia's population stood staring at the number. Concentrating on the countdown, as its seconds slowly wound backward until the minute was gone.

Ben found it difficult to tear his eyes away from the clock. It was not until the second counter showed thirty-nine of the next moment, that he found the will to avert his gaze directly to the numbers which denoted the hours. A bright red blinking nine sat beside the quietly descending minutes which read forty-eight. Nine hours, forty-eight minutes and twenty five seconds.

"Until what?" he thought out loud.

He'd spoken to himself, as he had for the last minute and a half been unaware of the presence of his two colleagues. It was Allen's voice that suddenly wrenched his mind back to the physical world they shared.

Ben looked around toward the sound of the rasping whispered voice. The words that were offered by the young family man were emphasized by the dark shadow in his eyes.

"Maybe it's more of a case of until 'where' Sir."

Wednesday 8.45 am

Larry was some minutes early. Glad as he stepped through the coffee shop doorway to see that Adam was in a similar frame of time. Adam greeted him with a light smile. It undoubtedly mirrored his own as he made his way through a mixed aroma of cooked food and steaming beverage. Adam stood to greet him.

There were few people in the café, and those that were held discussion between themselves. Captivating their attention to the extent they hardly noticed the warm handshake that joined the two men.

Larry looked about the room. He had expected the place to be busier at this hour of the morning. A second glance at the small, but boisterous party gave reason for its engagement. He voiced his observation to Adam as if in need of a second opinion.

"It might be that the night is too short for some?"

Adam looked toward the crowded table.

"They had better make the most of it. Their nights will soon enough grow long."

Larry looked at Adams face. The wisps of grey hair at his temples seemed to be complimented by the pallor of his nicotine soaked skin. The casual observer would guess Adam to be by far the elder, even though the two men were of the same age.

A television was perched on a shelf fastened to the rear wall of the coffee shop and he glanced at it.

"What's the story behind this digital clock on the television do you know?

Adam turned his head toward it.

"Yeah, it seems that the transformer gas bomb innovators have set the world to a deadline. Something is apparently going to happen at around five this afternoon, bastards."

Larry sat slack jawed gazing at the television until he was reminded of the present by a girl's voice. It cut the air and caught the attention of the occupants of the crowded table.

"See, there it is, the web clock. They're going to blow it up at five o'clock this afternoon. I told you so."

The volume was low, so the girl took centre stage as she explained to her friends her knowledge of the subject. She was at times frustrated by joking interjections by others at the table, but she persevered.

Her mention of time brought an automatic reaction from Adam, who glanced briefly at his wrist watch. Larry mistakenly took it as a signal to get down to business. He laid his briefcase upon the table top, and after raising its lid he removed a large envelope.

"I'll make the lodgment within the hour." Adam advised as he took the envelope from Larry's hand and placed it into his own briefcase. Larry took a sip from his coffee cup, and was about to speak again when he suddenly noticed a silence. It seemingly descended upon the room and he lifted his chin to listen intently.

Adam appeared to have also noticed a change in the volume, whilst looking in the direction of the party people at their crowded table.

Larry turned to see what it was that Adam had found to be of keen interest and was greeted by the sight of the young people. Their stillness seemed in tune with their sudden silence.

The only visible signs of life were the shifting of their eyeballs, as they gazed at and then evaded the eyeballs of those seated about them. He could see clearly that they sat in a silence brought about by their effort to hear. A brief glance at the coffee shop proprietor mirrored them, and proved that their effort had a contagious effect.

Larry listened, and then heard the sound on which they concentrated.

It was a siren.

Maybe an ambulance, which was now not all that far away and it seemed to be approaching. It sounded for a moment to stand still, like it had cause to negotiate traffic. Then the note of its wail changed, as if offering a signal announcing its freedom to progress. Larry was caught up in what felt to him like a listening contest, where each of the coffee shop customers were captivated contestants.

"It's the web clock," Adam whispered.

The words sunk slowly into Larry's brain and he recoiled as he understood the implications.

Sirens were an everyday occurrence in any city of the world. Sydney was no different, but that was yesterday. Today a siren bore a similarity to the V1 bombs that Hitler had rained down on London during World War Two.

When the inhabitants of London waited for a motorized missile overhead to run out of fuel and begin its descent. Then, after its explosive impact had echoed over the city, the Londoner resumed his or her day.

Larry's mind envisaged for a moment the trials of London town as he looked again at the crowded table. They instead waited to see where the siren would go. Would it drive right by here? Was it connected to the transformer that everyone by now knew about? Had the 10X gas bomb been detonated early? Was there gas out in the street now?

Suddenly it was obvious that the siren was bypassing this particular area. Its sound seemed to diminish with each slow breath of a second. Larry heard a comment made by one of the party at the crowded table. It was followed by a low laugh by one of the girls, before they picked up their belongings and quietly moved toward the door.

It seemed as though the siren had taken the fun out of their recovery party and had caused it to come to a quiet whimper of an end.

"I guess that now would be a good time to be out of the city," Adam offered.

"Do you think you'll move out until it's all clear?" Larry asked.

Adam looked thoughtful for a moment as he looked toward the hurrying pedestrian traffic through the shop window. "No, I think I'll hang around. I've nowhere else to be right now. Once you've organized our new company and we start to realize some cash from asset sales, then I will make a decision. I will have to. By then Lee will undoubtedly notice that his business is being dismembered and my people at work will start to ask questions. What about you?"

"Probably start with New Zealand, after that I don't know," Larry said, "I'll probably be on a plane and out of the country before this day is out, so I'll not get the opportunity to see Mum. Will you tell her I love her and that I had to leave just in case I got caught up in my client's troubles? I think she'll understand. Tell her I'll come back as soon as it's safe enough, and that I'll call her in the meantime."

"I shouldn't worry about her worrying. I think she'll be glad to hear that at least one of us is out of the country and harm's way while this gas bomb thing goes on. Or off," Adam added with a smile.

Larry had always envied his twin brothers dry sense of humour and he laughed lightly.

"If they do set it off, I think they'll do so right here as close to the cities centre as possible, where they'll expect the most casualties. So watch how you go, eh?"

He held out his hand and Adam grasped it.

"Yeah will do."

Adam looked at his watch. Expressing their feelings had always been awkward and now it became apparent again.

"I'd better get moving. Good luck, Larry." Adam turned and began the short walk to his office in the Australian Securities and Investment Commission building. A trek that he'd made for so long, he reckoned that by now he should be able to do it with his eyes closed.

As he watched Adam disappear into the growing pedestrian traffic, Larry felt again the disappointment of another opportunity lost.

On this occasion, the lost opportunity to express the importance of his brother's existence was crowned with the knowledge, that it may be a long time before their paths crossed again.

Larry suddenly felt alone.

He put aside his feelings and concentrated on a path through the oncoming human tide that washed the footpath before him.

A short walk brought him to his car where he built up the funds in its parking meter. Not because he couldn't afford a parking ticket. It was more of a need to cover his tracks. He'd stepped over the line and had put himself on the opposite side of the street to the Law. Now his hand went to his jacket pocket for the assurance that his passport, and the cash for his ticket out of town offered.

Larry was a little uncertain about the decision he had made, but as he stepped through the doorway of a travel agent he heard yet another siren and noticed that the girl behind the counter was listening intently.

Yes, he thought. Now was good time to be somewhere else.

It was obvious to him that the girl behind the counter was using both sides of her brain. She listened to his enquiry and also listened to the siren. It dawned on Larry that he too waited for a change in the direction of the mournful cry.

"Ah yes. I need to be in Auckland this evening please. One way."

*****

Lee had not slept well.

He'd awoken a number of times during the night and now wondered if it was due to the fact that he'd left the television on. Even though he'd kept the volume down, the sound of gunfire and the roar of an aircraft seemed to be more than whisper in his ears. He did know for sure that his dreams had taken place behind closed eyes, and therefore could not be associated with the television screen.

In the dream he'd been secreted behind a half closed door of a night filled room. Peering into the darkness outside which was then cut by a handheld searchlight. He'd watched as the light touched on walls of another building before it reached across the garden area. Briefly exposing trees and small bushes until it came to rest on the ground at the feet of its director.

It had brought to light the silhouette of three men. One of them held a dead bird by its lifeless legs and dangled it in an effort to distract his watch dog. Lee saw a figure he knew to be himself, move from a position by the half closed door, to a telephone where he might try to call for help.

A cold dread had swept over him when he found the line was dead. He was alone. He knew the end was near as he'd looked behind him to the half closed door. The inevitable flash of the searchlight finally pieced the darkness within the room and highlighted his presence.

As Lee broke from the dream he turned sharply on the office lounge, so much so, that his legs fell from it. He sat there motionless for some moments, blinking his eyes and getting in touch again with his immediate surroundings. Rising to his feet he made his way to his small bar fridge, and took from it a bottle of water. Then picked up the television's remote control and flicked through T.V programs until he found a news service.

He was greeted by a young woman with a heavily made up face. She sat at her news desk, while highlighted on a screen high behind her, a set of numbers in bold red counted down.

The numbers beckoned his eyes as he began to concentrate on the words she spoke.

"... brought to the attention of the Nation. It is still unknown what can be expected at the conclusion of the countdown. It was decided by authorities that the outcome for Australia might be made known by the outcomes in the other affected countries due to the difference in the time zones, but that has been discounted by the now known fact that there is only one web clock. It appears that whatever the outcome at the conclusion of the countdown, all the affected countries, Australia, Canada, the U.S, the U.K and the Philippines will without doubt be struck with the reality of the terrorists actions at the same instant..."

Lee flicked further into the programs until he found C.N.N, where he was met with the same thing. Only this time it was the President of the United States who stood at a podium and stated clearly.

"...they will not escape their fate. I will see to it personally that every step is taken. Every avenue which can be followed will be, and the terrorists responsible for this outrage will be hunted down and brought to justice..." Lee switched over to the B.B.C. It too, was focusing on the web clock countdown.

He sat back down on the lounge and stared momentarily at the floor, as if an answer might be found in the carpets design. There was nothing, but the red numbers encroaching on his peripheral vision.

A glance at his wrist watch told him it was nine thirty, and he wondered at his next move. A thought that dissipated rapidly as it was replaced by another. How come the police weren't crawling all over him by now?" He'd expected them to come, and for some unknown reason he became suspicious.

An overwhelming suspicion brought on by their obvious inaction. Why the delay, he thought. Surely they had made a connection between him and the crate that had been on his premises at Grey St? He'd been sure they would be knocking at his door. Particularly now, that the diabolical reasons for the existence of the crate had been made known."

Maybe they have enough on their plate in trying to find the contents of the crate, to bother right now as to how it came to be here? Maybe they have enough information to know it was all down to Sudovich and that Kane is the culprit?

"Whatever," he said quietly, "It's obvious they don't have enough on me to arrest me. If that's the case, then..."

He stopped speaking his thoughts and allowed them to linger in his head momentarily before he picked up his mobile telephone.

"Larry, what time do you expect those papers to be lodged? You've done it? Good man. No, that's all I need to know. I'll see you then."

Lee broke the connection and dialled another number.

"Tony. Is your boat available? I have a friend who needs to lay low for maybe two weeks, so cancel whatever you have on. I'll pay you double rates, cash. I reckoned you'd be happy with that. Listen he likes good food, so stock up today and be ready to sail by ten tonight, alright? I'll try to have him on board by nine."

He was sure. As sure as anyone, when it came to trusting another human, he could depend on Tony. It didn't hurt to hedge your bets though he thought. Just to be on the safe side, he'd felt it prudent not to give Tony the identity of his passenger. He'd find out soon enough.

Lee dialled another number.

"Shane. I want you to be available tonight at nine o'clock. I have two cars that need to be parked out of sight for maybe a couple of weeks. No, I'll ring you at about eight and let you know where I want you to be, alright?" Lee put the phone down and sat back in the lounge chair as he took another long swallow from the water bottle. He'd been on Tony's boat a few times and it was top value when it came to comfort. After all, if one is going to go underground for a while he may as well do it in style.

The red digital clock on the televisions screen added reason. Now is as good a time as any to go and do a bit of fishing. Lay low for a while and let all this shit blow over.

He paused for a moment and considered Sally.

"Fuck her," he whispered as he gathered fresh clothes from a steel filing cabinet and walked into his personal bathroom. "With any luck she might have shot through with her boyfriend by the time I get back. If so, then I'll at least know his identity and I'll have Dan to pay him a visit."

"Teach the bastard a lesson in good manners," he chuckled.

CHAPTER 19

Wednesday 9.35 am

Rodney Anderson knocked on Ben Preston's door, and before he was acknowledged he walked in with a look of excitement on his face.

"Boss, I've got a photo of the truck. It's not the vehicle that was photographed for the actual traffic offence by the speed camera, but it got caught up in the picture. The really good news is that it is almost entirely visible." Ben reached for the print out and looked carefully at it.

The truck was plainly in view, but the resolution was not good due to the aberration caused by the poor peripheral view of the cameras lens. He could not make out the vehicles shadowed number plate, but he could see the fork lift truck parked at the rear of the load tray. With a concentrated peer he could see a small corner of the wooden box, prominent like an ear behind the cargo barrier.

Ben's eyes moved to the windscreen and through it, he could make out the blurry shadows of the trucks two occupants. One of whom had his arm resting in the sunlight on the window frame of the passenger's side door.

He looked back at Rodney as he handed back the printout.

"Get the original down to the photo lab. Tell them we need to know yesterday, that number plate and as much as they can give us on the two blokes inside."

"Which way was it heading?"

"Towards the city Boss."

"Right. While the lab people are playing with the photo, get onto traffic. Have them check all the speed cameras on the way into town?" Ben pointed to the printout, "This gives them a start point with the time, and an E.T.A at the next camera and so on. As soon as you get hold of the number plate, make it known to uniform. Remind them they should check the records of all previous vehicle random stops, with emphasis on this morning and yesterday. They may have already done a vehicle check on it and unknowingly let it go."

Rodney turned to leave, but propped and listened once again to his boss. "Rodney, compare notes with Allan. He's found the previous owner of the fork lift truck. Get your heads together, and tell him that I complimented the both of you on your good work. Thank you."

Ben sat down at his desk again, and gazed through his office doorway as he scanned the mental impression left by the printout.

His mind's eye gazed at the shadowy figures who occupied the trucks cabin as he wondered. John Kane. You are a large man. Where were you on that day?"

*****

Larry walked the pavement to his parked car, where he stood for a moment undecided as to what to do next. The warmth of the morning sun drew his attention to the back of his scarred hand, and reminded him yet again, the necessity of his fair skins protection.

He quickly sought the shade offered by the roof of his car. Noticing almost immediately the absence of the suns warmth, as his rear end settled into its driver's seat.

The placement of his hand on the steering wheel made obvious the scarring left by the surgical removal of four shin cancers. A grim reminder of his latest test results, and his mind wandered momentarily before he glanced at his wristwatch. It was three minutes to ten o'clock and a look at the parking meter told him he had ten minutes of parking time credit. Ten minutes of time paid for, and his to use as he pleased. Nothing's for free he thought, as he gazed out through his cars windscreen.

His eyes focused on a clump of people who spilled from a shop and onto the footpath. He thought that maybe the shop had a sale on, and he watched people as they carried away their purchases.

Their vacancies in the clump were quickly filled by new arrivals. Who readily disappeared, as they were seemingly absorbed into the restless crowd.

Suddenly the clump of people became still. For a moment they stood quietly, like meerkats who smelt trouble. Larry watched as some of the faces turned to look down the street past where he was parked. He turned in his seat to see what it was that they saw. Nothing out of the ordinary, he thought, as he wound his window down an inch to allow some fresh air to flow into his car. After sitting in the morning sun, it had become a little stuffy. It was then that he noticed the sound of a siren. Its cry carried to him as it approached from the city. Suddenly it became more muted as if it changed course. As it began to drift away he saw the clump of people lose its short term still form, and regain its shuffling sense of purpose.

He watched one of the figures emerge from the clump, to walk the footpath towards where he was seated in his car. The man was carrying a cardboard box. As he passed by the passenger side window, Larry could make out part of the large lettered writing which described the boxes contents. Most of the lettering was obscured by the left arm of the man who held it, but the words 'HAZ' and 'SUIT' were all that he needed to see, to know the reasoning behind its purchase.

Larry looked again at the clump of people, and then ran his eyes over the shop front. He could see plainly in yellow paint the words 'ARMY SURPLUS'. His eyes shifted again, to another man who separated himself from the clump of people, this one carried in plain view a gas mask.

It suddenly became obvious to Larry what was happening.

It was the Anthrax scare all over again. He realized then why it had been difficult to get an earlier flight out of the country, as he remembered the words of the ticket sales lady.

"I'm sorry, Sir, but we're unable to book you a flight before seven o'clock tonight. It seems that everybody has decided that today's the day to go to New Zealand."

Larry watched the unhurried walk of the owner of the gas mask. He wondered whether the relieved expression was because of his escape from the clump, or security in the knowledge that he was safe from the event promised by the web clock. Probably a bit of both, Larry thought. He watched the man make his way down the footpath. Suddenly another man, who had been leaning against the car parked two cars ahead of his, lunged away from his resting place.

Larry winced as the second man's fist cracked onto the side of the first man's head, and then again as the first man's head hit the footpath.

The second man then wasted no time. He snatched up the gas mask and ran off down the busy street. In flight from an attack that was over almost before Larry realized what had happened. His grip on the steering wheel strengthened while the vision of violence lingered in his head. Suddenly that vision brought to mind Tom Lee. Lee's potential in the art of violence would make the attack by the second man look pale in comparison. Larry looked at the first man who lay still on the concrete not four metres from where he sat.

The man's look of relief was gone. Replaced by the blank expression of one who slept, and Larry watched as a small crowd of passersby gathered. Some of whom held mobile phones to their ears to make calls for medical assistance for the man who lay at their feet.

Their calls for help would no doubt bring to life the wail of a siren. This time it would not turn away in another direction. It would, for those who'd not seen the attack, arrive screaming into their immediate environment and heighten their fear of the unknown.

Even if the web clock was some kind of cruel April fool type joke, it was working. It was also proof that threat potential was enough to fill the minds of ordinary everyday people with unreasoned thoughts of self-preservation.

Larry fitted his car key into the ignition and drove off with the flow of traffic. Glad to be away from the place where people were beginning to show their darker sides. Knowing also, that he could expect to see those same signs at any given place in the city as the web clock countdown wore on. Signs that would undoubtedly become more evident as the mental infection spread.

He turned his car radio on. Hoping the music usually played on his favoured city station might soothe him. He was disappointed. A reporter's voice reminded him of the situation in an urgent voice with a revelation that police were causing traffic problems as they stopped and searched all small trucks. He tuned to another station only to hear a similar story. This time about emergency services switchboard congestion, as reports of wooden boxes and crates flooded in from all over the city. Larry tried three more of Sydney's major radio stations before he turned the radio off.

His finger hovered over the power button momentarily, almost as if he feared being disconnected. He put the thought aside, as he was sure that nothing would change until the web clock had counted down. The media would focus on speculation. Speculation based on guesswork, and that was information built on poor foundations in Larry's mind.

He thought of a clown's gun, which when fired just produced a flag upon which was printed the word 'bang'.

As he waited at a set of traffic lights he noticed some cars that were laden with children and camping goods. The young faces that peered out of the cars windows did not wear the excited expressions of those who looked forward to a holiday.

In one car, a station wagon, he could see clearly the collar cut and banded hats of school uniforms. They failed to blend in with the obvious sleeping bags and pillows piled high against the vehicle's rear windows.

Larry looked at the red traffic lights, and then at the brake lights of the car ahead. Suddenly his mind's eye beheld the sight of the bright red digits of the web clock. A moment later he felt a cold shiver pass through him as if someone had walked over his grave. It dawned on him that his devil may care attitude had just evaporated, with the realization that he too had become infected.

It was as if a he'd been enshrouded, and with it came an intense feeling of claustrophobia. He looked about at the surrounding cars which hemmed him in, and as his two white knuckled hands gripped the steering wheel, he suddenly had an overwhelming desire for wide open spaces.

Larry wiped the back of a hand across his brow, and felt his wet sweat cool under the breeze of the air conditioner. As he wiped his hand dry on the thigh of his trouser leg, he was startled as the horn of the car behind urged him on under a green traffic light.

After he'd surged through the intersection he gained a left lane, and then took the next left turn. It gave him a course for the nearest beach and he breathed deeply the fresh ocean breeze that swept in through his now open window.

The sound of the surf and the sight of the seagulls cleared his mind of the events of the day, and he gratefully accepted the taste of a fresh cigarette. Expanding his lungs with smoke as he picked up from the passenger seat the set of photocopies of the documents which Lee believed he'd lodged.

He double checked to make sure he'd put the right papers in the right pile, before retaining his own copies. After pushing them into an envelope he deposited them into the boot of his car. Where they would stay until he carried them as hand luggage upon his departure from the country at seven thirty-five tonight.

A little over eight hours away, five of which he would have to spend in the company of, or at least in close proximity to Lee. That was something he was not looking forward to he thought. Partly because of his fear of the events that would immediately follow his possible exposure, but mainly for the lack of confidence he felt in concealing his guilt.

Yesterday during his meetings with Lee, he had only to conceal the guilt of one who planned deception. Today he had crossed the line and would have to conceal the guilt of the deceiver. He knew he walked on dangerous ground and was scared of the consequences if he failed. As he watched freewheeling seagulls floating on a gusty sea breeze, it suddenly dawned on him that the web clock may be a blessing in disguise.

After all, it seemed that many people throughout the city were acting out of the ordinary. Why should he be the exception?

The seagulls squabbled over a small offering left behind by a frothy wave, until one of them disengaged itself from the crowd and flew out over the water with its prize. Its success reminded him of the man who'd carried the gas mask.

Larry wished quietly that seven thirty-five would arrive quickly. Then as he noted a slight discomfort where his shoulder blade came into contact with the cars seat back, he humbly withdrew the wish. Instead he moved his body a little for access and slid a hand over his shoulder to allow his finger tips to touch a lump which rose like a small hill on the broad plain of his back.

One should never wish away that of which there is a shortage he thought, as he turned the key in the car's ignition. With a glance at the paper pile that sat on the passenger seat, he drove off to meet with Lee, where he would emphasize his concern over the web clock.

Wednesday 1.15 pm

Ben Preston had lunched at a small café just a short walk from his office. It allowed him some form of exercise, and in turn offered him an excuse to add the flavour of a custard tart to his midday diet. After which he'd felt almost compelled by way of penance to take the stairs to his third floor office. As he pulled himself up and over the last few remaining steps, he wondered if a custard tart in exchange for a minute in the stairwell was a fair trade.

He noticed the way his hand wavered as he used his finger to poke the buttons of the electronic door lock. A definite sign that his body was well on its way to a use by date he thought, as he opened the door to the detective's operations room.

As he entered, he saw Allen intent on pressing the keys of his computer keyboard. Rodney stood beside him with one arm outstretched. His pointed index finger waggled once in the direction of the computer's coloured screen. Ben watched as a grin suddenly grew on Allan's face, and then again as Rodney stepped back a pace and punched the air.

He pulled the door closed behind him, and its sound, as it clicked into place drew the attention of the two men. They both wore broad grins as they looked up from the screen.

"We've got a lead, Boss." Rodney called as he punched with his closed fist again, this time into the open palm of his left hand. Ben made his way over to them and looked at the screen that had captured their attention.

For a moment he had little idea what it was he was viewing. It was a hazy picture of what appeared to be a double edged dagger with a ship's anchor as its handle. The hooks of which acted as the daggers guard, and offered support to a snake curled loosely around the weapons length.

"It's a tattoo, Sir. The people down at photo lab were unable to get a good look at the faces of the two blokes' in the front of the truck. They were too well shielded by the trucks cabin roof apparently. However, they were able to zoom in, and build a computer image of the passenger's left arm, which was exposed as it lay in the sun on the door window. They found this tattoo. Boss, it's great. Better than an eye witness." Alan supplied.

"Well, Kane was wearing a short sleeve shirt when we interviewed him, so he's not the owner of the tattoo. The other bloke, Wild, was in overalls. We didn't get a clean look at

Walters, although I doubt it is his. It would have been recorded in his police file. Unless it's new?"

Ben rubbed his chin in his customary manner before he ordered.

"Alan, get on to Hutchinson. He's running the surveillance on those three. Ask him to keep a look out for snakes and daggers."

Ben was about to speak again, when suddenly a not so musical note of a mobile phone demanded attention. Rodney lifted a small electronic device from his pocket. Holding it for a moment before realizing it was not his personal phone that called. His right hand disappeared into another pocket. This time he was successful in retrieving the wailing culprit. Its sound seemed to be echoed by another, whose call was somewhat more distant.

Ben looked up and away from Rodney's phone, to where the second sound seemed to originate. The echo issued from the doorway of his office, and as he looked toward it, his peripheral vision caught sight of Laura who waited for some reaction to the noise.

It immediately dawned on him what was happening. At the same instant that he spoke aloud the word.

"Cooper."

Rodney called out in a coarse whisper.

"Lee."

Ben looked for some seconds into Rodney's glistening dark eyes. Focusing on their sparkle as it seemed to intensify with each passing second. He looked away from Rodney's face to Cooper's phone, and watched with keen interest as a tanned thumb pressed its speaker button. Stillness seemed to descend upon the three men as they listened for connection confirmation. The seconds that drifted by, seemed to be slower and more drawn out, as if time itself was being in some way distorted.

Ben was relieved when at last he heard Cooper's voice. It came through to him in a calm controlled manner, offering evidence that she felt she was in no immediate danger.

Things can change Ben thought, and almost as quickly as it took for that thought to dissolve, they did. Proof of the speed that a situation can change came at the end of Beth Cooper's next sentence.

"Any documents, such as the ones you are offering me have to be signed by at least three members of the Sarah Ray Foundation's board. I don't have the power to make decisions without their cooperation, Mr. Horton." Ben was dumbfounded. He'd read all that there was to know of this man Horton. His army records, and of course the detailed police report on the savage intensity of the outback murders.

The feeling in his gut told him that Horton was no ordinary street crim who would give up when his back was to the wall.

No. This man would go out with all guns blazing and take as many with him as possible, man woman or child.

Time was still slow, and he heard as if from the distance a voice.

"Boss, are you O.K?"

Ben looked toward the sound and saw Allan's lips move. He felt a hand which rested lightly upon his shoulder before he took a deep breath and answered.

"Yes, I'm alright."

He looked at his two colleagues and spoke again, this time with the voice of command.

"Allan, get onto liaison and have them get Tactical over there. Point out that silent approach is of top priority. Let them know all issues, and that we might expect a hostage situation. Make sure they understand that Horton is extremely dangerous, and that he won't give up. Radio comms to a minimum. This Horton is well trained; he might have a scanner. Rodney, you're with me." Rodney picked up Cooper's phone and made his way to call up the lift. Ben followed close behind, until he detoured briefly to his office to collect his armour vest and retrieve Cooper's second phone.

As he left his office doorway he called across the room.

"Allan. Use your memory to draw up a basic floor plan of Cooper's office and pass it on will you. Also, see to it that photos of that tattoo are distributed."

They waited in the corridor for the lift, and as they passed through its now open doors Ben told Rodney, "This man Horton may well be the meanest bastard that either one of us is likely to meet, so you take extra care."

Anderson looked at his boss, realizing by the tone of Ben's voice that the advice was given as a friend and colleague, rather than that of a superior officer. It caught him off guard to the extent that he was unsure how to answer.

It seemed to him that he blurted out the words that finally came to his lips.

"I've read all there is available on him Sir, just as you have."

"Just making sure you understand the situation that's all." The lift doors opened and the two men made their way quickly across the underground car park.

As he went, Rodney could feel the situation in his bones. The adrenalin, which was already seeping into his bloodstream, told him in no uncertain terms that he had a perfect understanding.

There was something else too.

Something more like a sensation than a feeling in the back of his mind suggested to him that this day was going to be like no other, web clock or no web clock. Must be the adrenalin he thought, as he pulled the car into gear and surged toward the basement car park's exit.

CHAPTER 20

Wednesday 1.20 pm

Mika had almost finished her mornings work when Lee had called. His suggestion that she be in his office as soon as possible resounded in her ears, as might a plea. She sensed his frustration when she'd advised him that her arrival would not be for at least another hour.

When at last she'd darkened his office door way, she'd found him sitting behind his cluttered desk. He was gazing almost vacantly at the red coloured web clock. It seemed to cling to television screens like it clung to the minds of the inhabitants of the world. She'd quickly noticed the blank look on his face and had taken it as a look of defeat. That thought had been quickly dislodged from her mind when he'd turned to acknowledge her with a smile that suggested he considered himself to be still in command.

The look in his eye told her that he had a card up his sleeve.

She had cards also. In the form of aces, and she had decided that now was a good time to play one. If only to find out how his was to be used. After locking the office door behind her, she'd begun to unbutton her blouse as she'd moved across the room towards him.

He'd been receptive, and after a half an hour of what they both jokingly referred to as desk top management, they had gotten down to the reason for her summons. It had not been difficult to learn what his card was, and she'd been eager in her response to spend at least two weeks with him at sea.

She knew Lee well enough to know that it would hardly be in a row boat, and she had often thought it would be nice to relax on one of the luxury type boats often seen moored on the richer side of town. A decision she'd made without even a glance at the televisions web clock. Although now with afterthought, the web clocks blaring red digits did suggest that it was a good time to be out of the city. After all, who really wanted to be here at this time?

Where in the city was there a safe place?

After acceptance of his proposal Lee had handed her a brown paper bag full of cash.

"Take this and go shopping for the afternoon. I will not be going home, so buy everything you think we'll need. Don't worry about food or drink. Just concentrate on clothes for the both of us, both warm and cold weather, toiletries and such. You'd better get some books and DVD's because we'll have a bit of spare time. Raid the perfume place if you want, and get me a few boxes of cigars." He'd looked thoughtful for a brief moment before he'd added, "Mika, tell no one what it is you're doing. Take your car to do the shopping, and then be parked out the back by nine tonight. We'll transfer it all to the boat directly from your car. Charlie and Shane will be at the wharf, and they'll be looking after both of our cars while we're away." She'd checked her watch as she'd left his office. Its time suggested that a visit to a small snack shop located close to the club was in fact an order of necessity.

The table she chose on her return to the club was one that gave her access to the bar. She sat down to quickly eat her lunch, glad that she had worn her flat soled shoes, as she would be doing a lot of walking as the afternoon progressed.

The bar was relatively quiet for this time of day. Some regulars pushed their money into the slots of the poker machines, while others sat by the bar and nursed the amber ale of their choice. At times she acknowledged those who she knew to be employees of Lee's as they carried out their errands. Most of them carried bags into Lee's office, before reappearing again some minutes later, still carrying the by now much thinner and lighter bags. The number of visits by these 'errand' people had decreased somewhat, compared to that of the day prior. By which Mika surmised that Lee's street product must be nearly all moved. She wondered for a moment, at the impact on Lee's competitors when he'd flooded the market with cut price bargains. There were going to be some pissed off people out there, both Italian and Asian, she thought. She chuckled as she thought of Lee's expected attitude to them, if the fact that he was pissing people off was brought to his attention.

A crumb from her sandwich caused her to cough, and as she wiped her lips with her serviette she noticed Dan across the bar room. He had his back to her, and faced the wall by the bars public telephone. His body language suggested that he was involved in a very personal call.

There had been a rumour circulating the day before, and out of curiosity she lifted her mobile phone from her bag and pressed the speed dial for Lee's home phone. She was not entirely surprised to hear an engaged tone. Not proof though, she thought, as she placed her mobile onto the table top beside her glass of water.

Dan waved his free hand through the air. Mika followed it with her gaze as he let it drop to his side before he turned side on and suddenly, but not heavily, put the telephone back into its cradle. As he did Mika again lifted her mobile and hit the speed dial again. This time a ring tone rang in her ear once, before she cut the connection.

Mika watched Dan as he glanced towards the door of Lee's office. Then again, as he surveyed the bar room like a guilty school boy might, before he nervously walked out of sight toward the other end of the bar.

It was pitiful to watch. He was not in Sally's league and out of his depth, but Mika, having led the life that she had, knew she was in no position to bat an eyelid.

She had left home when she was seventeen, and now when she looked at the whole affair with hindsight, it was blatantly obvious the main reason for her departure was that she and her parents were basically incompatible. There was also the fact that her father was a messy slob. He spilt things, and farted with monotonous regularity, while her mother hated housework and smoked cigarettes incessantly.

Maybe it was that their star signs were different, she didn't know. She did know that the three of them could only remain in a room together in silence, and handy to a tin of air freshener. Then the silence itself became overwhelming, not to mention the air freshener.

Without higher education and having a complete disdain for jobs like factory work or shop assistant, she entered into the occupation of private escort. She had been very pretty and of good figure, so she lured top dollar as a tiny, well-endowed young girl, whose entertainment wardrobe consisted of school uniforms. It had worked well for nearly six years. Until one day it became obvious even to her, that she was becoming less able to be choosey with her clients. So she purchased a second townhouse and cut her clientele down to regulars.

It was about this time she had met Tom Lee, and although he often jokingly mentioned his disappointment at being five years late, he was happy to partake in the experience she had to offer.

It was almost as if he'd become addicted to her, and over the next four months he became more than a regular. His visits became so frequent, and unannounced that she had to tell him he was getting in the way of her business.

He'd listened to her grievance, and then had taken her completely by surprise by suggesting that he put her on a retainer.

It was an offer that at first she was sure she would refuse, but after a week of indecisiveness, she'd reckoned that her successful business life had grown on the back of her *executive* decisions, and she had obviously been right so far.

The fact that she'd not succumbed to the expensive and soul destroying habit of drugs during her career had been a wise decision also, and proof in the pudding.

Up until Lee's proposition, her plans had been to work for maybe another year, before retiring from it all anyway. She was almost at a point of financial independence. The rental income from two town houses would allow her to live quite well. Accepting Lee's offer for at least a year, if it lasted that long, would not really interfere with her plans.

Lee's offer was a little like a scenic detour.

She would still arrive at the same destination.

Lee didn't know about her townhouses, so if he was prepared to place her in suitable housing, then the rental income from both of them would double the bank loan repayments on the second one. It would restrict her cash income money laundering activities, but it was still icing on her cake.

So she'd accepted, on the condition they both undergo blood tests for H.I.V and Hepatitis B. She knew from her regular tests that she was clean, but she'd come too far in her business life to lose out now for want of double checking. Lee was taken aback a little by the suggestion, but when she pointed out to him that she was prepared to take the test partly for his benefit, then he should do the same for her, shouldn't he?

What could he say when she put it that way?

He'd smiled in acceptance, and a little in awe of her talent in the art of delivering a subtle check. She never risked confrontation with a checkmate, but sought compliance by gentle suggestion.

After her acceptance of his business proposal, she was more than a little surprised how things changed. She'd known from the very start that she would miss sleeping in every morning, but that lost pleasure was offset by the fact that she could now go to bed earlier. Almost every night if she wished, and as those initial days passed she discovered a new life.

A new life littered with free evenings. She'd used them to further her interests by taking night classes in cooking, computers and a camera course.

She'd even completed a course in real estate. Knowing in the back of her mind that her escort experience could just be the extra arrow in her quiver with which to complete a sale.

One of her new life's surprises struck her sense of humour at an odd angle.

She'd begun to put on weight to the extent she'd been forced to enlist the services of a local gym. Her diet had changed little, but the amount of effort needed to bring her body back into shape, had caused her to wonder if she may have underrated the actual calories needed to be a success in the sex industry. Her sex life with Lee had started out at a rate based on his passion, but had decreased steadily to a point where he'd go without for sometimes a week. Their time spent together began to feel more like what she expected a married couple of some years to experience.

Now, the one year she'd expected to work had turned into almost three. The retainer based relationship had become more of a liaison, with less emphasis on sexual encounters, and more on basic companionship. Not that she disliked it. It almost touched on a normal life for her, but in some weird way she sensed a danger of sorts. Like she was lounging in a sense of false security where there existed a possibility for her a lack of fulfillment.

Mika knew and understood that she was the other woman. She had been just that for her whole adult life, and had been taken aback by the restlessness she'd been experiencing over the last few months. The reason behind these new feelings had only recently become obvious to her. Its exposure was due to the company of the women and one man, who attended as adult students, her latest night class.

Up until that night she had believed that her restlessness had been associated with her maternal instincts. Prior that night, she had wrestled with them the same way she'd wrestled with them for almost the entire decade past. When, with success she'd argued her case, based on the principle that she would not ask her conscience to allow her to bring forth into the world a child through the canal that she sold for silver. This time, even after she'd delivered her case and repeated her promise, the feeling of restlessness still plagued her. Until last week's night class when one of the women asked the joke that Mika had heard many times before, of one of the men.

"How do you make an Irish woman pregnant?" Every person in the class had waited for, and expected the same old answer, but the man's response wiped away knowing smiles. It also blocked any chance his class mates had of light hearted ridicule.

Mika still smiled at her mental picture of him as he bided his time, and let his audience wait for some moments before he quietly announced.

"There are four ways to make an Irish woman pregnant, as far as I know."

"Rubbish," one woman cried, while the others waited. Unsure what comment was safe to make, without causing themselves to become the centre of the joke.

"Well." He said as he looked the woman who'd called out rubbish in the eye. A light smile touched his facial features as he added, "Firstly there's I.V.F..."

The woman begrudgingly nodded her head, and then remained quiet as he concluded his sentence.

"..or you can fuck her, have sex with her or make love to her." It was at that point that Mika realized it was not only maternal instinct that caused her restlessness.

Part of the reason for sure, but as she considered his answer, it dawned upon her. She'd had some thousands of men fuck or have sex with her, and she with them, but no one had ever actually made love to her. Nor had she made love to any man.

She saw his point clearly, and the way he'd announced his answer made it plain that it was a truth he'd learned by experience, rather than knowledge he'd gained by ear. A point that she'd felt she'd already known, but one whose significance was not obvious until explained. Maybe it was a point that one did not consider until they reached a stage in life to which such a point was applicable to them.

Either way, Mika had taken the simple wisdom on board, and with it the understanding that her life was overdue for change. She could not perceive her eventual destination, but she had a clear view of the necessary direction. It was nearly time for another *executive* decision, and even though her life now with Lee was comfortable, like favoured old shoes. It was unfortunate in a way that he was not expected by her, to be at her new direction's ultimate destination.

Mika was consuming the last of her sandwich when she noticed Larry push open the front doors of the bar to make his usual low key entrance. She had made a life of watching people's faces, and had learnt through necessity the need to read expressions.

An art form that had kept her safe more than once in her stranger strewn past. Strain clearly showed on Larry's face, but her study of his features became interrupted when a short sharp shriek of a siren suddenly stabbed at her ears.

Mika caught the startled look which cloaked Larry's face as he turned his head forward from where it had spun to allow him to see over his shoulder.

His expression had changed little from that which had preceded it. Now it was touched by fear. His initial expression, which now filtered through her mind's eye, had been shaded with a tinge of nervousness.

She wondered why Larry might be nervous.

He had little to fear in being an associate of Lee's. He was only the accountant, who like Mika herself could take all care and no responsibility. Regardless of how many policemen knocked on the door, because after all, they were both only Lee's whores. Her wrist watch reminded her that her twenty minutes for lunch was up, and it was time to get moving. She lifted her glass from the table and delivered it to Bo at the bar. He greeted her with his usual smile.

Mika liked old Bo. He was the quiet type of barmen who spoke only when he was spoken to, and then listened intently.

His working life was nearing its end, but she knew he would have to persevere until he was due his old age pension, in order to support his wife who was wracked with M.S.

"How's Kate, Bo?"

"Going downhill slowly Mika, but she's still as cheeky as ever," He grinned.

Mika undid her wrist watch and handed it out to him.

"This was two and a half grand a month ago. You should easily pick up one, one and a half for it if she needs anything, or if you like, she might like it as a pressie. You don't have to tell her whose arm it came off."

He looked at the finely worked piece in his hand.

"You're sure?"

"Yes," she said as she patted the brown paper bag, "I'm going to buy a new one this afternoon to celebrate change."

"Change?" he enquired.

"Long story Bo."

She turned away from the bar, and then turned again as he said.

"Mika, I'm sure that if she knew you as I do, I wouldn't have to fib."

She noted the apologetic look in his eyes before she smiled.

"I understand, Bo. Thank you for the compliment."

The trip away with Lee for the next two weeks would be like a last waltz. A brief holiday before she set out on a voyage of self-discovery. Find a man to love and become a legitimate clean living woman. She was still young and she had money. Now, after all the hard years the world was her oyster.

A laugh that was free and unbidden escaped her as she went out into the street to find a taxi.

"Time for some serious shopping," she told herself, as she walked light footedly along the less than crowded footpath.

CHAPTER 21

Wednesday 1.50 pm

Ben and Rodney made good time from the city. As they approached the Harbour Bridge, Ben saw why there had been concerns raised about possible traffic congestion, due to random truck searches.

Traffic was light at this time of the day, but as the afternoon wore on it was obvious there could be problems during peak hour. The police presence stole away the use of one complete lane. As they passed over the threshold of the bridge, a large red sign ordered each and every truck or van to the left hand traffic lane. Where a short distance further on, a uniformed police officer stood by a blue lighted patrol car.

Ben watched as the officer beckoned the driver of a light truck. It moved onto the stopping lane and travelled for another one hundred metres before it rolled to a stop. Directly behind another truck which was the last in a line of some ten.

The lead search vehicle on the Western side was almost in the middle of the bridge. Immediately opposite the lead vehicle of the short line of trucks which were parked on the Eastern side of the bridge.

It seemed to him that police manpower maximization was not the only reason for using only two search teams in the middle of the Bridge proper. It was good reasoning, that if the transformer was found, then the middle of the Bridge was an ideal place for containment. It was well away from the general population, well elevated and exposed to a constant sea breeze.

He checked his weapon and added further rounds to its magazine before looking forward again. Into a brief blue flash of their police light, whose issue from the roof above his passenger's seat reflected off the vehicle ahead.

Ben's occupation with his thoughts was interrupted by a word from Rodney. He looked toward him, and then followed the direction of his nod to the oncoming traffic on the opposite side of the bridge.

There were two Land rover vehicles and a set of four olive army trucks. Their drivers were waved through by the traffic patrolman, and Ben looked around to see that each of the trucks were full of army personnel. An armed presence on the streets of Sydney would have been considered highly unlikely just yesterday. He wondered at the wisdom of such a move, but then concluded that the cities citizens might well see the troops as a sign of their own securities benefit rather than a reason for further consternation.

A thought which dissipated as Ben wound down his window and removed their magnetically attached revolving blue light. He placed it onto the cars dash, before allowing himself to be pushed back into his seat as Rodney accelerated through the exit. Main street parking was a rarity in the central business district, so Rodney took advantage of a loading zone some twenty metres from the front door of Cooper's office.

Ben listened to Cooper's phone, where the conversation between Cooper and Horton was still being carried out in a calm manner.

It appeared to Ben that Horton had been up to that point in time, in no great hurry.

Ben listened to yet another protest by Cooper. Her argument being that she did not have the power to grant Horton his wishes. Horton's response was in a tone that suggested irritation.

As yet the footpaths had not been cordoned off as normal procedure dictated, so Ben's next move was based on the need to evacuate the other floors of the building.

"We'll go in, Rodney. You evacuate as quietly as possible the ground floor, while I do the second floor. When you've done that, meet me on the third floor and we'll try to at least get

Booth out." He paused and then asked, "Are you ready?" Rodney's quietness during the drive from the city was extended as he nodded. They left the car and made their way hurriedly through the light throng of pedestrians, until they reached the office block's main entrance.

Ben pushed at the heavy glass door and made his way into a small foyer. A direction sign of metal stood out on a dark brick wall, informing him that all of the offices, three on each floor were occupied. A quick mental calculation based on there being two or three people in each office, suggested that he and Rodney may have to move up to twenty people before they could concentrate their efforts on Cooper's floor.

There was an office to his immediate left. A second lay next to it though deeper into the building, while a third faced the second from the opposite side of the foyer.

Ben looked to his right, where the elevator's stainless steel doors stood defiantly. As he made his way to the elevator summons button, he pointed to the first office and quietly, with a nod of his head directed Rodney toward it. Ben was about to press the lift summons button, with the intention of bringing it to this floor and rendering it inoperable by pressing its stop button. Suddenly the lift mechanism whined into life, and he looked up to see the lift level light indicate that the lift was coming down. He had no idea why he had a sudden urge to move back from the lift's doors. As he did, his left hand went to the knot in his tie, hoping that in loosening it he would help relieve the constricting knot in his throat.

His hand dropped to his trouser leg to wipe its sweat away.

The lift stopped at the third floor and Ben took the opportunity to dash over to the office doorway that Rodney had disappeared through. He caught sight of his colleague and beckoned him. Rodney stopped what he was doing and waved his hand palm down to his immediate audience, ordering by way of mime that they all hit the floor. He made his way to the door, and after closing it behind him he took up a position off to Ben's right hand side where he copied his boss's attitude.

Ben's posture suggested a relaxed preparedness that might be expressed by all humans who waited for lift doors to open. Although a brief glance in his direction gave Rodney visual evidence to the contrary. He could see its proof on Ben's forehead, where small droplets of perspiration glinted under the artificial glow of the overhead fluorescent lights. It seemed like time was passing slowly, as if the lifts arrival might allow time to duck out and have coffee. Rodney's abstract thought was fleeting, and it disappeared as he rearranged the position of his feet on the carpeted floor.

The weight of his hand gun as it hung in a loose grip at the end of an extended arm seemed to drag at his shoulder. He readjusted, and moved it from beside and behind his right thigh to the small of his back by bending his elbow.

At last the lift reached its destination, and for a moment after its whine had ceased there was a pregnant pause of inaction before the stainless steel doors finally slid open. It seemed to be a cue for a drop of sweat to drip from Rodney's eyebrow and into his eye, where it emphasized its stubbornness by refusing to be readily blinked away. Rodney felt a shock of relief when his now unblinking eyes fell on Lynette's lovely face. His relief almost died when the expression on it betrayed the existence of immediate threat. He looked directly to the figure beside her, who for those few seconds had only existed in his peripheral vision.

Beth Cooper's expression, although similar to Lynette's, differed to the extent that it held more fear and less anger. A lone tear dropped from one of her eyes and travelled down through space, to where it splashed onto the hairy male arm which held her neck locked.

It was a right arm and Rodney had no doubt that it belonged to Horton. Although the man's face and most of his body was concealed by the lifts small front part wall where the lifts console was fixed.

The weapon that the man's left hand carried was more than conspicuous. Its size and black shape more pronounced by the white back drop provided by Beth Cooper's blouse. He noticed a dark stain of oil where the tanned hand pressed the cold steel of the weapons working slide firmly against her belly.

Rodney felt very exposed. Although the dark hole in the end of Horton's weapon was not pointed directly at him, he knew that his well-being was within an inch or two of its adjustment. Some seconds dragged by as muted sounds of passing traffic outside drifted into the building. Their impact on Rodney's eardrums was almost overpowered by the fast, even pounding of his heart, as his arteries delivered its noise directly to his brain.

Suddenly Horton's menacing hand moved. He pushed Cooper forward slightly in his effort to peer around the corner of the lifts console wall. Rodney's jaw clenched as he finally looked the mysterious mercenary in the eye.

"Who are you?" Horton demanded.

Rodney tried to hold the man's steady gaze. When he failed, he allowed his eyes to rest upon the end of the gunman's hooked nose. Then he made extra effort and stared into the man's eyes.

"My name is Rodney. I'm a Federal Police officer and I will point out to you that there more of my people outside, both front and rear. So there's no way out for you."

Horton glanced briefly to the glass door which led to the street, and noted the passing pedestrians. He spoke through a light smile which made a bold attempt at softening his somewhat harsh features.

"The amount of people passing by outside doesn't lend backbone to your argument, Rodney? If there were more of your kind out there they would have had the area cordoned off by now, wouldn't they?"

"You can be sure that they are working on it right now, Henry Horton."

Horton's smile faded with the mention of his name. His voice became more businesslike as he asked.

"What's in your hand?" Rodney pushed his luck as he held up his left hand. As he did he noted from the corner of his eye an admonishment in Lynette's facial features at his seemingly careless attitude.

"The other one smartarse!" Horton's limited patience was emphasized by a slight, but curt motion of the barrel of the black heavy weapon. It had been moved away from Beth's belly and was now held still and steady.

Rodney was unsure as to how he might stall the situation. He hoped the pedestrians might disappear and add some backbone to his argument. He felt some security in the knowledge that Ben was close at hand and wished his older colleague could take over the talking, but he knew that as long as Horton was ignorant of Ben's existence, then the trump card was at that moment in their hand.

Lynette's distressed expression had alerted Ben that the situation had suddenly become awkward. As the lift doors had opened, they'd revealed to him the bigger picture an inch at a time, until finally a clear view of Horton's elbow.

Ben had flattened his back hard against the outside wall of the lift bay as the lift doors had fully opened. He stood with his weapon trained along that same wall. The end of its barrel was just about flush with the point where Horton's head would be if he stepped from the lift's cube shaped room.

Rodney informed Horton of his next move.

"I'll lower my hand and show you what it holds, will that do?" Horton nodded his acceptance of the proposal as he thumbed back the hammer of his weapon. It announced its destination with an audible click. With it came Rodney's realization, that where his well-being had been dependent on an inch or two of distance, it now narrowed to a pound or two of trigger pressure.

His eyes noted yet again the semi-automatics big bore, and knew that if it exploded in fire and flame he would be blown from arsehole to breakfast time. With great care he slowly straightened his elbow and allowed Horton full view of his hands contents.

"Nice gun, but it's a bit small isn't it, Rodney?" Horton asked, with a tone that bordered on sour humour and malice, "Now are you going to get out of my way?"

A slight tremble became evident in Rodney's voice.

"I can't let you go. Even if I did, you'd not get past those outside. So how about you just put down your weapon and we can pull this up before it goes too far?"

"No. That's not going to happen, so back off now."

"Can't do that Henry. How about you leave the two ladies in the lift while you step outside? Let them go back up in the lift. Then we can sort this out between ourselves?"

Ben felt that Rodney was making headway with his suggestion of a trade. He would give it another few seconds to see which way Horton would go. Then let Horton know of his existence, and the fact that were two of them to get past.

It seemed that Horton was now pausing to consider Rodney's offer. It reinforced his decision to remain hidden, as he quietly prayed that the man would give up and they could all go home. Horton's silence seemed to stretch, even in this time loop where everything seemed to be in slow mode. Ben could not help but notice his watch's face. Its old and loose band had allowed it to turn to the inside of his wrist. Almost in direct line of sight as he viewed along the top of his cocked weapon.

It seemed to him to be odd, that it had only been a minute since the lifts doors had opened. The fact that his gun arm had not yet begun to ache certainly substantiated the short time factor.

Horton spoke.

"It seems that you leave me only one choice." Ben heard the words clearly, while wishing he could see the face of the man who issued the low toned menacing remark. He readied his mind to speak and let his existence be known, but was beaten to the crunch by Rodney who began a question.

Ben took his eyes away from the sighted top of his weapon and looked towards Rodney's face. In time to see his lips begin to form the word 'what', and then it seemed to be a second later that he actually heard the word. A split second later, his ears were assaulted by an explosion. In the enclosed area, the noise was magnified and it left him partially deafened, until an intense high pitched ringing invaded his brain.

He held his post as his gut seemingly twisted to sickness. From the corner of his eye he saw Rodney lifted from the ground. Slowly, with his hands held out from his sides like that of the Saviour, he flew backwards until he hit and crashed open the office door which he'd earlier closed.

Some screams issued forth from the occupants of the office as Rodney finally hit the floor. His once white shirt coloured by a bright red stain which exploded outwards from the base of his throat. Tears burnt Ben's eyes as he tried to focus again on the sight line of his weapon. A rage built within him like none he'd felt before, and he trembled for the seconds it took for Horton to evacuate the lift.

The ringing in his ears went on, until he felt that he would give anything to have free hands to massage the pain away.

At last Horton's closely shaved head came into view. For a short moment Ben saw sparkling intensity in the man's eyes. It caused Ben's brain to scream out for him to give way to his own vengeful need and gun the man down.

Ben's trigger finger, as if with a mind of its own strained at its own leash. It seemed to suck at his will until he nearly succumbed, but the need for complete satisfaction stayed his hand. He waited for Horton to notice his presence.

Horton did not look surprised when he turned his face toward Ben. He could not bring his weapon to bear because of Beth, whose knees buckled under her and dragged his gun hand down.

As he pushed her away from him, Ben could have waited for another second to see clearly his ultimate intention, but

Horton's fate was beyond him now. It was in the hands of someone whose existence Ben may have suspected, but up until this point in time had never known. It was this someone whose presence had been masked for a lifetime that pulled the trigger of his gun, and then watched as a small hole appeared in Horton's forehead. Almost immediately a second hole appeared as Horton's knees folded.

Ben's gun, as if by its own accord followed him down and he had to control himself so as to not keep punching bullets into the man. At last he raised the shaking weapon and sagged against the wall as if exhausted.

He looked down at the lifeless Horton for some moments until suddenly he looked up. Almost as if he'd remembered something. He kicked Horton's gun across the floor as he pushed himself away from the wall and walked like a drunken man across the narrow foyer floor.

Tears rolled down Ben's cheeks and his grief stricken hunch shouldered frame quaked as he tottered towards the doorway where Rodney lay.

He called as he went, through a constricted throat his friend's name. When he finally looked down upon the young man's body, he knew with sadness that the only answer he would ever hear would be one recalled from memory.

*****

A part of Ben's inner ears still issued its form of protest. The unprovoked assault on its sensitivity gave it license to emit an unrelenting high pitched hum. It was not a sound in the real sense of the word. A sound is normally detected by an ear, whereas this noise was, it seemed, being generated by the ear itself and heard by him and him alone.

He knew that sounds similar to these would undoubtedly be interfering with the thought patterns of both Booth and Cooper.

He hoped their sounds would at least be a distraction from the related violence of Rodney's end, rather than a reminder.

Laura had learned the outcome of events, and had greeted him with tear laden eyes as he'd made his return to his office. She had tried her best to be supportive, but Ben had seen through her applied efforts at strength and quickly reversed their roles. Relying on the sedatives he'd been administered by the Departments medical examiner to achieve his aim.

She'd expressed her grief in short sobs that had reverberated through to him. Until he'd disengaged the embrace and suggested she might like to go home early. At first she'd refused. As if it might suggest she was in some way deserting the team at crunch time, but relented when Ben pointed out that crunch time had already passed and he'd then, gently, ordered her to go.

Now as he sat at his desk, he secretly wished he could give himself the same order, but the bold red digits which occupied his computer screen reminded him starkly his priorities. Ben cursed the web clock and its instigators for forcing him to prioritize his mourning for his comrade. He was also secretly thankful for it in a way. It allowed him to postpone coming to terms with the fact, that although he'd acted in self-defense with Horton, he'd had murder in his heart.

A subject which, when finally confronted would bring into question his conscientious ability to act as a law enforcer. His report on the shooting would most certainly describe his actions as self-defense, but he knew in the back of his mind that he'd lost it and had stepped over the line.

Horton had been the first person to die at Ben's hands in a police career that spanned thirty-two years. In that time he'd most certainly shot people, but those occasions had been different because he'd felt some remorse after the event. Whereas with Horton he'd not only felt a lack of remorse, he'd felt something that bordered between exhilaration and satisfaction.

It was a worrying thought, but he'd slotted it away into a private recess of his brain and tried to concentrate on the web clock. Its existence was a reality that could not be postponed to a time of his choosing.

He sat and watched the web clock count down another minute, before deciding that it didn't seem to be the right thing to do. Rodney's time had come to an end and with it a reminder of his own mortality, which in itself was only a measure of time and certainly not time to be wasted.

His thoughts were interrupted when he noticed a stain on the cuff of his shirt that appeared to be dried blood. He looked closer and discovered more of them. It registered in his brain then, that his gun hand had been less than half a metre from Horton's head. In immediate range of the umbrella of pink mist that would have undoubtedly erupted as his bullets had impacted.

Ben wiped his hand across his forehead and then looked closely at its palm. It occurred to him that there had probably been hundreds of tiny particles of skin, blood and bone in the umbrella, and much of it would have fallen upon him. The need to wash it away suddenly became overwhelming. He snatched up the overnight bag which held his fresh clothing as a brief glance at the web clock alerted him that he would have to hurry.

In thirty-five minutes the bold red digits would become bold red zeros. The outcome of the countdown would then be made known to whole world. Everyone from the jungles to the deserts, from the icecaps to the open sea would make up the biggest audience that mass media had ever seen. Most of them secretly thankful they didn't live in, or near one of the five affected cities.

There would also be many amongst the audience who'd take great delight in seeing the West impacted upon.

Either way, he thought as he walked hastily to the showers. The whole world is waiting.

Wednesday 4.25 pm

Bo knocked gently on Lee's office door before he opened it and poked his head into the room. Lee was seated at his desk and although the numbers on the large screen television invited his attention, Bo would not be drawn.

Instead he gazed intently on his boss's face and took in the grey pallor that shaded its features.

Lee was silently listening to someone on his desk telephone and seemed to be totally absorbed in what he heard. Bo wondered if maybe a full minute had passed before his presence was noticed. Lee looked physically sick as he finally looked up and acknowledged Bo, and with a slow wave of his fingers beckoned him into the room.

Bo closed the door behind him and stood uneasily with his back near and toward it. He hoped his invited presence to Lee's office was not going to be bad news for him also. Something was seriously wrong he thought, but his basic understanding of the events of the day regarding the web clock would not allow him to speculate on what news could be worse.

He waited while Lee put his telephone back into its cradle, and then watched as Lee solemnly looked at his open hands whose backs lay lightly against the edge of his desk top. Lee gazed into his hands for some seconds before he let his fingertips touch. Then with a slow even motion he brought the two palms together and raised them to where the tips of his index fingers came into contact with his forehead.

A slow sigh came from the man who appeared to be in prayer, before he finally looked up and toward the door where Bo stood. As his face lifted, his hands retained their position so that his index fingers now rested lightly against his lips.

Bo had preserved the silence as long as he was able, but finally it overtook him.

"You wanted to see me, Mr. Lee?"

Lee's voice was quiet, and it sounded tired.

"Yes Bo. What is it?"

"You asked me to come to see you when I had a quiet moment at the bar."

"Of course. Sorry Bo, I've a bit on my mind at the moment." Lee paused to collect his thoughts before he continued, "Bo, do you remember a year ago when I took some time off and just dropped out of sight?"

"Yes. Mr. Lee," Bo answered, relieved that his requested presence had leaned toward a better outcome.

"Well I plan to do the same again. Will you be happy with the same arrangement that we had last time?"

"Yes, Mr. Lee."

"Good. You are to be my eyes and ears. Tell no one anything and keep me informed."

Lee took a new mobile phone from his desk drawer.

"I'll call you on this phone. Don't. Under any circumstances use it personally. You can't know who might be listening, and if you have to use it to call me then keep the calls short. Let me know if there's a problem and I'll get back to you. Understand?" Bo made a move toward the door when Lee asked.

"How's the wife?"

"I think she's coping Mr. Lee. Some days she's up, and then the next day she's down. She's cheerful enough though. Always been a fighter."

Lee had met Bo's wife Kate on two occasions, and he didn't like the woman much. He felt she played on her situation, which either went entirely unnoticed by Bo, or he put up with it for some reason that Lee could not fathom. With that thought in mind Lee felt that there was no reassurance he could offer that was not based on a lie, but rather than make no comment at all, he suggested.

"Don't be backward in coming forward if there is anything I can do for you Bo."

"Thank you Mr. Lee," Bo replied as if with hat in hand.

He lingered momentarily before he turned about to make his second attempt to exit. Then as with half a mind he paused by the closed door and politely asked.

"Mr. Lee? What about you?" Bo glanced at the floor before he proceeded, "I mean, when I was at the door and you were listening on the phone you looked like you'd seen ghosts. Are you alright, Boss?"

Lee's eyes showed telltale signs of sadness, and although his face suddenly produced a new mask in the form of one of his wide grins, it failed to address the windows to his soul.

"I'll survive Bo, unless this clock thing has substance. If so, then we've all got twenty-three minutes up our sleeves." They both looked at the web clock for a moment before Lee said with a light laugh, "Better check to see if any of our customers need a last drink. It might be a bit warm in the afterlife for some of them, don't you think?"

Bo was silent for a moment, and then his old face crinkled with lines of amusement.

"Mr. Lee, Louie hasn't turned up for work again today and I'm a barperson short....?"

Lee looked thoughtful briefly before he smiled lightly.

"Ah, yes. I'm afraid Louie didn't quite come up to scratch and his employment here has been terminated. You'll have to find someone else to take his place. You know the routine, so I'll leave it in your hands." As Bo closed the door behind him he gave Lee one last glance. Noting that the look of sadness had once again found its place in the man's green eyes, as his lips returned to rest on the tips of his two touching index fingers.

It seemed to Bo that there were more countdowns to inevitable outcomes within his immediate environment than just the web clock.

Dan was nervous, as was Larry the bean counter and now Lee looked like he had just lost his best mate.

It didn't worry Bo if any shit hit a fan.

After all, he was only the bar manager.

On second thought, Louie had only been a barman, and the way Lee had said terminated certainly had ring of finality about it. He was thoughtful as he made his way behind the bar, and helped himself to a shot of single malt from the bottle he kept below the bar.

One of his younger customers spoke out loud.

"You're looking pretty thoughtful, Bo?"

"Just thinking about a warmer climate mate, are you right for another drink?" His eyes shifted to the bar rooms television, where the red digits displayed an uncertain future.

As he watched, twenty minutes suddenly became nineteen.

Wednesday 4.48 pm

Ben Preston's skin felt flushed after his shower. He'd stayed under the steaming hot water as long as he'd been able to bear it, and after he'd washed his thinning head of hair twice, he reluctantly stepped from under the pressured spray. As he dried himself down, it occurred to him that for the first time in his long career he was guilty of washing away evidence. Under different circumstances it may have appealed to his dry sense of humour.

The thoroughness of his physical cleansing had allowed him the certainty that he was uncontaminated by a single particle of Horton. Now, as he looked carefully at a spot on his arm he realized, that for some time anyway, he would see his freckles and skin blemishes in a whole new light.

He'd stolen a plastic bin liner from the cleaners cluttered closet for his soiled clothes, and now with its weight at the end of his extended arm he made his way back to his office. Scratching as he went an irritation at the back of his neck where he'd forced his skin to accept too much soap.

As he walked through the open planned office area he looked about the room and noted the serious intent of his colleagues. They worked incessantly in search of the vital clue upon which theirs, and their cities well-being might hinge.

He was sure the awareness of their colleague's death was in all their minds at this very moment. Also, he was just as sure that they, like him, knew that now, like no other time in their careers they had to prioritize their actions and their thoughts. To be sure, they'd all at some time in their careers had to prioritize, but then it had always been on someone else's behalf.

It was their job to serve the public.

Today, at this the beginning of a new millennium, a subtle change had come about. They still persevered to serve that public, but the web clock made it more personal, in that it was aimed just as squarely at them as anyone else. His thoughts were interrupted by a sharp voice that for a moment issued forth from a television set. It had been wheeled into the airy room to allow all those present visual access to whatever was to take place in ten minutes.

The sudden loud sound, which was probably due to its previous user leaving its volume on high, caused everyone in the room to startle.

From where he stood he had a clear overview of the desk and computer laden detective's station. In the instant of the television being turned on and delivering its high definition noise, the eyes and minds of every person in the immediate area were forcefully dragged from whatever they'd been concentrating on.

Two of them, Ben noticed, had instinctively reached beneath their coats to where their weapons were concealed. One had wasted his coffee with a hapless hand and its flow flooded the papers and report folders that inhabited his desk top. No word was spoken, but Sean, who was in charge of linking the televisions screen to the A.F.P's central computer, became the centre of attention for the intense focus of a dozen sets of eyes. He apologetically held out his two hands and then almost as abruptly turned his attention back to his technical task.

Ben noted the tension and understood the pressure.

He was also heartened by the fact that none had made personal comment towards Sean. It suggested to him that although they felt the pressure, their temperament was far from being affected by it.

It also became startlingly clear to him, that although it is said that there's a comedian in every crowd, this small group of men was without one. Ben wondered what Rodney might have said if he'd been here. His comment and humorous light hearted wit had always softened the serious, and now, the lack of it made his absence more than obvious.

Ben suddenly and forcefully snapped his mind back to attention. As he raised his eyes from the point where they'd been focused on the floor, he began a short walk throughout the room. He enquired of some of his people short verbal reports on progress, before offering quiet words of guidance and support.

Knowing as he did so he felt no better than anyone else, but part of being the boss was to plant the basic seed of morale by advising that his door was always open.

He approached his team's youngest and newest player last. Allan had only been with the squad for a little under three months. He'd been Rodney's partner and on the job apprentice for the whole of his service career. Ben, through the sight of his experienced eyes, had watched as they'd become an integral part of his command.

"Anything new, Allan?"

"No Sir," Allan replied as he turned in his chair and looked up at Ben. "Reasonable news and bad news I'm afraid. I've run the best search programs available to us in an effort to track the website of the web clock, but it appears there isn't one. Sorry. That's impossible."

Allan paused momentarily and held his hands apologetically, as he made a second and more concise effort to explain.

"What I mean Sir, is that there must be one, but it's either hidden ultra-carefully, or it's camouflaged as something else so it appears not to exist."

Allan reached forward and tapped a single key on his keyboard. The script he'd been reading disappeared and was replaced just as quickly with a map of England. It was overlaid with a lightly coloured circle which encompassed an area stretching from Weymouth to the Scottish border.

He looked to his boss while he pointed an index finger toward the computer's screen.

"I talked to the wizards in our tech department. They informed me that the most they can confirm is that the web site is somewhere within this circle. Within this particular satellites footprint, and whoever is running it has a monster mainframe at their disposal. It seems their programs have been specifically written for this particular venture. So the bad news there is, we're up the creek so to speak." He paused again before he turned to speak eye to eye. "Sir, I know that what I'm doing here may appear to be a fruitless line of enquiry, but I'd figured that these people being as professional as they appear to be, must be linking themselves directly through satellite. I thought that if I ran a search and intercept program on that satellite, to sift out any information with Sydney addresses, I'd be overwhelmed. So I narrowed it down a little by setting the search task to exclude Federal, State and local Government departments, Western Religious groups, oil companies, Federal and State Police, banks and numerous others. I've also excluded private residents, other than those with a new connection less than three months old, but that search and intercept is running separately on Rodney's computer."

"And?" Ben asked.

"That's where it gets a bit sticky, Sir. This search and intercept program needs to be left running twenty-four seven if we want to catch our culprits with their pants down. If Kane is our man, then he will most surely expect that he's under surveillance and steer clear of his communication site. As it is almost countdown time, then maybe his part in the operation is near completion. If so, then his necessity for access might not be needed. Either way, I think we've missed him." Allan paused for thought for some seconds before he continued, "But. If he does use the site again, we'll have a fair idea where his computer is, and its hard drive will more than likely give the wizards downstairs something to work on for evidence against him, after the fact. If Kane is not our man, and the culprits use the site again, then at least we're not yet out of the race. That's the reasonable news, Sir."

"How long has this program been running?" Ben enquired.

Allan looked at the computers clock.

"Two hours and forty-five minutes."

"Can we have look and see what it's got to say for itself so far?"

Allan turned again to his keyboard and punched some keys. Ben watched as the map of England disappeared to be replaced with a list of mainly business names. It was a comparatively short list at this early stage of the programs running, and as the two men stared at the names of the list one thing became obvious to them.

"Maybe the back packers have given us something to go on." Ben suggested as he pointed to one, and then to another business name on the list. "People on the move are undoubtedly the ones who rely on an internet café."

"Alan, get in touch with Kane's surveillance team. See if they can furnish us with a photo of Kane, Wild and a fresh one of Walters. Tell them that I said it's extremely urgent. When you've got them, then pay a visit to all internet cafés within a mile of Kane's accommodation and Grey Street. See if anyone recognizes them."

"Yes, Sir." Allan replied as he again turned his attention to his computer. He was glad he had something to get his teeth into, but he had to turn toward his boss again as Ben offered congratulations.

"Good work, Allan."

"Thank you, Sir, but I should have thought of internet café's earlier."

"So should've I Allan, but it may have been overlooked altogether if not for your tenacity."

It appeared that Ben might say more, but he was suddenly interrupted by a call from the other side of the office. He turned to see that everyone's eyes were intent upon the televisions screen, as Sean's seemingly loud voice reminded him.

"Boss, the show's about to start."

CHAPTER 22

5.01 pm

Ben seated himself in a chair that Sean had made available. Along with his colleagues he waited expectantly as each second stretched its way into the next, until finally the web clock stated its conclusion with a set of four zeros.

Almost immediately the televisions screen became full of what appeared to be a small office. The cameras lighting was not of a professional standard, but it offered a clear picture of a shadowy figure who was reaching with extended arm towards the small room's ceiling.

Then, with a slow advance the camera operator moved closer to the side of the small room, all the while holding the shadowy figure in the cameras field of view.

Suddenly a fluorescent light flickered into life. It flooded the small room's interior with its glow, and exposed the shadowy figure as a man in an air tight chemical hazard suit. It seemed to hang baggily at the end of an umbilical airline which connected its helmet to the small rooms ceiling. Ben noted the silence that had engulfed the room about him. Then, along with his colleagues he realized, without surprise, that it was not only this immediate area that was being smothered by an invisible cloud of soundlessness.

The silence had taken the whole building in its grasp. For some brief seconds he listened to a sound of silence that seemed to have depth. It was as if the office area had suddenly acquired the expanse of an outback plain. At that moment the suited figure turned around to face the camera. It stood like an alien life form as artificial lighting reflected in small sheets across the curved Perspex of its helmets visor.

Ben gazed intently at the visor in an effort to pierce its shining barrier, but only met frustration at not being able to see the eyes of his aggressor. As if the camera sought to relieve him of his frustration, it offered his attention a substitute beacon by rotating in a short arc until it focused on the bulky steel, block like transformer.

It hovered briefly before moving on again, to where a nest of six rats fidgeted behind the glass of a small aquarium. The silence was suddenly shattered by a low voice that Ben recognized as a poor imitation of a Hitchcock impersonation.

"Good evening, world. Welcome to our version of reality T.V."

There was a brief pause before the voice continued.

"I undoubtedly have your full attention, so I will come straight to the point. I am sure that by now all of you have a basic understanding of the potential of the device we have at our disposal. We decided that the world's media was the most practical method to use, to inform you of the possible outcome if our weapon of mass destruction was actually detonated. Let me for a moment point out to those among you who believe that the media might at times exaggerate, or let us say in this instance, add colour to their reports. There is no need for exaggeration on their part in the case of this weapon. The media's descriptions to date are, I assure you, entirely accurate. So accurate, that their reports may have caused some concern to those who have a weapon in their midst. With that thought in mind we felt it only proper to deliver the good news we have for them."

The voice paused again, as if the speaker played cat and mouse with his audience.

"The good news is that we have no intention of detonating the weapon." A light hearted chuckle that seemed to border on sarcasm escaped his lips before he said, "I thought you'd all be pleased to hear that little snippet of information. It might lighten the situation somewhat, before I explain to you the bad news?" His voice suddenly sunk to a 'beware the bogey man' tone, as he said, "Oh yes, there is bad news."

"The small room that you see before you holds within it the weapon of mass destruction. It also is the temporary home for some rodents. Their reason for existence in this case is to give visual proof of the weapons destructive power. They will prove the effects of 10X gas on living beings to the people who will be participating in the auction that will begin directly after the demonstration. For some months now, our agents have been busy finding underground organizations and individuals who have a passionate desire to attack the West. Those people who, since the major event of 9/11, have not had access to a weapon with huge potential, or more importantly, the means for its delivery to a populated target area. Where its use might emphasize their fervour in confronting the biased polices and attitudes of America and its allies."

Ben's anger, which had begun its life as a seed at the beginning of the mono-toned delivery, had grown as the words grated on his eardrums. Each like single arrows, pierced the heart of the civilized side of his brain, and brought to life a primitive urge to take the voice by the throat and squeeze it quiet.

"The success of our agents can only be described as outstanding. They have found no less than a score of different parties who have expressed their wish to take part in the auction. Hence, here is the bad news for those in the five affected countries."

"As I have already stated, we who are in possession of the weapons have no desire to detonate them. Unfortunately, we will have no control over the actions of those who are successful in their bids."

Ben was forced to wait through a long moment of silence. It was broken once by a low voiced venomous curse from amongst the ranks of his seated officers. He had the desire to look in the direction of its issue, but his mind would not allow him to take his eyes away from the fidgeting rats, as they searched with uncertainty each corner of the aquarium.

Suddenly the voice started again. This time it came through with added annunciation, like that of an introduction to guests' who were about to embark on a tour of an art gallery.

"I think that it is now time to move on to the second part of our programming. It is mainly for the benefit of those who will be participants in the auction. For you, the general public, you should of course feel free to accept our invitation to sit back, relax and enjoy the show."

Ben watched closely as the camera panned the small room's interior. It finally settled on the man behind the helmets visor, who stood motionless as if waiting for direction.

It came with the voice's introduction.

"Our friend in the suit is Daniel." Daniel gave a wave of his plastic encased arm in a sarcastically friendly manner, as if the viewers had caught him entertaining at a family BBQ.

"We'll call him Daniel for the time being. He's the one in the lion's den as it were, and in charge of the finer points of the demonstration. I think he is about ready to now start."

Daniel lowered his arm and made his way through the small room to the transformers squat form. He lifted a cordless drill that was fitted with a socket attachment and began to remove four nuts which held in place a rectangular shaped steel plate. He removed a fifth bolt which appeared to have no reason other than to fill a bolt hole.

Another silent minute passed until he placed the rectangular plate onto the top of the transformer. As it clunked onto its new resting place, Ben wondered why it was necessary for such a plate that had no obvious purpose to be manufactured of such heavy steel.

Its reason became obvious some seconds later, as Daniel moved a short step sideways. Allowing the camera direct access to the dark steel box to which the rectangular lid had been fitted.

The voice, now without its sarcastic content, took its cue and began a description of the boxes contents. While Daniel's gloved left open-palmed hand guided the viewer's eyes to each individual object described.

"The package that Daniel is now pointing to is a small amount of plastic explosive. Its blast force will be contained within the steel box for less than a second, before it breaks its way through a seal in the firing tube and propels before it a litre of our gas 10X." Daniel pointed to the package, and then with a short wave of his gloved hand he invited the viewer's eyes to the firing tube.

Firstly, to the firing tubes entry point and then to a light gauge steel seal that lay flat on the top of the transformer. He held his hand palm side up, before lifting it upwards to express in mime the gases expulsion point.

The voice changed tact, to one whose tone carried like that of a person insulted.

"I'm sure that some among you have noticed there are no wires or detonator attached to the explosive."

The camera focused again, closing in on the explosive package, while the voice allowed a brief moment of silence before it stated threateningly,

"Be advised. We have overlooked nothing."

At that moment Daniel lifted a long bolt from the small tables top and held it up for the camera. The voice continued, its tone now suddenly back again to an attempted soft tongued charm.

"The bolt that Daniel now reveals is in fact the weapons detonator."

Ben watched as Daniel gently slid the long bolt into the fifth bolt hole. He left it naked to the camera's lens, where it appeared to be too long for the weapons requirements, until the voice healed all wounds of confusion.

"The detonator is in the tip of the long bolt, and is at the moment resting on a light tin seal. This seal will be gently pierced by the bolt as it is wound into its thread and the detonator will be slowly embedded into the explosive material.

The wires that you see at the head end of the bolt are those to which the power source will be connected."

The statement concluded with an attempt at sarcastic humour which accompanied a light chuckle that like the voice aggravated Ben's ears.

"We felt it necessary to transport the weapon in a disarmed state, in the interests of public safety."

The chuckle echoed hollowly in Ben's ears. In stark contrast, and seemingly in direct competition with the ringing buzz, that still invasively issued its constant protest to the explosive power of Horton's hand gun. Until some moments later it was replaced with a new vibration.

"Now for the juicy part." The voice cried out, like a miser who rubbed his hands together in glee. Then it suddenly dropped into a more explanatory tone, "I could go into the details of 10X history, but I think we are all interested in the present rather than the past. So without further ado, I'll let Daniel take over at this point. His actions will undoubtedly speak a thousand words." Ben watched Daniel remove a clear sided container from the firing tube. It appeared to be plastic and probably one litre in content. Daniel handled it very carefully as he turned toward the antics of the restless rodents.

Having set the container on to the table's top. He withdrew from a plastic pencil case a long stemmed glass tube that looked like an eye dropper, placing it within easy reach by the container.

Ben wondered at the deftness of Daniel's gloved fingers, as he watched him lift a rubber eye drop extraction cap from a small container. Then again, as he fitted it to the long stemmed glass tube and rested the single unit on the table's top.

For a short moment Daniel rested. His audience waited while he stretched to his full height within the baggy suit, seemingly to take a long deep breath. It expressed clearly, his understanding of the material in the litre container that he was about to uncap.

Ben, like the rest of the world watched as Daniel finally began to unscrew the container's lid with his right hand. While holding the containers base firmly onto the tables top with his left. Finally, after several short slow methodical turns he placed the lid lightly on the table top beside the open container.

The clear sided container was full nearly to the base of its neck and Ben wondered at the need for such a long eye dropper. The thought just as quickly dissipated in his mind as his attention was drawn back to Daniel's actions. Daniel lifted the eye dropper and for some seconds he allowed it to hover over the containers orifice, before he carefully dipped its tip into the leaf green liquid.

As he withdrew it again, it appeared he'd only just wet the end of the dropper. Like a showman he held it to the camera as it zoomed in, capturing the presence of the tiny drop that occupied a small area just inside the eye dropper's tip.

Daniel placed the eyedropper at rest on the pencil case's edge, and with great care replaced the lid onto the container, before again lifting the eye dropper.

Ben watched closely and saw what appeared to be Latex stretch its way in to the aquarium space, before it was pierced by the eye dropper's tip and it snapped back into its pre-probed place.

Daniel's left hand, whose palm edge rested on the aquarium's lid, partially hid the stem of the glass eye dropper. It supported and made steady his right hand, whose finger tips held their pinching position lightly on the rubber extraction cap. Ben noticed a slight movement of Daniel's glove which advertised the pinching of his fingertips, and his eyes went immediately to the tip of the long glass stem. There a tiny drop dangled for a brief second, before it escaped its hold and disappeared into the mess of litter and rat droppings on the aquarium's floor.

There was not time enough for a pregnant pause, before the rats realized that something was dreadfully wrong. Almost immediately there was a rush of activity as they bounded about the aquarium's glass frontier. Seconds later they suddenly appeared to be moving in slow motion. The slow motion had begun as their muscles began to seize, and with it severe lockjaw. The seizure interfered with the flow of air into their lungs, but it did not restrict the flow of white coloured foam as it bubbled out from between their teeth.

In seconds they lay on their sides, where it appeared they suddenly had an urge to stand on their toes as the seizure over took all and with outstretched quivering legs they died.

Daniel appeared not to have noticed the consequences of his single minded action. He replaced the eyedropper into the pencil case, and then returned the clear plastic container and its contents to the firing tube.

After replacing the steel plate, he produced two curved pieces of steel. They were shaped like suitcase handles, but with bolt holes in either of their ends. These bolt holes fitted the exposed ends of the steel plates threaded studs. He replaced the nuts and tightened the handles into place.

The fifth bolt replaced the detonator bolt before he used the cordless drill again to remove four other same size bolts. Then with two free hands he grasped the recently installed steel handles, and without effort removed from its place within the transformer, a steel box. Ben grimaced, and one of his colleagues cursed as the conspicuous transformer weapon suddenly became an easily concealed small steel box. Daniel gently placed the steel box upon the small table, before he reached under the table and produced a medium sized common cardboard carton.

He lifted the steel box and dropped it lightly into the cardboard box. It appeared to fit snugly, and as he placed the detonator inside with it the voice once again began its narrative.

"I did point out earlier the importance of weapons delivery to its populated target area. To which the bulk of the transformer may have suggested a contradiction, but as you have all just seen by the removal of just four small bolts, the weapon has immediately become much easier to transport covertly, without interfering with its effectiveness." The voice paused for breath before it continued.

"As you have also seen, 10X is effective. In fact, it is the best there is, and if any one of you feels that its effectiveness was enhanced due to our furry friends confined space? Don't be misled. It was designed to descend to ground level in open spaces, where moving masses might stir it up to nose and throat level, even days after its original dispersal."

"Oh! There are two other minor points that I should bring to your attention. Due to the restrictions placed upon us by the size of the firing tube, we took the liberty of using the 10X undiluted. That has allowed us to fit five litres of the original Russian militaries weapons grade 10X into a one litre container. We've also taken away its smell, so those who inhale it at least won't know what hit them, and that is a good thing I think. Wouldn't you agree?"

There was another brief pause, before the voice spoke directly to those who were expected to take part in the auction.

"Now that we've concluded our demonstration, the time has come to get down to business. Gentlemen, we have been informed by our sales teams that all interested parties have been furnished with our web address to which to make your bids. The auction will begin now. It will run for two hours. After the successful bidder's money transfer is confirmed, he will be notified of the weapons pick up point. Let the bidding begin."

Ben blinked as the television's screen suddenly became blank and the voices transmission terminated. He looked over to Allan who tapped on his keyboard.

"Nothing Sir, it appears they prefer to deal directly and privately with their bidders. We'll know nothing other than what they're prepared to tell us." Ben had known from the outset that things could get worse, but he'd never envisaged that the weapon itself might become smaller than a needle in his city sized haystack.

Before, they'd at least had the conspicuousness of the transformer on their side. Now, the situation became almost hopeless, and it rested heavily on his heart that they might lose the fight.

Two hours, he thought as a telephone's demand for attention wrestled with the constant hum in his ears for the right to be heard. Its sound stopped as its call was finally answered, and then he heard as if from a distance.

"Call for you, Sir."

Ben looked up and saw Allan with a telephone hand piece held out toward him in an outstretched hand. He envisaged it to be the Police Commissioner.

"Who is it, Allan?"

Allan face registered a look of serious uncertainty as he replied.

"It's John Kane, Sir."

CHAPTER 23

Wednesday 5.45

Sally had turned on her television for the first time this day, as a distraction while she painted her toenails, and had broken into a news program. It stated that the countdown was finally about to reach its conclusion. Half way through the art deco of her eighth toe she'd stopped to watch its final seconds.

Sitting on the edge of her bed, she'd forgotten about the cotton balls between her toes as she'd leaned forward towards the television. Her attention became totally immersed in the actions of the man in the baggy suit, until finally her jaw had snapped shut in disgust when the camera zoomed in on the rats.

Animals had never played any part in her life, other than the odd mouse that had on occasions invaded her kitchen. Sometimes a stray or leashed dog she was forced to avoid on the city's streets.

She was a city girl, born and bred. She'd never had a pet and had never been out of this city. The only farm animals she'd ever come in contact with were wrapped in plastic sheeting on refrigerated shelves in supermarkets. As a child, there had been the zoo of course, but the strong smell of animal body odour had tamed any enthusiasm. Not to mention the suggestion of skin irritation brought on by the animal's incessant scratching, which had over powered her senses to the point she vowed she would never return. She agreed with the man in the baggy suit, that rats, if they were to be in close proximity of man or woman, should be kept under some form of quarantine. Basic hygiene commanded segregation, and she had smiled to herself at the man in the baggy suit. Who, even by her standards was going a bit overboard by wearing such an odd shaped suit, as well as imprisoning the rats in a glass cage.

Her light smile had persisted for only some seconds. Until a man with a voice whose tone suggested it was not one to be trusted, suddenly beckoned her wary attention. Then he immediately grasped it with the mention of reality television. Sally liked reality T.V, and had watched most of the shows available to Sydney's networks. Taking part in them with careful consideration when the time came to SMS her decisions, as to who should be evicted or elected.

Her brow furrowed with light lines of confusion as she tried to guess what a reality program had to do with the news station.

As the voice continued, so did Sally's confusion. She retreated back across her bed, away from the scenes of the stiff legged rats, whose grinning frothy faces gave rise to her alarm.

She tried to tear her eyes away from the horrible sight, and for a brief second she succeeded, until her gaze was dragged back. To where it involuntarily set rock steady on the rats, whose rigid state proclaimed clearly in suspended silence their thousand words. Sally sat stunned as the camera operator redirected her attention to the actions of the man in the baggy suit. While two words used in the narration tolled like bells in the back of her brain.

Her mind wandered away from the events on the television's screen as she sought to seek out the significance of the two words. A conscious thought suddenly blossomed, and Sally's lips slowly formed into a quietly spoken question.

"What five cities?"

She pulled her dressing gown closer about her as she listened for more information, but it appeared that he'd said all that there was to say. Then the program finished as if its plug had been pulled, and almost as suddenly a well-dressed news presenter appeared.

He remained speechless for some seconds, like one whose thunder had been stolen, before he offered comment.

"Well there you have it," offered the news presenter. "Five cities have simultaneously been forced to accept the fact that they have within their midst a weapon of mass destruction. A weapon that will be presented on a silver platter to any lunatic terrorist who can come up with the enough money to win this madman's auction. In a moment we'll be speaking with Dr. James Wren. He is an internationally recognized expert on chemical weapons, who will expand on what we already know of the deadly nerve gas 10X."

"What five cities?" Sally demanded impatiently. She touched the remote control and brought to view another station. Its news cameraman was obviously viewing Sydney from the top of one of the cities high rise buildings.

She watched as the camera operators lens surveyed the Eastern Suburbs as it began a three hundred and sixty degree rotation. It covered the cities south, before it panned slowly across the Western Suburbs, until finally she recognized the leafy green suburb in which her own backyard lay.

A chill feeling swept through her as she heard the news reporter say, "...and it is suspected that somewhere within the circle our camera has just surveyed, that the weapon of mass destruction awaits its new owner...."

Sally felt physically ill and she hurried from her bed to the bathroom to wash away the sickly taste that had suddenly regurgitated to the back of her throat. Then a sense of panic touched her, and she rushed back to her bedside table where with a water wet chin she dialled her telephone. Her small hands clenched as she waited for her call to be answered.

"Tom, I've just seen the dead rats on television and I'm scared. I want to get out of here." She couldn't believe the calm in his voice. After all, the bomb thing could be right on his doorstep too, couldn't it?

"Ah! Sally. Finally woke up to the fact that the world has been spinning around without you for the last few days, have you?"

"What?" She was suddenly concerned at his attitude, "Tom. Don't play games. The newsman said that the bomb thing could be near the house, and the terrorist said that we have two hours. I need to get away."

"You have a car. Get in it and drive away."

"What do you mean, on my own?"

"Sal, I've always given you the freedom to do what you need to do, haven't I? Well, that freedom is still there. All you have to do is go where you wish to go." Sally's silence suggested to Lee that she was unsure as to whether she wanted to hear the answer he might give if she asked him to explain.

The silence that followed allowed Lee time to arrange his thoughts. He wanted to be tough with her, but he decided to play it cool for amusements sake. See where the conversation took them.

He realized the significance of the difference between their ages. In their time together she had come of age, while he had finally, and begrudgingly accepted his membership to the 'over forties' club.

Lee decided to pull the plug on her politely.

"Sally..." He paused as he reminded himself that his telephone might not be secure, before deciding to use that possibility to his own advantage and kill two birds with one stone, "Look Sal." The bomb that holds the gas that killed the rats was brought into the country by one of my companies..."

"You did it?" Sally asked.

"No of course not. I knew nothing about it. A man who worked for me whose name was Sudovich did it. He went behind my back, without my knowledge and used one of my companies' names to import it, but that's not important right now where you are concerned. The important thing is that the police might try to implicate me in Sudovich's wrong doings. That's why I think that now is a good time for you to take the opportunity to distance yourself from me. Get into your car and get away for a while."

Sally heard his words clearly, although her quiet consideration was not for them, but more for the seemingly mocking tone he used to deliver them. She suddenly and venomously accused.

"Bullshit, Tom Lee! You're up to something. You're ditching me, and making it look like I'm leaving you because you're scared of what I can do to you in a divorce court."

"Come on Sal. Why would I want to ditch you? You've done nothing serious enough to warrant a divorce" He allowed the words to sink in before he asked, "Have you?" Lee smiled to himself as Sally's sudden silence told him what he already knew.

"Damn you. You've got another woman, and you want me out so you can bring her to my house, haven't you? Well I'm not moving. You can go to hell." She screamed.

"What's happened Sal, did I hit a nerve?" Lee asked before he made a suggestion, "Listen. Why don't you call up your boyfriend, maybe he can help you?"

Silence reigned from Sally's end of the phone for some seconds until she threatened.

"Damn you, Tom Lee. You'll get yours. I'll bury you and when I do I'll be there to piss on your grave."

Lee listened as she slammed her telephone hand piece down.

"I think you've buried me already Sal," he whispered as he lowered his own hand piece onto its cradle.

London time.

Charles stood quietly behind Phillip. Watching the man's computer screen, and trying to relate its information changes to the increased speed of Phillip's fingertips on its keyboard. While he waited, his hands though dry writhed against each other as if to wipe away an imagined moistness. His tongue, as with its own attitude writhed against his lips in an effort to maintain moisture.

The silence of the large room was broken only by Phillip's keyboard tap, and Charles was forced to still an overwhelming desire to demand verbal commentary from one of the computer wizards. He looked to those console operators who sat with still hands. A few fingertips drummed quietly onto the table's top, as they waited with anticipation for their invitation to participate.

One of them whose hands had left the table to be wiped on the thighs of his trousers suddenly returned them to his keyboard where they came alive. As if to compete with Phillip's apparent involuntary effort, they created a second sound which claimed its space in the large high ceiling room. Some seconds later Charles's hands lightened their grasp as a third console operator's fingers added further voice to the keyboard chorus. Then a fourth added harmony.

After some minutes the chorus became like the rattle of out of time snare drums. Charles's hands rubbed together like those belonging to a miser who could smell money in the air. He moved away from his position behind Phillip and walked around the large table. Quietly pausing, and then peering over the shoulder of each of the console operators to digest the information posted on their screens. He strode on to the operations communications computer. It sat alone with its operator in a corner of the room.

"Stephen, advise Athol of seventeen hits, offering one million pounds at this time, but as yet early days." He waited while Stephen carried out his wishes and then ordered, "Let me know the minute our people are either in the air or on safe soil."

He turned again to the large table, and with the keyboard clatter now beating a rhythm of success, he smiled to himself as he thought, I love this job.

Wednesday 5.55 pm

Dan Sanic wished for a brief moment that he'd not drunk as much bourbon as he had. He wasn't drunk, but he wondered if maybe alcohol was the wrong thing to do to a stomach that felt queasy at the prospect of deposing Lee. The possibility of dying like one those rats was real too, he reminded himself.

Each as dangerous as each other, he thought.

He'd been at a loss for something to do for most of the afternoon after having dismantled another of Lee's meth labs. The stocks of chemicals had been stored for use at a later date, and unless Lee called him for a specific task he'd be at a loss for something to do for the rest of the evening. Just one more he thought, as he lifted his empty glass in the direction of Bo's enquiring eye.

Bo poured two more nips into the small glass as he quietly suggested.

"I can make you coffee if you'd like, Mr. Sanic?"

Dan picked up the glass and drained it before he considered its emptiness.

"As usual Bo, you are right. Coffee is a good idea. While you're going, you might heat me one of those chicken rolls, eh?" He wasn't hungry, but the hope that food might help settle his restless belly allowed him time to shift his thoughts. The interval was short lived, as after some minutes watching Bo's activity behind the bar, his mind once again chose its own path.

Dan felt wetness at the end of his fingers, and his eyes strayed to the reflection held in a small lake of spillage on the bars top. Maybe he should forget about popping Lee. Just take the terrorist's unspoken advice and leave the city, at least until its future was certain. He considered the options, and welcomed the thought of the easy way out, as well as the relief of worry that accompanied it. For a brief second he almost made a decision to leave his life as it was, uncomplicated in its entirety.

He smiled inwardly, then outwardly as a sense of relief seemed to descend upon him. Its invisible cloak enveloped him like a veil of warm security.

His return to relaxedness was suddenly interrupted by the vibration of his mobile phone. Dan lifted it to his ear.

"Dan, I've just seen the dead rats on the T.V, and they say that the bomb thing could be near me, and I rang Tom and he said that I should go away by myself 'cause he reckons that it's better for me, but I think he knows about me playing up, and I reckon that he wants me out of the way and I don't know what to do and I'm scared and…."

"Whoa whoa. Hold up a minute. Just calm down and take a deep breath." Dan turned away from the bar and walked towards the glass windows, where he watched the busy street while he waited for Sally to console herself.

"You better now?" He asked.

"Yes," She sniffled.

"Right. Now listen. Don't worry about the rats. If the terrorists decide to blow up the bomb they won't do it out in the suburbs, will they? They'll want to do it right in the heart of the city. Doesn't that make sense?"

Sally thought for a moment before she offered a quiet and un-assured, "Yes."

Dan looked about him for his own reassurance, noting quickly that no one was within ear shot before he spoke.

"What did Tom say?"

"He said that I was free to go where I want to, but it wasn't what he said, it was how he said it. He told me that a man named Sandwich had used his company to bring the bomb thing into the country, and that the police were after Tom because of it, and that was why he said that I would be better off away from him, but I think, by the way he said it that he's trying to dump me."

"What makes you think that he knows you're seeing someone else?"

"I told him that I thought he was getting me to go away so that he could say that I'd shot through on him, so he'd have a reason for a divorce. He asked me in his smart arse, know it all voice, if I'd done anything to deserve being divorced. Then he asked, "Have you Sal?" I didn't know what to say, and then I realized that he'd given me a trick question. If he wasn't sure before, then he knows now that something's going on. I told him that I reckoned that he had another woman, and that he was trying to get me out of my house to make way for her."

Nice house too, Dan thought before he began to visualize himself enjoying its comforts.

"What are we going to do Dan?" Dan's silence stretched as he took up the strain in the tug of war between what to do and what not to do. He felt the weight of conscience fall upon him as he explained.

"I'll have to carry out the plan that I told you about, and I will have to do it tonight. After it is done, I'll come to you."

He felt a tingle in his loins as she goaded him on with a low deep throated purr.

"Mmm Dan, my big man. Come to pussy."

"I'll be there baby. Now you don't worry about a thing. Dan will fix it."

"Hurry Dan," she said before Dan broke the connection. As he returned to the bar and his now hot chicken roll, a small voice cried out in his brain. Wrong way, go back, but his ears were no match for the tingling sensation in his loins when it came to a common sense debate.

While he slowly ate his chicken roll he devised the plan that when successful, he the heir apparent would have all that Lee had owned. He couldn't remember the name of the old black and white movie, in which the town crier had called out the phrase, but he had no doubt that he would fit the title.

"The King is dead. Long live the King."

CHAPTER 24

Wednesday 5.58 pm.

Ben Preston had not made comment to John Kane. After listening to the man's direction he'd made immediate contact with the Police Commissioner, who agreed with Kane's wishes that a Command meeting should be held at once. He'd then made his way to the boardroom where he paced the carpeted floor while he waited for the Commissioner. Some minutes later the door swung open allowing Commander Rusty Bates entry.

"What's happening Ben?" Rusty huffed as if he'd decided on the stairway rather than the lift.

"I've just had a call from John Kane, our chief suspect in the 'wooden box' inquiry. He asked for a meeting with the Commissioner. His phone call was brief, but he requested yours and my presence. Mine because we've met. He asked for you by name."

"Knows my name, eh? Did he say why he wants to meet?"

"No. He just said that a meeting was in all our interests, and that time was short." Their conversation was suddenly interrupted by the opening of the door.

The Commissioner entered, and then stood aside to allow John Kane's large frame to fill the doorway before me made basic introductions.

Ben stared coldly into Kane's shining excited eyes.

Kane withdrew from his jacket's top pocket a small note book which he held up for his audience's view as he said.

"Time is short so I'll come straight to the point. This notebook has, on its first page the directions needed to find the location of the transformer and the weapon." He paused briefly as the eyes of the three police officers stared greedily at the small notebook that contained the answer to all their prayers. "Unfortunately for you, the directions are all written in code.

You cannot possibly decipher it in the short time available to you before the weapon is handed over to its purchaser." He paused again in his delivery, and as he tossed the book through the air in Ben's direction he added, "Here you go Ben. It's all yours."

Ben caught the book, and quickly opened its blue plastic cover to see a series of numbers interspaced with a meaningless array of alphabetical letters. He passed the open book to his Commissioner, and then looked at Rusty Bates with a slight, almost undetectable shake of his head. Ben turned his gaze to Kane.

"What do you want?" He demanded

Kane smiled lightly, as if he was about to say something he knew would be taken as impossible, but the tone in his voice suggested otherwise.

"I expect free and unchallenged passage for me and my colleagues out of this country. After which the notebook's deciphered information will be made available to you via the internet." He glanced at his watch and added, "I should point out at this time, that you have a little over an hour to get us onto our private plane, receive your email and capture the weapon's new owner's agents."

"You are asking us to trust you?" Rusty Bates asked.

"No. You're the drowning man, and I'm the one who holds the straw."

Rusty cursed and Kane straightened. His hands turned into fists, ready to defend against possible attack. He held this stance until Rusty Bates brought himself back under control before he offered some reassurance.

"Don't feel as if you're the only one. An exact copy of this conversation is at this moment going on in four other countries." He drew breath before he continued, "Now. Let's get back on track shall we. The time for your decision has come and it has to be made. Your backs are against the wall. You have no choice other than to move now, or lose."

Ben looked to his boss and begrudgingly understood as the Commissioner slowly nodded.

"Excellent. Now with your permission I would like to take Mr. Preston with me as my personal escort. I'm sure that his seniority will ensure smooth transit. By the way, your surveillance teams are still on watch where they think I and my colleague are. I might suggest a refresher course for them in covert surveillance?" The Commissioner nodded his consent, at which Kane turned toward the door and opened it. He gestured to Ben his desire to leave.

Ben almost stepped forward, but suddenly he propped and put forward a question.

"If you've evaded our surveillance teams, why didn't you just take the opportunity to leave without calling this meeting?

Kane looked directly at Ben as he answered.

"I didn't want to take the risk of being cornered by Customs or your uniformed police and have to contend with their chains of command just to get here where I am now. Instead, with the importance of time in mind I chose a more direct route. We have achieved what we set out to, and we don't want to be held responsible for the actions of the weapon's new owners."

"What have you achieved?" Ben Asked.

Kane was thoughtful for a brief moment before he answered.

"That's a question best answered by my boss, Athol, if you ever have the opportunity to meet him." He pointed to the face of his watch and Ben immediately strode out the door, his mobile phone in hand.

"Allan. Have the police helicopter on the roof immediately?"

"Where are your friends?" Ben asked.

"They're waiting in a car parked across the road from the entrance to this building."

"Right, we'll get them and then make for the roof."

Twenty minutes later their helicopter touched down near a private jet which sat ready as Kane's band of men strode hurriedly toward it. Kane turned to Ben and spoke loudly against the whine of the idling aircraft, and the wind that blew a cold shower of rain.

"We expected interference from the police after we advertised the wooden box, but you arrived before we'd planned and surprised us. How did you get onto us so early?"

It was a good question Ben thought, as he walked quickly beside Kane toward the aircrafts steps. Suddenly the name of the man who'd directed his initial line of enquiry came to mind. He was thoughtful of the turn of events since the interception of a facsimile.

"A man by the name of Simon West unwittingly pointed me in the right direction..." He shouted before Kane noticed a veil of sadness which clouded his eyes as he added with a lower tone, ".".. and two of my apprentices." With that Kane lightly danced up the steps to the aircraft's doorway. He turned to see Ben's lips form the words of either one last question, or maybe a threat born of frustration at having to let an arch foe go.

He had no time to guess, and instead he issued the last words before he turned and disappeared into the aircrafts inner darkness.

Ben lost Kane's words in the plane's engines howl as it began its taxi to the runway. It left him with a mental picture of the words that had formed on Kane's lips as he'd stood at the top of the aircrafts steps. The image slowly transformed into the sound of Ben's own voice as he repeated the words to no one but the wind.

"Ask Athol."

"Fuck Athol," he thought aloud as he walked with a bowed head toward the police helicopter and its warm cockpit.

As he opened the aircrafts door its pilot inquired.

"Where to now, Sir?"

"Back to the shop and don't spare the horses."

The aircraft lifted off and turned in the cities direction

"Are you a praying man?" Ben asked its pilot.

"Recent events suggest I learn, Sir."

"Well practice while we go that there's an email waiting for me when we land."

London time

Charles turned toward the call of his name.

"Yes, Stephen. What is it?"

"The Australian operations team informs me that they are in the air. All their team is away and in the clear."

"Good. Send the weapons locations immediately."

"Ready to send!"

"Send," Charles ordered.

"Receipt of product confirmed all points," Stephen replied.

"Double check?" Charles asked.

"Confirmation definite, all points."

"Terminate internet connection"

"Internet connection terminated."

"Maintain sales team's emergency systems satellite access. All channels open, their priority."

"Emergency systems satellite access all channels open, sales team's priority."

"Situation report on sales teams?"

"Six teams are away and four still in country."

"Syria?" Charles asked.

"Syrian sales team is one of the four," Stephen looked up at his friend Charles and added, "He's is a tough customer Charles and he knows the country. He'll come through."

Charles nodded as he turned away to begin another around the table screen examination. The sound of keyboard activity was still heavy, and its sound, which had accentuated the whole operations success up to this point, now emphasized the fact that the game was not yet over. Until it was, total success could not be claimed.

In this game, total success meant no friends funerals or grieving widows.

Wednesday 6.35 pm.

Ben Preston had no part to play in the harnessing of the weapon, or those who may be found to be in its close proximity. While he waited for the specialist's to carry out their task, he'd decided to take refuge in his office to at least make a start on the previous afternoon's reports.

He'd begun his report on Horton, but as he progressed he found that he did not have the resolve to finish it. Rodney's savage end was still too fresh in his mind, and at the first sign of a knot in his throat he closed the file and concentrated on the wooden box and John Kane.

Kane's report was easy to write, but as he typed in his description of his meeting with Kane, he found that with each word he became angrier. The fact that the man had got away frustrated him. There was also the insistent nagging echo of the faceless name Athol. It tolled like a cracked bell, and undoubtedly it would do so for the rest of his life.

His mind was on a roll of sorts and he quickly filled the report before he paused to stare at the silent screen of his offices television. It presented the Police Commissioner's face, signalled with a caption which stated Press conference broadcast. Ben turned up its volume and listened intently for some moments. Before deciding that although he'd missed its beginning, it was obvious that he would learn nothing new. The carefully choreographed broadcast was like all the others he'd heard in his career. Press releases designed to deliver the least amount of information in as many words as possible. He lowered the volume again, and placed the remote control onto his desk top near Kane's notebook. Its nearness prompted his fingers to open its small front cover and view once again the presumed complex code.

The whole page was filled with numbers. Each set of five, sometimes six numbers was interspaced with an alphabetical letter.

The first line read e 96843 n 44892 a 53984 k 409843 k 922919 o 40922. After scrutinizing it for a minute, he rubbed his forehead as the thought of the too hard basket sprang to mind. He was about to close the book when his eyes read the letters n 399922 e 09344 b 20203 near the bottom of the page.

"Ben written backwards," he wondered aloud as he picked up his pen and wrote each letter in reverse order, beginning from the end of the last line. A moment later he read, *"Well done Ben now read the back of the book Kane."* Ben turned to the last page to find that it was blank, and then to the outside of the plastic back cover to find the same.

Without hesitation he held the books plastic cover while he pulled at the small pages. Almost immediately the books cardboard back cover released from its plastic sheath.

Its flap closed upon his thumb revealing a short list in a fine written hand.

He read quickly as his hand reached for the telephone.

"Rusty. Ben. Kane's code in the little notebook? It's just a sentence written backwards, which has directed me to the back of the book where there's information concerning the weapon. It says that the gas container is only filled with dyed water. The gas which killed the rats was only a small amount housed in a glass capsule. It was in the eyedroppers rubber extraction cap and was ruptured when it was squeezed. It also points out that the weapon will self-destruct the moment the bad guys try to insert the detonator..."

Ben's ears were again, for the second time that afternoon harassed by an explosion, and the sudden unexpected silence at Rusty's end of the phone caused him to call out.

"What's happened?"

Rusty's reaction to the shattering sound was an immediate order that goaded his men into action. It raced excitedly through the phone line and into Ben's brain.

"Go. Go. Go."

He knew the call and like an apprentice in respect for his master, he stayed silent as Rusty went about the business of commanding a raid. Ben glanced at his watch and noted the time. He wondered if the purchasers of Kane's weapon had twigged to the presence of Rusty's specialist team. The urgency in Rusty's tone certainly suggested so.

Then suddenly, his thoughts were confirmed by the sound of gunfire. Ben listened carefully to the very brief fire-fight which was accompanied by the sounds of shouting. A scuffle of feet sounded out before Rusty's heavy breathing took over and became the centre of his Ben's auditory universe.

Rusty finally spoke in an excited tone.

"Ben. How did you like the show?"

Ben hadn't noticed the dryness of his mouth, until he was forced to flick his tongue around in order to gain moisture.

"Sounds like you enjoyed yourself. What's the situation?"

"It would appear that you were right about the self-destruct button. There's nothing left of the weapon, just a hole in the floor and no evidence of the poison gas. One of the bad guys who came to pick up their purchase must have been wounded by the explosion, but he's still breathing. If there was gas, then he would be starting to cool by now. Anyway, it would appear that we have everything here contained. Transformer, trucks, dead rats in their aquarium, they even left the movie camera behind." He paused momentarily and took a deep breath before asking, "Are you at the shop?"

"Yes. Something I can do for you?" Ben asked.

"Yeah, if you could pass onto the Boss that we've got the whole thing under control, that'd be good. Let him know that we're all in one piece. Three bad guys' dead and one of them wounded. I'll update him the moment I get through here. Half hour tops."

"I'll duck up to see him right away. He'll be glad to have some good news for his next media presentation. It'll take the pressure off him a bit."

"Thanks Ben. I'd better get back to it. I'll catch you later."

The connection broke and Ben dialled the Commissioner's internal number.

"Sir, Ben Preston. Sir, I've just been on the line to Commander Bates and I need an immediate meeting please." Silence greeted his request, so he added, "It's all good news, Sir."

"Thank you Ben. Come straight up."

Ben put down his phone and picked up Kane's note book before he strode to the corridor. He pushed the lift's summons button and then suddenly, unexpectedly, stepped back from its doors, as sweat sprung through his forehead pores. It was accompanied by a cold shiver that ran like a ripple of seizure between his shoulder blades. He stared at the lift's doors for a brief moment. His teeth clenched as his mind flashed back to the events of the afternoon. They'd begun when stainless steel barriers similar to these had parted.

Ben turned away from the doors quickly. His open hand wiped his brow before its fingers pressed into his closed eyelids, as if to protect his eyes from an intense and oppressive light. He stood motionless for some moments, before he breathed deeply and tilted his face toward the ceiling. Then after checking the corridor to ensure he'd not been observed he decided to take the stairs.

Wednesday 7.40 pm

Larry Barrett was relieved to be in the air. He looked out of the aircraft's small window, half expecting to see a cloud of poisonous gas spread its vaporous fingers over the city.

Her lights were soon lost to his sight as the aircraft changed course, and Larry finally saw only darkness. It emphasized his reflection in the window, and he gazed at the picture for a moment before he quietly complimented himself.

"Well done, son."

The small folder which lay on his lap was gripped tightly between his thumb and forefinger. He turned his face toward it and opened its light cardboard cover. The papers within it were copies of the documents he'd lodged with Adam for fast tracking. He leafed through them, until he withdrew a single sheet which stated blatantly to him his major shareholding in everything that Lee had owned.

Even his bloody house he thought, before he suddenly laughed out loud. It caught the attention of some of his more serious fellow passengers. They saw little reason for amusement after escaping a city which could be at this moment enveloped in death.

Stupid bastards, he thought as he slotted the single piece of paper back into the folder. Surely the fact they have escaped is reason enough for celebration.

These people have a second chance. A new beginning awaits them. What more could they want? He patted the folder as he extended the thought. There is money, I suppose. Larry smiled as he closed his eyes and allowed his accountant's mind to calculate the best and quickest method to turn Lee's assets into cash.

*****

Athol lifted the hand piece of his phone and listened carefully as Charles brought him up to date.

"Sir, I can inform you that all of our operations and sales teams are on safe soil. However, it appears that one of our sales team leaders is missing."

"Where?" Athol asked.

"Syria Sir, it's Jamal. The other team members are off Syrian soil, but at this time they are out of contact. We'll know more when they report in."

Athol was silent for a long moment.

"We can only hope for the best and be optimistic at this stage, Charles. What about the others?"

There was a shuffle of paper before Charles answered,

"Total income for the night was a little less than eighty-five million pounds. More importantly, we had a total of twenty-seven bidders. Nineteen of which we've infiltrated and can gain access to at our leisure. We also have passwords for six bank accounts, and the names of twenty-three banks that were either used by bidders or nominated by them. Charles voice was replaced by the sound of his breathing and the shuffling of paper before he concluded, "There have been some interesting side issues, Sir, which I will outline in my final report to you, but in all, aside from the possibility of Jamal, it has been an outstanding success, Sir."

"You said six account passwords?" Athol asked suddenly.

"Yes Sir. It seems that one of our computer console operators decided to make it a bit more of a challenge. He made two bidders believe that they were each the winning bidder. I did chew him out for jeopardizing the operation. Would you like me to carry it further, Sir?"

"No. Not at this time Charles. No doubt you'll include it in your final report; along with your recommendations as to his best use to us in the future. When can I expect your final report?"

"A few hours Sir."

"Bring it to me personally, will you? Oh, one more thing before you go. Congratulations on a job well done."

"Yes Sir. Thank you Sir."

Athol put his phone down and gazed out through his office window at an aircraft winging its way across the city. It brought to him a feeling of déjà vu as he was reminded of a similar aircraft he'd seen some years earlier. With that reminder came also the memory of the moment he realized its huge potential.

As he turned toward his telephone to place another call, he thought to himself as his chuckling crowded the room.

"Outstanding success comes easy once you're provided the right environment."

CHAPTER 25

Wednesday 8.45 pm

Tom Lee glanced at his watch as he locked his office door and then rolled the carpet back. Soon the jingle of keys announced their presence as Lee pushed one into the padlock mechanism. It clicked open with its ease of newness.

After raising the boxes steel lid, he reached in and hoisted out the suitcase which he'd packed with the currency of the highest denomination. Its plastic handle carried the weight and he laid it to one side of the hole in the floor, before gazing momentarily at the second bag.

The thought of eggs in baskets flashed in his mind before he decided to leave it for the time being.

"It's as safe here as anywhere," he told himself as he relocked the heavy lid.

He grunted lightly as he lifted the suitcase onto the hand trolley. It looked out of the ordinary, so he threw a towel over it and then placed his attaché case on top. The back door was not far away, but he and the trolley would be in sight of the bar patrons prying eyes as he made his way. Not reason for discomfort he thought, as he gave his office one last glance. All the while knowing he'd forgotten nothing. The items stored in the attaché case had been chosen carefully.

There was an immediate bombardment of sound as opened his office door. It deluged his ears as he towed the trolley into the corridor connecting to the club's rear delivery door.

Noise from the front bar, with its loud voices of cheer and electronic poker machines combined with techno from a rave party upstairs. The corridor darkened as he approached the store room. He decided to leave it that way as he found security in the dim light.

Some moments later, he fumbled in the darkness for his key to the rear delivery door. The dull glow of a single light bulb greeted him as he opened it, and he stood still to peer into the darker areas of the clubs rear yard to ascertain his privacy. Confident that he was alone, he leaned back behind the trolley's weight as he made his descent down the loading bay ramp. At ground level he twisted the trolley, rolling on one wheel in an effort to back his way in the direction of his car's rear end.

He'd taken one step backwards, when suddenly a voice reached out to him from the shadows. A second later a big framed man stood up from his concealed position on the far side of Lee's car.

"Good evening, Mr. Lee. I wondered how long I'd have to wait."

Lee almost cricked his neck as his head twisted on his shoulders toward the voice in the shadows. He swivelled his body and felt a cold shiver of fear at the sight of the man's gun. It stated starkly that his intention was not of the social kind.

Lee swore as he peered toward the man's face, and even though he was sure that he already knew the answer, he asked, "Dan? Is that you?"

"Yes, Mr. Lee. It's me, Dan. Who is soon to be Mr. Sanic."

"What do you want Dan?"

"I want what you have, Mr. Lee."

Lee tapped the handle of the trolley.

"You want this bag?" He asked

"That too, along with everything else you own."

"That's impossible. You can't..." It suddenly dawned on him that there was one way to make that possible, and he spat venom as he cursed, "Fuck you. You're the one who's been screwing my wife. You prick. I trusted you."

Dan was feeling more confident now.

"Anything's possible Mr. Lee. You've told me that yourself a number of times." He paused as if searching for the next thing to say, "Don't take it as personal though, it's as they say, just business. Now throw me the keys of the car. I'm going to take you for a nice ride in the country." Lee remained still as he tried to realign his thoughts. Decide on the best course of action, but Dan was impatient.

"Throw me the keys Mr. Lee, or I'll drop you where you stand and get them myself." Lee's options were limited, and riding to the country alive rather than dead, might allow an opportunity to gain the upper hand and turn the tables. He reached into his pocket and threw the keys at Dan's feet.

"Always the smartarse, aren't you?" Dan said as he rested his gun hand on the boot of the car and leaned down to retrieve them, "Doesn't matter though, because it'll be the last thing I'll pick up for you."

"Dan, I didn't just throw them there for you to pick up. I threw them there to prove a point. You're a pick up man. It's in your blood. You'll never be a Boss man. A Boss man would have kicked shit out of me, and then made me crawl over to the keys. Then a Boss man would have said, while you're down there pass those keys up to me, arsehole. You're a servant, and right now you're Sally's servant, you fuckin' idiot." Lee spat.

Dan spoke quietly as he stood up straight again.

"You won't draw me, Mr. Lee."

"There you go again, you clown. You've got a gun on me, you're threatening to kill me and you're still calling me Mister. You won't be in business five minutes before you'll have those Italians breathing down your neck. Not to mention the Asians...."

Lee paused as Dan said in a matter of fact manner.

"I don't have to worry about them Mr. Lee."

"What? Have you gone in with one of them?" His voice quieter now and its tone registered disbelief, "It must be the Italians then, because the Asians wouldn't deal with you. They'd just cut your throat and take what they want. So in effect, you're trading in one Boss for another?" He paused for a moment before trying another angle, "Listen Dan. I've got another bag just like this one. Why don't you take it, there's enough to give you a good start somewhere else? Take Sally with you and start a new life with her. You can do that, because I finished with her today on the phone."

For a few seconds Lee thought that he might be making some headway. Suddenly he was jolted back to reality.

"Sorry Mr. Lee. It's gone too far. I can't go back now." As he spoke, Dan pushed a key into the car's boot lock and turned it, before using the key itself as a handle to lift the boot's lid.

It rose easily, as did the terrible eye watering smell that invaded Dan's nostrils. He involuntarily stepped backwards as a ginger shadow burst out of the boot and sought to cling to his arm. Its clawing paws flailing as they tried to find purchase. Lee was unsure as to what was happening, but he quickly grasped at the chance given to him by Mrs. Brown's cat.

He charged into Dan's big frame and grasped the pistol with both hands. His left hand held fast to the weapons grip, while his right hand grasped the barrel near its revolver cylinder. He tried to twist its muzzle toward Dan.

The cylinder began to move beneath his fingers. A warning to him that Dan had his finger firmly on its trigger.

Lee used all his force in that second and jerked the barrel.

Suddenly his ears registered the weapons explosive discharge. Then a deadening dull pain suddenly punched into his fingers, as percussion escaped from the pistols cylinder at the breech end of its barrel.

Lee cried out at the pain and instinctively pulled his stunned right hand away, while at the same time trying to will it back to its wrestling position. He'd almost succeeded when it suddenly became obvious to him that the fight had gone from Dan. The big man began to sag and Lee stood back a step, watching as Dan slowly slipped to his knees. The gun and his gun hand hanging loosely at his side.

Lee hunched over as his left hand went to his right, where it squeezed as if with pressure he might compress the pain away.

As he did he lifted his head, and through eyes squinted in pain he saw what appeared to be tears running down Dan's face. They glinted softly as they rolled in the glow of the single light globe.

He had an unusual feeling of pity, like that for a small child who'd been hurt. As he ceased wringing his hands he heard an utterance of coarse breathless whisper.

"Sorry Mr. Lee."

Suddenly, and with great effort, Dan brought the weapon up. Lee knew that there was no escape at this short range, and as Dan pulled the trigger Lee cried out.

"No."

Lee felt the impact of the bullet that took him side on in the ribs. As he fell, he caught a glimpse of a still kneeling Dan, who sat back on his heels with his head lowered to his chest like an altar boy in prayer.

Mika had been parked outside the club's back gateway, and had watched with fear and fascination as the two men had grappled for the gun.

She'd seen men fight before, but never to this extreme when two opponents had actually gunned each other down. After the second gunshot she'd climbed nervously from her driver's side door to investigate the outcome. As she stepped lightly and nervously along the side of Lee's car, she allowed her fingertips to slide gently over its paintwork, as if she was visually impaired and needed guidance.

Her mouth was dry as she finally rested her fingertips on the rear mudguard of the car, and leaned around its rear end to peer at Dan. He sat on his heels in a silence that seemed to her to indicate finality.

A sudden sound from Lee's direction made her jump, and she turned her eyes toward him in time to see him convulse in a short cough. Its sound was emphasized by a blossom of shining bright bubbles that glinted pink under the dull glow of the single light bulb.

"Tom?" She called softly as she bent over his face and looked down at his unblinking eyes.

"Mika. Is that you?"

"Yes Tom. It's me."

"I'm afraid you caught me at a bad time. Something's holding me down and I can't get up."

"Please Tom. Don't joke."

"I'm not joking baby. I think they'll carry me away from here boots first." Lee let out a little chuckle that ended in a short fit of coughing and another blossom of bubbles.

Mika was unsure how to offer comfort in a situation like this and reached out to touch his forehead. He saw her intention and cried out as best he could, "Don't touch me baby. Doctor called today and told me I'm H.I.V positive." Mika felt like she been kicked in the guts as his words spilled out in blood and she recoiled under their weight.

He coughed again before he continued.

"You don't have to worry though. You were always the smart one, with the condoms and that." Lee went quiet for a moment until more bloodied bubbles rose from his lips. "You always were the smart one Mika. One of the smartest girls I know. Why didn't we just run away together, go and live somewhere quiet. If I had my time over again, I'd whisk you away to the country."

He was beginning to ramble, and his mumbling became almost unintelligible when suddenly as if with new strength he cried out.

"Mika. There's a thing you have to do. The suitcase trolley is money, take it, get away before they come."

Lee went quiet again and she looked at his chest for bubbles for a sign of life. There seemed to be none until Lee called out one last time as he stared off into space.

"Remember me."

"I will, Tom." She spoke softly to his quiet face as she thought; I just hope it's for the right reasons.

With that she turned, and without looking back struggled with the weight as she wheeled the suitcase laden trolley away.

An hour later, with the suitcase crammed into the front passenger seat she headed north.

She drove with her mind in silence, and although she felt no sense of mourning, she noted something akin to a feeling like numbness. It seemed to be complimented by the darkness of the car's interior and it hung on her like a cloak. She chose the phone number stored under 'pizza', and listened to the ring tone until she spoke into the instrument.

"Mary. Both Tom Lee and Dan Sanic are dead." There seemed little else to say and she paused for seconds before she added, "Good bye."

A moment later, as a single tear ran down her cheek she deleted the phone number. She'd not need it again.

It was part of her past.

Just like the lights of Sydney, which were now lost in the darkness behind her.

Thursday 8.30 am

Sally felt as if her knees were about to buckle as her head swam in bewilderment. The tears that bathed her eyes brimmed over her eyelids. Blurring the image of the man who spoke to her words of encouragement as the steel barred door of the holding cell clanged closed.

She wanted to take hold of the bars. Push them away and gain access to her freedom, but they looked dirty and her hands hung in the air momentarily before she pulled them back. The cells smell was a cocktail of cheap perfume, body odour and vomit. It invaded her nostrils, as if it were attracted to the raw bile like taste that clung to the back of her throat.

Finally she blinked away some of the wetness and focused on the lips of the man. Their movement appeared dislocated and unsynchronized with the words she heard. Almost as if the air between them had become viscous, and the words had to force their way to her one syllable at a time.

"Don't worry, Mrs. Lee. I am absolutely sure that I can have you bailed within an hour or so. I also believe that the charges against you won't hold, as the court order for the phone tap was taken against your husband. On that fact I will file that the use of your conversation with Mr. Sanic should be classed as inadmissible evidence."

"Mrs. Lee?" The man waited until he was sure that he had her full attention. "I'll be back as soon as I can. You just hold on O.K?" He turned away and left her on her own. Complete with her overwhelming sense of desolation.

She stared at the tiled wall opposite her barred door. It stood stark white under bright cage enclosed overhead lights.

Suddenly a word formed in her brain. She visualized it in her imagination before she muttered with contempt through quivering lips.

"Promises."

And then she screamed.

CHAPTER 26

Thursday 11.47am

Ben Preston rolled over in his bed and stared at his bedside clock. He wondered if his oversleeping could be based solely on the sleeping pill he'd prompted himself the night before.

He still felt tired as he pushed himself to the side of his bed. Deciding then, that maybe the cascade of events during this very long week, had finally built up to a point where a reminder of his age was unavoidable.

The calendar picture of an ocean view gazed down at him from its place on the wall. As if to suggest that the early retirement option mentioned by the department's Medical Officer might after all be a good choice. He thought about it as he came to the conclusion, that if he was to put a voluntary end to his career, then the events of this past week would certainly make that end a memorable one.

"Early days yet," He mumbled as he rose from the side of the bed. After visiting his bathroom, he walked to the kitchen where he pressed a button on an old electric kettle. Then as he waited for it to boil he moved to his lounge room and picked up his television's remote control.

A glance at his watch told him that the midday news would have started on the A.B.C. So he changed channels and caught part of the stations opening story.

"...the Federal Police Commissioner also stated, that while the terrorist's weapon of mass destruction had been captured and destroyed, the threat of future attacks could not be ignored. He called on the Government to make funds available to improve the capacity of the countries Police and Emergency Services."

"While he commended the Police and the Emergency Services in the field, congratulating them on their capable and well drilled precision in dealing with an extraordinary situation. He pointed out that there was still work to be done in some areas of the essential services bureaucracy and communications. The Commissioner said that while a disaster had been averted, there was still room for improvement. If the threat had done nothing else, it had been exceptional value as a training exercise."

"At the press conference the Commissioner was also asked if the fatal shooting of a Federal Police officer on Wednesday was related to the terrorist weapon. Here's what he had to say."

As Ben concentrated on the screen he hoped the news hounds had not been too inquisitive. Any questions as to why the suspect in the outback murders, was in the building that housed the Sarah Ray foundation might cause complications.

"It won't take long," he thought aloud, "Someone's bound to make a connection."

The news reader disappeared and was immediately replaced by a taped version of his Boss, who spoke quietly and respectfully.

"No. The fatal shooting of one of our officers was in no way connected to the wooden box affair. It happened as two Federal Police officers carried out their duty and tried to arrest an individual who was attempting to abduct two women. The two officers confronted the man who was armed with a high powered weapon as he tried to make good his escape. Unfortunately, his cowardly attack has cost the community a well-liked, respected detective, friend and family man. He will be missed and remembered."

The news reader reappeared and continued on with the story. "The officer's name was Rodney Anderson, and his funeral will be held on Tuesday. He leaves behind a wife and two daughters."

Ben noted the day of the funeral as he lifted the volume, then turned to walk toward the kitchen and breakfast. He'd taken a step when suddenly the next item caused him to focus his attention once more on the screen.

"Gangster and leading underworld figure Tom Lee was found dead in the early hours of this morning at the rear of his Kings Cross club. According to police, Lee was shot dead by one of his gangland employees Dan Sanic. Sanic was also fatally injured during an apparent altercation between the two men. Lee, reputed to be one of the areas drug lords, remained elusive for nearly two decades from criminal prosecution due to lack of evidence and disappearing witnesses. A police spokesman told reporters that Lee had been under constant investigation, and that a recent telephone surveillance operation had uncovered conversations between his wife Sally Lee, and Lee's employee Dan Sanic which suggested an alliance. Sally Lee has since been arrested and charged, as a conspirator in the murder of her husband. The discovery of Lee's body was made just a day after water police found the body of another man in the Parramatta River. A police spokesperson told reporters that the man known only as Louie was an employee of Tom Lee. Investigations are still at an early stage, but it appears that the man was shot dead execution style. Authorities also stated that the man's death could not be discounted as a further escalation in Sydney's drug turf wars."

Ben was taken aback by the news of Lee's death.

Glad on the one hand that Lee had finally been taken down, but disappointed that Lee had not been ridiculed by arrest, before he ended his days behind bars.

He made tea, and as he sipped its heat he picked up his telephone and dialled.

"Miss Cooper? It's Ben Preston. I'm sure that you were asked to give a statement after the shooting. I need to know if you explained what you thought was the reason behind Horton's presence in your building?"

"I asked if I might be allowed to give my statement on the day following the shooting because of my shock at what had happened. Then overnight Lynnette suggested that in the best interests of the Foundation, we should just state that Horton demanded the opals that he believed had been stolen from him."

"Opals, what opals?" Ben asked.

"Simon uncovered a lot of opals when he was driving a bulldozer near Lightning Ridge. He gave them to me to use as base capital in getting the Foundation operational."

"Have you given the statement yet?"

"No. No one from the authorities has visited us as yet. I expect that everyone has been busy with the other things that have been going on." She paused for some seconds before she changed the course of the conversation, "Do you think that, that terrible man Horton will be the last one to die because of what Simon did?"

Ben considered Horton, the fifth person who was connected to the Foundations fortune and killed, without including Lee or Scott. He tried to choose his words carefully as he finally broke his silence.

"Miss Cooper. I think that if I'd been directly involved in an official investigation of the whole affair from its beginning, I would have considered the case closed at the time of Horton's death. I'm sure that anyone else who had an outside interest in the foundation's wealth is beyond caring now." He paused as he realized his failure in bedside manner, "I'm sorry. I would like to have sounded a little less blunt."

"No. Please don't apologize. I think that the one thing that both accountants and detectives have in common, is that they expect direct answers. It's a basic necessity, as with direct questions. I suppose the answer I was hoping for would be one that allowed me to concentrate on the Foundation's business without fear of more criminals turning up in the future. Thank you for giving me some peace of mind." She paused for a moment, and then again steered the conversation, "I'm sorry I seem to have interrupted your line of questioning. The statement, what should I do?"

"I think the best thing to do now, is for me to collect one of my people and meet with you as soon as possible to get your statements recorded. How about I meet you in about an hour and a half's time?"

"Both of us? I mean, Lynette too?" Beth asked.

"Yes, we'll need statements from the two of you. In the meantime, if anyone else approaches you for your statement refer them to me, O.K? Good, I'll see you around two o'clock."

Ben sat and pondered the theme for his meeting with Cooper. The address book that had belonged to Simon West would provide an innocent connection between the Sarah Ray Foundation and the outback murders, he thought. It, along with the opal story would most certainly prevent further police enquiries, and deter the newshounds from delving deeper.

"In other news," the news reader continued, "A British national thought to be a tourist has been found shot dead and mutilated in the Syrian capital Damascus. The man, according to local authorities had been in the country for some weeks, and was last seen alive by staff as he left his hotel supposedly en-route to Britain. Enquiries are continuing and the man's name has not been released."

Ben turned off the television, and as he dialled his telephone he wondered why people were stupid enough to go to the volatile Middle East for holidays. "Allan, can you meet me at Beth Cooper's office at two o'clock?"

"Yes, Sir," Allan replied before he asked, "Sir, I thought you were on compassionate leave for a few days?"

"That's right. Orders from above are that I take a week's leave along with some counseling. It has to wait though. There's a loose end that needs to be tidied," he explained before directing, "Allan, in the top right hand drawer of my office desk, there's a small yellow address book in an evidence bag. Get it and bring it with you, will you? By the time you knock off work this afternoon, we'll be able to consider the outback murders as solved, our early intervention in the John Kane affair as exemplary police work, and the Tom Lee investigation as an acceptable outcome."

"I thought we could consider that to be the case already, Sir."

"Not yet Allan. Not even when we've tied the loose ends at Cooper's office. We'll consider it done when we meet on Tuesday and farewell the third member of our team."

Allan understood.

"Yes, Sir. I think that that is fitting."

Both men remained silent in respect for their friend until Ben said.

"See you at Cooper's."

CHAPTER 27

A week later, and three days after Rodney's funeral, Ben climbed the stairs to his Police Commissioner's office. He was on time for his three o'clock appointment, and unsure as to the reason behind the Commissioner's invitation. A point he had wondered about until his exercise in elevation commanded his whole hearted attention. He paused to catch his breath and straighten his tie, before he announced his arrival with a light knock on the Commissioner's door. It was answered by an immediate bid to enter.

The Commissioner greeted Ben with a handshake before he waved in the general direction of a chair. Ben was glad to take the weight off his stair weary legs and allow his heart rate to slow, while the Commissioner opened a plain report folder and read its typed contents.

After a minute he turned another page, and then suddenly stole his bald spot from Ben's view as he lifted his head,

"I can't help but wonder why a foreign mercenary would fly half way around the world, and then travel to the States outback in search of stolen opals?"

Ben gazed back at his boss, like a school boy before a headmaster who expected a full confession. He gave a mental order to his hands to play their part in his body language, and remain motionless on his lap as he offered an explanation.

"Sir, the opals in Beth Cooper's possession are quite valuable according to the valuation she has made available. In her statement she points out that they are only a small part of the original large parcel she saw in Simon West's possession."

Ben allowed the Commissioner to draw his own conclusions, and then waited as another page of the case file was turned.

"Is this a copy of the valuation?"

"Sir, it is the valuation of just ten of the stones. They are the last of the parcel of eighty-eight that West gave to Cooper, and are those that Cooper had valued with the intention of financing a trust fund for Rodney Anderson's family."

The Commissioner was thoughtful for a moment before he asked.

"How did this man Horton know that Cooper had the opals? Do you know?"

"An address book was found on Horton's body. It belonged to Simon West, and had apparently been taken by Horton from the house where the outback murders took place. It appears Horton used it to follow up on Cooper after he escaped the explosion on Simon West's yacht." Ben decided to try and bring the interview to its conclusion, "There's no way we can know what took place on the yacht prior to the explosion. It is possible that Horton tortured Simon West or maybe West died while defending himself and forced Horton to follow his next best lead." The Commissioner gazed steadily at Ben before he again showed his bald patch and signed the police report.

"Ben, I would like to personally congratulate you for a job well done on winding up the outback murders investigation, and for your early intervention on the wooden box affair." Ben was about to express his gratitude, but clenched his teeth together as the Commissioner continued,

"Those two matters, plus the inevitable outcome of our friend Tom Lee must be for you a high on which to wind down a very successful career. I've spoken to the department's Medical Officer, and he informed me that he suggested to you the possibility of early retirement. Have you considered his suggestion at all?"

Ben felt his skin crawl at the question. I wondered why the medical officer might bring up the early retirement issue. You suggested it, but used the medical officer as a mouth piece, you prick. Although he felt the urge to grab his boss by the shirt and give him a Glasgow kiss, he knew that he was in a no win situation. Arguing with the referee was a waste of time, so instead he decided to bargain.

"Yes Sir, I did consider my options, but came to the conclusion there was no benefit for me in retiring any earlier than necessary."

The Commissioner smiled lightly at the realization he was being screwed, but he was prepared to pay.

"I could recommend promotion, effective immediately which would upgrade your pension plan by about forty percent."

Ben decided to make him wait.

"Could I have twenty-four hours to consider that option, Sir?"

"Yes. That sounds reasonable. Now I have someone who has requested a meeting with you." He pressed his intercom and asked his secretary, "Miss Johns. Would you kindly show Sir James in please?"

Ben stood as the door opened and a large rotund man strode into the room. He approached Ben with an outstretched hand.

As he did the Commissioner stood and offered introduction.

"Sir James, this is Ben Preston, one of our longest serving officers who brought to the Department's attention the wooden box affair. Ben, this is Sir James Tulluston. Sir James is in Sydney on the first leg of a fact finding tour to the five countries involved in the wooden box affair."

Ben noticed the moisture which had been transferred to his hand as he allowed it to fall to his side. He looked into the man's eyes a second time to see a brittle hardness which seemed out of place in his round jovial face. The Commissioner had no sooner finished his introductions before he, as if uncomfortable, gave reason for his need to be elsewhere.

As he left the room Ben momentarily wondered why he should appear uncomfortable. Maybe the Commissioner is a little pissed off at not being included in the meeting, he thought. He smiled lightly as he turned and faced a different kind of smile. It sat heavily upon Sir James lips, but did not touch his eyes.

The two men remained standing, which suggested to Ben that the meeting, whatever it was to be about, was most certainly going to be short lived. After a few moments of small talk Sir James began to beat about the bush.

"Ben, your Commissioner was accurate as to the reasons for my activities in your country. However, his knowledge on the subject is based on the limited amount of information I allowed him. For example, I did not let him know that I am the head of a branch which is among other things, directed at the 'Generals' of our enemies' army in the war against terrorism." He allowed this information time to sink in, and as Ben nodded his understanding he continued, "Now, part of my task in MI6 is to try to put myself in a terrorist's shoes so to speak. Not so much as to ascertain the reasons for their successes, but more to assess where they went wrong. Mistakes they made, no matter how small, which may be beneficial to our operations in the future."

Ben was unsure what was happening. He groped for understanding as to why this man was imparting obvious need to know information, to a soon to be retired, single pixel in the big picture policeman. He hoped the worry in his mind would not be expressed in his facial features, as he suddenly wondered if Sir James might be just plain nuts.

Ben noticed that the brittle hardness had left the man's eyes. It had been, at some stage of the discourse replaced with an excited shine.

In a second it became all too obvious.

Sir James was on a power high. Like a drunk in a pub who had just scored with the beautiful barmaid, and then had the overwhelming necessity to tell someone of his exploits. It became apparent that Ben was to be his subservient captive audience. That's why he used the word 'Generals' of the enemies' armies. He needs to rate his opponents high so he can elevate his own importance, Ben thought.

Sir James looked down his shirtfront to view the backs of his hands and his fingernails before he went on.

"I've been allowed access to your reports, and I have one question I would like to ask you."

He paused for some seconds, as if to allow Ben time to appreciate the importance thrust upon him by being allowed to advise the General.

"What was it that made you suspicious of the, as you call it, the wooden box? How did you get on to it so early?" Immediately, an almost identical question echoed in his memory, one that Ben had heard quite recently.

Ben looked again into Sir James's staring gaze. It shone like those belonging to one who expected that a brilliant plan could only have been thwarted by an even more brilliant manoeuvre. Ben was unsure what reaction to expect.

"I suppose the thing that clutched at my suspicious mind was the fact that Steve Walters was involved."

Sir James urged.

"Yes?"

To which Ben lied.

"And that was only because his name came up more or less accidentally."

"Accidentally?" Sir James voice dropped to almost that of a whisper, "You mean that you stumbled around in the dark and tripped over apparent evidence?" Ben nodded in an offhand way as he watched the fire go out of Sir James eyes. Then, just as suddenly it was replaced by the brittle hardness that had been evident at the beginning of their meeting.

"We were looking into another matter when Walters name came up, and as coincidence can only be stretched so far, we scratched the surface and discovered something we were not supposed to see."

As he spoke, Ben felt the almost habitual sensation that came with commanding an interrogation. He watched as bright excitement flared once again in Sir James's eyes as he completed his next sentence.

"The plan that John Kane and his colleagues carried out was grand, almost to the point of perfection, both in preparation and execution..." Ben noted the poker face which still clung to Sir James's features. An expression that didn't fit the look of almost joyous rapture that beamed in his eyes, until they suddenly clouded as Ben continued.

"But, they didn't look into the criminal background of the owners of the building they leased, and they didn't make sure that all of their members entered Australia under assumed identities. Namely Steve Walters, who was immediately noticeable due to the attention he drew on an earlier visit to this country. Two small flaws, which, in answer to your question as to our early intervention, were the only clues we had available to us. It was upon these we focused our attention and carried out some very fine police work."

Sir James suddenly turned on his heel and walked slowly to one of the office's windows, where he stood stock still and gazed out at the cloudless blue sky.

Ben allowed him his moment of thoughtful solitude, before he changed the course of his dialogue.

"Sir James, I've been a policeman for many years, and during that time I've learnt that all that needs to be read is written in the human eye. It clarifies the truth along with the lie. I've also learnt that usually the best way to have that writing displayed is to offer a compliment, deserved or undeserved. Either way it will almost always bring a result." Ben waited until Sir James turned to face him before he went on.

"The question that you asked was almost identical to one asked of me by John Kane. It was another surface that I felt the need to scratch. Habit I suppose, or curiosity. Just delving a little deeper to see if there is anything I am not supposed to see. I then offered you a compliment, and read what was written in your eyes." Ben wondered if he might be going too far, but he pressed on regardless, as his mind tried its best to persuade him to desist.

"I think that I've read enough to be able to ask you a favour?"

Sir James turned his head toward Ben and offered a slight nod of his head.

"Of course."

Ben was in two minds, like one who is about to bungee-jump, until suddenly the critical point has been passed and he went into free fall.

"I asked John Kane what it was that he'd accomplished, other than a financial wind fall. He suggested that I ask Athol, should I meet him." Sir James expression stayed intact, but he couldn't stop his short and immediate intake of breath. It sounded to Ben similar to a hiccough.

"What did you accomplish, Sir James?"

Sir James turned to face Ben and the fore finger which had lain across his lips, as if to guard their movement, began to scratch an imaginary itch high on his cheekbone as he explained.

"We've deprived the enemy of millions of dollars of their operational funds, placed moles in most of the computers which took part in the auction and accrued priceless information on their financial infrastructure. Aside from that, we provided a practice schedule for five Nations that will fine tune their emergency services in preparation for any future 'real' event."

Ben chose the wrong moment for levity.

"You've frightened the hell out of a lot of people."

Sir James voice hardened.

"We reminded the world that they, along with us, are at war. If a scare now and then is what is needed to make them understand that the war on terror is not a tongue in cheek affair, then so be it."

He suddenly relaxed, and as he turned away from Ben to gaze again out of the office window he wiped his forehead with a handkerchief before he offered quietly.

"Ben, the wooden box affair as you put it, was a successful strike against the enemy. We've dealt him a decisive blow, but it is just one battle in a war that is far from over." His pause emphasized the silence before he added, "We've had a victory, but do you know why it was not a one hundred percent success?"

Ben could only shake his head.

"It's because one of our men won't be coming home. I lost a good friend and colleague in the fight against terrorism, just as you lost a good friend and colleague in the fight against crime. You understand the seriousness of the situation. If I need to drive the seriousness of the situation home by scaring shit out of people, then I will. I'd prefer to do it that way, than have them come to the understanding the hard way like you and I have done. Wouldn't you agree?"

Ben mentally recoiled under the force at which the point had been driven home to him. It was accompanied by a flash in his brain of Rodney's flailing body, as it accepted the impact of Horton's high powered bullet.

He was stunned to silence for some seconds, and then suddenly an overwhelming feeling of weariness seemed to infiltrate his being.

His hand went to his forehead and came away wet with the sweat that seemed to have erupted from the pores of his skin. At that moment there was a knock at the door. He turned to see a face that was unknown to him.

"Sir James? Call from London, Sir. Urgent."

Ben noted the unknown man's English accent, and then listened as Sir James answered.

"Thank you Charles. Have it put through to this telephone will you?" He pointed towards the telephone on the Commissioner's desk.

Ben accepted the interruption gratefully, wishing already that he was somewhere else. Somewhere quiet where he could allow the after effects of the flash back to slowly dissipate and let him regain his sense of normality. He excused himself.

"I hope that I've been helpful in providing input for your assessment, and now, if you might excuse me. I have something of a personal nature that must be done right away."

Sir James face showed some concern as he carefully surveyed Ben's face and asked.

"What is that Ben?"

"The Commissioner believes that people our age are beyond our use by date, and I've come to realize in the last few minutes that he may be right. It may be time to move aside. Let the younger minds who feel they are in better touch with this new world do what they will. So I have letter of acceptance of early retirement to write."

Sir James stood with his chin nestled between thumb and forefinger. Into which he nodded his head before he lowered his hand.

"Yes, of course Ben. Thank you for your input."

"Thank you Sir." Ben said as he walked to the door. He took the stairs of the fire escape to where one floor down he suddenly thought. Quinn was right. The world had changed and nothing was what it appeared to be. Gone are the good old days when black was black and white was white.

He wondered at Quinn's unusual philosophy if he learnt that the wooden box affair was just a huge anti-terrorist sting operation. Put up by the British Secret Service. It then became clear to Ben, why the Police Commissioner had had the authority to let Kane go so easily, and without seeking advice. He was obviously in the know.

"Was Rusty Bates also?" He wondered aloud.

As the pressure of previous few weeks' uncertainties at last broke free, it left him feeling relaxed and inwardly content. He felt it in his step on the last of the stairs to his department's floor.

He could see his computer as he passed through the fire escape doorway, and he gratefully accepted the short walk to it and his new beginning.

CHAPTER 28

One-month later Ben left prints in wet white sand. Their existence was short lived as small waves, after delivering sounds of their destination, smoothed all proof of his passing. The wide horizon's fine line between the ocean and a sky of blue accepted his gaze for some moments. Until a seagull riding a wave of air overhead caught his eye and redirected his gaze inland, to where Peter Quinn sat looking in his direction. Ben waved as he changed direction and proceeded toward the small cottage. Soon he stood close enough to the porch to talk, but not to appear to be invasive of Quinn's space.

Quinn asked the inevitable question.

"Business Ben, or is this a social call?"

"Social call Peter." Ben removed his hat and exposed his perspiration to the sunlight as he searched for the right words to explain his presence. Without beating around the bush he offered, "I've retired from the Service. One reason being that the hierarchy feel that blokes my age are too old to function. Two, I stepped over the line to the extent that I felt unable to act conscientiously as a law enforcer. Thirdly, I felt that it was time to give some of my life to me, if that makes sense?"

"I understand perfectly, Ben. You'd best come on up and take the weight off your feet. I'll put the kettle on. Tea or coffee?" Quinn slid open the glass door, and as he passed through its doorway he called back, "I'll tell Justine you're here. She wondered if you'd come back."

Ben made his way to the stairs, and as he stepped over the lip of the veranda Justine glided through the doorway.

"Hello Ben. How are you?"

"Good thank you, Justine. How is your day?"

"It's a lovely day." She seated herself at the table and shortly after Quinn brought kettle and cups.

"Is it time for you to go fishing, Ben?" Justine asked.

"Yes. It came a little earlier than I expected." He gathered his thoughts before he added, "That is only part of the reason for my visit though." Both Quinn and Justine became noticeably still, interrupting Ben's explanation. He quickly went on.

"A second part is that I was sure that you'd like to hear the whole story, and the outcome of the Simon West's foray into the unknown."

Quinn nodded as Justine inquired.

"Who is Simon West?"

"I suppose that he's one of the heroes of the story, but it is a long story and it became connected to the wooden box that plagued the world recently."

"I think that everyone heard about that part." Quinn grinned.

"Yes," Ben chuckled, "But not the inside story."

"Sounds intriguing?" Justine questioned.

"It's also a rare story, but as I said it is a long story. So if you'll allow me I'd like to put it aside for the moment, and come to the third part of the reason for my visit?"

"Come on Ben, tell us." Justine cried. In way similar to Ben's eldest daughter when she thought she was being teased.

"I wanted to know if you know how to scuba dive?" He asked Quinn.

"Yes," Quinn said, "It's been a couple of years since I've done any, but yes I can dive. I don't have any diving gear though."

"We can get some if necessary." Ben said before he apologized, "Look I'm sorry to beat about the bush, but there are a couple of things I'd like to point out to you before I come to the point. Is that alright? Just so we know where we stand." Justine and Quinn nodded their consent.

"There may be treasure or there may not be. If you come with me and help me look for it, we might find it or we might not. We might find the boat that it was on, but we might also find that someone has beaten us to it. Either way we get the enjoyment of looking for it. That is, if you like a treasure hunt?"

"Everyone loves a treasure hunt, don't they?" Justine reminded.

Ben looked to Quinn who nodded.

"Even me."

"Then it's understood where we stand? You also understand that I'm not making any promises that we'll be successful in our venture?" Ben asked.

"Yes, fully understood." They choroused.

"O.K." Ben said, "Simon West's boat went down off the coast just a little North of Brisbane. I'm ninety percent sure he had a parcel of opals aboard at the time. I've bought a Bayliner, and I have the approximate location of the place where it sank, along with charts of the area. The plan is, load the Bayliner, drive up there and have a look."

"How approximate is your location." Quinn asked.

"G.P.S and compass reckoning given by the crew of the fishing vessel who saw the boat explode and go down. Who, I should add, may have gone back to perform their own brand of salvage."

"Possibly," Quinn replied before he asked, "What's it been? Five weeks?"

"Plus a few days," Ben added.

He could see that Quinn was interested in the search, but there was something holding him back.

As if he was cautious.

Ben decided the best way to find out was to ask.

"Peter, you look like you may be interested in the venture, but something holds you back?"

Quinn was silent for a moment before he formed his question.

"Can you think of any reason why it might be dangerous for me to go into Australian waters?"

Ben looked Quinn in the eye and said what he thought Quinn hoped for, while understanding the need in Justine's ears.

"No. Tom Lee is dead. He died in a gunfight with one of his men who attempted a hostile takeover. So you and your family are safe from any threats that may have come from that quarter." He added what he knew was for the benefit of Quinn's ears. "Sudovich is also dead. The report I wrote at the end of the investigation into his death states he more than likely died at the hands of those who were behind the wooden box affair."

"Did he?" Quinn asked.

"No. My report was not entirely accurate. I took a little poetic license."

Quinn read Bens eyes and inquired further.

"Do you know?"

Ben reached into the back pocket of his trousers and brought out a folded photograph. He handed it to Quinn.

"I knew before I made my last visit here. This photo was lifted from the security camera of a motel near a golf course. I deleted everything associated with the particular day of Sudovich demise. So the person in that photo has nothing to fear."

"Why?" Quinn asked.

"Initially I had bigger fish to fry, and my interview with you was concerned with that. The fact that you were so forthcoming with information was beneficial to my investigation. In a way you helped me get a head start on Lee, and I would have caught him red handed if he'd lived longer. You also helped me to discover the existence of Horton..."

"Horton?" Quinn interrupted.

"Yes, that was the real name of the N.C.O. He turned up looking for Simon's money. He also killed a close friend and colleague of mine when we tried to apprehend him."

"I'm sorry to hear about your friend, Ben."

The three remained quiet for some moments.

"What became of Horton?" Quinn asked.

"He's dead too."

"...and Simon's money?"

Ben smiled as he nodded at Quinn.

"It's safe."

"That's a good thing. A lot of people died making sure that it worked out that way though, didn't they?" Quinn offered.

"Many more will stay alive because of it." Ben suggested before he said, "The other part of your original 'why' question is, when I came here the last time Justine asked me if I was a friend, and I said yes." He paused and accepted her smile, as she realized her part in protecting her meaning in life, "As well as that, there is also, as I said earlier, the fact that I stepped over the line..." He didn't finish the sentence. Instead he looked closely at some freckles on his arm, before he rubbed his hand gently over them. Then, after another sip of his coffee he suggested, "Anyway I'd like to, at some stage of the game tell you both the whole story. Especially the scary part about the wooden box, and if I make known too many bits and pieces it might spoil the tale."

"Scary Ben?" Quinn raised an eyebrow as he asked.

Ben touched his lips as he thought for a moment.

"Do you remember on my last visit here, you talked about the way that the world was? Our paradise in the sun, cricket in the street, unlocked doors and such?"

"Mmm. Yes," Quinn replied.

"I think that your words were, "Suddenly we turned around one day and everything had gone?" Well, to put it as simply as I can. That is, without telling you the whole story. We've turned around again and everything has gone further. To the extent that, like me, you may have to reconsider everything..." Ben searched for words as he shook his head slowly from side to side, until he finally lifted his hands, palms up and said, "Everything, from past events through to whatever happens in the future." He took another sip of his coffee before he smiled lightly and excused himself, "As I said it's a long story."

Quinn understood the signs. He noticed Ben pass a hand gently over his freckled forearm for a second time and redirected the conversation.

"If we find the booty on board Simon's sunken boat, Ben, how do you want to divvy it up? I only ask because you made it clear that we should know where we stand."

Ben allowed his sense of humour to clear his mind of that dark place, "Aye. That I did me hearty and I'll tell ye. If the haul be huge, then I'll just take what covers expenses and you can have the rest. If the haul be small, then you two take it all and let me just have the adventure."

"That's a very generous offer?"

"Look at it from my point of view, Peter. If you don't come then I don't get to go, and if I went on my own then I can't dive when I get there. I don't need the money that the opals might bring, but I like the idea of the adventure. We'll keep to the coast on the way up and if for any reason you want out then we'll always be near a port. I know that a boat allows restricted space, but the whole time on the water might only be three weeks max, and that time will be split up between ports and islands."

Ben considered the trump card he was about to play.

One based on his lifetime experience of reading people. He delivered it for the benefit of Justine's ears.

"There is one other thing. If the haul be huge then you might never have to leave this place to work again."

He'd struck a chord with Justine's desire for security.

"That's settled then," she said, "Where do we start?"

Ben looked to Quinn who grinned back at him as they shook hands over the table.

"To new beginnings," Ben said as he raised his coffee mug in salute.

"New beginnings," Justine and Quinn replied with hopes raised high, as Ben's finger tips subconsciously touched his forearm.

EPILOGUE

The sun washed over current rippled sand flats, where soldier crabs moved herd like in their search for minute particles left exposed after the high tides recent departure.

Some young boys disturbed the crabs, as they enthusiastically picked through the thick liquid that spewed from a pump their father used to suck yabbies from below the sands surface.

Each one optimistic that the collected bait would offer sizable rewards from the ocean's inshore depths, while seagulls waited in small perimeter for the collector's leftovers.

The man who leant forward on the park bench overlooking the beach gave them a cursory glance. Before he again lent is gaze to the horizon, where distant sails of a yacht displayed white on a background of blue.

He suddenly turned his head. Looking over his shoulder towards the sharp noise of a teenager's skateboard as it clattered along the concrete pathway.

His thoughts relived the events of the past months as he tried once more to find some peace, while the faces of those lost to him lingered in full view of his mind's eye.

Burn scars from the explosion which destroyed 'der boat', displayed their story on the hand which held a bottle in brown paper wrapping.

The bottle held water, but the brown paper bag gave it the appearance of alcohol, and played its part in keeping regular passersby at bay.

It was a well-rehearsed and welcome ruse for he who wished to be left in solitude.

A power tool used by the gardeners in the caravan park suddenly let out an animal like howl. It caused the hairs on the back of his neck to stand, as the skin gave way to a crawling sensation.

Rising quickly from his seat he immediately strode across the park, and after glancing once more over his shoulder he disappeared into the bush.

Time was a necessity for his healing, and that time needed its companion, silence.

He was like a wounded animal that needed to lie up for a period of time, until he could once again reclaim his place in society.

Until then he must wait.

He looked back yet again before he listened to the quiet. Then silently moved to his bush camp, where dreams would wake him at night and visions haunt his days.